The King of the Spoil

of the Spoil

A MELITA VORONOVA NOVEL

WARHAMMER
CRIME

The
King
of the Spoil

A MELITA VORONOVA NOVEL

Jonathan D Beer

WARHAMMER CRIME
A BLACK LIBRARY IMPRINT

First published in Great Britain in 2023 by
Black Library, Games Workshop Ltd.,
Willow Road, Nottingham, NG7 2WS, UK.

Represented by: Games Workshop Limited – Irish branch,
Unit 3, Lower Liffey Street, Dublin 1,
D01 K199, Ireland

10 9 8 7 6 5 4 3 2 1

Produced by Games Workshop in Nottingham.
Cover illustration by Amir Zand.

A CIP record for this book is available from the British Library.

ISBN 13: 978-1-80026-202-7

See Warhammer Crime on the internet at

blacklibrary.com

Find out more about Games Workshop
and the worlds of Warhammer at

games-workshop.com

Printed and bound in the UK.

WARHAMMER
CRIME

It is the 41st millennium, and far from the battlefields of distant stars there is a city. A sprawling and rotting metropolis of ancient hives, where corruption is rife and murder a way of life.

This is Varangantua, a decaying urban hellscape, full of fading grandeur and ripe with squalor. Countless districts run like warrens throughout its cancerous expanse, from greasy dockyards and factorums to gaudy spires, decrepit slums and slaughterhouses. And looming over all, the ironclad Bastions of the enforcers, the upholders of the Lex and all that stands between the city and lawless oblivion.

To be a citizen in this grim place is to know privation and fear, where most can only eke out a meagre existence, their efforts bent to feeding an endless war in the void they know nothing about. A few, the gilded and the merchant-barons, know wealth, but they are hollow and heartless creatures who profit from suffering.

Violence is inescapable on these benighted streets, where you are either a victim or a perpetrator. Whatever justice exists can only be found through brutality, and the weak do not survive for long. For this is Varangantua, where only the ruthless prosper.

PROLOGUE

The King of the Har Dhrol was a big man, powerfully built in the chest and shoulders. Age and indolence may have added their weight to his gut and their lines to his face, but Nurem Babić still felt the familiar swell of dread as he entered the chambers of the gangster lord of the Spoil.

'Who's that?'

Babić jumped at the barked challenge. In his old age Andreti Sorokin's eyes had begun to fail him, and though he could have easily obtained the corrective treatment a man of his standing might enjoy out in the wider city, he had never sought it out. Instead, he pulled a pair of anachronistic lenses from a pocket and perched them on the bridge of his nose.

'Ah, Babić.' Sorokin's voice matched his size, a deep, creaking growl full of ursine power. Even the most banal of pleasantries sounded like a threat in that voice. 'What do you have for me today?'

Sorokin sat in his usual chair, half turned to face towards the domicile's door. The orange glare of sunset filled the thick glassaic in the lancet window in front of him, obscuring rather than revealing the squalor beyond. An inactive data-slate sat on the table beside him.

Babić fumbled with his own data-slate to avoid meeting his master's eye. 'Just a few things, sire.'

As far as Babić knew, no one could say who had first given the title of 'king' to Sorokin. Certainly, there had been no throne waiting for him when he first began to claw his way to supremacy. Even after he had conquered the Spoil, no less a feat than an Imperial crusade marching to victory among the stars, still no one had thought to call him anything other than his name. Regardless of whoever had first said it, the idea had stuck. Babić's robes, more suited to the receiving hall of a gilded mansion than the Spoil's wretched poverty and barely restrained anarchy, were a symptom of how completely the title had ensnared its bearer over the long years of his dominion.

'"A few things", eh?' Sorokin repeated, his pale eyes watching Babić as he crossed the room. He had a way of looking at someone like he was reading the thoughts off the back of their head.

Babić tried to ignore his mockery. 'The usual trouble in the Depths... The Iron Crones turned in a larger tribute this month than we'd expected. Amadan is looking into why... There's been a noticeable drop-off in raids across the Line in the past few weeks.'

'Hrm.' He had turned away, and seemed to be examining a patch of stone wall as he listened. 'What else?'

'Russov Bai has sent through another list of parts they need for the water treatment plant in the Onden clave. It's pretty steep, and we–'

Sorokin turned back, waving a hand dismissively. 'No, no. No. We do not argue with Magos Bai.' He clicked his fingers to get Babić's attention. 'You send them what they want, and you buy what we don't have. D'you understand?' Sorokin's voice dropped even lower. Babić had been the man's aide for almost four years, which was long enough that he no longer visibly startled at the sound.

'People need water, and not the filth that's pumped off the canal.' The old man climbed to his feet, and gestured at the window as if to encompass the entire Spoil. 'If they don't have water, they start to die. When they die, they can't work. And if they can't work, the whole thing starts to crumble, doesn't it?'

'Yes, sire.' Babić bobbed his head meekly.

Sorokin subsided, and lowered himself back into his chair. 'Well, carry on, then.'

A loud thump echoed from the chamber's door.

'What?' barked Sorokin. This time Babić did jump.

A ganger entered with a curt nod to Sorokin. His attire was just as anachronistic as Babić's; he wore a long tabard in the grey of the Har Dhrol alliance over a battered steel breastplate, along with more practical flak armour and heavy boots. He held the door open to admit a bent-backed maid carrying a silver tray of food.

'Ah, something important,' said Sorokin.

The serf wobbled towards Sorokin's desk.

'Anything else, Babić? Or will you leave me to eat in peace?'

Babić swallowed. 'Just one, sir. The Valtteri have sent word that they've got another convoy coming in from the Pans.'

Sorokin's eyes narrowed behind his lenses. 'How big?'

'Five carriages, sire, with the usual escort.'

'Hrm.' Sorokin thought in silence. 'When?'

'Tomorrow night.'

Sorokin grunted again. 'Fine. Tell Mercy, step up the watch on the arterial.'

'Yes, sire.' The necessary measures had already been put in place to secure the convoy's safe passage, but Babić had learnt that it was important for the king to feel that it was his word alone that made the world move.

A shiver of metal on metal made them both turn. The maid was struggling under the weight of the tray. Wrinkled hands were white-knuckled around the silver handles, which emerged from the depths of a robe that was far too big for her. The hood of the heavy fabric was drawn up, but enough light caught her lined face to reveal that she was grimacing with the effort.

'Help her, for Throne's sake,' growled Sorokin. The guard let the door close behind him and strode over to take the tray from her, but she shrugged him off and increased her shuffling pace. The man stayed at her elbow as she crossed to Sorokin's desk and placed the tray on the wooden table-top beside him.

The woman puffed, straightened, and with a strange flourish withdrew a folded square of linen that lay atop the flatware. One of the utensils was a knife, bone-handled and iron-grey, entirely out of place amongst the fine silverware.

It was an extremely sharp knife.

The maid bared her teeth in a gleeful, predatory smile, snatched up the knife, and rammed it into the taut sinews of Sorokin's neck.

Babić made a strangled croak of protest, eclipsed by the shocked, agonised gargle that burst from Sorokin's lips.

The guard went for his gun, but the maid released her blade and snatched up the metal tray. She whirled, launching food into the air, and its edge struck the ganger across the jaw. He staggered back, and in his momentary confusion the maid stepped forward and planted her closed fist against his chest. A flare of crimson light erupted from her hand and he fell, a small hole glowing red in the centre of his breastplate. He crashed to the floor, but not before the maid had wrenched the autopistol from his hand.

As the dead man struck the stone flags with the sound of a cracked bell's chime, the maid flicked off the pistol's safety catch and dropped to one knee, the gun gripped in both hands.

The door to Sorokin's quarters was pulled open by a second guard, his face showing concern more than alarm. Two shots boomed, echoing from the stone ceiling. The first round cratered the guard's armoured chest, and the second snapped his head back. He slumped to his knees, dead before he fell.

The maid raced over to the door and briefly glanced outside. Between her body and the door's jamb, Babić could see a gruesome mess of blood, brain matter and bone that painted the corridor's floor. She bent to haul the dead guard's body inside the room, armour squealing on the stone, then she pulled the heavy door shut.

Babić had not moved. He stood, frozen in place, chest heaving, breath sawing in and out. His stylus was still raised in his thin fingers over the day's report. His mouth opened and shut, gaping like a landed fish.

The woman turned with reptilian slowness, terrifying after the sudden burst of ferocity and speed. She stood tall, straight-backed, all vestiges of her disguise cast aside. A flicker of orange light caught that mocking smile, a cruel line between thin, bloodless lips.

It was the smile that finally broke Babić's paralysis. The data-slate fell from his hand. It struck the ground with a discordant clatter, appallingly loud in the sudden silence, as he looked for anything that might be a weapon, heedless of the tapered metal stylus still caught between his fingers.

There was a rustle of fabric and suddenly the maid was

in front of him. Babić jerked away, but his back struck the heavy post of Sorokin's bed. Her face was a hand's breadth from his, concealed by the shadow of her cowl.

With malicious patience, the woman reached up and pushed back the heavy cloth. Her skin was pale, unusually so for the equatorial girdle of Varangantua. She was bald; not a single hair marred the smooth curve of her skull. Deep lines ran from her eyes and creased her brow, but surely they were a trick of cosmetics given the speed and strength with which she had struck.

Babić felt a slight pressure against his chest, and looked down. The maid – the assassin – had lifted the stolen autopistol, and was pushing its muzzle into him, directly over his heart.

The stylus fell from nerveless fingers. The clerk felt a shameful warmth as his bladder emptied.

'Look at me.' She was so close, staring at him with wide, dark eyes. Her voice was deep, slow, each word spoken with care. It was a voice that was used to command, and Babić could do nothing but obey. Her pupils were huge, ink-black voids into which he was drawn.

She took a step back, pistol still held level with his chest, and moved to stand beside Sorokin.

Babić's master was dying, but he was not yet dead. The old man was pawing weakly at the blade lodged in his throat. Blood escaped from either side of the wound, trickling in slim tracks over the ivory collar of his shirt and down his flank. Babić could see his eyes reflected in the smoky glassaic of the narrow window, full of shock and fury and pure, naked fear.

Still staring at Babić, the woman placed the guard's pistol on the desk beside the stricken gang lord. Babić could have tried to reach for it, but fear kept him rooted to the spot. The woman stood behind Sorokin and leant over him, reaching across his body with her right hand.

'Look at me,' she said again, demanding Babić act as witness to her deed. He could not look away, even as he felt an awful wave of relief flood through his being as those big, black eyes turned from him to Sorokin.

Slender fingers curled, one knuckle at a time, around the knife's handle. She placed the palm of her other hand against the old man's forehead, tilting his head back with sickening gentleness. She smiled again as their eyes met.

Sorokin let out a pained gurgle and grabbed her wrist. Even now, with his strength ebbing out around the blade, he fought. The woman's smile broadened. Slowly, irresistibly, the knife sawed across his throat, the serrated edge tearing steadily through skin and muscle and cartilage. Blood washed down the old man's front, first a stream, then a torrent. Babić hadn't imagined one body could hold so much.

The woman pulled the blade free with a final grunt of effort and stepped back, triumphant. Sorokin's head lolled, half-severed. Bone glistened where the blade had cut through to his spinal column.

The woman retrieved the autopistol. She seemed calm, but he could see that her eyes were even wider than before, her breath shallow and quick. She walked over to the chamber's door, a strange lightness in her step, and eased it open. There was, somehow, no sign of alarm.

She turned back to Babić. 'Tell them what you saw.' She pulled up the cowl of her robe and ran from the room.

Babić remained standing for several seconds, until the coppery tang of his master's blood reached him. His stomach heaved and his limbs went slack. Nurem Babić fell to the floor with tears in his eyes and vomit staining his lips.

Andreti Sorokin was dead.

PART 1

CHAPTER 1

Haska Jovanic heard the tramp of footsteps on the stairs, and swore.

The walls of her domicile were made of flimsy compressed fibreboard, and were no barrier at all to the sounds of other people's lives as they stumbled up and down the hab-block's stairwell. She heard each step clearly, coming a few thumps at a time, then a pause as the climber caught their breath.

Haska swung her feet off the battered table that almost filled the hab's tiny communal space, and looked around for her boots. She quickly pulled them on, cursing her laziness. She had woken late, so late that the red orb of Alecto's star had already set, and although the brutal heat of the day had started to fade she had been wallowing in it, letting her mind turn over the usual bitter thoughts, one after the other.

The wall of the hab flexed inwards as the climber leant their weight against it. Haska could hear their laboured breathing, the cracked rattle that rasped across her nerves.

A key-stave clicked in the lock – a nonsense that would not have slowed any Spoil thief for even a second – and the door swung open.

A skinny woman in her middle thirties was framed by the doorway, slumped against the jamb. Her cheeks were red from the effort of climbing the stairs, stark against the grey, drawn skin of her face. Despite the heat she wore several layers of holed pullovers, and patched novaplas trousers.

'Haska? I wasn't… expecting you'd be home,' wheezed Verka Jovanic. After the climb to their floor, it would be a few minutes until Haska's mother could get a whole sentence out in a single breath.

Haska stood up. 'I was just leaving.'

Verka shuffled into her hab, blocking the doorway. She held a laden sack in each hand, and their combined weight bent her towards the floor. 'Hold on, just let me–'

She didn't finish. A hacking cough interrupted her, shuddering through her overtaxed body. After a moment, Haska took the sacks from Verka's shaking hands. Her mother gave her a weak smile of thanks, and sputtered out a few more breaths. Verka pushed the door closed behind her, then slumped into a moulded plastek chair fixed to the table. Haska dropped the sacks onto the hab's culina worktop.

'Let's talk for a minute,' said Verka, a false, almost urgent cheer in her voice. Her eyes roamed Haska's face, like she was checking for signs of illness, or as if she couldn't quite remember what her daughter looked like.

'I'm expected,' Haska said. She and Verka rarely crossed paths like this. Haska tried to make sure of it. She grabbed her plasweave jacket from the seat where she'd been using it as a rest for her head, and shrugged it on over her sweat-stained shirt.

'Have you heard?' Verka blurted out. 'He's dead.'

'Who's dead?' Haska asked, not listening for the answer. Death held no fear or mystery for anyone born inside the Spoil.

'Sorokin. It's... all over the clave.'

Haska stopped pawing at her sleeve, and slowly turned to face her mother. 'Sorokin's dead?'

For her entire life – for the whole of Verka's, in fact – one person had been the master of the Spoil. Everything flowed from and to Andreti Sorokin. He ruled the patchwork alliance of Spoil gangs they called the Har Dhrol. He gave the clave-captains the licence to run their territories, to extract their tithes from their tenants, so long as they paid their dues to him. His crews were the ones that controlled the generatoria and vox-exchanges, the dispensaries and waste-harvesters. His word was the Lex, and his gangers were its enforcers.

'How?' she asked.

'Assassinated, according to the street. Someone... got into his dorm. Cut his damned head off. It's probably hanging in a trophy case already.'

'That's dross,' Haska said immediately. Sorokin lived like a Throne-accursed merchant-baron. There was no way someone could have made it into the King of the Har Dhrol's compound with murder in mind.

Verka shrugged. 'Maybe. But Erastin has shut the factorum tonight. And he's told us all not to turn up tomorrow.'

Haska blinked. She had been so lost in the enormity of it, the impossibility that Sorokin might be dead, that she had not considered what even the rumour of his death would mean for the clave, and for her.

Chaos would rule the Spoil tonight. There would be blood on the streets, probably for days, at least until the clave-captains figured out who would take Sorokin's place.

It would be war.

Like most Spoil children, Haska had been part of a gang since she'd been tall enough to reach the hab's door handle. She and Lira and Katryn had outgrown their juve crew at twelve, and the three of them were a tight-knit little band, trying like so many others to break into one of the Har Dhrol gangs. War would bring opportunity. Dead folk left gaps, and Haska and her crew had spent years picking up odd jobs for the gangers. They were known to the local clave-captains. This could be their time.

She tried to ignore the creeping fingers of fear climbing up her spine. Haska was not blind to the danger of what was playing out in her mind. She had seen her first dead body when she was three years old, a putrid ruin Haska had found while exploring a disused hab-stack. She'd seen her first killing at seven. But for all that she was a seasoned street-rat, Haska had never shaken her reluctance to shed blood.

At sixteen, she was well past the age by which most Spoilers had found their niche. Some fell in with the narco-gangs, sneaking into the city districts with plastek bags of bliss and topaz sewn into their clothes or lining their stomachs. More became street-blades, those idling gangers who did their clave-captain's bidding and were always the first to die when a grudge could not be settled, or when an example needed to be made.

Most, like her mother, ended up in the workshops and factorums, selling the short span of their lives for a few meagre slates at the end of each day. They lived a pale, miserable existence, shackled to the hope that come the dawn there would be work, and that their wages would sustain them until the next sunrise.

A quick death on the street, or a slow one in the manufactorum. That was no choice, not really. And that was the thought that was never far from her mind, the kernel of bitterness at the world that she could not dislodge.

Haska realised she had been gripping the back of the chair, and let go.

'Are you hungry?' said Verka suddenly. 'I picked up what I could.' She waved a hand at one of the bags. 'Terra knows if the dispensaries are going to have anything left by morning.'

Haska's empty stomach momentarily pulled her thoughts away from gang politics and existential anger. 'What did you get?' she asked.

'Starch, stamp, sticks.' Verka forced a sing-song lilt to the refrain; the daily diet of the Spoil. Fist-sized blocks of starch, reclaimed from the dregs of the food-processing plants of the more affluent districts of Varangantua. Stamp, the all-encompassing term for reconstituted protein of even more dubious origin than the starch. And lho-sticks, to suppress the hunger of living at the literal bottom of the city's food chain.

Verka reached over to the yellowed sack and pulled out a small, dented packet and a cheap igniter. 'I managed to grab some vitamin supplements.' She paused just long enough to light a lho-stick and suck in a long, crackling breath. 'I even found a pack of carb-bars.'

'I... Thanks,' Haska said, stumbling over the unfamiliar word. She turned to hide her awkwardness, and broke open the box of carb-bars. She stuffed two of the synthetic sucrose slabs into a pocket, and after a moment's pause put a third on the table in front of her mother.

'Why don't you stay here tonight?' asked Verka. She reached out and took Haska's hand, who flinched at the unexpected contact. 'Please? It's been weeks since we've properly seen each other. It's going to be bloody out there.'

Haska pulled away. Her mother's thin fingers had been so

cold around her wrist, and Verka's pleading woke the guilt that Haska tried so hard to ignore.

'I can't. Lira, Katryn. I've got people who depend on me.' She could already imagine how Lira would react to the news.

Verka's eyes, brown where they weren't bloodshot, fixed on Haska's. She drew in a breath to launch into the argument. The same damned argument they had been having for years.

But the words didn't come. Instead the hacking started again, and this time it did not let up. Wet, choking coughs echoed around the hab, painful enough to make Verka's arms close in against her hollow chest.

A rush of panic filled Haska, a child's fear at seeing their mother in pain. She was torn between the urge to reach out and the need to run away. So she did nothing, standing in mute terror, until finally Verka managed to suck in a breath and not immediately lose it to the spasms that shook her.

Her mother turned away, watering eyes full of pain and shame. A streak of blood stained her lips, and smeared the inside of her cupped hand. She tried to cuff it away, but Haska had seen it.

Verka was dying. It was not the lho-sticks – although they didn't help – but rather the inescapable end for the hundreds of Spoilers in their clave who, like Verka, spent their days bent-backed in Ludoric Erastin's garment manufactorum. With every breath inside its low walls, Verka inhaled tiny, brittle synthweave fibres and the noxious fumes of poisonous dyes deep into her lungs. They were killing her from the inside out.

Verka's condition was the reason Haska spent as little time as possible in her hab. It was impossible to look at her mother's thin, wasted limbs, to listen to Verka's wet rasps and bloody coughs, and not see her own fate playing out before her eyes. To see the same futile, inevitable end that waited for Haska if she gave in to her fear of the street-blade's life.

Haska saw herself reach out a hand to grip her mother's shoulder, but the crash of rapid bootsteps on the stairwell made her turn. The hand instead slipped into her pocket, and emerged gripping her knife tightly. The blade snicked from its housing with the slightest pressure.

'Haska!' A fist hammering against their insubstantial door accompanied the familiar voice.

Haska folded the blade away, and crossed to the door with quick steps.

Lira Starikan and Haska Jovanic looked similar enough that they sometimes passed for sisters. Lira's eyes were a deep emerald green, whereas Haska's were her mother's dull brown, and Haska's bottom lip was creased by a tiny scar from her first proper fight. But they shared the same rail-thin figure, the same olive skin, and the same sharp, determined set to their jaw.

As ever, Lira's appearance at her door felt like a punch to the gut, making Haska's stomach churn and her pulse flutter. She smiled, without any conscious thought or intent.

'Have you heard?' Lira was practically vibrating with nervous energy. Evidently her mother, another one of Erastin's indentured workers, had brought home the news, just as Verka had. She didn't give Haska time to reply. 'Come on, we need to get to Lopushani's.'

Kronstantin Lopushani was the praetor of the Pit Snakes gang, and the clave-captain who controlled their block. The Pit Snakes were the main target of Haska's efforts to break into the Har Dhrol's ranks. She and her crew hung around the gangers, picking up the trivial jobs that others didn't want, taking their mockery and abuse.

Haska hated it. She hated the threat of the volatile, often stimmed-up street-soldiers, and the endless petty rivalries with other unblooded crews waiting for their chance. But she endured it for Lira's sake. Lira, whose fearless pursuit of rank and respect would have seen her sent to the crematoria-fields without Haska's restraining hand.

'Haska–' Her mother tried to make a final appeal, but the words died on her lips, lost in another bloody cough.

Haska turned back, and looked into her mother's watery, bloodshot eyes. At the skeletal fingers that clutched the trembling lho-stick. Verka was right: there would be blood on the streets tonight. And Haska had to make sure it wasn't her friends'.

She grasped Lira's outstretched hand, and let herself be pulled out of the hab.

Mattix held out his hand in welcome to a woman wearing an ensemble worth more than his yearly stipend. His noble visitor looked at Mattix's callused paw the way she might a venomous reptile, but in deference to the circumstances deigned to give it the briefest of touches. Anto, Mattix's aide, gratefully retreated from the office as soon as he had conveyed the woman inside.

'I am grateful for you seeing me at this late hour,' she trilled as she lowered herself onto the very lip of a chair. The silver chains that lined her half-cloak jangled softly as she settled herself as best she could. Her outfit was a riot of pleated purple silk, which narrowed to a punishingly slim bodice then flared outwards at her shoulders. Her eyes were half hidden behind a black mesh visor, held in place by a cobweb of silver strands woven through her sable hair. The impression of unrestrained wealth was completed by a heavy gorget worn atop her dress, engraved with the stooping hawk emblem of the Foreska Dynasty.

A pink-skinned cherub accompanied her, its vat-grown child's body held aloft by a subtle suspensor field. It bobbed beneath Mattix's doorway behind its mistress, then set off to explore the corners of his office.

'The night is young, mamzel.' Mattix sank back into his own seat, which was significantly more comfortable than the one on the far side of his desk. It was a petty jape but, as Mattix often reflected, in this city you had to make your own amusement.

His visitor cleared her throat. She was evidently keen to keep her visit to the squalid pens of Bastion-D as brief as possible.

'I hope you understand, Probator-Senioris Mattix – may I call you Thaddeus? – I hope you understand why this matter must be handled with the utmost discretion.'

'Entirely, my dear Annunziata.' The noblewoman wrinkled her nose at Mattix's use of her own familiar name, but he pressed on before she could object. 'A wayward child can be such a blight on a family's good name.'

Lady Annunziata Lesket Foreska and Probator-Senioris Thaddeus Mattix looked at one another over the scuffed surface of his desk, each calculating how much slate would change hands before their meeting was over.

The benefits of rank gave Mattix an office to himself, one of the shallow spaces that encircled the open chamber of probators' stations from which the noblewoman had been ushered. The room was painted in the same flaking, bilious sepia as the main hall, and the cogitator mounted on his desk was no better than that of the junior officers, but it had a door that closed, and that was worth a lot to Mattix.

Lady Foreska snapped her fingers. Her cherub attendant stopped its curious flight and bobbed over to her side. With pudgy hands, it withdrew an ornate fan from a satchel strapped around its distended belly and began to waft a rather overpowering perfume through the room. It was well into the noctis-shift, and most of the stations outside were vacant, but the level's ancient ventilation could do little to extract the day's accumulated heat, or the ground-in odours of sweating bodies and stale recaff.

Mattix liked to work at night – with fewer people around, it was easier for him to have conversations like the one he was sharing with the Lady Foreska.

'You must believe that he was led astray. My family's history in this city goes back twenty generations. There has never been a hint of disloyalty.'

Mattix held up a hand to gently stem any further protestations of innocence. 'I assure you, I am entirely aware of all that your clan has done for the district.' He was also aware of the jaw-dropping quantity of slate the Foreska Mercantile Association recorded on its ledgers each month. 'But the facts being as they are, a rather unfortunate inference could be drawn from your son's recent behaviour...'

Lord and Lady Foreska had three sons. Each of them was, in their own way, a disappointment and a liability to their noble name. But only one – Horetio, the middle child – was currently languishing in the Bastion-D gaol, on charges of sedition and distribution of inflammatory rhetoric. The severity of his crimes was such that his mother had come in person to the Bastion to plead his case. Mattix suspected Horetio's punishment for inflicting that indignity upon the contessa would be worse than any retribution the Lex Alecto's penal codes might exact, to say nothing of the Ecclesiarchy's precepts on apostasy and moral hygiene. Young Horetio had been up to quite a bit of mischief.

The noble lady had not liked his threat. Her eyes narrowed to pinpricks behind her visor, and she sat, if it was possible, even straighter on the edge of his cheap, stained chair.

'I am sure that no one possessed of any wisdom would seek to draw such an inference.'

'Of course not.' Mattix smiled to draw the tension from the conversation. She appeared to recognise his retreat, and granted him the briefest flash of perfect, polished teeth.

'As I said, my son has fallen in with an unfortunate crowd. They call themselves idealists – you and I would call them fools.' Another gleam of flawless white. Mattix wondered whether her teeth were her original set; she possessed the refined, ageless quality that was the gift of truly high-class rejuvenat treatment, and a lifestyle that rarely took her beyond her family's estates and the most select of Drago-syl's commercia precincts.

'May I be honest with you, probator-senioris? The fact is, my son is not a natural leader. He was not the architect or instigator of these... incidents.'

'Really?' Mattix's voice did not betray his interest, inviting the lady to play her hand.

'If you were willing to release Horetio into my custody, I am sure that I could convince my son to provide sufficient information for you to bring the true criminals in this affair to justice.'

Lady Foreska gave her son too much credit. Mattix had instructed the Bastion's chasteners to use only the gentlest forms of questioning, in anticipation of this encounter, but the young nobleman had already given up every one of his co-conspirators. He had gabbled out their names, renounced their dissident ideology, and pleaded for the chance to swear out a writ of testimony against them.

'That would certainly go a long way to demonstrating your son's desire to reform,' said Mattix carefully. With the opening moves made, Mattix leaned forward to reach for a mug of cold recaff on his desk with a patience calculated to infu-riate the noblewoman.

> Sorokin: dead.

The thin bead of text flickered into being across the top-left quarter of his vision. He barely glanced at the notification, pulled from his private dataveil node by his iris augmetic, but then the words settled in his mind. An unprompted surge of adrenaline set his heart rate racing.

'Do you see?' insisted Lady Foreska.

'Please, go on,' said Mattix, who hadn't heard what she'd said. He reached across his desk and struck a single key on his cogitator's built-in runeboard, and then another to open the waiting message. It was brief, just a few lines, but Mattix felt his heartbeat continue to rise.

'Is something the matter?' she asked after a few seconds of silence, her voice edged with irritation at his wandering attention.

'Hmm? Oh, not at all,' said Mattix. He stood suddenly, one hand extended towards the noblewoman. Lady Foreska rose as well, automatically matching his gesture. Mattix stepped around his desk and grasped the crook of her elbow, the touch straining the bounds of decency.

'I am afraid I must beg your indulgence, my dear Annunziata. I shall have my novus arrange the release of young Horetio in just a few days.' He pushed open his door and waved a hand to attract Anto's attention, who looked up from a stack of data-wafers with a grimace.

'But–'

'I'm so very grateful.' He gently but irresistibly propelled the woman from his office, her cherub burbling disapproval at such indecorous treatment.

The moment the door clattered shut on the noblewoman's protest Mattix had forgotten her. He dropped back into his chair and cranked his cogitator's imagifier to its full waking state, bathing his face in sickly green light.

The message was from one of his best sources in the Spoil.

It was time-stamped to less than an hour ago, showing when it had first been lodged within the vast etheric network of the dataveil. The runeboard's brass keys clattered as Mattix wrote a brief acknowledgement, along with a demand for more information as soon as it could be sent. Then he pushed back from his desk, rolling gently on his chair's castors.

It was a single source, but one he trusted. How long would it take to arrange confirmation? Too long, most likely.

When Mattix was deep in thought he would often rub his hands together, gently rasping one thick palm over the other as his mind explored a question. He was entirely unaware of the habit, but his colleagues within the Bastion knew to leave him be whenever they saw his hands slowly working away.

The murmur of rough skin filled his office for a long minute.

Mattix closed the message, then leant across his narrow desk and picked up his vox-horn from its cradle. He frowned in impatience until the crackle of static was broken by a loud click as the operator opened his line.

'*Caller and destination.*' The servitor's dry monotone carried poorly over the Bastion's ancient vox-net.

'Probator-Senioris Mattix for Castellan Hauf's office.'

'*One moment, probator.*' The desiccated voice did not give the platitude any hint of warmth. The line fuzzed once more with static until the connection was accepted.

'*What can I do for you, probator-senioris?*' murmured Kerimov, the castellan's long-suffering secretarius.

'I'm coming up to see him,' said Mattix.

'*I'm afraid that's impossible, sir. The castellan does not have a free moment for–*'

'I assure you, he has time for this.' Mattix placed the vox-horn back into the worn metal prongs of its cradle.

The walk from his office to Hauf's passed unseen, a hundred

possibilities playing out in his head. Fellow enforcers who greeted him received a quiet 'His Hand' in reply, if he bothered to reply at all. The flaking walls and tired faces went unseen because Mattix was thinking about a map, its runes and features as familiar to him as the lines of his own face.

The Spoil sat like a cancerous growth, or a knot of scar tissue, at the intersection of three districts of the city – Dragosyl, Korodilsk and Setomir. It was a neglected corner of the vast, continent-spanning immensity of Varangantua, and deliberately so; which of the neighbouring districts had once governed the Spoil was long forgotten, most likely on purpose. More pertinently, for at least two hundred years none of the district vladars had been willing to taint their fiefdoms by accepting responsibility for the sprawl of ruined manufactoria, exhausted mines, and teeming masses of destitute wretches that lurked on their borders.

Instead they had walled it up, in the case of Setomir's great line of boundary fortifications, or else left it to fester beyond the Rustwater Canal. The city had amputated a piece of itself, severing the crumbling region like a gangrenous limb. Anyone unable to acquire the residency papers necessary to escape to the more civilised districts had been left to fend for themselves. And so the Spoil had degenerated into a lawless den of criminals and their prey, a Zone Mortalis in all but official designation.

Until Sorokin had come along. By the time Mattix joined the ranks of the enforcers, recruited straight out of scholam, the man had already established himself as the pre-eminent power inside the Spoil, and had been well on his way to crushing his few remaining rivals. But unlike the petty warlords who had come before him, Andreti Sorokin had seen the potential in the decaying ruins over which he was master.

By its nature, the Spoil was a crossroads. For those willing to hazard the attempt, it was one of the few ways to cheat the city's strict border controls, allowing unregulated passage from one district to the other. It also lay across the Binastri Arterial, and was bounded to the east by the Rustwater, both once invaluable trade routes. These routes had been allowed to atrophy and die by the tri-districts' merchant-combines when the city withdrew its aegis from the region, forcing costly diversions of transported goods that had broken more than a few trading collectives.

Sorokin had reached out to the merchant-combines with an offer. He would rein in the engine-gangers and road agents, most of whom were now part of the Har Dhrol in any case, and allow the slate-hungry conglomerates to reintegrate the arterials and waterways of the Spoil into their webs of logistics and trade. In exchange, he demanded a cut of all goods that made the transit. It was a simple accord, and one that paid extraordinary dividends for the cartels and collectives who were willing to deal with the King of the Har Dhrol.

The agreement had been a masterstroke. Sorokin's power had grown, to the point that his favour had become vital for the continued commerce of the tri-districts. He was a man whose influence rivalled that of the vladars and burgraves whose offices had once left the Spoil to wrack and ruin.

Or, at least, he had been.

Mattix reached the Bastion's executive level, glided past Kerimov, and opened the office door without knocking.

Castellan Alber Hauf was not much older than Mattix, but he wore his years far worse. Genomics had cursed them both with thinning hair, but poor judgement led Hauf to scrape his grey skeins across his balding pate, whereas Mattix's servant shaved his scalp smooth each morning. Hauf's growing

paunch and pale, waxy complexion completed the contrast
with Mattix's tall, lean frame and dark skin.

'Yes, Mattix, what is it?' asked Hauf by way of welcome,
trying and failing to project an air of authority upon his subordinate. Mattix had long since trained Hauf to tolerate his
directness and his whims. Hauf was a political appointment, a
relative by marriage of some gilded grandee who had ensured
his rapid promotion through the ranks in exchange for the
usual favours and discretion that were within the power of
a castellan of enforcers.

Mattix did not resent Hauf for his unearned station. It was
the way of things, and throughout his career Mattix had been
careful to ensure that his achievements reflected just enough
of their light onto his castellan that Hauf was favourably dis-
posed towards him, despite his lack of deference.

'Andreti Sorokin is dead,' Mattix said quietly.

Mattix watched the reaction play across Hauf's face. He
could see the man's thoughts, as plain as day. First surprise,
then the momentary temptation to pretend that this was
not news to him at all; that he was not entirely reliant on
his subordinates for intelligence on the goings-on outside
the walls of his office. To Hauf's credit, he let the impulse
pass, and instead allowed a conspiratorial smile to add new
lines in his face.

'Shut the door,' said Hauf.

A pair of attendants pulled open the set of ornate doors as
Tomillan Vasimov approached, in time for a loud bark of
laughter to cut across the sounds of genteel conversation and
the strains of a viol quartet. Without turning his head, Vasimov glanced towards its source. It was Golnarok, making an
ass of himself as ever. He looked away as the burgrave gave
another discordant bray of amusement.

Vasimov stepped into the ballroom, pausing to let his gaze roam across the wide chamber. Wealth met his searching stare, in all its myriad forms. The ballroom was a monument to excess, a baroque fantasy of sculpted wood and black stone. The far wall was covered with enormous mirrors in golden frames, giving the assembled nobility every opportunity to marvel at themselves and their peers. A constellation of servo-skulls circled overhead, projecting the quartet's music along with a high-frequency privacy field.

Satisfied that there was no immediate threat, Vasimov began a slow circuit of the room's edge.

Several hundred nobles, merchant-barons, executrices, and seniors of the city's Administratum stood in tight clusters about the dance floor. Each was a riot of silk, lace and colour; this season's fashion tended towards the gaudy, at least in Vasimov's opinion. His sombre suit of black quivit wool was entirely eclipsed by the profusion of garish gowns, precarious wigs, and outlandish ruffs and collars on display.

Events such as these were a regular occurrence in the social calendar of Setomir, attracting guests of the highest strata of society from all over the city. Their frequency was due in most part to their vital role in the smooth operation of the tri-districts' business. There were other events and other venues for those merely seeking to revel in their opulence, but these galas were places for serious people making serious decisions. At least, it would be for a few more hours; after all talk of business was concluded and the night shaded into morning, the solemn and refined conversation would inevitably slouch into a debauch fit for the grandest voyeur and wastrel among them.

Attendants, for now in various states of tasteful dress, walked between the tight knots of conversation, bearing platters of obscenely rich food and tall flutes of opalwine.

No servitors were present at this function. Although their host for this evening, Lord Cherneski, and the assembled industrialists and merchant-barons could easily acquire the finest examples of the Adeptus Mechanicus' work, the current trend in the tri-districts was for fully human servants. Vasimov heartily approved. There were no ashen-skinned automata reclaimed from humanity's dregs to detract from the elegance and beauty on display.

Each attendant had been rigorously selected for their physical attributes, enhanced by chirurgeons where necessary. At the night's end, the most attractive among them would be adopted as body-servants and concubines and taken away for a life of luxury and indulgence for as long as they could hold the attention of their patrons. The rest would, in all likelihood, be traded by Cherneski's estate to one of the many flesh-purveyors who served the gilded houses, and head off to perform the same services as their more fortunate fellows but in greatly reduced comfort.

Vasimov completed his circuit of the dance floor and stopped beside two well-built men wearing sober suits of a similar, but marginally inferior, cut to his own.

'Anything?'

Andela Nedovic, his second for this evening's assignment, did not turn to look at him. 'All quiet. Except for that idiot Golnarok.'

His third, Vasil Seveci, said nothing, but silently stepped back to give Vasimov the space and deference due his rank. The three securitors stood in silence, stares roving across the mingling nobility. Formally, each man was bonded to the Reisiger, an association of securitors, bodyguards and mercenaries for hire. This made them valued servants of the Valtteri cartel.

The Valtteri was the name of an idea, although that did not prevent it from having the weight and bearing of the grandest gilded house. It had begun, as far as Vasimov knew, as an alliance between a collection of industrial concerns, agri-collectives, and the banking dynasty of Datsyuk-Bartosz. Over time, the alliance had grown into one of the most successful and ruthless examples of its type, a cartel that claimed effective monopolies over entire industries across the tri-districts. Hundreds of subsidiary corporations and merchant-combines contributed to the Valtteri's power, and guarded it from the jealous eyes and vengeful schemes of its beaten rivals.

This was Vasimov's arena. His role and rank as a senior securitor gave him a wide remit to explore and uncover threats to the interests of Valtteri. But his first duty was to safeguard the lives of the cartel's directors and executors, and that meant, on occasion, standing guard over a night of tense and intimate conversation, and the subsequent bacchanal.

Vasimov and his colleagues were far from alone. Other security officers and attachés stood at regular intervals around the ballroom's edge, clustered together beneath fluted stone arches. From time to time an aide would be summoned by some coded gesture, making a discreet sally out into the milling scrum of finely attired bodies to whisper briefly in their lord or lady's ear. Words would be exchanged, advice given or a decision noted, and then they would melt away and return to their stations.

Vasimov frowned. Several functionaries were making their way onto the floor at that very moment, and others were walking briskly away. More were sharing hushed conversations among themselves. An indefinable change in the air had taken place in the last few minutes; a new tension had settled across the assembled worthies.

He turned to Nedovic and murmured, 'Something's happening.'

Director Kriskoff Tomiç, the hereditary controller of the

Aspiry-Tomiç Trading House and Vasimov's principal concern for the night, reached up with an impeccably manicured
hand and casually brushed his thumb down the length of his
lapel. Vasimov stiffened.

'Find out what's going on,' he hissed to his subordinates.

While they scurried to obey, Vasimov waited for the requi-
site minute, and then set out at a calm but purposeful stride,
dodging between two inebriated justicii and their escorts.

He drew to a halt a few paces short of Tomiç, and clicked his
heels together sharply. The old man made him wait another
thirty seconds before deigning to give Vasimov his attention.
Vasimov inclined his head to bring him intimately close to a
man whose merest whim could alter the destiny of millions.
He did not blink at the cloying odours of perfume and sour
sweat that lingered around his shoulders.

Tomiç's voice was barely louder than a breath. 'What is
happening?' He, perhaps even more than Vasimov, was
attuned to the currents of these gatherings.

'I don't know, sir.' The admission hurt.

The old man looked up, giving Vasimov an instant of eye
contact as sharp as the rapier concealed within his cane.
'That is the last time I want to hear you speak those words,
Tomillan.'

Vasimov did not blink at the rebuke. 'Of course, sir. If you
will permit me a moment.' He straightened and dipped his
head in a curt bow, then spun and marched off the ballroom floor.

Seveci backed away as Vasimov reached him.

'Well?'

The man spread his hands in a gesture of ignorance. Vasimov felt the powerful urge to strike him, but checked his
hand as Nedovic hurried over, his gait caught somewhere
between a dignified stride and an outright run.

'Sorokin's dead,' Nedovic said breathlessly.

'What?'

'Sub-Marshal Gutzko's attaché has it from an agent in Dragosyl. Someone's killed the King of the Har Dhrol.'

Vasimov couldn't believe it. The Valtteri were the Har Dhrol's most powerful patrons. They had been the first to see the gains to be made from an alliance with an ascendant Sorokin, and had invested considerably in his tenure at the summit of his organisation. In return, Valtteri convoys constantly traversed the Spoil, bringing vast quantities of goods from the high-intensity agri-fields and ore extractors beyond the Pans to feed the insatiable tithe demands of the tri-districts' Administrata. The cartel's monopoly on the Binastri Arterial passage was integral to their dominance over their rival conglomerates.

The securitor pulled a sleek data-slate from a jacket pocket and opened his message feed. A screed of text flicked into life. Vasimov scanned the feed quickly, then swore under his breath.

He turned to his aides, gripping the surface of the data-slate in a white-knuckled fist. 'Find out where the hells Voronova is, and why I'm learning about this from Sub-Marshal Gutzko's attaché and not from her.' The two men almost ran to carry out his command.

Vasimov seethed. He had warned his masters repeatedly of the danger in their over-reliance on the woman Voronova. On most nights, he would have taken great pleasure in being proved right, but this failure transcended that petty instinct. Sorokin's death had the potential to rock the Valtteri to its foundations.

The securitor took a breath to master himself. Then he returned the data-slate to his pocket, plastered his neutral servant's expression across his angular features, and set out to inform Director Tomiç that one of his most important vassals was dead.

Vasimov considered himself to be a man of rigid self-discipline. Nevertheless, as he strode across the priceless floor, he allowed himself to utter a brief but powerful curse against the person of Melita Voronova.

Edi Kamensk released a low, impassioned curse, and hammered his fist against the heavy steel door. 'Voronova, for Throne's sake, are you in there?'

He waited for an answer, but did not expect one.

Night had fallen over Dragosyl many hours ago, but it was far from dark. The lumen-posts in this part of the district all worked, and a massive chameleon-screen on the roof of the opposite building blazed with advertisements, in between the mandated exhortations to duty and vigilance. Warmth radiated from the hab-tower's brickwork, and from the crowds that thronged the street at Edi's back. It was the dry season in the city's equatorial reaches, and the narrow streets had soaked in the day's heat, ensuring no respite even in the early hours of the morning.

Even without the glare of artificial light, there would be little to distinguish night from day on the fringes of Dragosyl's expansive mercantile district. Business, like so many other things in Varangantua, did not sleep. Crowds of suited merchant-combine lackeys mingled with robed Administratum officials heading to and from their places of work, cursing the clusters of off-shift revellers that formed knots of sweat and noise outside the entrances to joy houses.

It was a night on which the sanctioners would be busy, if Edi was any judge. Which he was; for thirty-two years, Edi Kamensk had carried the seal and shock maul of the Sanctioner Corps, the arm, and more often than not the fist, of the Lex Alecto. On a night like this, the heat would make people thirsty, and the drink would make them unruly. And then it would be necessary for his former comrades to step in and return order to the streets.

Melita Voronova had her office on the ground floor of a squat tenement in the Ubrava habclave of the Dragosyl district. In similar buildings the street-level unit would be a refec-house, its walls fronted with plex and catering to the hurrying legions of stipend-men and manufactorum labourers going about their day, or a habclave overseer's office. In this one, it was an info-broker's lair.

Edi slammed his fist against the door once more, but there was still no reply.

With a sigh, he reached over to a discreet panel beside the door and flipped it down. Inside was a small, hollow space, with the bottom surface smoothed into a depression. A series of tiny needles, barely visible in the light of the nearest lumen-post, lined the depression.

Edi pulled off one of his gloves and pressed his thumb into the space.

Nothing happened for several seconds while the gene-lock tasted his blood, then a loud buzz crackled as the electromagnetic locks holding the door closed clicked off. Sucking his thumb, Edi pushed the sea-green steel back on its hinges.

'Bloody hells.'

The room was in its typical state of utter disrepair. The office lumens were dark, but the light from the doorway revealed enough. The far wall was stacked high with cogitator units of every description and function. The rear of the office was dominated by a desk piled with yet more equipment, some of it disassembled. Reams of parchment and data-wafers were strewn across the floor, along with recaff mugs, discarded food wrappers and dirty clothes.

Amid the mess, Melita Voronova lay sprawled on her cot, half a dozen blisters of topaz scattered across the tangled sheets. A cotin inhaler lay in her open palm, and its cloying odour hung in the air.

Edi stepped inside, and let the door swing shut. The metal made an almighty bang as it closed, but that drew no reaction from the unconscious info-broker.

'Melita!' He strode over to her and clapped his hands beside her head. She stirred, but did not wake. He checked her pulse, and then the blisters of topaz; fortunately, only two had been drained. Edi flicked on a small glow-globe mounted on the wall above the cot and swept up the unused packets, each about the size of his callused thumb. He slipped them into a pocket, out of her reach.

She seemed to Edi to be very small, and very young. Her hair, lank and greasy, had fallen across her face, although it was still no more than brown fuzz on the left side of her head after the surgery. The scar that curled from her temple along the edge of her shaved hairline was raised and livid, at odds with her waxy, pallid skin. She never saw the sun; Edi had known her to go for days without leaving the cesspit of her office. Her loose shirt was tangled around her, as though she'd been thrashing in her sleep, and her tight-fitting breeches were stained and torn.

With a sigh, Edi went into the office's tiny ablutions chamber, and returned carrying a metal bucket. Then he plucked a slim case from a pocket in his jacket, and withdrew a chromed injector.

He leant over Melita's prone form. 'I'm running out of patience with this,' he said quietly. Then he jammed the injector hard into the meat of Melita's thigh.

'Gah!' She lurched upright, one hand grasping her leg in pain. She looked around, surprise momentarily banishing the narcotic stupor in which she had been wallowing. She looked up at him, eyes still unfocused. 'Edi? What the hells?'

'Brace yourself.'

'What–' Then she pitched forward, retching into the pail. Weak hands tried to grasp either side of the bucket, but Edi held it stable in her lap as Melita's body was wracked by heaving spasms. There were detoxicants that did their work more gently, but they were expensive, and Edi was a believer in direct action.

Amid the noisy convulsions, Edi felt the urge to reach out and stroke her head, but stopped himself. Theirs was not that kind of relationship.

After a while, the stream of vomit slowed. Melita coughed up a final mouthful of bile, then pushed the bucket away. After a few deep breaths, she managed to stammer out a few words.

'For Terra's sake… Why?'

Edi set the pail down carefully beside her cot, and knelt to look her in the eye. 'Sorokin's dead.'

He watched the two words filter through the remnants of topaz that still clouded her senses. After a moment's delay, her brow furrowed, and her eyes gained a fraction of their usual hardness.

'Shit.'

CHAPTER 2

Melita stood in the ablutions chamber on unsteady feet, both hands gripping the metal basin. She didn't look at the mirror, because she knew what she would see.

'Here.'

She turned to find Edi holding out a pair of blue lozenges, each the size of her thumbnail. She reached out and took them, disgusted by the tremor in her hand.

'You carry a detox kit around with you?' she asked. Her voice was a hoarse whisper.

'I do these days.'

She dry-swallowed both tabs with a grimace. She knew from bitter experience how harsh the hangover from a detox-icant injection could be. The lozenges would stimulate her body to start replenishing its needs, which had been stripped from her system along with the topaz. They wouldn't help with the shakes, though.

She rinsed her mouth with water from the basin – the municipal water supply in the Ubrava region was regularly tested, and was more or less safe to drink – and spat into the noisome bucket beside her.

'He's really dead?' she asked, still not looking up from the basin. The scuffed metal caught her reflection, but only barely, showing anonymous streaks of colour for her hair and face.

'So they told me.'

'Who told you?'

'Vasimov. Someone on his staff, at any rate.'

Melita swore under her breath. Of all the malicious, ambitious, narcissistic officers of the Valtteri cartel, it was her poor fortune to have been leashed to Tomillan Vasimov.

'Who killed him?'

'I think that's what Vasimov wants you to tell him.'

Melita swore again.

She finally looked up. The face in the mirror was pale and drawn, with a stray smear of vomit clinging to her cheek. She wiped her mouth and turned away.

Edi was looking at her, not trying to keep the judgement from his face. Or maybe it was concern. Either way, she ignored him. She kicked a pile of unwashed clothes aside as she crossed to her desk, and slumped into her chair.

The old sanctioner opened the small fridgerator under the office's culina counter and retrieved a plastek container of water, and a bottle of jeneza. He placed the water deliberately on the desk beside Melita, and took his beer over to the cot. There were no other seats in the room besides her chair; this was where she came to work, not to meet clients or entertain friends. If she'd had any friends.

The two of them sat in silence, Edi holding his beer, Melita cradling her head in her hands. The aches of her abused body demanded her attention. The two punctures in the crook of her elbow were the worst, at the same time itching and throbbing. She felt feverish; sweat was beading her brow despite the cold that seemed to emanate from her bones.

'A bad time for one of your benders,' Edi observed, into the silence. His voice was a bass growl from a lifetime of cheap lho-sticks and roaring orders at recalcitrant citizens.

She looked up at him. 'That's not helpful, Edi.'

'What prompted tonight's session?' he asked, ignoring the warning tone in her voice.

Melita shook her head. 'It doesn't matter.' She threw herself back into her chair. The cracked and faded synthleather hugged her thin frame like an old friend.

'The aug acting up?' That was an excuse she had given before. In truth, the scar left by the implantation of her iris augmetic three months earlier was a fierce ache through the left side of her head. But that wasn't why she'd reached for the first blister of topaz.

'Just leave it, Edi.'

He nodded, relenting for the moment. 'You should drink that,' he said instead. He gestured to the water on her desk, while taking a pull on his jeneza.

It was good advice. Melita cracked the bottle's top and took a long swallow, before reaching out to flick switches and dials. The banks of cogitators and data-looms around the office began to hum, growing in volume and tempo as the machine spirits of her equipment awoke. The fog in her head was starting to clear, creating space for her to grapple with the enormity of what Edi had told her.

'When did they find you?' Melita asked without turning round from her desk. There was a feverish urgency in her question. She needed a timeline, to know just how long she had been out of the loop.

'An hour ago, more or less.'

'How?'

'A messenger. Two, actually. I gather they'd already tried you, but you weren't at home.'

She ignored that.

So, an hour for Edi to be roused and to reach her, and assume at least another hour for Vasimov's runners to reach him. How long would it have taken for word to have reached the securitor, if not through her? How much could have happened that she had missed?

The first imagifier finally clicked into life, and Melita reached for the runeboard with a desperate hunger.

She knew that the Valtteri had other info-brokers on their payroll, but none were as well connected as her. Over the course of six years, Melita had built a network of paid informants that spanned the tri-districts, and particularly the festering tumour of the Spoil that lay between them. She knew that since they had press-ganged her into their organisation, the cartel had come to rely on her for insight into the Har Dhrol over and above their other spies and spy-masters.

She was not proud of that position; in fact, she actively resented it. She had not developed her web of contacts in order to satisfy the Valtteri cartel's thirst for intelligence, nor to aid and defend their dominance of industry and commerce in the tri-districts.

Melita Voronova had, before the Valtteri had claimed her, been an independent agent, a go-between for individuals and organisations of every kind. She had worked for jaegers and bounty-hunters, gangsters and assassins. Even an enforcer or two, when they were pursuing some extrajudicial mission beyond the bounds of the Lex. But mostly she had been a broker, an expert in bringing together two parties who each had something the other wanted, and pocketing a tidy sum for her efforts. The challenge had been uncovering who wanted what, and it had been those skills that had brought the Valtteri to her door.

She specialised as a cipher-knife, a hunter of secrets lodged within data-looms and information manifolds, a subverter of all systems electronic and technomantic. She had a gift for it. She had spent years honing her craft, and gathering the tools and machinery necessary to make her a danger to any data-bunker. But those skills would not be needed tonight.

Nine times in ten, slate was a surer way to obtain information than the subtle arts of the cipher-knife, although admittedly of more variable quality. For some of her informants, particularly those in the Spoil, Melita was their main source of income. For her more affluent sources, her slate was a bonus, a tidy supplement to their annual stipends to be concealed from the Ecclesiarchy's tithe-collectors, a way of subsidising their losses at the rajet tables, or funding their other illicit habits. Slate flowed through Melita's hands like water. For some it was a trickle, and for a few a mighty river, depending on how greatly Melita – and the Valtteri – valued their insights.

The cogitator-bank's hum kicked into a higher frequency as Melita sought out what insights they could give her now.

As a rule, Melita's informants did not contact her directly. Instead, she created places where they could leave her messages, trusting to her ingenuity and the sheer scale of Varangantua's infosphere to conceal them. With rapid, clattering strokes on her runeboard and the arcane processes of her brass-bound thinking machines, Melita delved into isolated dataveil nodes, forgotten storage units, enforcer closed-case vaults, merchant-combine records-towers, and in one case the private and rather insecure archive of a senior cleric of an Adeptus Ministorum mission in Korodilsk.

She worked in intense silence, while Edi quietly nursed his

jeneza. That was the way between them, and for the most part, it worked.

Edi Kamensk had come into her life four or five years ago, one of several bodyguards she had contracted as muscle for a job that had brought her into contact with more guns than she was comfortable with. Unlike the rest of the mercenaries, Edi had actually stuck around until the job had been done, and probably saved her life in the process. After that, she had hired him more and more, until, almost accidentally, he had become her permanent bodyguard, and she his only protectee.

She wasn't sure why, exactly. For her part, Melita valued having someone in her life that she wholly trusted, whom she knew was entirely in her corner. Why Edi put up with her, she couldn't say – Melita knew she was hardly the easiest person to be around. During his years with the enforcers he had been married, but the district's census records did not record any children. If she was an outlet for his pent-up paternal feelings, Edi had chosen poorly.

In any case, since she had been forcibly inducted into the Valtteri cartel, Edi's presence at her back had become a source of comfort, when he wasn't being judgemental and overbearing.

After an hour of ferocious activity, she leant back from her desk, rubbing her eyes with the heels of her palms. The night had given way to the deep hours of early morning, and the topaz blackout from which Edi had roused her could not be called a form of rest.

She let out a loud sigh.

'Well?' Edi asked. If she had caught him napping, he hid it well.

Melita was too tired and strung out to conceal her frustration. 'The city believes that Andreti Sorokin is dead.

Beyond that, I have no idea. If anyone knows anything real, they haven't told me.'

The majority of her informants had reported in over the past few hours, most with brief, breathless missives that simply passed on the rumours that had come to them from their own sources. Few had any first-hand information, and some had included their own speculations that were easily interrogated and dismissed.

'What about your inside man?'

Alone of all her informants, Melita had given one person the means to reach her directly. She had invested considerable time and energy setting up one of her sources in the Spoil with a way to reach her day or night. Someone on whom she relied to corroborate any hint or rumour concerning the Har Dhrol's operations.

'Nothing. Not a word.' The absence of any contact from her principal informant was deeply troubling.

'Are they alive?'

She shrugged. The prospect that they had been caught up in the spontaneous and chaotic violence that was undoubtedly sweeping the Spoil was not out of the question. A full-scale coup against the Har Dhrol leadership could be underway, and she would have no way to know it.

'So. What do you know?'

Melita had to smile. Edi had an uncanny steadiness to him. He seemed to absorb her vocal agitation with a gruff, weatherbeaten calm. It made him a useful sounding board.

She plucked a slim black lho-stick and an igniter from a silver case on her desk. It was a bad habit, and one she'd tried to stop more than once. But without a runeboard under her hands – or an injector against her arm – she felt restless, her fingers tying themselves in knots. The sticks gave her hands something to do.

'Oh, plenty. The gangs are mourning, or celebrating, and

each of them is fighting everyone else. All the clave-captains and anyone of sense has gone to ground, so there's no one to rein them in.' The igniter clicked on and off, and she drew in a deep breath of hot, bitter smoke. 'The Grenzers are closing the bridges.'

That had been the one useful nugget of information she'd acquired. An enforcer dispatch operator had sent her a copy of a deployment request from Bastion-D to the Grenze Guard, directing them to lock down all of the Rustwater Canal crossings into Dragosyl. The Grenzers were the division of the city's great administrative machine that maintained the watch on the border between the tri-districts and the Spoil. In years past, they had been held in the same regard as the district enforcers, but since Sorokin's rise their prestige and readiness had suffered, responsible for a duty that most in positions of power preferred to see done poorly.

'That's smart. Best to keep things contained,' Edi offered.

'Yes, but only for a little while.' Melita leaned forward, suddenly animated as she started pulling on the thread. 'The Spoil lives on imports. Food, medicaments, fuel for generatoria. The dispensaries are going to run dry, and anyone who's stockpiled is going to either get rich or get raided in short order.' She could see it in her mind, the irresistible pressures of hunger and anger breaking down all the rules that Sorokin had painstakingly erected. 'The clave-captains will need to get food into their territories quickly or they will lose control entirely. That will mean more raids, on Dragosyl, on Korodilsk. Into the Line. And if they fail, we'll start to get people looking to escape. There's always some movement into the districts, but this will be a flood.'

Melita drew in another lungful of smoke and exhaled it into the space between them. 'Things could get very bad, very quickly.'

Edi nodded slowly. 'So, what are you going to do about it?'

Melita blinked. She had not considered that question.

One of her cogitators released a tinny chime as a new message winked into existence at the top of her feed. Melita spun around, feeling hope rise, only for that hope to be punctured when she saw the sender's ident-tag. She stared at the blinking line of text, but there was nothing to be gained by putting it off.

The message was a hololithic recording, so with a brief sequence of commands she transferred it over to Oriel. A loud metallic crunch echoed from the corner of Melita's office, as a silver-plated servo-skull pulled itself free from its docking station.

Oriel had been Melita's companion for the whole of her life, in one form or another. In her infancy she had been cared for by a nursemaid named Jerilla. When Jerilla was finally consumed by the vindictive blood disorder that had plagued her life, Melita's parents had chosen to honour all that she had done for their daughter. They had given her body to the flesh-crafters of the Adeptus Mechanicus, who returned Jerilla to the Voronova clan as Oriel, a tireless, macabre guardian servo-skull. Melita had had much cause to thank her parents for their generosity and foresight; the needle-gun projecting from beneath Oriel's chromed palate had saved her life more than once.

The anti-grav plates contained within the servo-skull's lobes propelled it up into the office's rafters, then down to hover at head height. The ruby-red glow of its ocular sensor dimmed, and at the same time a blue gleam in its other eye socket bloomed. After a moment, the hololithic projector flickered into life.

'Voronova. The situation in the Spoil is rapidly deteriorating. I hope this is not news to you.'

The upper half of Tomillan Vasimov's body wavered in the air between her and Edi, like the busts of civic leaders and benefactors that decorated so many Administratum buildings. Oriel's projector was fairly high-grade; although all colour was reduced to hues of laser-blue, the tri-D image was sufficiently clear to carry every twist of scorn in Vasimov's face.

Melita hated him. Even the sight of his projected image in her office felt like an intrusion, a violation of her sanctuary. Of her life.

The projected Vasimov proceeded in ignorance of Melita's glare. *'The directors believe that intervention may be necessary in order to ensure a smooth transition of power within the Har Dhrol.'*

Melita had to smile at that, although there was no amusement in it. Finding someone from among the ranks of the Har Dhrol's leadership caste who could keep the rest in line, and who would be willing to maintain the much-hated union with the Valtteri, would be far from easy.

Her smile faded as she realised that Vasimov might hold her responsible for finding such a candidate.

'The directors desire a briefing on the situation. I have arranged transit for you from Ubrava. Present yourself to the Lariel Skyport at oh-three-hundred hours for transport to the Xeremor.'

Just like that, she was summoned. Called to heel. Vasimov, more than all the other Valtteri lackeys she had dealt with, seemed to enjoy reinforcing her status as a servant of the cartel, a tool with as little agency as a hammer or an auto-quill.

Vasimov adjusted the set of his shoulders, and his sneer grew into a predatory leer. *'You should know that your failure to predict this crisis has been noted. If your capabilities prove inadequate to the coming challenge, I am authorised to terminate your relationship with the organisation.'*

The tri-D image played on for a few more seconds, then

froze. Vasimov's cold, mocking eyes glared from the still image, then guttered out as Oriel's projector clicked into somnolence. Melita stared at the space where Vasimov had been, not seeing Oriel's impassive skull as it bobbed in place, awaiting her next command.

She was under no illusions about Vasimov's threat of expulsion from the cartel. The Valtteri was a city-spanning alliance of merchant-combines, industrial concerns and trading entities, but it operated on the same logic as any gutter gang. If they no longer needed you, there was no amicable parting of ways. The Valtteri could call on any number of cut-throats and assassins who specialised in killing people they didn't know. That threat, after all, had been how Melita had ended up working for them in the first place.

'You should go,' said Edi, puncturing the silence.

'Why?' she replied immediately.

Edi's face shifted into the tense, locked-down expression he wore when he was containing his exasperation. 'Vasimov was pretty explicit on that front.'

'Fuck him.' That was reckless and petulant, but Melita's strung-out body was aching and her mind was fizzing. She climbed to her feet, lifted by frustrated energy. 'I'm supposed to jump whenever they call?'

'There are worse things in life than taking orders.'

'You think I don't want to go because I'm being contrary?' Although there was, she had to admit, some truth to that.

'But you can help!'

'Why would I want to help the damned Valtteri?'

Edi said nothing for a long moment. 'Sit down,' he said finally.

Melita bridled; she had had more than enough of men telling her what to do in her own damned office. 'No.'

Edi sighed, and pressed on. 'A lot of people are going to die in the next few days.' He leaned forward, rolling the empty bottle of jeneza between his hands. 'You're too young to remember the Spoil as it was. Hells, it's a distant memory for me. I'd been in the Corps for less than a year when Sorokin finally brought the Redfort gangs to heel. But I remember what it was like.'

She leaned back against her desk, letting curiosity overtake her anger. Edi rarely talked like this, and when people wanted to talk, Melita let them.

'The Spoil was poor. And not poor like it is now. They had nothing. The borders were warzones. The Spoil lived off the raids into the Line, into the districts, just like you're saying will happen. The gangs weren't just trigger-happy men and juves looking to build a reputation, they were mothers and grandfathers. That kind of desperation is a more powerful force than you can imagine.

'I had comrades in the Corps who saw whole families sent to the penal battalions for managing to cross the canal. I detained a father who was stealing unformed starch in buckets out of the waste bins of a processing plant. Neighbours would kill each other just for the chance to go out on a raid into Setomir, despite barely a third of them ever making it back across the Line. A verispex once told me that in those days, by the Bastion's estimates, the sale of bodies to the crematoria-fields was the Spoil's fourth biggest export, behind topaz, black ice, and people with blades who would do anything for a fistful of slate.

'So when I say that you can help, that's what I mean. If you have to swallow your self-respect and lick Vasimov's boots to save Sorokin's damned gang and stop all that from happening again, you should do it.'

Edi stopped, all at once. At some point in his speech he had stood up, and now folded himself back onto her cot.

Melita watched him for a little while. 'I wouldn't expect an enforcer to be such a humanitarian,' she said mildly.

He snorted. 'I'm retired.'

She had listened throughout Edi's speech, and had been surprised to feel herself shamed by it. Since hearing the news, she had only considered Sorokin's death in terms of herself. What would the Valtteri do because of her failure to predict it? How would she escape that retribution? Even as Melita had been describing the Spoil's descent into chaos, her mind had been turning over the commercial implications, the million connections between suppliers and producers and consumers in the tri-districts that would be disrupted by the coming anarchy. That was where her instincts led her, because amid that anarchy was her place. Right now, she should be deep inside trading ledgers, searching for new deals, helping to forge new connections to keep the eternal cycle of commerce moving. To spot the advantage in the situation, wherever it might be found.

It had never been Melita's role to be a shaper of events. She merely reacted to them, and found a way to scrape her percentage while avoiding the crash of the falling wave. The lives lost in the churn had never been a part of her equation. She had never cared, because caring would not have changed anything.

Or, at least, that was what she had told herself.

'All right,' Melita said.

'All right, what?'

'I mean, let's be humanitarians.'

'You're going to the Xeremor?'

'No.' Melita had decided that the moment Vasimov's message had demanded it of her. Not just because she resented his high-handed summons, but because right now she had nothing substantive to present the cartel's lords. In all likelihood, she would be delivering herself to a death sentence for failing in the duty they had demanded that she discharge.

'No, I need facts. Solid information, something I can give them. Whoever killed Sorokin didn't do it out of revenge or at random. They wanted to start something.'

'You don't think your employers will be upset that you're standing them up?' asked Edi, trying for one final time to be a voice of reason.

'Probably. But I can't help anyone from a spire in Setomir.'

Edi crossed his arms, admitting defeat. 'So what are you going to do?'

Melita spun and sat down heavily again, hands already reaching for the runeboard. 'We'll need a groundcar.'

CHAPTER 3

Fire was the elemental fear of every Spoiler, an indiscriminate predator that tore the guts from domiciles and ravaged factorums. It was inexorable, unstoppable, particularly in the dry season when there wasn't even the hope of an Emperor-sent rainstorm to fight the inferno. The rumour of an arsonist stalking a clave was one of the few things that could unify the Spoil's fractious populace, calling down lynch mobs on anyone unfortunate enough to be accused.

'Stay back!'

Haska and Lira stopped in their tracks, even though the command had not been for them.

They had smelled the smoke as soon as they left their hab-block, but hadn't started running until they realised its source. They had been looking for Katryn, as there had been no answer when they tried their friend's domicile in the neighbouring building.

'She'll be with her man,' Lira had said with a mocking grin. The third member of their crew, Katryn Muscher, was sweet on Aryat Karamenko, one of Kronstantin Lopushani's young soldiers and the nephew of one of the praetor's key lieutenants. Aryat would undoubtedly be found clinging to his uncle's coat-tails, and she with him.

Flames billowed from the windows of Aryat's hab-block. The plex was gone, shattered by overpressure, and black smoke poured in torrents from rooms lit red from within. The hab was six levels high, and the top two were barely visible between curling ribbons of fire.

Hundreds of people lined the street, impotent witnesses to the destruction of their homes. Even from a distance, Haska could feel the flames. A half-hearted cordon of gangers kept the crowd at bay, although most were staring upward, gripped by the same horror and fury as the block's residents. The hab-block had been one of the Pit Snakes' own stacks, home to dozens of blooded gangers and their families.

A tall girl with a shock of blonde hair pushed her way through the crowd, heading for Haska and Lira. At the sight of her, Haska let out a heavy sigh of relief.

While Haska and Lira shared a resemblance, the same could not be said of Katryn Muscher. Her father had been famed across the clave as a pit fighter, and Katryn had inherited his height, his broad shoulders, and his devastating uppercut. She was a year younger than Haska and Lira, but was by a considerable distance the best fighter among them, the victor of a dozen brawls with rival juve crews.

She cannoned into her friends, wrapping them in a tight embrace.

'Are you okay?' Lira asked, slightly muffled by her friend's arm.

Katryn released them. 'I'm fine.'

'The boy?' The insult slipped out, and Haska immediately regretted it. She and Aryat did not get along. Like so many juves pretending to be men, Aryat was a fragile and easily offended soul, and Haska had little time for his posing. But this was not the time for that pettiness.

Katryn's expression soured. 'He's fine too. We were down at Morsanyi's joy house when we heard about the king. We came back to... this.' She looked up at the burning building, in time to see a wall collapse inwards. A serpent's tongue of flame boiled from the new wound.

'What the hells happened?' Lira asked. 'You think that has anything to do with Sorokin?'

Katryn didn't answer. There was no way to know, but it hardly mattered. The Pit Snakes would assume this was an attack of the most savage type and respond in kind, even if they had no idea who their attacker was.

There would be blood on the streets tonight, just as Haska had imagined.

'Where's Lopushani?' she asked.

'Not here. At least, I've not seen him. The talk is he's run for a safehouse, same as every other clave-captain with any sense.'

Lira nodded understanding. 'So who's in charge?'

'Does it look like anyone's in charge of this?'

It did not.

'What about Karamenko?' Haska asked. The ruined hab-block was in Aryat's uncle's territory. Everything in the Spoil was someone's possession, from the street corner held by a single favoured crew to an entire clave claimed by a captain, all the way up to Sorokin, the master of all he surveyed. At least, that's how it had been.

'Over there,' Katryn said, pointing towards the far side of the street where Aryat and Karlo Karamenko were locked in tense conversation.

The older man was an inch or two shorter than his nephew,

but much more powerfully built, like a barrel on legs. He wore a heavy coat despite the night's heat, thickly padded at the shoulders to emphasise his frame. His face was dominated by a short beard, which Haska was certain he dyed to an unnaturally deep black. The iron trim on the armoured panels of his coat displayed his status as a lieutenant of the Pit Snakes, along with the gang's viper icon picked out in silver on both shoulders.

Haska had an instinctive dislike for and fear of Karlo Karamenko. He was too slick, too vicious. She knew the clave's smile-girls avoided him if they could, and Haska could easily see why.

'What are they talking about?' Lira asked.

'I don't know,' said Katryn, 'Karlo grabbed Aryat as soon as we got here.'

The elder Karamenko had his hand on his nephew's shoulder in a grip that was domineering rather than familiar. The boy had a nervous frown on his face, which looked absurdly childish beside his uncle's stern scowl.

Aryat glanced towards the hab-block and noticed Haska and her crew. He turned back to his uncle, gesturing their way. They spoke for a few more moments, then both headed towards the knot of juves.

Haska steeled herself. Through unspoken agreement, she had been the leader of their little crew since the three of them first banded together. And that meant being the one to have to deal with men like Karlo Karamenko.

'Jovanic,' he said by way of greeting. The old man's top lip was split by a nasty scar, which could not be concealed by the thick bristles of his beard.

'Karlo.' Haska tried to give his nephew a reassuring nod, but Aryat didn't acknowledge her.

'It was Stoyano. That bastard Stoyano.' Aryat spat the name

like a curse. He was a handsome boy, lithe where his uncle was stocky, but with the same piercing eyes and coal-black hair.

Vagif Stoyano was the captain of several claves that neighboured Lopushani's territory. The Pit Snakes and Stoyano's Forge Fiends had been circling each other for years, two rabid canids forced into close proximity. The undercurrent of their conflict broke out in violence every few days – crews getting into scuffles that turned bloody, raids on one another's holdings, threats to tenants paying protection to the rival gang. The sort of thing that made life in the Spoil so tense, and so brief.

'How do you know that?' Haska asked.

Karlo glared at her. 'Because I do.'

'We're going to hit him back.' Aryat looked to be on the verge of tears; his domicile was one of the habs now burnt to ashes. Katryn reached out and took his hand, and he gripped it hard.

'We are?' said Lira, half scared, half excited.

Karlo gave the briefest nod. 'The rules have changed. We know where he is, and we're going to kill him.'

'I want you all with me,' said Aryat in earnest. He gave Katryn's hand another squeeze, and she looked at Haska and Lira.

Blood on the streets, thought Haska.

CHAPTER 4

Melita and Edi drove along the eastern edge of the Rustwater Canal, the tyres of their groundcar just yards from the cliff-edge.

The border road barely deserved the name. The narrow ledge of rock followed the course of the waterway that marked the western boundary of Dragosyl, and its surface had been allowed to erode into gravel and dust by the district's authorities. The canal itself was far below them, an expanse of grey mire hundreds of yards across, slick with accumulations of spilled promethium, human sewage, and the oxidised run-off that gave the Rustwater its name. The canal ran for over three hundred miles, from its terminus beneath the shadow of the Redfort, to its junction with the Drav River. There the two polluted streams curdled and became one, and ran on into the dark waters of the distant ocean.

Edi steered manually, not trusting the machine spirit of their borrowed Grappia Noxus on the broken asphalt and loose scree. Ordinarily they would have taken *Katuschka*,

Edi's prized Dymaxion Model 34. The painstakingly maintained antique was ideal for making an impression, and for a fast getaway, but for this day's work they needed something that was less conspicuous. The Noxus' bodywork was corroded back to the flaking steel and its synthweave seats were torn and stained, but there was a reliable engine slung within its rusting chassis. Edi and Melita sat up front, with Oriel clamped to a mobile charging rig that was secured inside the groundcar's storage compartment.

Entering the Spoil was proving to be harder than Melita had predicted.

This, in itself, was an emphatic indicator of the impact of Sorokin's death. As a matter of district policy, the bridges over the Rustwater were purposefully ignored, although as a result they were in varying states of disrepair. The largest of them, like the crossing between the Kerysk subdistrict and the Spoil-side clave of Abbotsfeld, might be monitored on the Dragosyl side by a picter hooked into the Grenze Guard data-trunks, or by a bored youth with a vox if the controlling Har Dhrol clave-captain felt like going to the trouble.

The reason for this purposeful neglect was obvious. There was sufficient slate invested – from both sides of the Rustwater – in the free and unexamined movement of traffic through the Spoil to ensure that no one wanted to pay close attention to the ways in which it got in and out.

It had taken just one death, and one night, to change all that.

Opportunistic crews of gangers had built barricades across the first six bridges Melita and Edi came to, evidently hoping to shake down or, more likely, hijack any uninformed travellers. The bridges not barricaded on the Spoil side were blocked by the city. Enormous Bulwark riot-wagons, their armoured prows extended to either side to form impromptu battlements, were posted at the largest crossings. Squads of Grenzers stared with undisguised hostility at the gangers who jeered beyond the range of their shot-cannons. Edi and Melita slowed as they passed these roadblocks, not wanting to draw any attention to themselves.

Finally, Edi took them to the Wasaran Locks, a narrow series of swing bridges which leapt across the canal a mere fifteen yards above the foetid waters. The crossing, as he'd predicted, had not yet been occupied on either side, for a reason that became apparent as soon as they started down the sheer approach road.

Melita gagged. The reek of the canal's putrid water had been foul from the cliffside, but so close to its surface the stench was thick enough to make them both retch. Edi fairly raced from one rotting stanchion to the next, the Noxus' tyres clattering over the Locks' loose deck plating. Finally, they reached the far side, and followed the bridge's curving path down into the tangle of canal-side wharfs and warehouses.

Melita coughed as she finally sucked in a full breath.

'Bad, isn't it?' Edi chuckled, although he wheezed just as hard. 'My father's father worked these docks. I never met him, but my pa talked about him a lot. He'd come home each day wearing a stink that made his eyes water.'

Tears were, in fact, streaming from Melita's eyes. 'I didn't know the Rustwater was still active back then.'

Recollection's warmth faded from Edi's smile. 'It wasn't.'

In a time well beyond living memory, the Spoil had been the industrial heartland of the tri-districts. Manufactoria and smelteries and forges had turned out materiel in quantities to match any district of the city. But its true wealth had lain in the substrate beneath these mammoth complexes.

Iron, carbon, aluminia. These elements were common enough, veined throughout Alecto's continental shelves. But the city's ravenous hunger for the base materials of industry could never be sated, and they had been found in gargantuan quantities throughout the region that quickly became known as the Spoil. Open-cast mines were delved by the extractor-behemoths of the Adeptus Mechanicus, and armies of serf-labour were imported from the tri-districts to haul the coveted ore free. The foundries of the Spoil were unequal to the task of processing such volumes, and so the greater part of the planet's bounty had found its way to the Rustwater Canal.

Melita stared up at the iron skeletons of gantry cranes and ore elevators as they passed beneath their rusted frames. The city was already beginning to bake in the morning heat, and everything outside the groundcar was streaked with chem-rich rot and filth. It was hard to imagine the docks as they had once been. The colossal silos of the Rustwater had, so local legend maintained, fed hundreds of cargo vessels each day, great macro-ships that carried the produce of the enormous quarries to the Drav River, and thence to every corner of the city.

Those times, if they had ever existed, were well and truly over. The mines had been exhausted centuries before Melita's birth, and the great cargo vessels plied other waterways.

'What did he do?' Melita asked. She was tense, nervous questions chasing one another round her head, to say nothing of the lingering aftershock of Edi's detoxicant. Edi's gruff storytelling was a comforting distraction.

'Hmm?'

'Your father's father. What work did he have down here?'

'Same as now,' he said. 'Taking whatever the gangs wanted moving down to Korodilsk, or brought up from there.'

'A rough trade.'

Edi shrugged.

Since its decline, the vast majority of employment within the Spoil was in unlicensed manufactoria and narcotics plants, and in the warehouses and depots that supplied them. These were grim, dirty places set up by grim, dirty people, hoping to undercut their competition in the tri-districts through access to a workforce desperate for slate, in a location with non-existent safety standards and no Lex oversight. Most folded before too long, unable to match the sheer output of the merchant-combines, or else were forced out by a more established rival who was jealous of their niche. But there were always new speculators moving into workshops recently vacated by the last entrepreneurs, with plans in mind that needed cheap labour and no questions asked by the city's bureaucracy. And always the Har Dhrol street-soldiers were there, demanding prompt payment of the building's rent regardless of success or failure.

Edi kept the groundcar moving, turning off the dockside and up through the paved storage fields and warehouses. Melita saw Edi watching corners and the tops of buildings for signs of ambush. The docks were the haunts of smugglers and the stevedores that helped them export the illicit produce of the Spoil across to the buyers in Korodilsk and Dragosyl. But this morning the wharfs were all but deserted. Habless vagrants and oblivious rek-heads lay slumped in doorways, immune to the wider politics and fears of the street, but the crowds of day-labourers who would usually be trudging towards the docks at this hour were nowhere to be seen.

Melita shifted in her seat. 'I don't like this.' The strange emptiness was unnerving. Life, such as it was in the Spoil, was lived on the streets, at least during the daylight hours.

'No work's getting done today,' Edi said. He was right; Melita had a sudden image of a great mass of people crammed together in their squalid hab-blocks, roasting in the heat,

raging at the day's lost slate thanks to the death of one man
and the volatility of his would-be successors.

The arterial they had been following finally left the rust-
encrusted domain of the docks and entered the first of the
habclaves and their slumping tenements. At Melita's urging,
Edi accelerated, and they plunged into the Spoil.

Almost an hour after they had crossed the Rustwater, the
groundcar's machine spirit pinged, and Edi turned off
the empty arterial road and into a tangle of side streets.
Buildings of every description and use crowded in above
them. Their walls were daubed with territorial markings and
lewd runes, where they weren't crumbling to rubble. There
were more people here, sullen faces in patched clothing who
tucked themselves into alleys and corners as they approached.
Groundcars were rare in the Spoil, and those that owned
them would not think twice at running down anyone who
did not get out of their way.

Then, almost without warning, the narrow street opened
onto a small square, perhaps thirty yards to a side. The groundcar pinged again, signalling their arrival at their destination.

'Pull in here,' said Melita.

Edi gave her a look, but slowed their borrowed groundcar to a stop.

Like so many similar spaces across the Spoil, Merdiç Square
had seen better days. The boarded-up frontage of an abandoned commercia precinct formed one side of what had
probably been intended as a public platz, a shared space
for the occupants of the neighbouring hab-blocks to spend
their slate. Now it was the haunt of narco-pushers and their
buyers. Even at this hour of the morning, a pair of distressingly young street-blades lounged against one wall. Their
grey trousers had heavy synthleather panels sewn across the

thighs, marking them as aspirants of the Forge Fiends gang that controlled the Merdiç clave.

Melita and Edi pulled up in the shaded side of the platz, disturbing a knot of glowering juves who were lounging on the steps of the arcade. After a few seconds' deliberation, one of them rose in what he clearly thought was a predatory fashion. A short-bladed knife was strapped to his thigh, and something bulky was concealed beneath his jacket.

Edi unhurriedly climbed out of the Noxus, and leant casually against the door.

'Morning.'

The juve scowled at Edi's unconcerned greeting. 'You picked the wrong place to break down, upclave.'

The juve half-drew his blade, but as soon as his hand touched the hilt Edi slammed the groundcar's door closed and swept back the hem of his coat to reveal his holstered hand-cannon. He said nothing, just staring at the juve, who had frozen mid-advance.

The boy's gaze travelled from the gun to Edi's face, then back to the gun. Then, with a sullen grunt to his comrades, he turned and shuffled further along the precinct's steps. Melita watched the juves retreat from inside the groundcar, grateful as ever for Edi's restraint. When she was sure they had received the message, she climbed out of the Noxus and looked around.

A seven-storey hab-block formed the south side of the square, opposite the arcade. Its face was festooned with narrow balconies, each one barred from top to bottom. More than a few of the balconies had fallen away, leaving voids like broken teeth in the building's facade. Men and women stood at every window, and in every broken space, looking down at the square or out across the Spoil. Not one of them was speaking.

Melita stood very still, listening to the unnatural quiet. It was almost funereal. Sorokin's death had thrown a pall over the Spoil.

No, Melita realised as she looked up at the grim, drawn faces. They weren't mourning. That was entirely wrong. They were waiting, waiting for the next move, the next phase of the crisis that had shattered what amounted to normality for their benighted lives.

She felt as though every eye in the square had turned on her. She wasn't known here, and that made her one kind of threat or another. The silent watchers were weighing up how she fitted into the new complication that the Spoil had imposed on their lives. Melita logged that feeling, tucking it away for further thought. She was no stranger to the Spoil, and she flattered herself to think that she could blend in with a crowd when she wanted to. But there were no crowds here, just the strange stillness and hostile stares.

Melita leant against the groundcar's door. It was starting to get hot, even in the shade. Between the choking haze of smog above them and the walls of the surrounding buildings, the square seemed to trap the heat, reflecting it back from every surface.

'Are we here for anything in particular?' asked Edi. 'Because we're drawing a lot of attention.' He gestured at the far side of the square, where the two narco-pushers were staring with predatory interest at their groundcar.

Melita frowned. 'Give me a second.'

She blinked, focused, and a wash of text overlaid the sight in her left eye. She felt a pang of vertigo as she tried to look at the interface and the square at the same time.

Melita had had the surgery almost two months earlier, but accessing her iris was still an unusual, heady experience. It wasn't that it was painful, or particularly difficult.

Just thinking about the tiny augmetic buried in her skull was enough to wake its machine spirit, and to throw a curtain of text over the world. Rather, it was the potency of it, the almost giddy thrill of power it gave her.

As an info-broker, Melita had always been tied to cogitators. The world of data in which she moved had been confined to imagifiers; her ability to interact with it constrained by the physical limitations of runeboards. The iris had changed all of that. Though she still occasionally wore her old vambrace-mounted data-slate on the inside of her forearm, it was out of habit rather than necessity. Now, with a thought, Melita could touch the vast wealth of information that raced along the city's data-trunks, or pore through her own prodigious archives with an ease she would never have believed possible.

With a blink and the subtle movement of her fingers, she linked to the dataveil via the closest noospheric access point. This turned out to be a communications tower installed on the roof of the commercia arcade, which was evidently used to pirate the city's entertainment vid-feeds for distribution to the Spoil's various taverns and illicit joy houses.

As soon as she had decided to ignore the Valtteri's summons, Melita had lodged a message on the half-hidden node that facilitated the exchange of messages between her and her chief informant within the Har Dhrol. The message had, in no uncertain terms, made it clear that she needed a report, and had given the arcade's loc-ref as the place for them to meet.

'By the bloody Throne,' she hissed. Nothing. No reply, not even an acknowledgement that her source had seen the message. She blinked the iris interface away.

'It's time for us to leave,' Edi said urgently. Two more gangers had emerged from the basement access of the hab-block. They were half-dressed, their overalls undone and sweat-stained shirts flapping free. But, crucially, they were armed.

The crackle and grumble of unshrouded engines announced more new arrivals before Melita saw them. A pair of dirtcycles roared into the square, two riders on each. All four were wearing dark synthleathers bulked out by thick armour, and their faces were concealed behind full-faced flak helmets.

'Get in the groundcar,' said Melita, in the same moment as the passenger of each dirtcycle lifted an autogun and started firing.

The ripcord crackle of automatic fire hammered at Melita from every surface, appallingly loud in the tight confines. Melita saw two of the Forge Fiends soldiers go down beneath the opening volley. They barely had time to clear their weapons from their holsters before the blaze of bullets tore them both to bloody ruin.

'Fucking hells!' Edi swung into the Noxus' driving seat. Melita did the same through the passenger door.

Screams greeted the gunfire, but more out of shock than fear. The people at the balconies had already vanished inside, acting on the collective instincts that anyone who lived in the Spoil needed in order to survive. This, finally, was what they had been expecting, ever since they had heard the news that Andreti Sorokin was dead. The first act of bloody violence that marked the start of the next era of the Spoil.

Edi gunned the engine and the Noxus leapt forward. The juves on the steps dodged aside, and then they were past, flying along the edge of the square. In seconds they were swallowed by the relative darkness of another narrow alley. Edi kept the engine roaring for several minutes, until they had left the bloodstained platz and its murdered folk far behind.

'What was that about?' he asked as he throttled back. The groundcar lurched as he threw it round a corner.

Melita pushed herself into the passenger seat's fraying synthweave, and tried to calm her racing heartbeat.

'It's starting to fall apart.'

CHAPTER 5

'Aryat!' Haska hissed his name as a command, but the boy ignored her.

He swaggered over to the heavy-set old man who had climbed out of the groundcar, a Grappia Noxus with heavily rusted body panels. Haska heard the boy say, 'You picked the wrong place to break down, upclave.' His hand dropped to his knife, more for effect than a threat of violence. That was the body language of the Spoil: showing someone your weapon without drawing it was a signal for them to take the conversation seriously, nothing more.

It was clear even to Haska, for whom the enforcers were a distant, almost mythical threat, that the man was a former sanctioner, evidently working as a hired gun for the ill-looking woman who remained in the groundcar. With a speed that shocked them all, he slammed the Noxus' door with a thump that echoed around the square. In the same movement, he took a half-step forward and revealed the truly enormous hand-cannon holstered at his hip.

He said nothing, just stared into Aryat. Whether the old sanctioner was familiar with Spoil street etiquette or not, he made his point. Aryat raised his hands and backed away. Haska and her friends retreated further along the commercia precinct's wide steps. The boy joined them, cheeks burning.

Her crew had arrived in the platz a little after dawn, lounging on the steps of the arcade, playing the part of a young man out to impress his lover and her friends. They were strangers to the clave, but they had bought some blisters of topaz from the Forge Fiends narco-pushers to justify their presence. Fortunately, no one had challenged them as they sat down to wait for the sound of approaching engines.

'What now?' Katryn asked,

Aryat looked at his chron, a loan from his uncle along with the shot-cannon concealed behind his coat. 'They'll be here any second.'

They had set themselves up very deliberately on the arcade's steps, opposite the hab-block and the alleys that led further into the Merdiç clave. Throughout the morning they had played their role, pretending to crack the topaz and bask in the chemical high. But one of them always had an eye on the door to the under-level of the hab-block. According to Aryat's uncle, when the news began to swirl of the king's murder Vagif Stoyano had fled to the topaz still located beneath the block.

Haska swore. It was a simple plan, but the groundcar was going to ruin everything.

She could see the two Fiends talking, evidently as curious about the unexpected upclavers as Haska. Har Dhrol crews of every stripe were opportunists, and even a rusted hulk like the Noxus appearing in their midst was a gift from Terra.

One of them signalled to a juve on watch in the second level of the hab-block, who disappeared inside. Lira saw it too.

'Shit.'

'What?' asked Aryat.

'The shooting's going to start sooner than we thought.'

A minute later, two more Forge Fiends emerged from the hab-block's under-level in their shirtsleeves, the straps of their overalls hanging down to their waists. At a nod from one of the pushers, the two street-blades began to advance on the groundcar.

As they took their first steps, the tinny crackle of engines began to burble along the alley's walls. As the Forge Fiends hesitated in their advance, the dirtcycles ripped into the square.

The two narco-pushers were closest to the riders. They had no chance at all.

The Pit Snakes riders opened up as one. The report of the autoguns was horrific, rapid-fire blasts that seemed to detonate around Haska's head from everywhere at once. She froze, all her swagger and experience of a life on the Spoil's streets deserting her in an instant. The pushers seemed to dance in a hail of bullets, bodies twitching left and right as they fell. Haska watched, horrified, as they dropped like puppets whose strings had been cut.

There was a grumbling roar to Haska's left. Lira grabbed the collar of her jacket and hauled her back a bare second before the strangers' groundcar sped past, its corroded side panels mere inches from her face. Haska tumbled back until she struck the stone steps. Pain shot up her spine, but Lira still held her collar and pulled her bodily behind one of the pillars that held up the commercia precinct's roof.

The two street-blades who had come to investigate the upclavers were as unprepared as the pushers, but they had their guns in hand. They too went down, the air around them misted with their blood, but not before one of the Pit Snakes on the dirtcycles took a bullet between the plates of his armour.

He slumped forward against his rider, who took off with another rattle-can burr of revving engines. The other dirt-cycle followed, racing along the face of the hab-block and out the far side of the square.

Haska's breath came in short, shallow bursts. She thought she would pass out. The thunder of her blood was loud in her ears, as loud as the reverberating crash of autoguns firing. Lira stayed with her, holding Haska in a crouch behind the pillar, still pretending to be the fearful juves they were.

They had set a simple trap, and it relied on Stoyano valuing the lives of his gangers enough to risk his own.

As the dirtcycles' echo faded, four more gangers burst out of the basement level of the hab-block, weapons drawn and panic on their faces as they sought the sudden danger in their midst. They ignored Haska and her crew, just as they were supposed to. Vagif Stoyano was among them, the distinctive notch missing from the bridge of his nose marking out the praetor of the Forge Fiends. The architect, apparently, of the arson that had claimed a Pit Snakes hab-stack.

Aryat's jacket flared as he stood. The snub-nosed shot-cannon that had been hidden against his body was in his hands, held low at his waist. The boy looked terrified, but his finger found the trigger.

The cannon roared. A fan of shot crashed into the knot of Forge Fiends just as they reached their fallen brethren. The morning light caught every droplet of blood and splinter of bone that burst from their bodies, a horrific spray of crimson that was appallingly vibrant against the gravel and dust coating the square.

Aryat racked the slide, and fired again. Lira and Katryn joined him, the cough of their pistols eclipsed by each thunderous boom of the shot-cannon.

Stoyano and his crew were dead, they just didn't know

it yet. They turned towards the sudden threat, but far too slowly. Round after round cut the air, a horizontal hail of metal. Most went wide – Haska's friends were hardly marksmen – but that didn't matter. The square was a killing floor, a murder-field, the bare rockcrete devoid of any cover that might have bought Stoyano's men a few more seconds of life.

The praetor got one shot off, which flattened itself against the ground as he crumpled. His autopistol fell from his lifeless grip, and skittered away across the rockcrete.

Aryat, Lira and Katryn kept on firing until the last man fell.

The square was a charnel house. Blood ran in rivulets along the cracks between the paving stones. The bodies had fallen almost one atop another, forming a heap of dead flesh at the very centre of the square.

Haska looked down at the gun in her hands.

All morning, the borrowed autopistol had been a hard, awkward shape lodged against her hip bone. She had worn a knife since her sixth natal day, but she'd never had the connections or the slate for anything more potent than a blade. She had feared the pistol when Karlo had handed it over, and had felt pathetically childish as Lira and her friends confidently inspected their own borrowed weapons.

As the last echoes of gunfire died away, Haska realised she hadn't fired a single shot. She had been paralysed, stunned into inaction by the ferocity of what her friends had unleashed.

First tentatively, then swiftly once he was sure the gangers were down for good, Aryat came out from behind his pillar. He walked unsteadily down the precinct steps towards the broken bodies, shot-cannon held loosely at his side.

'Aryat?' Katryn called after him, but he gave no sign that he had heard her. He stopped beside Stoyano's body, but still said nothing. Maybe he felt proud, his vengeance taken for his ruined hab. Haska couldn't say.

Then Katryn screamed. One last Forge Fiend had emerged from the basement.

Time seemed to slow to a crawl. In that brief second, it seemed like Haska could see every detail of his face, caught in the harsh glare of sunlight. He stood transfixed by the horror that Haska's friends had wrought. He was a juve, no older than Haska, the first weak attempts at a beard framing his jaw. His black hair formed a greasy halo around his head. He wore a thin undershirt but heavy synthleather trousers, as though they had caught him while still dressing for the day.

Aryat was alone, standing over the bodies of half a dozen Forge Fiends. The juve raised the shot-cannon in his hands, the mirror of Aryat's, his expression hardening from shock to fury.

Haska's pistol bucked, so hard it almost leapt from her hands.

Her bullet caught the juve in the throat, blowing out the side of his neck in a welter of blood. He collapsed immediately, his legs folding beneath his dead weight. His head struck the ground with a sickening crunch of breaking bone.

Katryn crashed into Haska, mouthing a wordless sob of thanks.

'Get off me!'

Katryn recoiled as though she had been stung by a razorbriar.

Haska felt suddenly angry, furious even. The rage seemed to boil up within her, physically rising through her body hot enough to make sweat bead on her forehead. The feeling came on so quickly it scared her. She wanted to keep firing, to riddle the body with bullets for daring to make her feel so afraid, so angry. For making her feel, for a fleeting moment, so terribly proud.

'I'm sorry, I...' Haska trailed off. 'I'm sorry.'

Katryn nodded, perhaps in understanding, then ran over to Aryat's side. Lira was still crouched beside her, watching Haska with wide eyes.

The juve wasn't dead. Blood continued to pump from the ragged tear in his throat. Haska couldn't look away. It just kept coming, a pulse at a time, as his heart laboured in futility against what she had done. She felt her stomach lurch, threatening nausea.

Some instinct made her look up at the face of the hab-block. There were figures at the windows again, curiosity and anger overcoming their fear now that the shooting had stopped. They looked down in silence. Not judging, not shouting, or threating abuse or reprisal at Haska and the others. They were simply silent, mute witnesses to the latest turn of events in their corner of the Spoil.

'Haska!' Lira's shout gave Haska the excuse she needed to look away. Katryn and Aryat were running for the corner of the square, and she and Lira set off after them.

They had left their groundcar, a Shiiv Grigga borrowed from Aryat's uncle, blocking one of the side streets close by, and the four of them bundled inside. Haska and Lira clambered into the back seat, and Katryn leapt into the front beside Aryat. The boy passed his shot-cannon to Katryn, and hit the accelerator.

None of them spoke as the Grigga's engine coughed into life, and they took off down the alley. Haska thought she heard Katryn stifle a sob. She definitely saw Lira cuff at her eyes, but her friend kept her face turned towards the ground-car's window so Haska couldn't see her tears.

Haska looked down at her hands. Slowly, almost painfully, she uncurled her fingers from the pistol's grip.

CHAPTER 6

'That's close enough!'

A voice, shouting from somewhere out of sight, greeted them with less welcome than Melita might have hoped for, but less hostility than she had feared.

The rest of their journey had been more or less uneventful. After the ambush at the commercia, Edi and Melita had agreed that it would be wiser to stay off the main arterials, expecting that engine gangers and opportunists would be on the prowl. While that had likely been a wise decision, they had had to backtrack multiple times as they encountered roaming packs of street-blades, and habclave communities constructing barricades across their alleys and back streets. Drawing lines between Us and Them, hunkering down for what Melita and Edi knew had already begun.

They had climbed out of the endless nest of habs, yards and warehouses of Merdiç, and into the foothills of the Ashbani clave, once the domain of the more affluent – or, at least, less poor – denizens of the Spoil: scholam tutors,

Ecclesiarchy curates, manufactorum overseers, and the purveyors of amenities that such folk attracted. The narrow streets had begun to broaden. The rows of looming tenements had given way to shorter, finer buildings with the cracked plex frontages of abandoned salons and emporia lining their ground floors. And, finally, they had emerged into the Saint's Square.

Edi brought their groundcar to a stop, careful to keep his gloved hands visible atop the steering column. Melita could see at least a dozen men and women, weapons raised, watching from the once ornate cafes and parlours that bordered the square.

Once they reached a certain size and standing within the highly stratified order of the Har Dhrol, most Spoil gangs adopted some kind of affectation to mark them out from their peers and rivals. Most were fairly literal. The Forge Fiends they had encountered in Merdiç Square stitched panels of synthleather over their clothes in mimicry of foundry workers' overalls. The Salt Dogs that haunted the claves that bordered the Binastri Pans wore dust goggles, often as part of full-faced masks in the shapes of gargoyles and canine grotesques. It was a uniform, as much as a sanctioner's armour or a missionary's surplice.

The gangers who watched from the square's edges wore the grey sashes and paired bandoliers of Sorokin's own gang, now effectively his household guard.

Melita climbed out of the groundcar, hands raised. 'I need to speak to whoever's in charge.' She shouted up at the gatehouse, ignoring the sentries who were conspicuously approaching either side of their groundcar.

A window opened, high up on one of the gate's two crenellated towers, and a servo-skull wobbled out into the air. It descended quickly, dropping out of the sky to hover a few yards in front of the Noxus. Its lower jaw was locked open, and a vox-emitter was wired between its teeth.

'I don't know you,' said the skull. The vox distortion was minor, enough for Melita to hear the scorn and false bravado in the words. Whoever was speaking through the skull was trying to talk himself into feeling brave.

'Well, go and find someone more important who does.'

The skull said nothing. She took that to mean that the speaker had followed her suggestion, and so she waited, standing in the crook of the groundcar's door.

The Saint's Square had once been paved with clean, dressed stone and ornamented with imposing statuary, like so many public spaces funded by the largesse of the Imperial Church or gilded benefactors hoping to impress their peers. But the statues were gone, and the elegant flags long since prised up and carted away to more fortunate quarters, and it was now covered in an uneven patchwork of gravel and poured bitumen. The Har Dhrol had added to this state of disorder with rows of fat rockcrete bollards, stout enough to stop a Bulwark riot-wagon in its tracks, or at least seriously incon-venience it. A path through from the square's edge to the gatehouse was discernible.

The skull suddenly croaked into life. *'That you, Voronova?'*

Melita forced a small, tight smile as she recognised the voice of Kiren Rasyn. 'In the flesh,' she said.

'What do you want?'

The man himself was still out of sight, but she glared at the servo-skull. 'For Throne's sake, Rasyn!'

After a few moments of petulant pause, the skull croaked again. *'Fine.'*

Evidently a command was voxed to the square's sentries, as they lowered their guns and grimly directed Melita and Edi towards the opening of the path through the bollards. Melita climbed back inside, and Edi slowly and carefully steered the Noxus towards the opening gates.

Despite herself, Melita had always been impressed by Andreti Sorokin's lair. Though the Spoil's fall had tainted so much of Ashbani, the former seminary of Saint Eurydice had endured under the stewardship of successive Spoil warlords. Sorokin had been the latest to occupy its expansive grounds and towering spires. Though the Adeptus Ministorum had removed its relics, its tapestries, and the other riches when the city abandoned the Spoil, Sorokin had wanted the seminary itself. It was a fitting seat for the man who had come to rule the entire Spoil as a self-styled king.

St Eurydice's was not simply one building, but a sub-clave in its own right. A perimeter wall almost three miles in circumference enclosed the seminary's grounds, its shrines, classrooms, oratories, small-scale agri-domes and priory-habs, ensuring that the faithful could remain securely segregated from the faithless. Above them all loomed the church of the saint herself.

St Eurydice's was a humble chapel compared to some Ecclesiarchy structures, lacking the patrician elegance of the Basilica of the Three in Setomir, or the grand decadence of the Church of the Merciful Emperor in Nearsteel. But as a statement of authority, both temporal and spiritual, it could scarcely be rivalled within the Spoil. Black granite buttresses, veined through with silver, climbed from the paved court-yard, lifting sharp pinnacles and fluted towers that loomed over the encircling wall and the low apartments beyond. The twin heads of a great granite aquila, wings spread wide, glared from above an ornate arched entrance. Melita knew that the doorway was carved with the lamenting faces of sinners on one side, and the beatific expressions of Imperial martyrs on the other. Saint Eurydice stood at the arch's apex, dividing and guarding the Emperor's chosen from the heathen.

The seminary had served Sorokin and the Har Dhrol well, and he had ensured that it was properly respected. Melita knew that his household – the equal of any gilded baron or dynastic scion – employed many Spoilers whose only function was to maintain the church and its grounds. As such, the compound was unusually clean by Varangantuan standards. No graffiti marred the walls, no refuse lay in wind-blown heaps. There were even ornamental trees and plants studded throughout the grounds, kept alive at presumably ruinous expense. As Melita and Edi drove beneath the gatehouse's imposing shadow, they seemed to leave the Spoil entirely.

Edi brought the Noxus to a stop just inside the courtyard, which stretched away for several hundred yards towards the entrance to the church. Half a dozen heavily armed street-soldiers blocked their path, Kiren Rasyn amongst them.

Rasyn was almost three times Melita's age, which was truly ancient by the standards of the Spoil. She knew he often bored young Har Dhrol aspirants with the story of how he had once spared a young Andreti Sorokin's life when he had caught the king-to-be raiding a storehouse under his crew's protection. He held the trust of almost everyone of any importance in the Har Dhrol, mainly because he was no longer capable of offering any threat to them.

He did not look happy to see Melita, but in her experience he had never looked happy. Both she and Edi climbed out of their groundcar, the latter loosening his hand-cannon in its holster at his hip as a gentle warning to Rasyn's companions.

'We'd expected you sooner,' said the old man by way of greeting. He walked with a profound limp, and the hand that gripped a battered metal cane was missing the bottom two fingers.

She was only slightly perturbed that the Har Dhrol had predicted her coming into the Spoil. 'Streets aren't safe,' said Melita instead. 'Barricades are going up.'

Rasyn nodded. 'The old ways never really go away.'

'You would know.'

Her attempt at cheer fell utterly flat. 'I survived the Fires, the Clave Wars, and I lived to see young Andreti's rise. Shame to live long enough to see what he built fall apart.'

Melita tried to control her surprise at his fatalism, but evidently not well enough.

'You live long enough, you know nothing really lasts,' he said. Melita noticed one or two of his crew, much younger than the veteran ganger, nodding in agreement.

'Who's in charge?'

Rasyn merely shrugged, and gestured towards the grandly arched entrance to the church. 'Don't expect much from them.'

Melita raised an eyebrow at that, which only made the old man's scowl deepen.

'They spent their lives in his shadow. Hard to step out of it.'

'We can go down?' she asked, feeling more awkward by the moment.

Rasyn nodded, and turned back to the gatehouse without any sort of farewell.

'Bloody hells,' said Edi as soon as the doors of the Noxus slammed shut.

'Can you blame him?' Melita was trying to process what Rasyn's defeatism might mean.

'I suppose not.' Edi roused the groundcar's engine. 'Doom and gloom come easy to old men. I should know. But his crew...' He left the thought hanging as they rolled the short distance to the church's steps.

Melita felt an unusual pang of pious awe as they entered

the chapel's shadow. She was usually too much of a cynic to be moved by Imperial iconography, but the sight of the aquila, carved in glittering granite, was enough to stop the breath in her throat. The eagle's vast wings were unfurled, the pinions extending across the church's full frontage. Beneath the unwavering stares of both heads, their raptor eyes sharp for any sinners that might approach this holy place, Melita felt a powerful urge to genuflect.

A figure in an elegantly cut suit of black cloth was waiting for them at the top of the church steps. He looked down imperiously, framed by the church's archway and the stern figure of the guardian saint. The stone faces looked down on Melita and Edi with no greater scorn than the brutally scarred man beneath them.

Juri Amadan was one of the Kadern, the cohort of gangers who had fought Sorokin's vicious war for supremacy at his side. He, like Kiren Rasyn, had survived to endure the ravages of time and age, and enjoy the spoils of dominion.

'Hello, Juri.'

'We'd expected you sooner,' the old man said, just as bitterly as Rasyn. His eyes were sunk in their sockets, and though he held himself stiffly, weariness seemed to bleed from him.

Melita smiled, trying her hand at charm. 'Me, or the cartel?'

Amadan was not taken in. 'What's the difference?'

'I–'

She was about to launch into a spirited defence of her independence when Oriel's auspex pushed an alert into her iris. She blinked the message open, then looked up into the ochre haze and let out a deep and profound curse.

Four flyers were descending rapidly, almost dropping out of the sky. Amadan, from his vantage atop the church's steps, followed her gaze, then looked back to Melita.

'What were you about to say?'

Overlapping cries of alarm rang around the courtyard as gangers spotted the approaching aircars. Some ran for the cover of the encircling buildings, while others called out to their fellows to arm themselves. Others came running across the courtyard from the church's outbuildings.

'For Throne's sake, calm down!' Amadan's voice hammered across the grounds, cutting through the chaos. 'You are acting like unblooded children.' He paused, glaring up at the dark shapes that grew larger with every second. 'These are simply more uninvited guests.' He flashed a bitter glance at Melita. 'Get back to your posts, and try to look like you know what you're doing.' Melita felt the scorn radiating from the old man.

Amadan turned away, not waiting for the new arrivals to land. Melita stayed where she was, Edi at her shoulder, wishing she could do the same.

The flyers slowed in the final seconds of their dive, turbines flaring to arrest their descent. They were coming down inside the seminary's courtyard, between the gatehouse and the church. Melita held up a hand to shield her eyes from the grit being thrown up by the downdraught, but she didn't move until Edi's hand on her shoulder gently pulled her back and up the steps.

The church's courtyard was wide enough for all four flyers to land in neat formation, although the collective downdraught rocked the Noxus on its suspension. Each craft was at least three times the size of Melita's borrowed ground-car, to account for the massive turbines on either flank and the passenger chamber slung between them. The nose of each aircar narrowed to a cockpit that overhung its body like an avian's beak. The design put the vehicle's single pilot in an almost standing position, surrounded on all sides by thick plex. The flared ailerons that rose from the rear completed the impression of predatory, iron-grey birds stooping into the courtyard. The flyers were a variant of the famed Valkyrie-class transport, used across the galaxy to carry the God-Emperor's Astra Militarum into battle. Laneus-Avier, one of the more powerful constituent organisations of the Valtteri, built them under an exclusive licence granted by the magi of the Adeptus Mechanicus, in strict adherence to that order's mysterious tenets. The Teridon, and its more luxurious sister design, the Terilli, were two of their most successful products.

The roar of their engines rose to a sense-abusing pitch in the final seconds before the aircars touched down on the pale stone, landing struts unfurling at the last moment. The stomach-shaking whine started to fade as the flight engines cycled down.

Mercenaries emerged from doors in the rear of each Teridon at the moment of contact with the ground. All of them were armed and armoured like Astra Militarum elites, their features concealed behind full-face helmets. They quickly formed a perimeter around the four flyers, high-powered lasguns in hand but not levelled. The Har Dhrol gangers still outside, though more numerous than the Reisiger men, appeared to recognise the futility of trying to threaten those whose equipment and panache far outclassed their own.

The Reisiger were the Valtteri cartel's enforcers, their own private army. Most merchant-combines in the tri-districts maintained their own security forces – by Melita's reckoning, Dragosyl's Sanctioner Corps was only just equal in size to the various incorporated guns for hire. The Reisiger were, as befitted the Valtteri's status, pre-eminent within the tri-districts, trained and equipped to a level that outstripped even the Alectian Planetary Defence Corps.

Tomillan Vasimov stepped out of the lead Teridon as the

drone of the engines dropped from unbearable to merely deafening. He stood inside the ring of mercenaries, a few steps ahead of his aircar, and looked around the church's plaza. Anyone who didn't know him would have assumed that the disdainful sneer on his face was directed at the gangers, who looked back at the new arrivals with undisguised hostility. But Melita knew that it was merely the default expression with which the man greeted the world.

Vasimov took in the imposing presence of St Eurydice's, then finally deigned to acknowledge Melita at the foot of the steps. His sneer twisted into a sinister smile, and with one hand beckoned her over.

His gesture made her lip curl, but there was no backing away from the summons.

'Want me to come with you?' asked Edi softly. She made no sign of hearing him, and was more than a little piqued by his question. Melita preferred to stand on her own when dealing with the Valtteri's many minions, and Edi knew that.

'Get Oriel out of the groundcar,' she said instead.

The Reisiger men – Melita knew that the mercenary collective almost exclusively recruited male veterans of the Alectian Planetary Defence Corps – did not try to stop her approach. Vasimov waited in the shadow of his Teridon, but Melita was determined to get in the first word.

'Do you think that was wise?'

The securitor's expression did not change, but Melita could see the flicker of anger behind the condescending smile. He was handsome in a vicious, aggressive way, his angular features and cold grey eyes conveying an air of targeted disdain. Melita's subtle investigations into his habits had revealed that Vasimov spent at least three hours of each day in the Reisiger complex's expansive gymnasia, and it showed in his broad shoulders and narrow hips. His hair was carefully lacquered and swept back from his face, and the line of his real-fibre suit emphasised the swell of his chest. His status as an executor of the Reisiger organisation was displayed by a silver half-cuirass bound tight across his torso, though he was undoubtedly also wearing a ballistic weave beneath the suit.

In short, he looked rich. Along with the flyers and elite mercenaries, Vasimov's entire entrance and presence seemed calculated to project an air of overbearing wealth and superiority.

'I do.' The man's voice was distressingly deep, to the point where Melita suspected that it was the product of deft surgery to artificially enhance the unconscious tones of command.

'Do you even read my briefings?'

'Extensively,' he replied. He had not yet made eye contact with her, ostensibly scanning the chapel's steps and outbuildings.

She continued as though he had not spoken. 'These people are defined by their inferiority. Anything that implies that you view them as beneath you is only going to make things worse.'

'That is one interpretation,' said Vasimov.

'What?'

He finally turned his grey eyes towards her. 'I would say that it is more important that we remind them that they *are* beneath us.'

Melita gaped, but he continued. 'Our arrangement has never been an agreement between equals. Andreti Sorokin knew that. Whoever takes his place must understand it as well.'

The arrogance was staggering. 'And that's why you've been sent? To put the whole of the Spoil in its place?'

Vasimov's cool visage finally cracked. He bent at the waist, bringing his sudden snarl to within inches of her face. 'I've been sent into this foetid sump because you failed to foresee this calamity. I'm here to fix the situation before it becomes irretrievably fucked.'

As quickly as he had lost control, Vasimov recovered himself. He straightened, and smoothed the line of his elegantly tailored jacket.

'You were ordered to attend me earlier this morning. Your inability to follow even the simplest instructions has been noted.'

'You pay me for information. I can't gather any from the top of a starscraper.'

As she had expected, Vasimov showed no sign of yielding to her argument. 'Well, do you have anything to offer before I go in?' He gave her a cold, mocking smile.

'Would you listen if I did?'

Vasimov's smile became colder, and even more condescending. He was used to immediate, unquestioned submission from all his subordinates, and Melita had never – would never – give him that.

'Do you know who killed Sorokin?'

Melita ground her teeth. 'No.'

'Do you know who will succeed him?'

'I wouldn't be so sure that–'

'Stop.' He interrupted her. He actually held up a hand to stop her speaking. 'When you have something of use to say, then I will listen.' And then he swept past her towards the church steps. A pair of mercenaries left their positions in the ring around the aircars and fell in behind him without a word of command.

Melita was left furious and impotent in his wake. She stared after him as he started up the steps, choosing a course that forced Edi, now with Oriel's imposing presence at his shoulder, to move out of his way.

The preening, effortless arrogance was stunning. She told herself that his rebuke should mean nothing; less than nothing, given the contempt she held for him. She told herself that the greater concern was the damage and danger Vasimov's egotism could cause.

It was this train of thought – that without her, Vasimov would likely doom them all – that allowed Melita to convince herself to follow him up the steps and into the Har Dhrol's lair.

CHAPTER 7

Mircea Iliev. Juri Amadan. Harol Toskanov. If Andreti Sorokin had been the King of the Har Dhrol, they, undoubtedly, were now his regents.

The three gangers had been Sorokin's lieutenants since the earliest days of his rise to power, and they looked it. Their clothes were a curious blend of gilded affluence and street-fighting practicality: brocaded waistcoats, linen shirts, rare-metal tie pins and jewellery combined with sturdy synth-leather boots, tightly clipped hair, knives and pistols near at hand. But it was their scars that marked them as Har Dhrol veterans. Iliev's left eye was an augmetic, of surprisingly good construction. Toskanov's left arm ended just below his elbow. The stump was capped with a socket for an augmetic, but the metal limb sat lifeless on the hololith table in front of them. Amadan was missing nothing, but the old man made up for it with surpassing ugliness, nose and cheeks and ears battered by a life immersed in violence.

Toskanov was the youngest of the three, and he was at least

sixty, Terran standard. But, like Edi, they had been hardened by time, rather than bent by it. That was how it worked in the Spoil, and for most Varangantuans, for whom rejuvenat drugs were a myth. Folk were either worn down by the years or toughened by them, becoming gnarled like the twisted spiatrees that stubbornly clawed their way from barren dirt.

That hardness appeared to have deserted the regents of the Har Dhrol.

They were gathered around a circular wooden table just inside the church's entrance, their faces bathed in a hololith's blue light. Toskanov had his one remaining hand flat on the tabletop, and looked as though it were the only thing keeping him up. The woman, 'Mercy' Iliev, hid her exhaustion better; Melita saw the gleam of fury in her eye as she and Vasimov approached.

A cloud of gangers hovered around the three regents, waiting for guidance and orders. As Melita and Vasimov entered the hololith's glow, a pair of runners were dispatched by a wave of Amadan's hand. Others crowded forward, but were ignored as the old man turned to the interlopers in their midst.

Iliev made a show of checking her chron, a fine timepiece held by a golden chain attached to the old woman's waistcoat. 'You took your time,' she said by way of welcome. 'I was sure the Valtteri would be here to dance on Andreti's ashes before they were cold.'

Melita bristled at being counted amongst the Valtteri's delegation, but she could hardly deny it.

'You do us a disservice, Madam Iliev.' Vasimov took her anger in his stride. Melita knew that the securitor had never met any members of the Har Dhrol's leadership – she wasn't sure he had even set foot inside the Spoil's borders before today – but he stepped up to their table as though they were the intruders, and he the host. 'I assure you, no one is more distressed by this loss than the directors of our organisation.'

'Was that little display outside meant for us?' asked Toskanov, as though Vasimov hadn't spoken. He had a cracked, reedy voice – the souvenir of an especially vicious back-alley brawl in his youth, if Melita's information was correct.

'Only as a demonstration of how seriously we take the situation,' Vasimov said smoothly. 'I have been sent as the representative of my organisation's directors. I am empowered to offer whatever aid may be of use to ensure the stability of the Spoil.'

His gesture of false humility did not seem to impress the gangers.

'To that end, I am authorised to confirm that the long-standing arrangement between our organisation and the Har Dhrol can and will continue, as long as you do not seek to amend it.'

The silence that followed this pronouncement was finally broken by a single peal of loud, humourless laughter.

'I see that your distress at Andreti's death was not hollow after all, Messr Vasimov.' Mercy Iliev scowled at the securitor. 'You're even more scared than we are.'

Melita could see a muscle twitch in Vasimov's cheek. 'I'm afraid you are overestimating your importance to us, Madam Iliev.'

'Is that so?' said Amadan. 'It could be argued that the Valtteri need the Har Dhrol more than we need you.'

Vasimov took the bait. 'Not by anyone of sense.'

'Really?' said Toskanov, taking over smoothly. 'For the past decade, an eighth of your agricultural and raw-material imports have come via the Binastri Arterial. For several of your manufactory combines, it's as much as one-third, to say nothing of your down-chain reliance on the goods they process. Your monopoly on the arterial – which we provide – accounts for a substantial proportion of your cartel's tithe contributions to the Setomir, Dragosyl and Korodilsk Administrata.' He threw out these figures with such ease and confidence that Melita felt certain that he had rehearsed them.

'So don't come here and graciously offer us your aid,' said Mercy Iliev, a good deal more angrily than her fellow regents. She stared across the table with undisguised loathing. 'We know why you have come. Andreti may be gone, but what he built will endure.'

Tempers were already starting to fray. Melita looked between Vasimov and the gangers, wondering how, and on which side, she ought to intervene.

'For how long?' said Vasimov, leaning forward, planting his hands on the tabletop, his sharp cheek bones bathed in the hololith's light. 'How long could your band of criminals last without our support? From where would you source your arms? The replacement components for your generatoria? The swill you people call food? Could the Spoil afford so much as a carb-bar if it wasn't sold to you at a cut rate by one of our member combines?'

Vasimov stopped suddenly, letting his thoughts catch up with his choler. If he had been despatched by the Valtteri as an emissary, he was failing spectacularly in the role.

'You're not the only gilded bastards who would like to make use of the Binastri road,' said Toskanov darkly.

And there it was. The threat was made.

It was a good one. The Valtteri's pre-eminence in any number of industries across the tri-districts was unquestionable, but not unassailable. Power drew rivals like moths to a flame, and the Valtteri's dominance blazed like a torch in the night. Jealous conglomerates and finance compacts sought to undermine the cartel at every turn. The tri-district's political class switched their favour as often as they changed their clothes. The multidimensional wars of commerce, flattery and industrial espionage the Valtteri waged with their competitors were no less ruthless than the gutter brawls of the Spoil.

In many ways, Melita knew, the Valtteri's position mirrored that of the Har Dhrol. The cartel, like the alliance of gangs, was strong because it was united, made greater than the sum of its parts through the sharing of effort and strategy. But to have that strength required each constituent organ, be it a merchant-combine or a street-corner gang, to willingly surrender the freedom to act solely as they wished.

Melita doubted that anyone at the table would be receptive to that observation.

'You think you can find a… partnership more agreeable to you than our organisation?' asked Vasimov.

'You made us into a damned vassal!' Iliev shouted. The old woman started around the table towards Vasimov, but was gently restrained by Amadan. 'You treated us like serfs. We will not stand for your contempt any longer. We can survive without Andreti, and we can survive without you,' she said.

'No, you can't,' said Melita softly.

Vasimov had been drawing breath to reply, but while he scowled at Melita's interruption, he did not try to stop her. The old gangers turned as one, their ire finding a new target.

'Without one, maybe. But not without them both.' Melita took a step around the table, creating distance between herself and Vasimov, for what that was worth. 'Sorokin held the clave-captains together through fear, and by sharing the wealth your alliance creates. His is the face of the Har Dhrol. An entire generation of Spoilers has been raised in a world where he was the king. On stories of the blood you shed to make that happen. And now he's dead.' She paused. 'He was killed, by someone who is trying to undo what he made. What you all helped make.'

She paused again, to let that sink in, although surely no one felt Sorokin's loss and the threat to his legacy more than his closest companions.

'No one wants to be in league with the Valtteri. Believe me.' She could sense the furnace of Vasimov's anger beside her, but pressed on. 'But you need them. You need the continuity, the stability they can provide to keep the praetors' trust in you alive.'

'Half of them think Andreti deserved to die for shackling us to the cartel. To you,' Amadan added pointedly. 'Continuity is not what they want. Even your presence here, now, will only serve to remind them that we are not, and have never been, free.'

'Do you want to be free, or do you want to survive?' Melita could not believe the words were coming out of her mouth. She hoped that the bitter tang of resentment in her voice would help convince the old gangers that she was sincere. 'You remember what the Spoil was like before Sorokin came. Before *you* came. The clave-captains will remember as well. They don't want to go back to that any more than you do.'

'One of them evidently does,' said Amadan.

That was a useful insight into their thoughts, and Melita filed it away for later consideration. 'And who did that? Who killed Sorokin?'

'Does it matter?' Vasimov asked, pulling all eyes back to him.

'Of course it matters!' Iliev bellowed. The old woman looked to be a short step from leaping across the table and throttling the securitor, whose coming had finally offered her a target for her rage.

'Why? You need to be seen to respond, so do so.' Vasimov

had regained his calm, and spoke with the cool, collected measure of one used to offering guidance to the powerful. 'Which captain was most vocally opposed to Sorokin and our agreement? Make an example of him. Or her,' he added, in patronising deference to Iliev's glare.

'And leave the true villain free to wreak more havoc?' asked Toskanov.

'To give yourselves time to bring the situation under control. Inaction is the worst of all possible states. Every hour you dither, the ties that bind your little federation fray even further.' He paused, evidently more comfortable in the role of patronising advisor than diplomatic envoy. 'In moments of crisis, stability is the only goal that matters.'

'We have no proof that a clave-captain is behind the assassination,' said Amadan, although the thoughtful tone in his voice did not suggest that he was averse to Vasimov's proposal.

Melita, though, was practically shaking with repressed rage.

Two years ago, the Valtteri had been under attack, their security assailed on all sides by what they had thought was a highly skilled cipher-knife. Their response had been as Vasimov now described – to scorch the earth, and kill anyone at all with the means to carry out such attacks, rather than attempt the more difficult task of finding their vulnerability. A dozen skilled info-brokers had died before Melita, herself on their kill-list, had identified the true culprit. In doing so, she had ended up press-ganged into the cartel's labyrinthine network of agents and actors.

Such ruthless indifference was why Melita was here, shackled to a sociopath who would kill because it was the easiest course to take. To hear the same logic that had led to her enforced servitude spoken so dispassionately was almost more than she could bear.

'You disagree, Mistress Voronova?' Iliev asked. She had noticed Melita's anguished expression, and could not pass up a chance to sow discord.

No force short of the God-Emperor's intervention could have stopped her speaking.

'Yes.'

She looked from the ageing gangers to the securitor, and back to them.

'You need to find the traitor in your ranks, because what you need more than stability is trust. The Har Dhrol is an alliance. Your clave-captains are cowering in safehouses, fearing that they might be next. Indiscriminate murder will not keep the Har Dhrol together, but the truth might.'

'I agree,' said Toskanov, after a long, tense moment.

'As do I,' added Iliev. 'I will kill whoever was involved in Andreti's death, but I want to know I have the right person under my blade.'

Vasimov absorbed this, and his anger swiftly turned into sly agreement. He turned towards Melita with a predator's slow poise. 'Then I suggest you get started,' he said.

'What?' Melita sensed, too late, the error she had made.

'Go. *Investigate*. Employ the skills you spend so much time extolling. Bring us Sorokin's killer, or the man behind him.' He paused. 'That is, of course, if you would accept the Valtteri's aid?' he asked the regents of the Har Dhrol.

'We have our own people,' snapped Iliev.

'But we would not be averse to a pair of fresh eyes,' said Amadan, over Mercy's objection. He gave Melita a smile that was oddly disturbing. It looked wrong in a face so notched and scarred by back-alley blades. 'Andreti liked you.'

'He did?' Sorokin and Melita had met perhaps half a dozen times. He had always made a point to goad her, and mock her state as a shackled thrall of the cartel.

'Indeed. And he respected your skills,' he added as a pointed rebuke of Vasimov's disrespect. Melita gaped, wrong-footed by the sudden turn in the conversation. She wouldn't know where to start.

Which was, of course, the point. Vasimov's devious smile made that clear. She had contradicted him and his proffered course of action, and in return Vasimov had seized on her argument as a chance to rid himself of her dissenting voice. Moreover, if she failed to find the instigator of this chaos, just as she had failed to predict it, that would be one more black mark against her in the Valtteri's eyes. One more argument the vindictive securitor could use to justify her expulsion from the cartel – a death sentence in all but name.

'I could be of more use in uniting the clave-captains around a successor to Sorokin,' Melita said. She had stepped into the trap, but that didn't mean she wouldn't struggle against it.

Amadan's smile disappeared. 'We have that under control,' he said coldly.

Melita strongly doubted that, but could hardly say so. 'I will need unfettered access to the seminary, and Sorokin's household,' she said, trying another angle.

'That will not be a problem,' said Amadan. 'After all, we are allies in this.'

There was no way out.

'I'll do what I can.'

'Good,' said Vasimov, triumphant.

Amadan nodded. 'We'll have someone assist you.'

'If you will excuse us for a moment.' Vasimov stepped away from the table, one arm extended to pull Melita with him. She allowed herself to be herded until they reached the church's entrance, where Vasimov bent to whisper in her ear.

'You would do well to remember why you are here,' he said softly. 'It was not my doing.'

She rounded on him. 'I'm here to stop the Spoil degener-
ating into chaos.'

'As am I.' He straightened. 'Now get to work.'

He turned back to the map table, leaving Melita with her
ineffectual anger.

Edi detached himself from an alcove in which he had
ensconced himself during the discussion. He had evidently
overheard enough. 'Not the outcome you were hoping for?'

Melita continued walking, heading nowhere. 'What the
hells do I know about investigating a murder?'

'You might surprise yourself.' Edi's bluff confidence
admitted no doubts. 'And you were right. The best way to
end this quickly is to find who's behind the assassin and bring
them into the light.' That was the enforcer in him.

Melita conceded that she had not been making a hollow
argument. Whoever had orchestrated Sorokin's murder was
likely capable of more acts of carnage, and while they and
their motives remained unknown, everything the regents and
Vasimov did to salvage the situation was imperilled. But she
had not anticipated that she would be manoeuvred into the
centre of that struggle.

She turned at the sound of footsteps on the smooth granite.
Juri Amadan limped towards them, trailed by a watery-eyed
figure swamped by a voluminous grey robe.

'I believe you know Nurem Babić, Andreti's aide,' Amadan
said. The man was indeed familiar to Melita. He had been on
hand, hovering in the background, at all of Melita's meetings
with Sorokin over the past two years. 'He will assist you.'

Babić did not seem happy about it. 'I was there. When she
killed him.'

The event had evidently left its mark on the man. 'I see,'
Melita said.

That did not seem entirely sufficient. What did one do

when asked to find a murderer in a den of killers and criminals?

'I want to know what happened last night. And I want to see him.'

INTERLUDE

Miloš Kuranov watched the missionary's approach, concealing his contempt behind the impassive mask with which he faced so much in this corrupt, benighted world.

The proselytising fool was not alone. His mobile pulpit, whose iron-shod wheels raised him high above those to whom he loudly ministered, was yoked about the shoulders of four straining men. They wore penitents' sackcloth beneath their harness, and if one of his human beasts of burden appeared to slacken in his effort the missionary leant over his lectern and applied the length of an electro-whip to his back.

The pulpit trundled along the via vulgaris flanked by half a dozen Ecclesiarchy bondsmen, whose mauls and cudgels ensured that none of the pedestrians who shared the street's pavement would impede its progress. A mob of worshippers trailed behind, hands raised in supplication and chanting in time with the priest's bellowed sermon. Many wore the same penitents' hoods as those shackled to the pulpit, while others scourged their flesh with barbed lashes, or walked naked and barefoot along the clave's untended streets.

Such was the religion of Varangantua.

As the wailing procession passed the refec-house in which Kuranov sat, one of the trailing zealots stepped out of the crowd and into the alley beside the eatery. Kuranov felt the slightest twinge of a smile cross his lips. His mistress' sense of blasphemy was impeccable.

He waited for a minute, then wiped his mouth clean of paraja crumbs, waved his slate-stick over the scanner embedded in the counter-top, and left with a purposeful but unhurried stride.

As he stepped out into the dry furnace of Korodilsk in mid-morning, a woman emerged from the alleyway. The penitent's hood was gone, replaced with a stiff comb of black lace that all but encircled her head, which he knew was bald beneath the long sable wig that curled out around the comb's edge. A long gown of dark green silk clung to her slim frame, and despite the heat a fur-edged pelisse was draped across one shoulder.

Her eyes, mercifully, were concealed behind thick, smoky lenses. Despite their years of intimate familiarity, meeting his mistress' eyes was still an act that taxed Kuranov's will.

He fell into step behind her, the two immediately assuming the roles of noble lady and dutiful lifeward. They headed in the opposite direction to the migratory priest, whose thundering denunciations of sin and vice still echoed from the plex storefronts of the commercia precinct.

Kuranov followed at his mistress' shoulder, close enough for whispered words to pass between them.

'You left a witness.'

Her high comb made it impossible to tell whether she took offence. 'I will not explain the significance of that to you.'

'Was it ego?' Kuranov was the only person on the planet who would risk speaking to her in such a manner.

She said nothing, and Kuranov did not press further. He knew the limits of her patience, likely worn thin after a month immersed among the Spoil's savagery.

'Your conveyance across the canal?'

Again, she ignored his question. The barge that had carried her downriver was doubtless at the bottom of the foetid mire of the Rustwater, along with its crew and any who had witnessed her alight from its deck.

They wandered for over an hour, passing in and out of boutiques, emporia, and the many vapid distractions that catered to the highest stratum of the tri-districts' degenerate populace. Kuranov was no stranger to concealing his identity, but he marvelled at how completely his mistress disappeared into each disguise she wore. She commiserated with other gilded patrons about the declining standards of a long-established millinery, spat waspish instructions to terrified attendants, and exchanged barbed pleasantries with justicii, vladars, and the scions of dynastic clans both young and old.

Their idle motion between commercia precincts led them, seemingly at random, to the offices of a merchant-combine. Plex and steel reared over Kuranov in a display of petty, empty power.

For the first time since emerging from the alley, she turned to face him. 'You understand your role in what follows?'

'I do.'

'I will send instruction as required.'

Kuranov frowned. 'You risk too much.'

She stared at him through her lenses and placed a cold hand upon his cheek. The touch was gentle, but its meaning was not. Kuranov did not flinch, but he could not fight the malicious memory of the first time she had laid her hand upon him. The horrifying clarity of purpose, the burden and joy of true knowledge in her gaze.

'Events are in motion. None of us, not even I, know where the pieces will fall. That is the sublime beauty of our calling.'

He bowed his head. Kuranov had faced horrors that would drive the cattle that passed them into madness. He had thought himself immune, or at least inured, to the sharp, electric frisson of fear.

In his mistress' service, Kuranov had learnt how false that belief had been.

She released him, though the burning ache of her touch remained. Without another word, she turned on her heel and strode towards the spire's soaring entrance.

Kuranov permitted himself the slightest sigh of relief. Though she was alone once more, an aircar waited atop the building's roof to carry his mistress back to the security of her compound. Her work, or at least the tasks which took her beyond the walls of her dynastic home and amongst the city's filth, was done.

His, however, was just beginning.

PART 2

CHAPTER 8

Their footsteps rose towards the distant ceiling as they strode through the church's nave, echoing from thick columns and finely carved statues of notable Adeptus Ministorum servants.

Cherubim and seraphim glared from shadowed buttresses, but their stony judgement was wasted on Melita. She was not a woman of significant faith. Or, at least, she was no more religious than was performatively required to keep the Ecclesiarchy's tithe collectors from her door. Edi, she knew, was a deeply devout man, as evidenced by his tentative manner as they walked beneath a bas-relief carving of the Three Sons, and his scowls for the gangers that they passed, indifferent to the works of worship above them. Melita found Edi's faith by turns touching and naive, but she didn't envy him. Never that.

The church's interior was a vast, vaulted space that, despite the Har Dhrol's occupation, showed few signs of abuse or neglect. She knew from past visits that many transepts and chapels branched off from the church's central aisle. Even a minor house of worship in Varangantua was a great, sprawling place, with baroque cloisters and discrete chapels for bishops and clerics to sequester themselves in, to consider the God-Emperor's will, and how they might pervert it to their own ends.

These spaces had been easily adapted to the various demands of maintaining a criminal empire, and to administering a territory equal in size to any of the tri-districts. Melita, Edi and their escort passed dozens of gangers, either in the anachronistic robes that Babić wore, or else in the more usual synthleathers and faded novaplas of the Spoil streets.

Babić, their guide, turned suddenly, heading towards a discreet arch tucked into a corner beside a penitent's box. The arch led to a stone staircase that spiralled towards the church's upper levels.

'What happened to your face, Nurem?' Melita asked as they slipped beneath the arch. As they had walked, the hood of his robe had slid back to expose the dark mottling of bruises along his jawline.

He answered hesitantly, with a furtive glance to see who was nearby. 'That was Mercy,' he said. 'When she... When they found Sorokin.'

'What happened last night?'

As they climbed, Babić relayed what he had witnessed in Sorokin's chamber.

'"Tell them what you saw,"' Edi repeated, after the man had told his tale. 'Not very professional.'

'No,' said Babić shakily. 'She definitely wanted a witness.'

They reached the stairs' third full turn, and crossed from one stone shaft to another. The opening to another set of steps, opposite the first, was barred by a heavy steel gate. Babić unlocked it with a slim metal key-stave inserted into the gate's hasp, and they resumed their climb.

The stairs narrowed as they ascended one of the church's fluted towers, until they emerged in the clerestory. Melita had never been permitted to enter this most private part of St Eurydice's, and she was entirely unprepared for the sight that greeted her.

The corridor was a blaze of colour, dazzling after so much forbidding stone. Glassaic lined the hallway in place of walls, and though the morning sun was diffused by the yellow haze of smog, each window was a marvel. Even Melita, so rarely moved by Ecclesiarchy imagery, was captivated by the images of Imperial saints, and of the God-Emperor in His aspect as Vengeance vanquishing the Trinity of Hatreds.

There was one flaw in the otherwise carefully preserved clerestory, where a window frame held plain, unadorned plex in place of a work of pious brilliance. It was a reminder of the fragility of the entire display, and of St Eurydice's itself. Of the Spoil, in fact. Even in the hands of Sorokin, who had evidently tried to maintain the seminary and its works, when the city abandoned such a place, what was left for it but degradation?

The corridor's far end was an octagonal space lined with more beautiful glassaic imagery, and a single door. Melita guessed that they were directly over the centre of the church's domed apse.

'What's this, Babić?' Three men had been idling outside the door, involved in some card game, but they climbed to their feet and put hands to weapons as Melita and the others made their way along the hall.

Babić held up a hand to placate them, but with little authority. 'They're Valtteri, Novak. They're to see him.'

'Why?' Novak, the biggest of them, stepped across the doorway, a stub pistol held meaningfully in his crossed arms. Though they had shown little sign of respect for who they were guarding, now that outsiders were in their midst they closed ranks.

'Because we're going to find out who killed him,' said Melita. She may have had little confidence in her ability to do so, but Melita had never responded well to being told no.

'Mercy and the others have given their permission,' added Babić.

Invoking Sorokin's regents had the desired effect, and the three men grudgingly stepped aside. Babić withdrew his key-stave again, but hung back. He looked paler than ever.

'I'm sure you can wait out here if you'd prefer,' said Melita.

He seemed to deflate, and nodded his thanks. He unlocked the door, then stepped aside. His fellow gangers seemed less than pleased, but did not try to stop Melita, Edi and Oriel entering without an escort.

Sorokin's chamber might have been called elegant if it had been in any other part of the city. Melita assumed that it had been the domicile of St Eurydice's abbot, before the Ecclesiarchy had abandoned the Spoil to degeneracy. It was the size of a modest hab in any tenement in the Spoil, but with thick stone walls instead of pressed fibreboard, and refined, understated wealth in place of heart-aching poverty. The vaulted ceiling climbed to a tall peak, giving the room an air of space and grandeur that belied its size. The few furnishings were made of real wood, and upholstered in real, ruinously expensive fibres.

Opposite the only door was a private chapel, partitioned from the rest of the room by a wide, ornately carved archway. An enormous window, through which light poured in a hundred shades of colour, depicted Saint Eurydice, arms open in benediction, her spear clasped in one hand and the gospel of the God-Emperor held in the other. How the fragile image of the saint had survived in a place as violently degenerate as the Spoil was no mystery to Melita – even the most ardent vandal would have turned their weapon on themselves before damaging such an artful object of mankind's faith.

An enormous bloodstain painted a patch of the priceless rug that covered the flagstones. There was a strange shape to the stain, an oddly sharp line between unspoiled weave and blood-soaked fibres. Melita realised that a desk or other piece of furniture must have stood there, but had been removed since Sorokin's death.

The body had been placed on his bed, a grand four-poster that would not have been out of place in a merchant-baron's quarters. A shroud of grey realweave linen had been laid over him, and two tallow candles burned on either side of the bed.

'Edi, would you...?' She gestured at the linen. Despite repeated exposure, Melita had never become comfortable around death and its many forms. The old sanctioner was decent enough not to comment on her squeamishness as he gently pulled back the shroud.

A horrendous, jagged line snaked its way across Sorokin's throat. She turned away, one hand to her mouth and the other on her trembling stomach.

Edi indulged her for ten seconds, but no longer. 'You have to look,' he said, in a firm but not unkind tone, as though he were still a sanctioner sergeant and she a hesitant recruit. Melita turned back.

The body was disturbingly pale. That was her first and most immediate thought – Sorokin had been exsanguinated, his skin drained to almost alabaster white.

She forced herself to step closer, to see the detail instead of being repulsed by the gruesome whole.

The old man's head had been almost completely severed. The ragged cut extended almost to his spine. His body had been cleaned, but the cleanliness of the appalling, gaping slash across his throat made it somehow worse.

'Not much to be learnt here,' she said, trying to cover her discomfort with bluff professionalism.

'Not without a verispexy team, at any rate,' replied Edi. He had bent at the waist to examine the grisly wound more closely.

'Amadan could probably find one.' There were plenty of back-street chirurgeons in the Spoil, not to mention the private practitioners of the macabre medicae arts who would come if the Har Dhrol compelled them.

Edi straightened, shaking his head. 'Waste of time. All this will be decided one way or another before they could tell you anything useful.'

'I wish I had your confidence.' She looked around, wondering if she should take a closer look at his clothes, or his papers. But to what purpose? What was she supposed to do with this dead lump of flesh?

Melita's experience was with data-tables and cipher-chains. With finding the intersection between a person's ambitions and their fears that would push them towards a decision that favoured her end. She wasn't a probator or a jaeger. She thought of Vasimov's sly smile, and cursed him once again.

Edi, sensing her frustration, sidled out of the room, leaving Melita alone with the body.

She felt no inclination to speak any words of condolence or respect. Sorokin had been canny, vicious, ruthless and ambitious. He was an exemplar of what one needed to be in order to thrive in Varangantua, and by necessity that had made him a man to be feared, not loved.

She had respected him, in the way that adversaries who had never quite come to blows could recognise one another's skills. He had achieved something remarkable in the course of his blood-soaked life. He had brought order to an orderless place. Affected, maybe even improved, the lives of hundreds of thousands of people, even if those lives were spent in servile toil. He had shed rivers of blood and ruled through terror, but that hardly distinguished him from the autocratic district vladars and the detached, brutal oppression of the Lex.

But had he really built anything? The Har Dhrol were collapsing. Iliev and his other lieutenants seemed lost without his guidance, and the clave-captains were evidently backsliding into their old instincts of pettiness and mistrust. All he had made seemed to be ending with him, and that, in Melita's view, was a damning epitaph.

Melita captured a few picts with her iris and had Oriel take an active scan of the room, for whatever use they might have. Then she tugged the linen back across Sorokin's face, and turned away.

The Har Dhrol men watched Melita leave their former master's chambers with undisguised hostility. She felt she had to break the silence.

'What funerary rites will be held?'

'He'll go to the crematoria-fields,' said one of the guards, immediately and emphatically. 'That's our way.'

Melita nodded, as much to placate him as agree with him. The different strata of the city's society had their own rites and practices for the dead, and Melita was not surprised that Sorokin would, either by his own preference or the demands of his followers, go the way of the common Spoiler.

'What about the others?' asked Edi. 'The two guards who died with him.'

'Them as well,' said the ganger.

'We should see them too,' said Melita to Babić, thankful for Edi's unsubtle suggestion. 'If they haven't already been taken?'

Babić shook his head, and led them back along the clerestory to the level below. Novak, the tall ganger who had

blocked their entrance to Sorokin's chambers, insisted on following them down, evidently mistrustful of the two outsiders
around the bodies of fallen comrades. The corridor was lined
with heavy doors, which presumably opened onto dormitories that had been the servants' quarters for the church's
bishop. Babić evidently knew which one to take them to,
although no gangers guarded the cell.

The dorm was surprisingly austere. A pair of beds, metal
lockers at the foot of each, and a bare glow-globe hanging
from the ceiling. No furnishings or decorations. The cell was
as sparse as when it had hosted acolytes of the Ecclesiarchy.

Each bed held a body. These also lay beneath shrouds,
although theirs were common synthweave rather than the
prohibitively expensive linen beneath which Sorokin rested.

'Their names?' asked Edi.

'Vinko Zorić and Andor Markovi,' said Babić, from the
corridor. 'Blooded into the Warhawks eleven and six years
ago, respectively.' That made them Mercy Iliev's men.

Edi pulled down their shrouds with appropriate solemnity. Both were still wearing their armour, anachronistic steel
chestplates over heavy-duty synthweave jackets. Zorić had a
large-calibre hole in the centre of his forehead, which Melita
did not try to examine. She felt another churn of nausea at the
sight of the ragged edge of bone where the back of his skull
had been blown out, and awkwardly turned to the other man.

Markovi looked oddly serene. There was no sign of injury or
struggle, and the mirror surface of his armour was unblemished.

'What's that?' asked Edi, bending closer to the breastplate.

There was, in fact, a small hole, half the width of Melita's
little finger, which cut straight through the metal.

'No lasgun did that,' said Novak, who had crowded into
the cell behind them.

That much was obvious. A lasgun's discharge was bright,

hot and diffuse. A las-bolt would have melted the man's breastplate to slag and driven flash-melted steel into his heart. This, by contrast, was almost surgical. The edges of the hole were smooth, indicating an exceptionally high-powered weapon, but with a tiny aperture.

'Babić,' said Edi. 'Tell us again how this man died.'

The aide relayed the assassin's sly entrance to Sorokin's quarters. The awful moment when she'd plunged the knife into the old man's throat. The burst of light that had struck Markovi dead in the blink of an eye.

Edi and Melita looked at one another, each coming to the same conclusion. 'A digital laser.'

'A what?' asked Novak.

'A miniature lasgun, the size of a ring,' said Edi, as much to himself as the ganger. 'Thirty years in the Corps, and I never saw one. Heard rumours, the few times the Bastion got involved in gilded business.'

No one in the Spoil, not even Sorokin himself, could have got hold of such an impossibly rare device. They were the preserve of the absolute elite. The cost would be unimaginable, enough to buy an entire merchant-combine outright.

This was a complication she had not expected, and did not want.

'Only the cog-heads could make something like that,' said Novak, looking as though he might spit on the floor to ward off the evil he had named.

The Adeptus Mechanicus had only one enclave of any significance in the tri-districts, out in the north-east of Korodilsk, close to the border with Nearsteel. Mechanicus crimson was accordingly rare on the streets, most of all in the Spoil, and mystery bred contempt and fear.

'What about Bai?' she asked, the ganger's casual slur sparking a connection in Melita's mind.

In a criminal empire that ran its territory more efficiently
than many district Administrata, where the Har Dhrol's
rules were enforced with more diligent brutality than most
Bastions applied the Lex, there was one novelty that stood
out beyond the rest. Russov Bai had once been a member of
the Adeptus Mechanicus, the secretive and near-omnipotent
order that hoarded the secrets of technology, science and
industry behind high walls and hardened data-manifolds.
Bai had been exiled from their ranks, but how and why they
had fallen into Sorokin's orbit were the subject of almost as
many rumours as Sorokin himself. Melita, despite her years
amongst the Har Dhrol's upper echelons, had only met the
ex-magos twice, and they had never exchanged words.

Babić answered haltingly. 'That seems unlikely.'

Melita agreed. She assumed that the Mechanicus could
build digital weaponry, but there was no possibility that one
of their exiled members could have made off with something
so rare, nor kept it secret for so long.

Edi and Melita followed the hulking Novak out of the cell,
and Babić pulled the door firmly closed behind them.

'What have you done with the rest of Sorokin's staff?' asked
Melita, groping for another angle from which to approach
the problem.

Babić answered hesitantly. 'Most were inside the wall
when... when it happened. They're under guard in the
priory-habs. Those few who were outside the seminary are
being tracked down.'

'We'll need a list of those,' said Edi. 'And anyone who
shared a duty with the assassin while she posed as a maid.'

'And who vouched for her,' added Melita. The require-
ments for sponsorship into any of the Har Dhrol's gangs, and
in particular the household of the king himself, were as strict
as the most rigorous of gilded lodges.

Babić frowned, fingering the cuff of his heavy synthwool garb. 'We already have the two men who arranged for her to join the household in our custody.'

Melita blinked.

'You could have led with that,' said Edi.

CHAPTER 9

Like any Ecclesiarchy mission, St Eurydice's possessed an extensive dungeon.

As they descended into the building's bowels, Melita felt the oppressive weight of the ancient stone around and above her, a sensation that was not alleviated as they emerged into the church's undercroft. Unlike the granite and marble grandeur of the church's nave, the squat space was lined with grey, unornamented brick, the walls curving deeply to form a series of domed chambers beneath the church's bulk. Each chamber led to another, and Babić led them on a twisting path through the warren.

The narrow tunnel was lit by orange sodium lumens at intervals, creating deep pools of shadow and harsh spots of light. The effect was unpleasant, as, no doubt, it was intended to be.

'How did you find them?' Melita asked.

'Zbirak was in his dorm in the priory,' said Babić. 'He was brought down here immediately, and confessed to everything.

Fortunately, we moved quickly, and we picked up the intermediary before he could run.'

After several more domed chambers, the tunnel opened onto a large, semicircular gaol, where a brace of Har Dhrol gangers sat in grim silence. Unlike their comrades outside Sorokin's quarters, these gangers were alert, but no more welcoming of Melita and Edi's presence. As in the clerestory, the guards yielded to the names of the interim rulers of the Har Dhrol.

The chamber's edge was lined with steel doors, each one opening onto one of the dungeon's cells. Melita noticed that the space in which they stood was marked in places by low plinths, empty bolt-holes, and other evidence of the equipment of Ecclesiarchy torment that had once occupied it. One of the gangers indicated the two cells in which the captives were held.

'What's his name?' asked Edi, looking through the first cell's spyhole. The old sanctioner was undaunted by their forbidding surroundings. In fact, Edi seemed entirely at home – as, she supposed, he should.

'Janis Zbirak,' answered Babić. 'He's the one who vouched for... for her.'

Zbirak's eyes jerked open as the cell door swung open. He flinched as Edi and Melita entered, and positively recoiled from Oriel's silvery leer floating behind them. He was old by the standards of the Spoil, nearer to sixty than fifty. He cringed inside a robe that seemed far too heavy for his wiry frame. One side of his face was horribly bruised, mottled black and purple from jaw to hairline.

Melita's lip curled in disgust. She turned to leave the cell, anger boiling up within her, but Edi caught her before she could leave.

'There's nothing worth saying.'

'But—'

'Just leave it,' he said firmly.

'You're Janis Zbirak?' Melita asked instead, more brusquely than she'd intended.

The old man nodded. He sat on the cell's bed, knees tucked beneath him, hands lost inside the robe.

Edi knelt down, not trying to get closer to the traumatised man, just squatting down to his level. 'What do you do here, Janis?'

'I... I'm Andreti's cook. I was...' Tears welled in the man's eyes.

'You were his cook,' Edi repeated. 'For how long?'

'Twenty years.'

'What happened?'

'She was just an old woman!' he howled. He held his arms up over his face, as though warding off the blows he expected to fall. 'I watched her for three weeks! She lived with her daughters down in Highgate, but they died of the flux. She wasn't capable of something like this! You have to believe me.'

Edi said nothing.

'How did you meet her, Janis?' asked Melita.

He looked from Edi to Melita, tears threatening again. 'I... I had debts. Rajet, and the pits. Someone found me at Lugborta's, covered some of my bets. Said that they had an aunt that needed work. I... I believed him.'

She didn't press him on that, but he broke down anyway.

'They were going to break my hands!'

Melita looked down at Edi. The old enforcer shook his head, and hauled himself to his feet.

'Will they let me out?' Zbirak asked. 'Please let me out!'

The cell door was slammed shut by one of the gangers.

Melita took a breath, and then rounded on Babić, who

backed away with his hands raised. Edi gently steered her towards the next cell.

The other captive was in a much worse state. He had clearly been beaten, and not lightly. Blood caked his face and hair, and one eye was swollen shut. As he turned towards the opening door, Melita saw him tuck one hand protectively against his chest, although he glared up at them in sullen anger and spat a gobbet of blood onto the cold brick.

'I've told them what I know,' he said through reddened teeth. 'If you're going to set that bruiser on me for spite, just get on with it.'

'We're not here to beat you,' Melita said. The smell of blood was thick in the cell, and she could feel the mixture of disgust and outrage stirring the pit of her stomach.

The beaten man stared up at her with his good eye. 'I know you.'

Melita forced herself to look at him. Though his face was a mask of dried blood, Melita realised she knew him too. Troian Horvaç. He worked as an overseer for a small factorum near the Kerysk canal crossing, but moonlighted as a fixer. She had used him once or twice, several years ago, when her own web of contacts had been insufficient to the task at hand. She had never liked him, but he had done good work.

'You do,' she said. 'And all we want to know is what you've already told them.'

'Then talk to them.' Unlike Zbirak's, there was no bed or blanket in this cell, just the brick floor and a bucket. He tucked himself further into the corner, looking sullen.

'We'd rather hear it from you,' said Edi.

'And what can you do for me?'

'We can stop them coming back in.' As with Zbirak, Edi's voice was perfectly neutral. Melita had rarely had a need to see this side of Edi's skillset, but she was becoming more and more grateful for it.

Through the blood, Horvaç gave a grudging nod.

He had been approached by an anonymous man at his regular joy house. Description: tall, dark skin, and rich – far too rich to be anything other than the agent of a merchant-combine or some upclave group. Horvaç had not tried to find out who. He had been asked to arrange for a woman – whom he hadn't met – to join Sorokin's house, and he'd been given the funds to make it happen. Zbirak had been easy to find, and desperate for the slate. By the standard of his usual jobs, this one had paid better, and had been much easier.

'It's remarkable what a man is willing to do for a stack of slate from someone he's just met,' he said finally.

Melita nodded. 'It is.'

He gave a wheezing chuckle, then hissed and hugged his fractured hand closer to his chest.

'And that's it. You didn't keep anything back from the gangers? Or from us?' Edi asked.

'It's pointless asking me for who. I don't get who, so I can't pass it on when this happens.'

'How noble.'

Melita had listened in silence, letting Edi prompt Horvaç when he started to slow down. His description of the agent who had approached him did not match anyone she recognised, but that was hardly surprising. But something about what he had said triggered a thought.

'How were you paid?' she asked.

The man's one open eye glared at her. 'How d'you think?' he said.

'With a slate-stick, credit account, what?'

'We only deal in hard currency round here, upclave.'

Her hope grew. She may not have been a probator, but one axiom was true for all forms of investigation – follow the money. 'Where is it?'

'Where's what?'

'The slate, you bloody idiot.'

He scowled. 'Throne knows. These bastards must have found it when they found me.'

Melita stepped out of the cell to find Horvaç's gaolers. 'Where is it?'

'This is definitely it?'

The ganger lifted the black synthweave sack he had retrieved from wherever in the church's expansive dungeons it had been stored. 'You think we just keep slate lying around like this?'

Melita knew they didn't. She was counting on it, in fact.

Babić had excused himself, citing a summons from one of the regents, and they had been left with one of the gangers who had been guarding the prisoners. He was a tall, heavy-set man with teeth stained almost black, who did not seem to take issue with escorting two outsiders through the undercroft.

Edi took the bag from him, and grunted in surprise. 'This is all of it?'

The man shrugged. So much slate, taken from the hands of a traitor, couldn't spend half a day in the company of gangers without some of it disappearing into their pockets. The fact that the weight of slate inside was still so great spoke of a sizeable pay-off to Horvaç.

Edi changed his grip on the sack, and carefully tipped its contents across the table.

Slates tumbled out in a grey-green wave. Each chip was no wider than Melita's thumb, and an eighth of an inch thick.

Splashes of red and blue surfaced within the heap, the higher denomination chips standing out like buoys on an ocean.

'That's a lot of slate,' Edi said dryly.

'We'll focus on the high-value slates. They're the least likely to have been passed around.'

Melita picked up a red chip, whose value approximated the stipend of a low-grade manufactorum labourer for a month. She rubbed it between her thumb and finger. Each slate was marked with High Gothic text on one face, and the city's serpentine crest on the reverse.

She tossed the slate back onto the pile, and then scooped them back into the sack with Edi's help. She reserved a handful of high-value chips, caging them within her steepled fingers in a short column. She grinned. This was a lead she could work with.

She turned to the ganger. 'I have to speak to Russov Bai.'

The sophistication of the Har Dhrol's operation did not extend merely to extorting rents from hab-block slumlords and workshop owners, and maintaining mid-yield generatoria to provide light and power to their beholden tenants. Sorokin, cut off from so much of the city's infrastructure, had created his own. Including a banking system.

Only a handful of the Spoil's denizens had access to equipment that could connect to the city's noospheric network. Even if they had, it was not a trivial task to obtain a credit account with one of Varangantua's byzantine financial houses, particularly without ident documents provided by the Administratum. As a result, almost all transactions on the Spoil's streets were made with hard slate, passed from hand to hand.

The supply of currency in circulation was finite, and so its control was a lever held firmly by Sorokin's hand. Early on in his rule, long before Melita had set out on her career as an info-broker, one of the Valtteri's rival conglomerates had sought to undermine the cartel's gangland allies by flooding the Spoil with low-denomination slate. The inflationary effect of this tidal wave of currency had seismic consequences for the stability of the Spoil until, as Melita had it, Sorokin's lieutenants had tracked down the source and dealt with the problem in an explosive and public fashion.

Sorokin, too, learned from that experience, and had set Russov Bai, his exiled acolyte of the Adeptus Mechanicus, to work. There had always been cash houses across the length and breadth of the Spoil, stashes where the narco-pusher crews and territorial gangs gathered together their ill-gotten gains. The magos had taken their hoarding instinct and turned it on its head.

Within two years, it became possible to trace the journey of a single slate from one Har Dhrol ganger to another. Each chip's serial code, stamped in minute runes on one face, was recorded when it entered one of Bai's banking houses, and logged against the account – how that idea must have vexed Sorokin's hardened street-soldiers – of the depositor. When it was transferred from one storehouse to another, it was tracked. When it was cashed out, it was noted. This web of transactions, daunting in its complexity and astounding in its omniscience, became Sorokin's greatest tool for monitoring the activities of his underlings.

Of course, each Har Dhrol ganger, from the senior praetors down to the lowest street-blade, kept their own caches of slate. But for sanctioned business, and for the monthly tributes that flowed from the Har Dhrol's limbs to its heart, and back out as Sorokin's largesse to the captains, they had to use the money deposited in Bai's banks.

'I need Bai,' Melita said again. Despite her best efforts, she had consistently failed to penetrate the layers of noospheric defences that protected the network of vox-links and hard-wired cables that underpinned the Spoil's economy. To track down the source of the pay-off – if the slate had been drawn from the account of a Har Dhrol ganger – she would need the former magos' cooperation.

The black-toothed ganger spread his hands. 'I don't move in such exalted circles.' He hawked up and spat a gobbet of phlegm into the room's far corner.

Melita tried not to let her disgust show. 'Who does?'

He looked up at the undercroft's stone ceiling.

'Right.' Melita turned to Edi. 'You think there's anything more we can get from Zbirak and Horvaç?' Not that Melita had any desire to go back into the miserable cells.

He shook his head. 'They were broken before we got in there.'

Melita agreed with him, and jerked her head towards the dungeon's door. The ganger cleared his throat, and gave a crooked grin. 'The slate stays here.'

Edi glanced down at the sack, still in his hand. 'We might need to take another look at that later,' he said as he passed it over. The ganger's black grin broadened.

After their escort had unlocked the barred gate and vaguely directed them back to the church's nave, Melita and Edi set off in pursuit of their lead.

'How'd you make out?' Melita asked quietly as they started up the stairs.

Edi's reply was a soft click of slates from within his pocket. 'You?'

Melita said nothing, fingering the rounded edges of the chips clutched within her closed fist.

CHAPTER 10

Hot, dry air greeted Melita as she emerged from the church's catacombs. Hot air, and the sound of voices raised in anger.

Nothing stirred as she and Edi crossed the nave, Oriel silent in their wake. In the undercroft the weight of stone above their heads had given a degree of blessed relief from the heat. With each step across the polished floor, the furnace of noon grew worse, stultifying in its intensity.

Amadan and Toskanov stood at the top of the steps, just inside what little shade was cast by the massive stone aquila above them. Below, Mercy Iliev was berating a man at least half her age, and a full head taller. They were surrounded by a mob of gangers, all of them yelling just as loudly. Most, Melita could see, had taken cuts and blows to their head and arms. These seemed to be the targets of Iliev's anger.

'What happened?'

The two old men acknowledged Melita's arrival with curt nods. 'Idiocy,' said Toskanov. His lip curled at the squabbling men and women, but he did not try to intervene.

Amadan was more sanguine, or, perhaps, more resigned. 'One of Mercy's crews was replenishing a dispensary, no more than a mile from here. Someone saw the hauler, thought that they were removing stock instead of adding to it, and...' He trailed off, gesturing at the wounded half of the arguing mob.

'And?'

'Two of the crew are dead. Terra knows how many in the crowd.'

'And the dispensary is up in flames,' spat Toskanov.

Melita waited, expecting more. But the two men, who had each lived for three-quarters of a century amid the Spoil's vicissitudes, had nothing else to say. It was clear that they would take no action. Not to sanction the gangers who allowed the situation to arise, although Mercy evidently had that in hand. Not to rush aid to the clave whose occupants would soon start to look at their neighbours, wondering which were prudent enough to hide away stores for a day such as this. Not even to organise a reprisal against the Spoilers who had caused the deaths of two of their own, the most basic instinct and law of any gang.

She looked sidelong at them both, at their impotent dismay. They really were lost without Sorokin.

Footsteps, sharp as snares against the church's tiles, made the three of them turn. Vasimov strode through St Eurydice's as though it were his family's private chapel, flanked by a pair of his mercenaries and followed, at a discreet interval, by Babić.

'What is this?' he asked. He stopped uncomfortably close to Melita, peering with distaste over her head at the arguing mob of gangers.

The two old men pointedly turned away at Vasimov's tone, leaving it to Melita to relay the tale.

'I see,' he said, in the manner of a gilded grandam who

had been forced to observe the squalor that persisted beyond their estate. 'Unfortunate. But not, I think, your most pressing concern.'

The regents of the Har Dhrol turned back. 'What now?'

Vasimov indulgently stepped back to make space for Babić. The aide came forward hesitantly, but evidently too slow for the securitor's preference. 'At least two of your gang captains are dead,' he said.

Babić cleared his throat. 'I've checked, lords, and it appears to be true. Lopushani of the Pit Snakes, and Stoyano of the Forge Fiends. And there's a rumour Ravshana Lurkova's body was found strung up from the Draven Bridge. I've sent riders to find out what happened.'

Melita absorbed the news alongside the two praetors, factoring it into her mental map of the Spoil. Lopushani and Stoyano were rivals, each moderately influential but far from the most powerful of the players within the Har Dhrol's vast, complex web of fealties and enmities. Their territories nestled against one another in the shadow of the Redfort, which marked the Spoil's north-eastern corner. What significance did their deaths hold? Were they the result of internecine conflict, the settling of scores now that Sorokin's restraining hand was lifted? Or had whoever killed the old man murdered these two as well? To what end?

'It gets worse,' said Babić.

'How?' asked Toskanov.

The younger man told them.

Several major infrastructure works – the data-trunk junction in Merdiç, a bio-waste generatorum in Vamasse, and a groundcar maintenance shop in Toskanov's fief of Bégna – had been attacked by street-soldiers in Har Dhrol grey, leading to a lot of dead on what were now two sides. Engine-gangers had been sighted on the Binastri Arterial, and several other major

highways through the Spoil. There had been clashes between
several hot-headed crews and belligerent Grenze Guard on
three of the Rustwater bridges. Crowds had been reported in
a dozen claves, presumably rallied by local rabble-rousers for
the purpose of one form of trouble or another.

The picture was grim, and clear. The Har Dhrol were losing
control of the Spoil.

'This has to stop,' Iliev said, once Babić finally finished. While
the aide had spoken, the old woman had finished berating her
crew, and had joined her fellows in mute disquiet as the litany
of calamities rolled on. 'Regardless of who instigated this chaos,
we must unite. We need to convene the praetors.'

'I have cautioned against that.' Vasimov's intervention was
as predictable as it was unwelcome.

'Yes, you've said your piece,' snapped Iliev. Amadan and
Toskanov remained silent, leaving it to the old woman to
lay out their position in adamant, furious tones. 'This is our
way. It's what he wanted.'

'And what if this conclave installs Sorokin's killer in his
place? Would he want that?'

'What news on that front?' asked Amadan, in an attempt
to defuse the gathering tension.

It worked. All eyes turned to Melita, and she had a moment
of sympathy for Babić, who had been subjected to the same
fervent hunger for knowledge, for the critical fact or discovery that would allow the regents to suddenly make sense
of all that had befallen them.

Like Babić, Melita cleared her throat. 'It is safe to say that
an actor outside the Spoil is involved in Sorokin's death.'

Vasimov was the first to challenge her. 'Your evidence?'

'One of his guards was killed with a digital laser.'

He cocked an eyebrow at that, but, to Melita's surprise, did
not challenge her assertion.

The securitor's mute acceptance made Melita wonder, not for the first time, whether the Valtteri were behind Sorokin's death.

If anyone in the city could lay their hands on such a device, it would be the cartel's executors. Vasimov had spoken truthfully earlier – what the cartel wanted and needed from the Spoil above all else was stability. Sorokin had been nearing the end of his natural life, his control over the Har Dhrol fraying – Melita's own reports had told them so. Would the Valtteri directors accept some necessary disruption in the short term for an assurance of hegemony for the future? Certainly, assassination was not beneath them. The loss of life, both specific and collateral, was hardly a concern for an organisation whose indifferent reach touched the lives of millions.

But Vasimov's glare suggested that he was struggling to understand the shape and direction of what was taking place just as much as Sorokin's regents. And, Melita reasoned, if the cartel had eliminated the King of the Har Dhrol, their next move would have been immediate. The ground would have been prepared, all obstacles subtly eliminated. Their chosen successor would have been sped to St Eurydice's before word of Sorokin's death had even reached the tri-districts, to affirm their new status and secure the loyalty of the remaining clave-captains.

Sorokin's death did not feel like the final act of a coup long in the making. It felt like the opening salvo of a war.

'Such a weapon had to come from outside the Spoil,' Melita said, into the silence. 'But we can't rule out the likelihood that whoever is moving behind this also has allies within the Spoil. That's why I need Russov Bai.'

Melita noticed that Babić chose that moment to take his leave of his masters, a finger pressed to the vox micro-bead in his ear.

'Bai?' asked Toskanov. 'Why?'

'I need them to interrogate the records of your banking system. It is possible that the slate used to pay the agent who smuggled the assassin into your midst was drawn from their own accounts.'

'That's thin,' said Toskanov.

Melita could hardly disagree. 'There's little else to go on.'

'I'm not about to lay bare our finances on the strength of wild speculation,' said Iliev, although with less steel than was usual for her defiant pronouncements.

Melita frowned. 'I did say that I would require unfettered access.'

'To the seminary, not to one of the fundamental pillars of our organisation.'

'Enough,' said Vasimov, in the tones of a justicius laying down a pronouncement. 'You do not have Bai.'

Toskanov was the one to finally break the silence that followed. 'We haven't heard from the esteemed magos since Andreti's death.'

'Holy Throne.' Melita gaped. Bai was the architect of the Spoil, as famed – if not as feared – as Sorokin himself. Every power plant, vox-relay and sewage reclamator was drawn from the jealously guarded secrets of the Mechanicus that Bai held inside their head. Their design, and Sorokin's ambition, had reshaped the Spoil, and in large part had allowed it to become what it was. Their loss was a grievous blow to the Har Dhrol's ambitions for the Spoil, although at least one of Sorokin's regents did not seem to be particularly dismayed.

'They're dead, taken or fled,' said Iliev brusquely. 'In any case, we will proceed without them.' She deliberately turned away from Vasimov and Melita. 'We need to send crews to the clave-captains, or even go out to the territories ourselves. We have to get them to attend the conclave.'

As the three regents retreated into the cooler interior of the church, heads bent in discussion, Melita took Vasimov aside.

'Was this you?'

He evidently took exception to her tone, but answered nevertheless. 'No.'

Her scepticism was plain to see, and Vasimov relented.

'We received intelligence regarding Bai's whereabouts.' He paused, to allow Melita the chance to ask from where such information had come. She didn't give him the satisfaction. 'I issued orders for a team to pick them up, in anticipation of their utility in whatever may yet come. But we were too late.'

He pulled a slim data-slate from his jacket, and called up a set of images. A Spoil hab in disarray. The detritus of broken machinery beside an overturned workstation. Shell casings, bright against a bilious green carpet, its pile worn down to coarse fuzz. An empty dormitory, clearly Bai's – a red robe was hung with deliberate care in the room's storage unit.

Vasimov tucked the data-slate away. 'I would say that that line of your investigation – such as it is – has been closed.'

'You don't think this is evidence of a wider conspiracy? Whoever got to Bai first may have done so precisely because they would be able to trace the source of the slate.'

The securitor's patience for her presence was clearly starting to wear thin. 'Perhaps. But what does it matter? They are gone. You will not be able to find the kidnappers.' He drew himself up. 'Your role here is ended.'

Melita was a contrary soul. She had refused to heed Vasimov's summons to the Xeremor. She had resisted taking on the search for Sorokin's killer when it was forced upon her. Now, faced with Vasimov's dismissal, she felt that same streak of perverse stubbornness rising once again.

'Not necessarily.'

CHAPTER 11

Haska had never seen the inside of a scholam. Her mother had taught her to read from a tattered hymnal that circulated through the hab-block, the golden aquila that had once adorned its cover long since worn away by the many hands it had passed through. She had nothing that the upclave snobs would recognise as an education. Certainly, she had never studied what collegium lecturers and cultural wardens termed the higher arts, such as aesthetics, history or psychology.

Nevertheless, Haska understood in her bones that Imperial architecture was built to overawe. Every building exuded power and dominance, regardless of its specific function. Each looming bastion, titanic manufactorum and towering basilica was an expression of authority, a declaration of strength and permanence stamped with steel and stone into the earth, and into the minds of all who stood beneath their sheer walls and leering gargoyles and spread-winged aquilae. They told every citizen of Varangantua that the Imperium had endured since long before the birth of their forgotten ancestors, and would continue to stand when the dust from their bones had settled back into the dirt.

Even in its broken state, with its iron flanks daubed with layers of filth and etched with gang slogans, Haska felt an involuntary urge to cower as they drove into the shadow of the Redfort. Though the Spoil's long neglect had taken its toll upon its greatest statements of Imperial might, some crumbling examples remained.

The walled enclave occupied a wide knurl of land that lay above the Rustwater's terminus. It had guarded the canal since the earliest days of the Spoil, if not before. Haska had heard of dozens of locations across Varangantua that purported to be the site of the First Landings, ancient conurbations that claimed to be where the original colony ships the God-Emperor had dispatched from distant Terra had finally set down. As far as most Spoilers were concerned, the Redfort had as strong a claim to that sacred title as any.

It was likely that the Redfort had held a grander title to go along with its rumoured history, but these days everyone simply called it what it was. The Redfort was not one building but a subdistrict in miniature, enclosed on all sides by iron ramparts that might once have equalled those of a Defence Corps citadel. Those disintegrating fortifications, which were gradually sloughing their flaking metal into the poisoned filth of the Rustwater, suggested an obvious name to the unimaginative folk of the Spoil.

Its man-made cliffs marked the north-westerly point of the Spoil. Shanty towns clustered around its corroding foundations, but they quickly gave way to the barren strip of empty land that emphatically delineated the abandoned region's border with its wealthy and disdainful neighbour, Setomir.

Aryat drove their struggling groundcar up a switchback ramp that climbed the southern face of the wall. Haska was keenly aware of the dark shapes of crenellations above them, the last vestiges of the palisades that had once guarded this quarter of the enclave. The murder-holes and projecting turrets had been robbed of their guns long ago, but they were a reminder that the Redfort did not welcome visitors.

The people that lived within the walls had a shared identity that was separate from the rest of the Spoil. They were sneering and proud, despite the wretched state of their decaying home. As well they might be: the Redfort had been the last bastion of resistance to Har Dhrol control, denying Sorokin's demands for submission for several bloody years.

Street lore held that Sorokin, tired of the constant cycle of raid and reprisal that gnawed at the corner of his domain, had called a parley with the leaders of the Redfort combine. The King of the Har Dhrol had arrived in a Sullaina-model limousine, wearing a finely tailored realweave suit, and escorted by a crew armed and armoured in gear that outclassed even the elite companies of the Alectian Planetary Defence Corps. He also brought with him a pair of smile-girls for each of the Redfort warlords, bearing satchels containing the prostitutes' own weight in coin. It, and they, had been presented as gifts to Sorokin's enemies as evidence of the advantages of finally accepting unity with the rest of the Spoil. It had been a potent display, and persuasive.

The rumour further ran that within two years, the gifted smile-girls had murdered every one of the former gang lords in their beds. But by then Sorokin's lieutenants had thoroughly dismantled his former adversaries' organisations, and the Redfort was just one more clave in Andreti Sorokin's kingdom.

Their groundcar finally reached the summit of the winding ramp. Aryat showed an uncharacteristic degree of caution as he slowly drove their wheezing vehicle beneath the gatehouse, evidently as intimidated by the broken fortress as Haska.

On the far side, the road was littered with shards of plex and metal, and its surface was scored with sets of parallel tracks. Four burnt-out groundcars were untidily drawn up on either side, sitting on broken axles that had gouged marks in the asphalt. The Redfort's gangs had presumably set up a substantial barricade across the gatehouse's mouth, but something or someone had persuaded them to remove it. There were a few gangers milling about; Haska didn't know the Redfort crews sufficiently to identify them from their green head-crests and complex, swirling insignia. They made no attempt to stop her crew from entering.

They had driven in silence since fleeing the ambush in Merdiç Square. Haska supposed that they should have felt victorious. They had killed a rival praetor and avenged those who'd died in Aryat's hab-stack. They would surely now be blooded into the Pit Snakes as fully fledged soldiers.

Haska stared down at her hands, knotted together in her lap. She couldn't shake the memory of the juve she had killed. The pool of crimson beneath him, growing inch by inch with each weakening pump of his heart.

She didn't feel like a victor.

'Do you know where you're going?' asked Katryn, so suddenly that she made Haska jump. They had taken half a dozen turns almost at random, and although Aryat seemed to be choosing the widest roads at each junction there was no sign they were approaching any landmarks.

'The loc-ref says the Soldier's Square.'

'Where's that?' Katryn persisted. Haska was glad that one of them had given voice to the nerves they were all feeling.

The groundcar's engine chose that moment to give a rattling sort of cough, and Aryat swore at the vehicle's machine spirit

rather than reply. He was clearly as unfamiliar with the labyrinthine streets as Haska and the rest of her crew.

'Well?' asked Lira, once the engine's gurgle and the boy's
string of profanities subsided.

'I'm following the loc-ref, okay?' He stabbed a finger at
the Grigga's centre console. A series of runes blinked from
its tiny read-out, although they seemed to display only the
distance to their destination rather than a set of directions.

The Redfort was a honeycomb, a ramshackle collection
of buildings that were as tired and broken as the encircling
walls. It was the first time Haska had been inside, although
she had looked at the walls often enough; the fortifications
dominated the skyline from the tops of the tenements in
her clave.

Everything had more up and down to it than Haska was
used to. Steps emerged from sublevels and concealed doorways to climb into hab-blocks, or disappeared into narrow
gaps in brick walls. The streets twisted back on one another
without any pattern or design. After fifteen minutes Haska
was completely lost, until she spotted the sheer line of a ram-
part between two buildings and realised that they were no
closer to the Redfort's centre.

And yet, through luck more than Aryat's sense of direction or the aid of the Grigga's machine spirit, they found the
Soldier's Square.

They emerged from yet another twisting alley and found
themselves at the top of a broad, open mall, with more people
than they had seen all day crowding towards its far end. The
change was so sudden after the claustrophobic tunnels and
empty streets that Aryat slewed their groundcar to a jerking stop.

Hazy sunlight filled the square, though it served only to
catch each grime-streaked window and wind-blown refuse

drift. Stone paving, grey where it wasn't coated in a film of dirt, sloped away gently towards a stone column and what had clearly been the local Administratum precinct in ages past.

The column was a truly wretched sight. It rose thirty feet or more above the crowd, and its upper third was streaked with palumba droppings. From the square's name, Haska assumed that the column had once supported some tribute to the mighty and innumerable ranks of the Astra Militarum, the hammer of the God-Emperor's enemies. Perhaps a Guardsman urging his fellows on, or a general calmly surveying a battlefield, rendered in bronze or granite. Haska had heard that such statues were common in the rest of the city. But here, as with so much of the Spoil's old wealth, whatever had crowned the column's plinth had been removed long ago. There were no symbols of Imperial glory or majesty to inspire the Spoil's citizenry, except for those too large and cumbersome to be stolen away.

Haska climbed out of the Grigga, and sweat immediately started to bead her forehead. Heat hammered at her from the cracked paving slabs, and from the walls of the buildings that enclosed the plaza on all sides. It had been hot inside the groundcar, but the Soldier's Square seemed to have been designed to trap the heat, perhaps in twisted echo of the fires of war through which the Imperium's warriors marched.

The baking air danced above the heads of the crowd, which had gathered in some numbers. Hundreds were shuffling towards the column and the clutch of groundcars arrayed around its base.

'We're supposed to meet your uncle here?' asked Lira. She and Katryn and Aryat had also climbed out. The boy nodded in reply, evidently as surprised by the congregation as the rest of them.

Lira pointed down the slope. 'Are they giving out food?'

Haska followed her disbelieving stare. Someone was, indeed, giving out food.

Serving stations had been set up on the open tailgates of six low-slung light haulers, and pairs of gangers were passing out mugs of stamp broth and fist-sized loaves of spun starch. Lines of disbelieving Redfort denizens, wretched in their ragged clothes, were filing past, grabbing all that they could carry. The haulers had been drawn up in such a way as to funnel people further down the mall's length, and Haska could see other vehicles on either side of the palace, similarly mobbed by hungry bodies. There must have been a thousand people gathered inside the rough perimeter formed by the haulers, and more waited with thinning patience outside.

'What's going on?'

'Let's go and find out,' said Haska. She slammed the Grigga's door shut, and started down the slope.

'What about the groundcar?' asked Aryat. He had grown attached to the vehicle in the few hours since his uncle had handed over the access stave, no doubt hoping that Karlo would let him keep it once their job was over.

Haska hesitated. 'You and Katryn drive it down, meet us over on the western side. We'll find Karlo.' She and Lira set off, roasting in the furnace heat of the square.

The smell of the broth made her empty stomach growl. Charity of this kind was rare in the Spoil, but not unheard of. As Haska walked closer, drawn as much by curiosity as the smell of hot food, the memory of a similar handout came to mind. When she had been no more than seven or eight, a group of philanthropes had occupied one of the abandoned commercia units near her hab-block with the aim of setting up an alms-refectory. They had been sponsored by some gilded house or saintly mission in Dragosyl, and they had wildly misunderstood the nature of who they hoped to help. It took less than a day for the word to get round the clave, and as soon as night fell no fewer than five competing crews broke into the unit to loot the refectory's supplies and equipment. A fight had broken out between the almshouse guards and the gangs, and somehow the entire building had ended up on fire. The philanthropes had not returned to Haska's clave.

Whoever was running this event had taken greater precautions. Each hauler was flanked by another pair of gangers, cradling autoguns and shot-cannons to keep tempers and appetites under control. Interestingly, they did not seem particularly hostile towards the crowds, although Haska saw an elderly couple shoved roughly out of the line when they lingered in the hope of picking up another hunk of starch. The street-blades were repeating the same refrain as the gangers who were acting as servers.

'Take it, and listen! Take it, and listen!'

She and Lira drifted through the crowds, unchallenged as long as they did not try to join the scrums around the heavy vats of broth. As they followed the general movement of the crowd, vox-distorted words drifted over the racket and clamour behind them.

A figure was standing on the roof of a groundcar, speaking into a vox-horn whose coiled cable led to a nearby servo-skull. He was stripped to his undershirt in the furious heat, but wore a wide sash in Har Dhrol grey around his narrow waist. Another strip of fabric was draped from one shoulder like a bandolier, from which hung a brace of short knives holstered in red synthleather. Other servo-skulls ranged above the crowd, broadcasting the man's speech loud enough for the words to echo back from the encircling buildings.

'I am grateful to you, my friends, for braving the heat, for braving the violence that plagues the streets, to join me here today. I am a stranger to your clave, but you have welcomed me like a brother.'

'That's not Lopushani.' Haska had to almost shout to be heard. They had ended up just a few yards from one of the skulls, and each word bored into Haska's head with a tinny burr of distortion.

'That's Damor Saitz,' replied Lira, at the same volume. 'A clave-captain in the Deiten chapter of the Red Knives.'

Saitz was no great speaker. His eyes darted from face to face, too rapidly to make any connection, too wild to imply command or wisdom. He spoke too fast, spitting each word so that they fizzed and popped from the vox-grilles of the servo-skulls hovering above the crowd. He reminded Haska of the itinerant preachers that sometimes braved the streets of the Spoil, fiercely proclaiming the greatness of the God-Emperor of Mankind, exhorting the weak and the sinful to abandon their treacherous ways and give themselves over to His grace and mercy. Few people paid them any mind, but here the crowd seemed sincerely rapt. They stood in clusters, drawing nearer to his platform as the crowd grew. Although all were quick to drain their tin mugs of steaming broth, Haska saw that most were lingering to listen.

'I ask you to look to the north. Beyond the Redfort's mighty walls. What do you see?' A few people turned to follow his gesture, as though they might actually look through the monumental ramparts of their prison-home. 'Do you see the Chimneys? The heartsblood of the Spoil, the wellspring of our food, our power, our hope?' Saitz waited. 'No, you do not!' He practically shrieked the words. 'You do not see them, because they were stolen from us! They were taken, excised by borders and hidden behind walls and guns.'

Haska had heard this brand of rhetoric before. It was a

common theme for anyone who could spare the breath from complaining about their own, more personal troubles. The northern border of the Spoil was an industrial and agricultural treasure trove, and the oldest name for the miles of rocky ground was the Chimneys. It came, she had heard, from the pillars of steam that had once risen out of the ground, which somehow made it ideal for power and heat generatoria. Alongside them had risen huge growth vats and cattle pens. When the city retreated from the Spoil, well back in the opaque mists of history, Setomir had taken the Chimneys for its own.

'But if we dare to take some morsel of what is rightfully ours, to snatch some of the scraps that fall from their table, we are chased back into our holes. We are shot like vermin, if we're lucky, or sent to be fodder aboard the Navy's slave-hulks if we are not. Who among us has not lost friends to the Grenze Guard?'

He stopped abruptly. Evidently, he had not meant the question to be rhetorical. A few voices answered, muted cries of affirmation that dropped into the rapt silence.

'I ask you, who among you has not suffered at the hands of the city?'

More people joined in, dozens and then hundreds shouting in anger. This was what Saitz had wanted. He stood with his arms open, eyes half-closed in an expression of sincere empathy, and let the tales of loss and pain spread through the crowd.

Saitz had been wise to come to the Redfort for his rabble-rousing. It was a breeding ground for street-blades, and with the Chimneys in sight of the walls, it had historically been a hub for the forays into Setomir, and for the sale of whatever they could bring back, if they came back.

'We can't even raid any more!' cried someone from within the crowd, drawing the loudest and bitterest cheer yet.

'You're right, my friend!' Saitz seized on that. 'Sorokin, for all his merits, held back our collective strength. We know, you and I, that it is only right that we claw back what we can for ourselves. You cannot steal from thieves!'

Even Haska conceded that that was true. Sorokin's edict had curtailed the raids across the Line, the price of his deal with the upclave merchant-combines who poured slate into the Har Dhrol's hands. That had hurt the Redfort, in particular. Haska would have bet a heavy fist of slate that whoever had shouted had been planted in the crowd.

Saitz fell silent, apparently feeling his audience's hurt as his own. Haska revised her opinion of him. He may have been a poor speaker, but he knew how to play a crowd.

'Sorokin is gone. Some of you may mourn him. But I do not.' He let that sink in. 'I tell you, I do not! For too long, he shackled us. For too long, we have been held by chains of his making, while he enriched himself on the bribes of the upclavers.'

Saitz was running a risky line. Even with the Redfort's history of independence, denouncing the dead king so openly was inviting a loyal street-soldier to take a shot at him. But no one did. In fact, the crowd seemed to cheer all the louder. Saitz seemed to have judged his audience very well.

'He is gone, and we are free of his fetters. We can set our own course. It is time the Spoil took back what is rightfully ours!'

They roared. Haska had never heard, never felt a sound like it. It was as though every voice in the Redfort cried out as one, a physical force that echoed around the square. Such a display of unity was utterly alien. It exhilarated and frightened her, all at once.

She grabbed Lira's arm. 'Let's go.'

'We can't leave now,' said Lira.

'Why not?'

She gestured up at Saitz. She was clearly riveted by Saitz's rhetoric.

Haska caught her shoulder. 'We need to finish the job. Remember? We came here to find Lopushani.'

It was clear that Saitz was far from done, but Lira nodded.

Haska set off through the crowd, shoulders set to push aside anyone who got in her way.

She eventually spotted Karlo Karamenko among the ring of gangers that encircled Saitz, and headed towards him. Aryat and Katryn had already found him, and were both staring up at Saitz, rapt.

Karamenko saw them approaching, and waved them through the ring of gangers who were keeping the clave-captain's keenest adherents at bay. 'It's done?'

'It's done,' said Lira.

'Where's Lopushani?' asked Haska. She recognised several of his soldiers among those clustered around the groundcar on which Saitz was standing, but she couldn't see the Pit Snakes' clave-captain.

'Doesn't matter,' said Karamenko.

Something in his voice made her push back. 'It does to me.' It did not; Haska had no love or loyalty to the man, but she had an instinct, and she wanted it to be confirmed.

Karlo met her eye. 'He's not here.'

Haska's skin crawled.

'Where's our slate?' Lira asked, showing more sense than Haska.

A cheer from the crowd interrupted Karamenko's reply. It wasn't loud or particularly jubilant, but grew and grew, gathering momentum as it echoed from the surrounding buildings.

'I hope, my friends, my brothers and sisters, that you will join me.'

Saitz stepped off the groundcar roof, one hand raised. The cheers continued long after he disappeared from sight. Some in the crowd even surged forward, provoking angry responses from his praetorians.

A member of his crew, a Red Knife whose signature crimson-hilted razor was strapped across his chest in the same manner as Saitz's trio of blades, handed his clave-captain a short jacket, its supple synthleather decorated with scarlet flashes. As he shrugged it on, Haska took the chance to examine this ganger, a man she had not heard of even half an hour earlier, but who had somehow drawn a Spoil mob together through the power of his voice and vision.

Saitz was fairly short, only an inch or two taller than Haska or Lira. He was of an age with Haska's mother, but probably no more than that. His black hair was cut short, above a thin, serious face. He had no real scars, but he had the slight bend to his nose common to so many gangers that came from a lifetime of taking blows to the face. His eyes were narrow and shrewd. They were never still, filled with the same manic energy that had animated him while atop his stage.

'Damor,' Karamenko called.

Saitz freed himself from the clutch of bodyguards that closed around him. Karamenko bent close as the clave-captain came over.

'It's done.'

'Good, good.' Up close, his voice was a low murmur, hoarse from his furious oratory. 'And who are these?'

'Pit Snakes aspirants. They pick up odd jobs. They were part of the hit.'

Saitz smiled, a slow bearing of sharp teeth. 'And do they have names?'

Haska frowned. 'Haska Jovanic. This is my crew.'

They introduced themselves. Saitz made a particular point

of nodding when Aryat spoke, as the boy put emphasis on his family name. Haska reckoned he had taken it badly that Karlo hadn't pointed out their connection himself.

Saitz inclined his head like a gilded patron. 'I am grateful to you.'

'Why?' Haska asked. She didn't like the clave-captain's manner. The morning's violence and the crowd's furious baying had unlocked something reckless within her.

He smiled, evidently unused to being challenged by a sixteen-year-old juve. 'Why what?'

'Why have us kill Stoyano and his crew?'

His calm humour was replaced by a look of stern judgement. Haska got the sense that this was another face of his performance. 'Vagif Stoyano was a villain, and a blight upon those unfortunate enough to live within his claves.' Haska had heard stories about Stoyano and his excesses, but there were stories and rumours about every clave-captain. 'In this time of change, it was right that he die with the old era.'

'And Lopushani?'

'Haska...' Lira hissed, but Haska ignored her. She had an urge to push this man. She did not trust his rhetoric, particularly given the effect it had had on her friends.

'Lopushani was... necessary,' he said. Was the flicker of regret that crossed his face sincere, or another put-on?

'I'll have the guns back,' said Karamenko brusquely, to shut down any further interrogation Haska might attempt.

'Keep them,' Saitz said, reviving his false humour. 'You've earned them. And, no doubt, you'll make good use of them.'

That was no small gift for an unsponsored crew of street-blades. Lira and Katryn beamed, and Aryat, the shot-cannon hanging from its sling inside his jacket, looked positively jubilant.

Gratitude was an unusual feeling for Haska. Saitz's gesture

fed, rather than subdued, her suspicion. 'And our slate?' she demanded.

Karamenko looked at Saitz, but the clave-captain gave another soft, almost indulgent smile. The older man pulled a black synthleather pouch from his jacket and tossed it to Haska. It was promisingly, thrillingly heavy.

'What's your clave?' Saitz asked.

'Bérault,' said Lira, before Haska could stop her.

The man nodded, as though he walked through the clave's streets every day. 'Do you know the junction between Urilad and the Gorstad factory?'

'Yes.' Aryat nodded, agreeing for all of them. That was where two wide roads joined to become the Urilad Arterial, one of the main thoroughfares through the Bérault clave, less than a mile from Haska's hab-block.

'We'll be mustering there tonight.'

'Mustering?'

'I meant what I said. It is time the Spoil reclaimed its birthright. I hope you'll be a part of that.'

'We'll see.' She gently put a hand on Lira's shoulder, trying to push her towards the rear of the crowd.

Saitz caught Haska's eye. 'You're not convinced.'

'No.'

'I understand. Change is hard to imagine for those who have never seen it.' He favoured Haska's crew with another smile, then turned away.

'Aryat,' the boy's uncle said. 'I'll be seeing you later.'

The boy nodded eagerly. 'You will.'

Karamenko nodded back, and gave Haska a withering, victorious glare. She was finally able to set her crew moving.

'Let's get out of here.'

CHAPTER 12

Melita finally cornered her target on the second level of St Eurydice's north-east aisle. He had fled from her, hiding for almost three hours in the priory-habs at the far side of the seminary's complex. But she had finally forced him to break cover with a seemingly innocuous request to Harol Toskanov. Unable to disobey a summons from one of his masters, he had returned to the imposing majesty of the church, and there she caught him.

Edi crashed through the door, one hand gripping the scruff of the man's heavy robe. He looked left and right, eyes swivelling in desperation. Melita had found an unoccupied chapel, a tiny space by comparison to the rest of St Eurydice's grand halls of worship, but it would serve her needs very well. She leant against the back of a stone pew, arms folded in triumph.

'Hello, Nurem,' said Melita.

Recruiting Nurem Babić had been one of Melita's earliest and most valuable coups.

The Spoil's joy houses were the preferred amusement of a

particularly reckless class of gilded sensualist, who sought out unfettered narcotics, blood-soaked spectacles and the shiver of violence amid the squalor. The young Babić had been one such rake. And as with so many tourists to the Spoil, heedless of just how much danger they were in when they crossed the Rustwater, Babić's life had taken a dark turn.

Babić was a victim of ident-theft. He had been kidnapped, drugged, and over the course of several days stripped of every facet of his identity. His residency papers and ident-cards were stolen, and his mind addled by drugs until he yielded the location and pass-phrases to permit entry into his family's dynastic home. His blood had been drained and his bone marrow harvested for transplant into whomever had funded the theft; Melita had never found out who it was that now wore Babić's name. Even his face was no longer his own. The gangland chirurgeons had cut, broken and altered his features sufficiently to render him unrecognisable to even his closest associates.

Grievously hurt, bereft, and unable to return to the comparative safety of Korodilsk without risking arrest by the district's sanctioners as an undocumented itinerant, Babić was left adrift in the seething mass of unfortunates that washed up in the Spoil.

Through either luck or resilience, he had escaped or endured the many humiliations and injustices the city heaped on such people. By the time Melita had encountered him, Babić had already managed to worm his way into the Har Dhrol. His scholam education and experience of the city's labyrinthine bureaucracy were rare in the Spoil, and he had found a niche as a clave-captain's tabularius. With Melita's subtle assistance, he had risen through the Har Dhrol's ranks, to the point where he had become her first and best source of information on Sorokin's organisation.

Or, at least, he had been.

Edi carefully closed the chapel's door behind them and stood across it, blocking Babić's line of retreat. The clerk twisted to look at him, then spun back to Melita with a pleading, apologetic smile fixed in place. 'I'm sorry, okay?'

'Sorry, Nurem? What could you have to be sorry for?'

'It was chaos! Mercy almost shot me when she found the old man's body. And then there was the manhunt. I had no chance to get to my cell.'

Babić, alone of her expansive network of contacts, had the means to reach her directly. The noospheric relay for a specially configured data-slate had been a sizeable investment in his worth as a source. Of course, it was a risk for Babić, since its discovery would have immediate and terminal consequences.

Melita waved a hand, dismissing his excuses. 'I need to know where Bai is, Nurem.'

The pleading fell away, replaced by a fragile and false display of anger. 'How the hells would I know?'

Melita scowled. Given his fearful performance earlier in the day, she had half expected him to crumble at her first question. She had almost grabbed the man when he had appeared as her appointed guide through the church. With each step through St Eurydice's halls she had wanted to shake him, to demand the reason why he had so spectacularly left her to twist in the winds of a gathering storm.

Of course, she knew the answer. Part of it, at least.

With an unspoken command through her iris, she had Oriel draw closer. The leering silver skull bobbed towards the once gilded rake, now grovelling aide to gangers and criminals. Oriel's needler jutted prominently from beneath its teeth, and the clerk's gaze flicked rapidly between it and Melita.

'You didn't tell me Sorokin was dead. You didn't make our

rendezvous this morning.' She ticked off his lapses on her fingers. 'You've failed, Nurem, at every turn, to help me get a handle on this crisis. Why is that?' The accusation hissed through gritted teeth. 'Who are you working for?'

The clerk backed away, and bumped into Edi's silent bulk. The old sanctioner placed both gauntleted hands heavily on his shoulders.

'You, of course.' The fear in his eyes was all the confirmation Melita needed.

'I know about the other account, Nurem,' she said quietly. 'The flash-transmissions along our node that you think are hidden. The meetings you slip away from the seminary for.'

'You had me watched? By who? When?'

His panic was justified: if someone in the Har Dhrol knew that he passed their secrets to Melita, or to anyone else, his life was held in their hands. Melita didn't answer his question, but instead homed in on his fear.

'You know what the Har Dhrol do to traitors? I can step outside that door, and you'll find out.'

He blanched. The wine-dark bruise across his jaw stood out all the more against his pale skin. 'You wouldn't. I'm your best asset!'

'You were, Nurem. But if I can't trust you, you're nothing to me. With one word, I can have your guts spilled across that holy floor.'

Melita saw the fight go out of him. Babić wilted, shoulders curling out of Edi's grip. He stared at the grey flagstones of the chapel's floor.

'Mattix. His name's Mattix.'

There were no info-brokers operating in the tri-districts under that name; she would know.

'He's a probator. In Dragosyl.'

Melita looked to Edi, who met her gaze with a complicated

expression. She had never considered the possibility of the Lex's involvement in the crisis that had befallen the Har Dhrol. The district's castellans, like the Valtteri, were too invested in the stability Sorokin had brought to the Spoil. To say nothing of self-interested – since long before Sorokin's rise, the region's gangs had paid the vladars, enforcer superiors and other city authorities to ensure that the tri-districts did not try to involve themselves in the Spoil's affairs.

'For how long?'

'Five months. Maybe more. He found me, I swear.'

Five months. Melita suppressed her shock. She had only spotted the trail of betrayal a few weeks earlier.

'Does he know you work for me?'

Babić didn't look up from the floor.

'What have you told him?'

He shrugged, childlike. Edi gave him an ungentle prod in the back. Babić finally met her eye. 'Answers to his questions about the gangs, about Sorokin. He wanted to know about the Kadern and the other praetors.'

'What else?'

His resentful pout became more pronounced. 'Whatever I gave to you, I gave to him.'

A cold knife of suspicion cut its way through her thoughts. 'And what did you give me, Nurem? A pack of lies? Whatever this Mattix told you to sell me instead of the truth?'

'What?'

'You've been feeding me shit for months.'

'No!'

'Did you know he was going to kill Sorokin?'

'No! You have to believe I didn't know. I was in the room, for Throne's sake!' A low moan interrupted his protestations of innocence as he relived the killing once more. 'I just needed his help,' he said weakly.

Melita waited until his sobs sputtered to a halt. 'Why?' she asked finally.

'Because you said you'd get me out!' Babić's resentment spilled over. 'I've languished in this Throne-accursed sump for eight years, playing the role of servile menial to scum! I have to get out, and you were never going to help me.'

A cruel, barbed anger stirred in her, to match Babić's own choler. 'You think that this Mattix or anyone else is going to get you out of the Spoil? Give you new residency papers, maybe even get your face back? I keep you here because this is where I need you, and he will do the same. You only have value because of where I've placed you. You're a tool, Nurem. My tool.'

She fell silent, shocked by the suddenness of her temper, of how far she had gone so quickly. Each of her contacts needed their own form of handling, and with Babić she had always tried to make him feel valued, a partner in her work. She had always been conscious that it was his life at risk. Her promise to eventually help him escape the Spoil had been sincere, or so she had told herself. But now, having said it aloud, Melita knew it was the truth – she would never have made good on that vow. He had been too useful to let go.

Babić pulled away from Edi. He fled into a corner of the chapel, sullen and silent. Melita had no choice but to press on.

'What did you tell the probator about Bai, Nurem?'

'Fuck you!'

Oriel chose that moment to make its ocular sensor flare, casting the briefest flash of ruby-red light over Babić's face. He flinched away as though the burst had been a las-bolt, his angry defiance immediately undercut.

'Where would Mattix take Bai if he had them? If he couldn't get across the canal.' That was a big assumption. But if Bai had been abducted in Onden, far from the Spoil's border zones, Melita was hoping that this probator would not risk crossing the full breadth of the Spoil. If Mattix had got Bai to a bastion or one of the subdistrict blockhouses, they were lost to her.

Babić opened his mouth to utter another protestation, but she stopped him. 'I don't want to hear, "I don't know." *Think*, and then tell me.'

The clerk's expression grew sullen, but, at length, he spoke. 'He uses a safehouse out west, in the Slahin clave-hub. I've been there a few times for meetings. He pays the local crew for protection. They're not Har Dhrol.'

Melita's knowledge of Spoil geography momentarily failed her, but she thought she recognised the name. 'And?'

'And what? I can't tell you what I don't know.'

Melita subsided.

Babić looked at her from the corner of the chapel, wounded pride and betrayal plain to see. 'What about me?'

'What about you?' Melita snapped, and his ashamed, almost childish cringe deepened. She sighed. 'Go, for now. We'll talk more soon.'

She hadn't needed to threaten Babić, to force the details of his second master from him. Melita had almost certainly burned one of her best assets. She would never again be able to wholly trust what Babić gave her.

Edi stepped aside, and Babić fled.

Sanctioner Sergeant Edi Kamensk, Retired, cleared his throat. 'I know what you're thinking.'

Melita pushed her nagging shame to the back of her mind. 'That's because it makes perfect sense.'

She had already sent a noospheric query to her office's archive spools. She kept records on all of the significant figures inside each of the tri-district Bastions, and Probator Thaddeus Mattix was an influential figure within Dragosyl's echelons. His rank gave him a wide remit to pursue infractions of the Lex. Orchestrating a coup against the leadership of the Har Dhrol was, by any measure, overstepping that remit, but that did not make it an impossibility. Perhaps he was seeking fame and promotion, to be the man who single-handedly brought down a criminal federation.

Edi shook his head angrily. 'No Bastion castellan would ever sanction this. For one thing, they all make a lot of slate out of the Spoil treaty as it is.'

'Perhaps that's his motive. Maybe he's a lone crusader.' There were always rumours of puritan enforcers on a mission to purge their Bastions of the taint that riddled them, like worms coring rotten fruit. They were few, and their stories never ended well.

Edi was adamant. 'An enforcer wouldn't kill like that.'

The image of Sorokin's butchered throat rose unbidden, and she tried to push it aside. 'You believe that?'

He did. He said nothing in reply, but Melita could see it in the wounded expression that crossed Edi's weather-beaten features. Despite the institutional corruption, the excess, the abuse of power he had seen in a thirty-year career behind the seal, Edi still believed in the mission and the honour of the enforcers. That was either touchingly naive, or dangerously foolish.

Regardless, Babić had given her a lead to follow. Enforcer or not – good man or not – Melita wanted to meet this Mattix, who had turned her best asset, and may well have toppled an empire.

Melita strode across the seminary's courtyard, boots clicking on the warm flagstones. Vasimov was deep in low conversation with the captain of his mercenaries beside one of their flyers as she approached. He glanced over his shoulder, and made her wait until he was finished.

'What?' he said finally.

'I need some of your men.'

CHAPTER 13

They drove through the boundaries of the Slahin habclave with the running lights of their groundcar shrouded. The throaty grumble of the vehicle's engine felt appallingly loud on the empty approach roads, reverberating from the tar-black walls despite Edi's light touch on the accelerator plate.

She and Edi led the way in their borrowed Noxus, followed by four of Vasimov's mercenaries riding slim two-wheeled cruisers they had retrieved from the interiors of their flyers. Two more of the hired guns were an uncomfortable presence in the groundcar's rear, their matt-grey lasguns held awkwardly between their knees.

They had driven out to the furthest reaches of the Spoil, with the sickly smear of smog at their backs lit by the setting sun. They were close to the eastern fringes, where the great expanse of the Binastri Wastes slowly chewed its way between wind-blasted hab-towers and abandoned freight depots. The arid dust of the Wastes in the air was a novelty after the choking effluence of the Spoil's hills and valleys.

Melita was on edge. Her hands were restless. Her nails picked quietly at the cracked synthweave of her seat, or else drummed out fragments of words against the yellowed weave as though it were a runeboard. She had distracted herself during the gradual descent from the Spoil's interior by reviewing Oriel's scans of the seminary's interior on her iris, but that had only worked for so long, and there was nothing of particular interest in them.

The forced inactivity during the drive had given her time to think, and for her anxiety to grow. In Melita's judgement, saving the Har Dhrol was all but impossible.

So much of her assessment of the patchwork alliance of gangs had turned out to be flawed. She had believed that the clave-captains would see the value of the unity Sorokin had imposed. She had assumed that the scale of his achievement was self-evident, and that ambition would make the best of them aspire to replace him. She had expected, come his death, a brief and bloody civil war, but nothing that would upset the fundamental nature of the Har Dhrol itself.

She had thought that because Sorokin had built a throne, those that came after him would fight over it.

Evidently, she had been wrong. Toskanov and the other Kadern could send all the emissaries and missives they liked, but they could not contend with the flaw that lay at the heart of all that Sorokin had made.

His pact with the Valtteri had, undoubtedly, been the lynchpin of his longevity. It was not just the slate, but the legitimacy their accord had granted him in those first early years, which had been the groundwork upon which all his dealings with the tri-district merchant-combines had rested. But the cartel had overplayed their hand. They had too visibly made the Har Dhrol an extension of themselves, treating the gang like a vassal rather than an ally. A thrall, to be managed and placated, but ultimately expected to be subservient. They had not counted on the pride of the clave-captains, the pride of the Spoil itself. Even the destitute could afford to resent the rich. The powerless could see the powerful in their towers, even if they could never hope to tear them down.

Melita realised that she was gripping the seat's fraying fabric with white knuckles, and forced herself to unclench her hands.

Perhaps unmasking the architect of Sorokin's death would alter things. She might, with Bai's help, be able to give the captains a common enemy from within their ranks, as she had said. But Melita knew there was little hope of that. Vasimov's arrogant arrival at the seminary could not have been more calculated to remind every member of the Har Dhrol of their place within the Valtteri's world.

The Noxus' machine spirit pinged, loud in the relative silence, and Edi slowed the groundcar to a crawl.

They were on a wide road, bordered on each side by tall brick warehouses. They were close to the Slahin Junction, one of the first freight terminals the Binastri Arterial reached after crossing the saltpans. Everywhere, the skeletons of industry loomed against the darkening sky. Silos that once housed goods of every description sat empty beside raised arterial roadways. The rusting frames of gantry cranes stood like sentinels alongside row after row of roofless warehouses, depots and magazines. The groundcar's tyres thumped across narrow-gauge rail lines that criss-crossed the road, running between the yawning mouths of countless loading bays and sorting facilities. This had been where the produce of the east had reached the needs of the west, to be sorted, repacked, and dispatched to hungry mouths and machines throughout the Spoil and far beyond.

The groundcar's console pinged again, a sharper tone. They were only a few hundred yards from their target loc-ref.

'Pull over here,' she said.

Edi nodded, and swung the groundcar off the road and into the open maw of the nearest loading bay.

The building's interior was pitch-black, except for the bilious yellow glow of sunset striking the topmost window panes. The Valtteri mercenaries followed them inside, the engines of their cruisers popping as they cycled down. They dismounted immediately and fanned out, searching the gloom for any sign of occupation. One of them flicked on the stablight attached to the barrel of his lasgun, and a spear of white light struck a row of long workbenches. The metal was bright where gusts of salty dirt had worn away the corrosion.

'Shut that off,' hissed Edi as he climbed out of the Noxus, a moment before their commander gave the same order. The man clicked the lumen off, and continued his search.

The leader of the squad of mercenaries was named Andela Nedovic, and he had been one of the two sullen passengers in the Noxus with Melita and Edi. Nedovic was a grim sort. He wasn't much taller than Melita, but he wore his black flak armour easily across a broad frame. Melita knew that Reisiger, the syndicate to which Nedovic and Vasimov belonged, was populated almost exclusively with Defence Corps veterans, and Nedovic fitted that stereotype to perfection. He had steadfastly refused to meet Melita's eye since Vasimov had ordered him to accompany her on this mission, a petty form of condescension that deeply annoyed her.

Melita blinked, consulting her iris to get her bearings in the darkness. She oriented herself towards their objective, but paused at the groundcar's rear. She opened the storage unit, and Oriel detached itself from its cradle. The servo-skull took its place at her shoulder as she headed towards the abandoned warehouse's far end. Edi fell in behind her, followed at a begrudging distance by Nedovic.

They left the squad of mercenaries with their vehicles, and ascended a set of stairs loosely bolted to the north wall of the warehouse. They awkwardly clattered up to a gantry that ran around three walls of the building's interior, and made their way along until they reached an exterior door. The door yielded after Edi pressed his weight against its rusted surface.

Melita stepped out onto a rickety staircase that climbed the building's side, grimacing slightly. The night air had not yet lost the day's heat, and the warehouse interior had been pleasantly cool, if scented with the usual melange of Spoil odours. Edi and Nedovic stepped out behind her, crowding the small landing. They stood in silence for a moment as they looked towards their target.

'Ugly,' grunted Nedovic. It was the first word he had spoken to Melita since they had departed St Eurydice's. He had a gruff, clipped mode of speech, which Melita assumed the Defence Corps taught its cadets alongside marksmanship and formation marching.

The Slahin clave-hub was indeed a squat, brutal thing. It rose to no more than fifty yards at its tallest point, but sprawled away from them for at least a mile. It had been built to house workers for the Junction. Now, like the freight terminal, it was a ruin, although no more so than similar warrens across the Spoil. The clave-hub was not one building, but dozens, probably hundreds, all crushed together until any sense of architectural intent had been entirely lost. Reinforced rockcrete stairs ran in all directions, connecting the various levels that collided with one another without any suggestion of design or planning. The clave-hub reminded Melita of an insect's nest, the overlapping and interwoven layers of unpainted rockcrete forming tight pockets into which habs were set.

'Your magos is in there?' asked Nedovic.

Melita had no idea if Babić's new paymaster had been the one to snatch Russov Bai. Nor, if he had, whether he would have brought them here. She couldn't even rely on Babić's word that Mattix's safehouse was somewhere inside the vast jumble of domiciles.

'Yes,' she said.

The mercenary spat over the railing. 'That' – he jabbed a finger at the dark outline – 'will be an absolute bastard to fight through. Sentries, barred doors, false walls, and every one of the scum inside will be armed. The place could swallow a company.'

Melita took this in without comment, but she noticed that Edi silently nodded his agreement. A clave-hub of its size would be home to thousands, and given the day's violence there were bound to be lookouts on guard for any interlopers.

'They could hide in there for weeks, and we wouldn't know it,' Nedovic pressed.

All sense – and Nedovic's blunt assessment – told her to back off. But she needed Bai; without him, there was no chance at all of tracing the assassin that had started this unholy mess.

'We're not laying siege to the place, we're just looking for one person,' said Melita.

Nedovic finally deigned to look in her direction. 'Do you have a plan for how to accomplish that?'

She met his eye. 'I do.' She'd had time to think about that in the groundcar, at least.

With a flick of command through her iris, she had Oriel purr through the air between her and Nedovic, and was gratified when he lurched back in surprise. The silver skull reflected the last glimmers of the day's light as it came to rest, its anti-grav plates humming gently. Nedovic, embarrassed, gave it a sceptical glare, but said nothing.

Melita put her back against the warm brick, and sat down on the staircase's grating. She brought her iris interface into focus, letting the clave-hub's outline fade.

Feeling vaguely self-conscious with Nedovic and Edi standing above her, Melita mouthed the terse couplets of the Benediction of Connection. Melita had never trained with the Adeptus Mechanicus, nor did she subscribe to the Machine Cult's principles or its secretive, elitist practices, but she understood the respect it was necessary to show the machine spirits of all mechanisms. Particularly the ones that were embedded within her skull.

'How long is this going to take?' asked Nedovic.

Melita did not look up at him, as the loss of focus would disrupt her link with her servo-skull. 'Get comfortable,' she said quietly.

With her iris fully synchronised with Oriel's cogitators, she opened its ocular feed. Seeing herself through the servo-skull's eye was still unfamiliar, and Melita felt a lurch of vertigo, particularly when she tried to tilt Oriel's view down and instead watched herself bend at the waist. She tried to ignore how sallow her skin looked, how thin and drawn her face was, and turned Oriel towards the clave-hub.

She gave the servo-skull its instructions, and let its machine spirit guide itself. It swooped away, taking Melita with it, up into the night sky and towards the tops of the clave buildings.

After a few moments, she strangely found herself starting to relax. The night was no hindrance to Oriel's ocular sensor and its many vision modes, and it was easy to forget that she was back at the warehouse, at the end of the noospheric tether, and not soaring away into the air. She felt some of the tension in her gut uncoil as the servo-skull climbed higher.

It covered the distance quickly, and took up a position a hundred yards above the flat, boxy shapes of the tallest hab roofs. Oriel's augurs detected motion, which Melita's iris interpreted as wavering outlines at some of the clave-hub's outmost habs and atop the grey roof. Melita switched to a heat-sensitive filter, and the outlines became colourful shapes, glowing starkly against the still-warm rockcrete. There were four people-shapes on the southern edge of the clave-hub roof, pacing slowly in the manner of sentries, and a larger clump further in near one of the many access points into the clave-hub's depths. Melita tightened Oriel's focus, and the clump resolved itself into a pack of juves, with a large canid at the centre of their attention.

Oriel, a slave to her instructions, veered away from the clusters of heat and movement, and towards one of the gaps where two sections of the clave-hub did not entirely meet. Melita had a second to worry about how far the low warble of Oriel's suspensors would carry on the still air, and then the servo-skull dropped into the tangle of habs.

The skull drifted down into an open-air walkway lit by a single flickering lumen-strip several yards away. Melita was glad to be at such a remove from what Oriel was showing her. Huge patches of the unpainted rockcrete were black with mould, and what was not streaked with filth was daubed with graffiti. What wasn't stained by organic waste or cracked from years of neglected maintenance was strewn with refuse. Evidently the more civilising features of the Har Dhrol's dominion did not extend to the fringes of the Spoil.

Oriel began a swift, auto-generated search pattern through the walkways, alert for any sign of movement or the approach of the clave-hub's occupants. The servo-skull sent out a continuous, low-yield auspex pulse that quickly built up a detailed tri-D rendering of the building's layout, which Melita hoped would be useful should she be able to track down Bai.

Although she had dismissed Nedovic's concerns, Melita

had only a tenuous plan for how to locate them, if they were indeed somewhere inside the massive complex. As she had feared, the thermal sensor was useless. Although she knew from past instances when she had surveilled the former magos that their core body temperature was significantly lower than that of a baseline human, the reach of the sensor was too low to efficiently search the hundreds of habs for Bai's distinct biorhythm.

She flicked Oriel's vox-receiver through a range of frequencies, hunting for anything out of the ordinary. The clave-hub was alive with short-wave transmissions, and the fuzz of leaking microwave radiation from poorly shielded culina heating units. Rising higher, she caught snatches of conversation, the burr of coded transmissions, and even the official propaganda broadcasts from distant Dragosyl, although they were barely received and heavily washed by static.

After fifteen minutes of fruitless meandering, Melita's growing desperation overcame her caution. She triggered Oriel's auspex to run an active scan for dataveil receivers. It was a risk – anyone with a device or implant capable of connecting with the noospheric network would know that someone was seeking them – but one worth taking.

The pulse of electromagnetic radiation thrummed out, silently and invisibly scything through the clave-hub's rotting bones. Immediately, Oriel detected two receivers, very close together, high up on the western side. Intriguingly, both returned no ident-codes or diagnostic data. The information for each of them had been masked at the source, suggesting a sophisticated understanding of the workings of the dataveil.

Half a mile away, Melita smiled to herself.

She sent the skull buzzing along more cracked corridors and climbing through urine-stained stairwells, drawn on by the electronic scent of the receiver-units. At several points, Oriel lurched to a halt, sensing the presence of some of the clave-hub's denizens in its path. Rather than waiting for the servo-skull to navigate around them, Melita impatiently took control and started setting out its route, tracing her way through Oriel's expanding map of walkways, ventilation ducts, and maintenance shafts.

The skull was no more than fifty yards from the two receivers, racing through a narrow crawlspace between two rows of domiciles, when it came to a sudden stop.

Melita blinked. She sent a pulse of command to resume its course. Nothing happened.

Fingers dancing in mid-air, she triggered a series of diagnostics, asking Oriel's machine spirit to probe for any mechanical errors that would account for the loss of movement. Each one returned its results almost immediately, identifying no issue. She tried to direct Oriel forward manually, but still it did not obey.

'What's wrong?'

Edi's voice, shockingly loud and jarringly near, only added to her rising panic. She was halfway through a second series of diagnostics when flat, yellow runes flashed into existence across the very centre of Oriel's ocular feed.

> Mistress Voronova, this is Russov Bai. I have commandeered your familiar. Please remain calm.

Melita's fingers froze in mid-gesture.

'Bai?' she said aloud. Back at her body, she felt Edi and Nedovic startle above her.

> Please enable your augmentation's audex-capture function if you wish to converse vocally.

She briefly divided her attention between Oriel and her iris interface, and awoke the necessary component. 'Magos?' she said tentatively.

> It is I.

'Am I broadcasting through Oriel's vox-emitter?'

> No, I have disabled that functionality to preserve the clandestine nature of our connection.

Melita sighed in relief. Then the pendulum of her emotions swung back towards anger. 'How the hells did you get inside my servo-skull?'

> I would not insult your intelligence, nor the animus of your familiar, by suggesting that establishing this bond was a trivial task.

Melita did, in fact, feel distinctly insulted, and made a note to review Oriel's security algorithms as soon as possible.

'Where are you?'

> Transmitting location.

A string of alphanumerics followed, which her iris was able to capture and display in relation to her current position. Oriel had indeed been homing in on Bai's position inside the western sector of the clave-hub.

'I've got them,' she said, for the benefit of Edi and Nedovic. 'What's happening?'

> I am being interrogated regarding my knowledge of the Har Dhrol's operations.

'By whom?'

> They have not identified themselves.

Melita felt a sharp burst of alarm. 'Magos, could your interrogators be aware of our conversation?'

> No.

If it was possible for a single, written word to convey scorn, Bai's reply did so.

'Are you hurt?'

There was a slight delay in the exiled Mechanicus acolyte's reply. > I am uninjured.

'Magos?'

> I am uninjured.

Melita wanted to probe further, but pushed that concern to one side for the moment.

'Can you use this connection to show me who's with you?'

There was a very long pause before the reply ticked across her vision. > I lack the necessary augmentations to facilitate transmission of my visual cortex.

The shame radiating from Bai's words was palpable, and Melita felt a pang of sympathy. Her life was centred on her access to information; on her ability to cut, dredge and scour the infosphere for the data she sought. She could not imagine the gifts that Bai had once possessed as an initiated member of the Adeptus Mechanicus, nor the frustration they must live with now that they were confined to the mundane senses of their mortal, barely altered form.

'Fine. Can you describe the people interrogating you?'

> Certainly.

A ream of text scrolled down her sight, character by character flashing into existence at the speed of thought. Melita read each line aloud, and dimly heard Edi and Nedovic conversing as she spoke. When she exhausted the information Bai had offered, she relayed their questions to the exiled magos, who duly answered in precise, terse detail. A plan began to coalesce, and after several minutes of back and forth, she heard Nedovic disappear inside the warehouse to brief his men.

'Magos Bai, do you understand your role in this?'

> I comprehend.

'Good. In which case, I must ask you to relinquish control of my servo-skull.'

Bai once more took their time before replying.

> Very well.

There was no sign, no sudden lurch or aural cue to indicate that Bai had withdrawn their hold on Oriel's operations.

But when Melita tentatively reached out, she was pleased to find that it immediately responded.

'Are you still there?' she asked.

> I am.

'Good. We'll be with you shortly.'

Melita issued a recall command to Oriel, and when she was certain that it had climbed free of the clave-hub's interior she severed her connection with the servo-skull. She held out a hand and Edi pulled her to her feet, making her senses swim as she briefly looked at two moving spaces at once.

Edi was smiling at her, a tight grin of pride. She ignored him.

'Let's get to work.'

CHAPTER 14

Melita passed Edi a strip of det-cord, then wiped the sweat from her forehead. The narrow crawlspace was a humid, reeking cavity in the clave-hub's wall. Melita was hemmed in on all sides by leaking pipes and the night's furnace heat.

Her flak vest did nothing to help the situation, although Melita was willing to accept the discomfort. The heavy weave was a reassuring pressure on her chest, even as she sweated through the shirt beneath.

'I could have done this without you,' he said, his deep voice pitched at a whisper. He fixed the det-cord in place across two cables, each the thickness of her thumb and encased in thick insulating plastek. The cables ran from a roughly drilled hole in the floor, up the wall, and out through the crawl-space's ceiling via another bore-hole. Using Oriel's augur at its most sensitive, she had traced the main power lines from the clave-hub's generatoria, labouring away somewhere in the building's bowels, up to the block where Bai was being held.

They had had this argument back at the groundcar. 'You

could,' Melita said, just as quiet. 'But in here with you is less dangerous than out there with Throne knows who. Or what.' Spoil rumour was always alive with tales of mutants and other monsters that escaped their rightful fate by hiding in the most wretched corners of the region.

Edi accepted that, or at least chose not to argue any further. The explosive strip in place, he retrieved the detonator from a pouch of his own flak vest and pressed the tines of the vox-receiver into the malleable explosive.

'Set?'

Melita saw a rune in her iris flick into life as her augmetics sensed the detonator's connection, and nodded. The charge they had placed against the cables was tiny; hopefully it would be sufficient for their purposes without doing too much damage to the surrounding network of pipes and ducts. Melita had no wish to add to the miseries of the inhabitants of the Slahin clave by further degrading their building's deteriorating infrastructure.

She backed away, twisting her shoulders to turn around without scraping against the mildewed pipes. Edi, his considerably larger frame bulked out further by his own vest, had to awkwardly shuffle backwards.

Melita emerged from the grimy space carefully. Two of Nedovic's mercenaries – they had given their names as Skala and Petisov, but they were wearing matching matt-black armour and full-faced masks, so she had no idea which was which – were crouching back to back at the opening, each watching one direction along the corridor.

They had split off from the rest of Nedovic's mercenaries after a heart-stopping run across grey waste ground, breaking cover from the neighbouring warehouses while Oriel's auspex informed them that the rooftop sentries were out of sight. The others had begun the climb up a reeking stairwell towards

the section of habs where Bai waited, while she and Edi anx-
iously worked their way through the ground levels to set the
charges that would cut power to the domiciles.

Short stalactites crowded the roof immediately outside
the crawlspace, thick nodules of accumulated condensation
from the leaking ducts that evidently survived the brutal heat
of the dry season each year. The white nubs were vaguely
disturbing, and Melita turned her eyes down to the level's
cracked and stained floor as she waited for Edi to emerge.
He stiffly freed himself from the cavity's interior, then tapped
one of the mercenaries on the shoulder. That one nudged
the other, and the four of them rose in unison and set off
towards the nearest stairwell.

Fortunately, they had not encountered any of the
clave-hub's occupants on their trek through the rancid bowels
of the buildings. At first, this had surprised Melita, given the
presumably cramped and sweltering conditions that must
exist inside the habs. However, after five minutes had passed,
her surprise had faded.

The clave-hub was typical of so many cheap, hastily
constructed living quarters throughout the Spoil. It had
been built in segments of roughly poured rockcrete, forming oblongs into which domiciles had been crammed with
no regard for comfort or natural light. The meeting points
between segments were a reprieve, of sorts, from the dank,
claustrophobic stone. Short walkways spanned the gaps,
bridging open-air cavities that descended from the roofs down
to the bare dirt. Unfortunately, these spaces also seemed to
be refuse dumps for the clave-hub's occupants, and the foetor
of rotting waste pervaded the lowest levels enough to make
her gag.

If Melita had lived here, she wouldn't have spent much
time outside her hab either.

Melita and Edi followed one of the mercenaries, with the other bringing up the rear. Edi had his Sulymann Engager out and gripped in one hand. The enormous hand-cannon was as familiar to Melita as Edi himself, as was the grim expression the old sanctioner wore. As they stopped at the stairwell's opening, he gave her a questioning look. A glance to check that she was okay.

Melita ignored him. She had to put a stop to that. She would have to do something soon to reassert the proper dynamic, to rebuild some of the barriers between them. Edi was her bodyguard, not her father. As with so many things, it was probably her fault. Over the years, and particularly since her entrapment into the Valtteri, she had come to rely on Edi more than was wise, treating him like a confidant rather than a contractor. That was dangerous.

They entered the stairwell, and Melita recoiled. The sharp reek of urine and other bodily waste saturated the clave-hub, but it was particularly acute in the switchback stairs that climbed steeply between levels. She held a hand to her face as they ascended, still alert for any of the Slahin's occupiers.

After six gruelling levels, the leading mercenary jerked to a halt. One of Nedovic's other men was waiting for them at the top of the stairwell, barring their path. He nodded to either Skala or Petisov, and made space for them to get past.

The rest of the Reisiger men were clustered just outside the stairwell, kneeling with guns raised, faces hidden behind their masks. Lying face down on the scuffed rockcrete, unremarked by any of the mercenaries who knelt beside them, were two bodies.

Melita stopped, making Edi bump into her. It was a man and a woman, both wearing torn and faded ochre overalls. The man was obviously in his early twenties, his gaunt cheeks showing the ravages of rekanine addiction, or else just the waste of gradual starvation. The woman's face was obscured by the fall of her hair, thin and brown where it wasn't matted with dried blood. A small puddle of crimson had pooled between them.

Nedovic had been the one guarding the stairwell, and he came to Melita's elbow with the visor of his helmet raised. 'Set?'

'Are they dead?' she asked, although Oriel's augur gave her the obvious answer to her question.

Nedovic said nothing, evidently annoyed that she felt the need to call attention to the bodies lying at their feet.

She turned her head, looking into the mercenary's eyes from a bare hand's span. 'Was that necessary?'

He returned her stare, his disdain weighing against her disgust. 'Are we set?' he repeated.

Melita's glare was unwavering, but she finally nodded.

'Good.' He turned away, snapping his visor down. He issued an order, muffled by his mask. Four of the mercenaries immediately set off along the corridor. Two of those that remained grabbed the bodies, and started pulling them towards the stairwell.

Melita stood in their way, until Edi gently placed a hand on her shoulder.

'Come on.'

She allowed herself to be moved, then a flicker of anger made her shake Edi's hand away and stomp ahead of him.

The mercenaries left the bodies slumped beside one another on the piss-stained stairs, then hefted their guns and formed up beside Nedovic. She and Edi fell in with them, and set off without a backwards glance.

Melita felt foolish, angry, at herself and at Nedovic. She had been shocked by the bodies, and that surprise had sought expression as stubborn outrage. But when she probed that feeling she knew that it was shallow, arising more from the mercenary's callousness than her grief or regret. To him, they had simply been in the way, obstacles to their objective and so eliminated without hesitation.

The worst thing wasn't that Melita felt guilty about their deaths. Securing Bai was more important – to the Valtteri, to the Har Dhrol, to the Spoil – than the lives of the wretches who inhabited this stinking ruin. They were only being stealthy because it was the best way to achieve that goal. If they had not been concerned about discovery, no doubt Nedovic and his men would have cut a bloody trail through the clave-hub, and Melita was not sure she would have tried to stop them.

That was the worst thing.

Melita trailed behind the mercenaries, just a passenger on their mission. Nedovic and Edi had put this plan together, and Melita trusted Edi, at least, to do it right.

They had split Nedovic's men into two groups. The bulk of them had been sent towards the north side of the clave-hub, aiming for the target hab's entrance. Melita and Edi accompanied Nedovic and one other Reisiger man – Melita thought it was Petisov – around to the south. Each group was following the tri-D map Melita had exloaded into a pair of data-slates from Oriel's data-spools, and though they moved quickly she saw Nedovic check his wrist-chron more than once as they hurried through the filth-encrusted passages.

Melita's iris pinged as they came within fifty yards of Bai's dataveil signal. She was about to signal to Nedovic to slow down, but then a gale of laughter and puerile insults echoed along the corridor. Melita and the others flattened against the wall.

The passage ended a few yards ahead, opening onto one of the communal spaces where two blocks met. A thick, hip-height wall encircled the cavity between them. Melita edged Oriel forward, and looked through its eye at the source of the sounds.

Two juves were leaning far over the rail to throw chips of stone down at a lower level. Elaborate and graphic obscenities were being shouted back at them, along with a scattered and ineffective return fire. One of the juves responded by brandishing a makeshift shot-cannon, made from a metal pipe and a jury-rigged trigger. That decided the battle, as the juves' victims on the level below evidently retreated amid another chorus of jeers.

After a few seconds listening to loud, self-congratulatory boasts, Nedovic gave a muffled command. He and Petisov rounded the passage corner and raised their lasguns.

'Wait.' Melita pushed past Edi to kneel beside them.

'Why?' Nedovic's deep voice was barely audible through his visor.

'They're not with Bai's captors.'

'Who cares? We're already behind schedule.' There was no hatred in his voice, no disdain or bloodthirsty frenzy. He simply saw killing the two juves as the quickest way to remove an impediment from their path.

Melita reached out and placed a hand over the barrel of his lasgun. 'Give me ten seconds.'

She took his silence as assent, and removed her hand. Her eyes unfocused as she opened her iris. With a swiftness she would not have believed possible before her augmentation, she called up a preset algorithm within Oriel's code. It took another moment to modify it, and prepare the command for release.

'Ready?'

Nedovic's impassive mask stared back at her.

'Fine. Be ready.'

She blink-clicked a rune, and Oriel sped away.

The silver skull kept low, below the height of the walkway's parapet, its suspensors humming. It covered the distance in seconds, then jerked up on a pulse of antigravitic power. The juves had just enough time to notice the sudden motion, but not nearly enough to react.

Oriel's sinus cavities contained, among the compact cogitators and logic engines, a pair of small plastek magazines. One held slivers of an appallingly lethal poison, suspended in crystalline shards. The other carried a potent neurotoxin, twice as expensive as the deadly kind, that would render a stimmed-up pit fighter unconscious.

The needler that jutted from beneath Oriel's golden front teeth spat twice. The two juves clapped hands to their exposed throats, and then the paralytic took hold.

Nedovic and Petisov burst from cover the instant Oriel lurched up to take its shots. They raced the distance to the juves, their footfalls muffled by their polymerised boot-treads. They were not fast enough to reach the juves before they struck the rockcrete, but Nedovic managed to catch the improvised shot-cannon before it hit the deck.

Edi started running just a second after the mercenaries, one hand on Melita's collar to lift her to her feet. Melita's heart was thundering. She felt appallingly exposed. All it would take was for one person to leave their hab, one scream of surprise, for their rescue to become a bloodbath.

The Reisiger men had secured the juves' weapons and were hunched over them, lasguns trained on the hab doors they had just run past. Edi reached them, stifling a wheezed breath. Alarm added to Melita's fears, and she grabbed the old sanctioner's arm. He shook off her hand, even as his body juddered with another suppressed cough.

Melita dropped into a crouch next to one of the children,

whose eyes remained open in blank, unseeing stupor. She brought Oriel over to join them, and the familiar throb of its suspensors was oddly reassuring. She had the skull scan them; both were breathing, but their hearts were drumming in syncopated panic.

Seconds ticked by in painful double-beats of Melita's pulse. Nedovic and his companion watched left and right, lasguns tracking, ready to lance shots into anyone unfortunate enough to leave their homes.

'Skala, status.' Melita just caught Nedovic's whispered command into his vox. She didn't hear the answer, but evidently it was positive. The two mercenaries rose to their feet, moving with the strange jerking motion born of haste and stealth. They each pulled a det-charge from pouches on their flak armour, and pressed the clay-like blocks into the wall's rough surface a few yards further along the gangway.

'On our signal.' He nodded to Melita as he and Petisov retreated, and pulled his visor down.

Melita took a breath, and pulled her small snub-nosed laspistol from its holster. She held it in both hands, seized with sudden concern that she would drop it. She called up her iris, and remembered just in time to open her connection to Oriel. She sent three words, then tensed into an even tighter crouch.

> Magos, brace yourself.

> I am prepared.

Edi placed one heavy, gloved hand on her shoulder. Melita wanted to pull away, but instead she gave him a tight smile, and blink-clicked a rune.

Down in the bowels of the clave-hub, the det-cord flashed with magnesium brilliance, severing the power cables. The lumen strips above them immediately died, plunging the level into total darkness. A second later, Melita felt as much

as heard a dull thump travel through the habclave's structure. In the same moment, Nedovic triggered their breaching
charges.

Later, Melita would check her iris' internal chronometer
and discover that less than a minute passed between the first
explosion and the final burst of gunfire.

Her world disappeared. Two blasts, a fraction of a second
out of sync, deafened her with a double-punch that seemed
to come from everywhere at once. The hab wall was vapor-
ised into fragments of rockcrete and a dense plume of dust
that tasted hot and foul as she sucked in a breath. Chips of
pulverised stone stung her face, and Melita flinched away
from the assault on every one of her senses.

Nedovic charged into the horizontal column of debris,
with Petisov right behind him. The two shapes disappeared
instantly, but bright bursts of las-fire illuminated the billow-
ing dust from within.

Shouts emerged from the cracked-open hab, cries of pain
and roared expressions of alarm and rage. Edi kept a hand
pressed to Melita's shoulder, holding her painfully in a
crouch. She wanted to stand and join the fight. She wanted
to hide. More than anything, she wanted to be anywhere
but the cramped, reeking walkway on the festering fringe
of the Spoil.

More gunfire crashed out of the void in the wall, the deep
cough of solid shot and the snap of high-powered lasguns.
Several hard rounds twitched the dust as they flew through
the hole, to flatten themselves against the walkway's far side.
Then something like the sound of vellum ripping, and shouts
of alarm that were cut off by a pair of shots.

And then nothing.

The silence stretched on for several seconds, until finally
Nedovic spoke.

'Clear.'

Edi stood, releasing his hold on her shoulder. He looked around, alert for the occupants of neighbouring habs who might choose to join the fight. Evidently nothing alarmed him, as he pulled Melita to her feet and over to the ruined hab wall. He briefly glanced inside, then gestured for Melita to step through.

The hab was dark, and even more choked with rubble and dust than the walkway. Nedovic's mercenaries had their muzzle-lumens on, which cut stark beams that weaved through the darkness. She could just make out the shape of the room, a rectangular space larger than she would have expected for a Slahin domicile. Someone had evidently removed at least one interior wall in the hab's recent past. A corridor disappeared into the smoke-shrouded darkness, and beside it a waist-high divider split a culina quarter off from the room they had broken into. One wall had a gaping hole torn through the flakboard. Several bodies were slumped in front of the gap, too slow to evade the mercenaries' opening shots.

Sat in the very centre of the room was Russov Bai, restrained to a metal chair by manacles fixed to their wrists and ankles.

They were naked to the waist, revealing pale, almost ashen skin and a bare, androgynous chest. Deep, puckered scars threaded their way up, along and around their chest, and steel glinted from several sockets embedded in their flesh.

'My robe.' Their voice was high, strained, and unmistakably human.

Melita looked away, pulling at the cuffs holding them in the chair. 'Who has the key for these manacles?'

'My robe, please.'

'Magos, we need to free you first.'

They looked around, then indicated one of the bodies with a terse nod of their head.

'Edi,' Melita said, sympathy giving her voice almost as much pleading as Bai's.

Nedovic's mercenaries seemed to have checked all the dead gangers, and were taking up positions by the corridor and the gap in the hab wall. Edi walked over, and warily nudged the body with his foot.

Which suddenly spun, and from within a fold of its coat drew an enforcer-issue Tzarina laspistol that was thrust into Edi's face.

'My name is Probator-Senioris Mattix. Drop your weapons.'

CHAPTER 15

Two of Nedovic's men were standing by the ragged hole that had been punched through the hab's rear wall. Two more were near the entrance, dragging a third inside the domicile. The mercenaries' leader was in the centre of the room, caught midway through delivering orders into his helmet vox.

None of them had a weapon even slightly aimed towards the man who had Edi at the barrel of his gun.

'Put it down.'

Edi's Engager was in his hand, but Mattix had the drop on him. Not taking his eyes off the laspistol's barrel, Edi slowly crouched, placed the hand-cannon on the ground, and gingerly pushed it towards the corner of the room. The hiss of its stock along the worn carpet was strangely loud, the only sound in a room that had rung with gunfire mere moments before.

'The rest of you, guns on the deck.' His voice was deep, commanding, with a trace of the Dragosyl streets.

'Not a chance,' said Nedovic. He and his men had frozen,

not daring to move, but their weapons were clenched in readiness to avenge Edi's death. 'No hard feelings, Kamensk.'

'None taken.' Edi's voice was as tight and humourless as the mercenary's.

Melita had not moved, still bent at Bai's side with her hands around a manacle at their ankle. Oriel, however, was slowly rotating to align its needler for a killing shot.

'I can see the damned skull,' Mattix snarled. 'I promise you, I can end him before it ends me.'

Melita stilled Oriel's movement.

'All of you, guns on the deck and back off, or your man dies.'

He seemed to fidget as he spoke, his eyes darting left and right as though seeing things the rest of them could not. Melita recognised the pattern of syncopated blinks, and hurled a command to Oriel's cogitators. The skull emitted a soundless screech, flooding the vox and noospheric transmission frequencies with static.

Mattix frowned, which suggested that she had successfully choked off whatever message he had been sending. Melita noticed that Bai winced as though the jamming field were a physical pain.

They were at an impasse.

'What did you say your name was?' Her voice came out cracked and hoarse, and she coughed to clear her throat of dust.

'Mattix. Probator-senioris.'

'You have unusual friends, probator,' she began, gesturing at the bodies of the gangers beside him.

'Thaddeus Mattix,' said Edi, cutting across Melita's tentative opening. 'Bastion-D. You broke up the Pasc Scorpina flesh-smuggling ring eleven years ago.'

He looked up at Edi, evidently seeing him as more than a target for the first time. 'You weren't stationed in Dragosyl.'

'No, Bastion-K. But word got around.'

They stared at each other some more. The old sanctioner rubbed a gloved hand across his chin, the thick synthleather hissing against the day's stubble.

'You're in a poor tactical position, sir. Outnumbered. No backup, or so I'd guess. You can shoot me, but that's your only option from down there on the floor.'

Mattix didn't respond.

'Better to talk this one out.' Edi's voice was a gruff, no-nonsense growl, as though he were giving advice on which fighter to back at a gambling den.

'I'd be showing a lot of trust. Are your colleagues the sort to take this personally?' Mattix asked, gently nodding towards Nedovic. He too sounded remarkably relaxed, although he held his off-hand against his chest, and his knuckles were tight around his pistol's grip.

'I shouldn't think so.'

'What about you?'

Edi shrugged.

'And her?'

Edi glanced over at Melita. She had stood helplessly throughout their exchange, trapped by indecision.

'No,' he said carefully. 'She won't fire.'

Mattix waited for a long, tense moment. Then he deftly spun the laspistol around, and offered the grip up to Edi.

Nedovic's men immediately swung their guns towards him, but Edi stepped across their line of fire.

'Back off!' Edi barked, as sudden and loud as a blast from his hand-cannon. 'This is an officer of the Lex.'

Edi waited, glaring, until Nedovic and his men visibly untensed, then plucked the gun from Mattix's hand and stepped back.

'Take him,' Nedovic ordered, and two mercenaries charged

across the room to lift Mattix to his feet. He grunted as they grabbed him, and when they pulled his arms apart to search him for other weapons, one palm was slick with blood.

Melita stood to go over to Edi, but then remembered Bai. They had sat in silence throughout the tense exchange, but Melita could see their distress at being so restrained and on display.

'The control for these,' she said, gesturing at the cuffs about their wrists.

One of the mercenaries patted Mattix's coat, pulled out a slim stave, and tossed it to her. With the press of a button, the manacles fell free.

Bai leapt to their feet. 'My robe!'

One of Nedovic's men emerged from the hab's corridor holding a heavy stretch of scarlet cloth. Bai snatched the robe from his hands and swept into the darkness of the culina. Melita turned away, oddly embarrassed, and walked up to Edi.

'Are you all right?'

The old enforcer gave her a grim smile by way of reply, and crossed the room to retrieve his Engager.

'Can I see his gun?' she asked.

Edi looked at her with suspicion, but held out Mattix's pistol.

What Melita had taken for a Tzarina laspistol was, in fact, a remarkably expensive custom model. There was the tell-tale bulge of an overamped charge pack in the weapon's breech, and the line of its barrel tapered more delicately than anything that would typically be issued to heavy-handed enforcers.

Melita weighed the weapon in her hand, then turned to the man who had co-opted her most valued informant, and had held her bodyguard hostage.

Nedovic's men had sat Mattix on the same chair in which Bai had been secured, and bound his hands with his own manacles. He was doing his best to sit upright, but the wound in his side was clearly causing him pain. She walked over and knelt down, one hand resting on her knee, and casually pointed the probator's weapon up into his face.

'As it happens, I did take that personally.'

'Voronova!' Edi was at her shoulder, but didn't try to pull her away.

Mattix looked at her, the pain in his eyes vanishing behind a facade of cool detachment. But as the impassive stare fell into place, she saw a flash of recognition in his eyes at Edi's use of her name.

'Why are you out here, probator?' she asked.

The probator leaned back. 'I think we have a common acquaintance, Mistress Voronova.'

She didn't reply.

'No hard feelings, I hope.'

Her frown deepened.

Nedovic, helmet visor down, appeared at Melita's side. 'The Teridons should be overhead.'

In the sudden shock of Mattix's hostage-taking, she had forgotten the final element of their plan. Before they had begun their infiltration of the clave-hub, Nedovic had sent a coded vox-pulse back to Vasimov. His master had responded, and the aircars had been on their way to extract them before the first shot had been fired.

Melita stood, and handed Mattix's weapon back to Edi. 'Then we'll take him with us.'

'Voronova...' Edi started to object, incensed by the notion of kidnapping an officer of the Lex. Edi Kamensk would always be an enforcer.

'I want to know what he knows,' she snapped. 'Where's Bai?'

At the mention of their name, a red-robed figure stepped into the cone cast by Nedovic's stablight. Their face was hidden within the folds of the hood, their hands concealed within voluminous sleeves. No hint of the human within the cloak could be seen.

'I am… grateful for your assistance,' Bai announced to the room.

Melita was uncomfortable with sincerity at the best of times, but managed to force a smile. 'You are quite welcome, magos. Now, let's go.'

Two Reisiger men led the way, with a wounded colleague slung between two more and Nedovic sticking close to Bai. Melita and Edi brought up the rear, with the ex-sanctioner's thick gauntlet gripping their captive's collar in spite of Edi's respect for rank.

They trooped out through the hab's ruined entrance, past the bodies of the gangers Mattix had presumably hired. The corridor was pitch-black, except for the mercenaries' muzzle-lumens. Melita heard doors slam shut as they approached; fortunately no one decided to involve themselves in their extraction.

'You took quite a risk coming out here,' said Melita to Mattix, as they reached the closest stairwell and began to climb.

The probator made a kind of facial shrug. 'So did you.'

'I had my reasons.' She wanted to let the silence extend, to see if she could draw Mattix out. But they didn't have the time for that kind of patient interrogation. 'What were yours?'

'Hmm?' He made an irritating noise, feigning ignorance.

'Why do it? Grabbing Bai, coming out to the far fringe of the Spoil. Just being here breaks the accord.'

Sorokin, and the gang lords that had come before him, had

paid their bribes to the castellans and Administratum officials for a range of reasons, but one was paramount above
the rest. The accord was simple: no sanctioner or probator
crossed the Rustwater or the Line.

'I hardly think that matters now. The rules have changed.'

'How's that?'

Mattix glanced at her, evidently wondering whether Melita's pretence of ignorance was sincere. She couldn't tell which
he decided. 'Sorokin's dead. The Spoil reacts. And so does
the city.'

'So what does that make you?'

He said nothing. That appeared to be all the explanation
she would get.

The howl of the Teridon's engines as they circled was
audible all the way down the stairwell, and as they reached
the summit gusts of hot air billowed through the rockcrete,
deeply welcome after the odious dank inside.

Melita stumbled as she emerged onto the roof. Two of the
aircars had landed and more of Nedovic's men had fanned
out to secure the landing space. The juves and lookouts that
had been posted had fled into their warren, although they
doubtless were watching from hidden corners.

'The enginebikes, sir?' Nedovic and one of his men had
their heads bent together.

'Trigger the charges to detonate. I'm not having the scum
here stripping them for parts.'

That seemed needlessly spiteful to Melita, but she agreed
that it was probably for the best that they beat a hasty exit
from the Junction, rather than try to retrieve their vehicles.

'The groundcar?' Edi asked her.

She thought of Oriel's cradle in the Noxus' rear. 'We'll
have to leave it.'

He didn't argue. Whomever Edi had borrowed the vehicle

from would be annoyed, but that was far from her gravest concern.

Nedovic and his men trooped aboard, leaving Melita and Edi with their captive. Melita sent Oriel inside the nearest Teridon, fearing that the swirling jetwash would interfere with its suspensors.

Mattix looked at her expectantly.

She waited another moment, hoping that something in his calm composure might slip. Then she nudged Edi and gestured at the probator's hands. 'Cut him loose.'

There had never been any question of bringing him with them. The Valtteri's power was essentially limitless, but she doubted Vasimov or anyone else in the cartel would use an ounce of influence to spare her from the enforcers' wrath if she orchestrated a kidnapping of one of their officers, even one who engaged in what she was sure – almost sure – was an unsanctioned operation.

'You're going to leave me here?' he asked, after Edi deactivated the heavy manacles.

Melita looked at him quizzically. 'You want to ride with us?'

Mattix grinned. 'No. I just wanted to see if you'd offer.'

He started walking back towards the nearest stairwell.

'Probator!' Edi called out, making Mattix turn. The former sanctioner stepped across the still-warm hab roof, and handed over the probator's laspistol.

Mattix said something that Melita couldn't hear, and turned for the stairwell. Edi, entirely unashamed, started back towards the waiting aircar.

'If you're finished?' Nedovic called out.

Melita watched the enforcer disappear into the darkness. Then she and Edi clambered up the Teridon's ramp, and heard Nedovic shout for the pilot to lift off.

CHAPTER 16

Haska eased open the door to her hab, braced for a barrage of scolding or weeping. Instead, all she heard was the rhythmic wheeze of her mother's laboured breathing, carrying through the tiny domicile from her dorm-chamber.

The last of the day's light pierced the grime-caked windows, illuminating the hab just enough to allow Haska to creep in without fear of disturbing anything. She pushed the door closed, making every movement with exaggerated care. She had not wanted to return to her hab, fearing the sight of her mother's anger or disappointment, but she had had nowhere else to go.

Saitz's words had not left Haska's head on the journey back from the Redfort, not least because Aryat and Katryn had not stopped repeating them.

It had been clear that Aryat would follow his uncle – he planned to park the Grigga somewhere safe and then immediately head for the mustering. Haska had been happy to let him go. But Katryn wanted to go with him. She was the one who had argued the case, echoing Saitz's words in the square. Whether she truly believed his heady rhetoric or not, Katryn had chosen her man over Haska.

As hard as it had been for Haska to hear, she had at least suspected it was coming. Katryn had been pulling away for months. But she had not been prepared for Lira to join them.

They had stood beneath the arch of their hab-block's entrance, Aryat and Katryn watching from a distance.

'This isn't like sneaking into a dispensary and stealing a pack of lho-sticks, Lira. Saitz is going across the Line. No one's done that for years, and even when they did, hardly anyone came back.'

'They were raids, one or two at a time. You heard him. We'll be part of an army.'

'Why do this? You're going to get yourselves killed, and for what?'

'For pride,' said Katryn softly. Both of them turned to look at her. 'We're going to take back our pride.'

Haska felt the temptation that had clearly captured her friends, but the truth was too hard to admit. Haska was afraid.

She had always been afraid. Every day, every time Lira pulled her out of her hab. She acted tough, did what she needed to to front off with whoever threatened them. But it was always Lira that found the marks, that drove them to find their niche within the Pit Snakes. Haska made herself the leader of their little crew for the simple fact that it was the best way to protect them.

And now she was losing them because they had finally reached a step that they could take, and she could not.

She couldn't admit that, even to her closest friends. 'You trust Saitz?' she had said instead. 'He had Lopushani killed.' She had no evidence of that besides the look in Karlo Karamenko's eyes, but that was all the proof she needed.

'So? Think of what we'll find. This will change things, just like you always say you want. Don't you want to be a part of that?'

She did. There was something pernicious in Saitz's vision, a truth that had wormed its way under her skin. All her life she had felt a great, depthless anger at the world, and Saitz had offered her a target for all that rage. Like her friends, she felt the temptation to accept it. To follow, for the simple reason of having something *to* follow.

But then Haska's hand had brushed against the butt of the gun at her hip. The gun Saitz had let her keep, the gun that had killed someone. The pit inside her yawned open at the memory, swallowing the temptation and leaving only the fear.

Leaving Lira standing at the step of their hab-block had been the hardest thing she had ever done.

Haska's stomach growled, loud enough to almost match her mother's snores. She headed into the hab's culina, hunting for the carb-bars Verka had brought home that morning. She froze. A bundle of half-stitched novaplas was heaped on the communal space's table, a needle glinting in the dying light.

Of all things, it was the sorry bale of fabric that changed Haska's mind.

Like everyone at the manufactorum, Verka brought material home with her. She spent the few precious hours between sleep and her shift still working, her chapped and calloused hands still labouring to earn a few more slivers. Even on a day like this, when the Spoil had been turned upside down, Verka had not stopped. She could never stop. Every second of her existence was a struggle, a back-breaking grind to bring home slate, to have enough to feed herself and her ingrate of a daughter, so that she could go out the next day and repeat the cycle. Each day took a little more from her mother, and gave back nothing but pain and misery.

Haska could not do that. She would not. She couldn't say whether it was too much pride or too little, but she refused to submit to that hopeless, arduous existence.

What, then, was left for her? The street war? Haska had pretended to enjoy that all her life. Perhaps, occasionally, she had. The adrenal rush of violence frightened her to her core, but it also made her feel alive.

An image of the juve she had killed in the safehouse rose again. His limp body, the blood draining weakly onto the dirty rockcrete. That was the fate that awaited her, as sure a death as her mother's bloody flux. Haska had worked for so long to gain a foothold within the Har Dhrol. She had convinced herself that it was her means of escape, a way to live for herself and her friends, to dole out the beatings instead of taking them. But the day had made it clear that the struggle for dominance between the clave-captains would only grow, and their foot-soldiers would be the ones doing the dying.

She thought about Saitz's words to the crowd inside the Redfort, whipping them up into a frenzy of rage and bitterness. If she had to die, would it be better to die for a cause? To spit defiance at the people who engineered the city to their desires, who kept from her and her kin any semblance of hope for the future?

Haska had not liked Saitz. His self-serving nature had been obvious; he would spend the lives of those that rallied to his banner as freely as any other clave-captain or factorum baron. Was there anything better about dying for his cause, throwing herself onto the lasguns of the gilded, than in dying in some pointless back-alley brawl with a knife in her ribs or a bullet in her guts?

There was. Haska felt the answer boil up inside her, so fierce and frenzied that she almost shouted it into the hot, dry silence of her hab. Her hands trembled with the force of her resolve, with the sudden clarity that gripped her.

She would go on Saitz's crusade, wherever it led, and she would die. Because she chose to.

Part of her realised that it was macabre, perhaps even perverse, to find joy in setting out on a path that she knew would lead to her death. But the manner of their death was the only decision any Spoiler ever really got to make. If that was true, then she had made hers.

Haska turned to leave, and a wet, heaving breath groaned from her mother's dorm.

She knew Verka deserved more from her. She should wake her, explain where she was going and why. But Haska also knew she would not be able to face her mother's pleading. She had never been able to face her, to look Verka in the eye and put into words the shapeless anger and gaping fear Haska lived with, birthed from her mother's fading life and her own hopeless existence.

But she deserved something.

She silently rummaged through her mother's ragged bag of tailoring supplies until she found the pale white stick Verka used to mark lines, and a large scrap of dark fabric. She picked up the stick and spread the black novaplas out across the table-top. She awkwardly held it taut, pinching one edge against the table with her stomach and stretching it out with her forearm.

She spent a long time thinking of what to say. Finally, in big, clumsy letters, Haska wrote three words.

I am alive.

It was all the hope she could offer, the only gift she could give. Regardless of what would happen to Haska, her mother could cling to the belief that her daughter lived, that she was thriving somewhere out in the world, free of the miseries and indignities that Verka endured each day.

Haska paused. Hope wasn't the only gift she could leave the woman who had raised her.

She rifled through her pocket, and pulled out the slate Saitz had given her. It was more than Haska had ever held; more than Verka would earn in a year of labour in Ludoric Erastin's poisonous garment manufactorum.

Haska piled the chips beside her message, gently placed the chalk on top, and then crept out of her hab for the last time.

Haska found Lira at the bottom of the hab-block's stairwell. She was looking out at the darkening street, one hand toying with the handle of her knife. When she heard Haska on the stairs she turned, the blade out. Haska held up her open hands. Lira relaxed, but then raised her chin defiantly.

'I'm going.' Her green eyes gleamed in the light of the street-lumen.

'So am I.'

Lira blinked.

'You were right,' Haska said. It was an easy thing to admit. In fact, everything seemed easier. Each step Haska had taken down the stairwell had felt lighter than the last, as though she had shed some enormous weight from her shoulders. She felt... not happy, but something like it. She had a course, with a definite, inescapable end. There was a kind of comfort in that.

'I was?' Lira asked.

It occurred to Haska that her friend could have left at any time, but instead she had been standing in the stairwell until Haska joined her.

She smiled, and reached out to squeeze Lira's hand. 'Come on.'

The two of them walked through the empty streets. If the day's violence had touched Haska's habclave, there was little sign of it. Night had fallen, and the occasional street-lumen only sharpened the darkness of alley mouths and tenement doorways. Above them, occasionally visible through the smog-clouds, glittering trails showed the paths of void trawlers and orbital tenders. They were as far out of Haska's reach as ever, but now, with her decision made, the sight did not have the same bitterness.

They heard the muster before they saw it. Three big cargo-8s were drawn up in a rough line at a crossroads, blocking the street heading north. At least two hundred people were milling about behind the heavy-goods haulers, each of them shouting at somebody else. Every few moments, a figure broke away from the press of bodies, and was directed into one of the interiors of the heavy vehicles, which were already loaded with people. They were helped aboard by big, grim men and women, who wore dark fatigues that Haska recognised from Saitz's companions at the Redfort. In the yellow glare of the street-lumens, they looked like some kind of uniform. Each of them had a lasgun or a shot-cannon slung over their shoulder, and were looking at the crowd with ill-disguised contempt. Haska spotted one or two of the soldiers – that was the only word that seemed to fit – from Saitz's rally.

Haska and Lira pushed their way through the crowd, which began to part when it became clear that they were heading for the haulers. A few people gave Haska wary looks of pity, others of envy. No one tried to stop them, but Haska caught snatches of angry conversations as parents pleaded with children, and husbands begged with wives. Haska hunched her shoulders and kept moving.

She shoved her way between two tall, elderly men arguing with one another, and she suddenly found herself at the front of the crowd. Lira's breath on her neck reassured her that she was close behind.

'You coming?' A broad woman with jagged lightning-bolt tattoos decorating her shaven head approached them, evidently sizing them up. Haska squared herself up, and turned her body to show the pistol at her hip. The woman seemed unimpressed, but did not turn them away. She pointed at the hauler at the far end of the line. 'Mount up, quickly. We'll be heading out soon.'

Haska followed her gesture, and spotted Aryat and Katryn in the open rear of the hauler in the middle, a Shiiv Raxis that had had its rear cut down. A nearby street-lumen cast harsh shadows on their faces, but Haska could see that they were clasping each other's hands. Katryn looked up, her face a picture of uncertainty, and she spotted Haska and Lira in the crowd. Instantly her expression brightened. She nudged Aryat, whose own smile seemed sincere and unforced.

'We want to go on that one,' Haska said.

The woman briefly glanced at the Raxis. 'It's full.' She gave Haska's shoulder a shove towards the vehicle she'd indicated.

'We want to go on that one,' Haska repeated. The woman wasn't much taller than her, but she was much heavier, with a strength to her shoulders and chest Haska couldn't hope to match. Haska stared her down regardless.

'Fine.' The woman shrugged. 'Get on, now.' She stepped aside to let Haska and Lira run past.

Aryat and Katryn shuffled awkwardly into the hauler, raising angry curses from others who were further in. Katryn reached down and pulled Haska up, and then the pair of them helped Lira climb inside.

They had made it just in time. A minute after they had settled onto the hard metal floor, the hauler's engine coughed into life, and the deck juddered beneath Haska's feet. She sank back on her haunches, and wormed her way into a small space to lean against the hauler's metal siding. The woman

who had ushered them on board appeared beside her, and
swung the loading gate up into place. The crunch and clatter
made a few of the passengers start in alarm, prompting others
to laugh at their nerves.

Haska did not join in. She was looking down the length
of the street, over the heads of the shouting crowd. Behind
the righteous anger that had propelled her out of her hab,
and the nervous, infectious excitement of the hauler's passengers, she could feel her old fears, the urge to second-guess
each choice.

She could still get off. She could climb over the flatbed's
rear, drop to the ground, and be back amongst the crowd
in moments. She'd watch her friends drive away to their
deaths, then slink back to her mother's hab. Go down with
her to Erastin's when the morning rose, and start the day
that wouldn't end until she coughed her last breath.

The cargo-8's engine grunted once, twice. Whatever waited
for her in the darkness, whatever form her death might take,
it was better than that.

The Raxis shook as it set off.

INTERLUDE

Andrusha Kazansi entered the study, silent on slippers made of off-world velvet. The lights were low, but he had become used to that over the past few years. The meagre illumination provided by a small table-lumen and the scattered brilliance of the city lights beyond the room's window were sufficient to let him find his way.

He walked towards the lumen, and the grandly arched chair beside it. It faced the window, the tall real-leather back to the door. This place was for the contemplation of the world beyond, not the tawdry business of maintaining a gilded house.

His mistress sat in the chair, relaxed but upright, like a felid awaiting its prey. Her month-long absence from the dynastic home had been noted, but not commented on. Whispers and gossip among the household staff seemed to find their way to the mistress' ears, and the past sanction of guilty parties had been exemplary.

Kazansi halted a few paces from the side table. The scratch

of a quill sliding across vellum was the only sound in the chamber, the motion and activities of the household purposefully shut out of this place. Kazansi did not glance down, keeping his gaze firmly on the grey expanse of the city beyond the tall window. He knew that the papers were within his sight if he chose to look. They had been placed there either as a temptation or a test, but long years of service had instilled an iron sense of discipline.

After some time, the quill ceased its movement, and Kazansi steeled himself to break the silence.

'Mistress, this was delivered by courier.' He placed a tightly folded sheet of vellum on the side table, to avoid an accidental brush of skin against skin.

He returned his stare to the middle distance. The folded parchment matched the paper on which his mistress had been writing: insubstantial, liable to burn quickly, or dissolve effortlessly in water.

'Do they wait for a reply?'

'Yes, mistress.' The courier was typical of the breed that came more and more frequently to the tower's entrances: plainly dressed, inscrutable, and possessed of a disconcerting emptiness behind the eyes. He waited at the tower's mid-level carport beside a sleek, two-person aircar that had touched down with barely a whisper of anti-grav thrust.

There was a rustling of papers as they were collected, ordered, and slipped inside a plastek sleeve. Kazansi braced himself.

'Tell them to see that these are enacted.'

The voice, impossibly deep, bade him look down to acknowledge the order. The dark eyes were waiting for him, black like pools of ink. They looked up at his, and for an instant the world spun away.

He mastered himself with an effort, and took the sleeve

from her grasp. 'At once, mistress.' He bowed, and turned on his heel. Kazansi felt the eyes chase him across the chamber.

The servant did not know what the packages contained. He didn't need to know. Andrusha Kazansi had served the household loyally and discreetly for his entire life, the same as his parents and his grandparents. He was the scion of one bloodline, bonded to another in perpetuity as imperious master and favoured slave.

He was tempted, though, as shameful as he had been raised to find such a thought. As he shuffled soundlessly across the thick rug and then cold stone, he felt the slim weight in his hands and wondered what devilry they contained. He mistrusted this woman, his sworn mistress, who seemed to wear shadow like a veil, and hoarded secrets like slate.

The house had always been known for its eccentricities, its lavish and exclusive gatherings that tested the fringes of sanctioned thought and explored the taboos of Imperial society. But since the mistress' return four years earlier, unlooked for and, in truth, undesired by most members of the household, the temper of the dynastic home had changed.

The parties had become more sombre, more concerned with subtlety than scandal. The visitors had become more frequent, and more stealthy, stepping from aircars in the dead of night for whispered conference behind locked doors. Kazansi had, to his consternation, lost track of whether all who entered the tower's vaulted chambers left once morning came. More than once in recent months he had noticed footsteps knock within rooms he knew to be disused, and heard quiet voices that ceased their conversation as he passed.

Kazansi became aware that he had paused at the door, distracted by his fearful and disloyal thoughts. As tempted as he was, he would not open the sheaf of orders. He was blood-bound to his strange mistress' will, and he would see it done.

PART 3

CHAPTER 17

Melita was woken by heavy blows on the cell door, rousing her from dreams of las-light reflecting in the dead eyes of Slahin clave-hub juves.

'What?' Her voice cracked, and her mouth tasted foul.

'They're arriving,' Edi said from outside.

She tried to lever herself up from the bed's hard surface, but a savage pain daggered through her head, and she slumped back down.

'Melita?'

'I heard you.' She lay in silence for several seconds, trying to bring her thoughts together. Her breath came in slow, laborious heaves, as though she were finishing a foot-race rather than rising from sleep.

'Bai?' She had left the magos running searches through the Har Dhrol banking system to trace the pay-off slate.

'Still at work, so I gather.'

She checked her iris' internal chron, and found that it was approaching midnight. After the flight back to St Eurydice's in the Valtteri aircar, and the brief explanation she had given Vasimov, she had sloped away to a room Edi had found for her high up in the church's dorm-block. She had no idea which ganger Edi had turned out to find her the space, but in the dead of night, she hadn't cared. After barely three hours' sleep, she still didn't.

Melita swung her legs off the cot onto the cell's freezing stone. She yelped, and tucked her feet back up. The sudden shock only compounded her headache, setting off a vicious shiver that travelled through her body. She slumped back against the cell's stone wall. It was just as cold as the floor, but somehow less punishing.

The sleeper had been a mistake. The injector sat on the scarred surface of a nightstand, the sleek chromed cylinder mocking her for her weakness.

The second she'd laid her head against the cot, the room had begun to spin. The Slahin juves, Mattix's knowing smile, the crash of Edi's hand-cannon and the snap of Nedovic's lasgun. It had all flooded in, her keen memory and overtaxed nerves merciless in their recall of the desperate fight to save Bai. There had been no conscious choice, no private struggle within her. She'd simply reached for the injector and pressed it to her arm, welcoming the happy oblivion that had swallowed her almost immediately.

Fortunately, she knew herself well enough to plan for this. The sleeper dose she had brought with her into the Spoil had been a small one, just enough to knock her out when she needed it. There was a hit of topaz in her jacket to banish the hangover and get her moving again.

With her eyes closed to try to clear the sharp spike drilling through the centre of her skull, she reached for her jacket. Her questing hand found only the bunched blanket that she'd kicked off in the night.

She forced her eyes open. The synthleather, which she had hung from the cot's end, was not there.

'Edi?'

The door swung open.

'Where's my jacket?'

He didn't say a word, but tossed the synthleather onto the cot beside her and closed the door.

She waited until the heavy metal slammed shut, and patted the outside pockets. Then she checked inside. She shook it, hard, and finally she threw it down on the cot in frustration.

'Fuck.' She looked up at the closed door. 'Fuck.'

Melita stepped out of her borrowed cell, jacket on and Oriel silently hovering at her shoulder. She walked past Edi, who fell into step behind her.

She was furious, and the brutal pain that was digging its way into her head was not helping.

'Have you slept?' she asked, but there was no concern in her voice.

'I'm fine.' His reply was equally terse.

Despite the late hour, there seemed to be more Har Dhrol in the church's corridors than the previous day. Some were clad in the thick robes that Babić had worn, while most wore the heavy synthleathers and battered sidearms of the typical street ganger. They moved with more purpose, too. Evidently the coming gathering was being taken seriously.

'How are you feeling?' Edi asked as they turned a corner.

She rounded on him. 'What the hells are you doing going through my jacket? You had no right!'

'No right? You're getting high in the middle of a goddamn warzone!' He fished around in a pocket and pulled out the dose of topaz. 'You can't be trusted with this shit.'

A small, craven part of Melita made her want to snatch it

from him, but she crushed that impulse without hesitation. 'It's an aid, to get me going. Do you know what it's like to have this thing buzzing in your head?' She gestured at the scar that cut its way along the side of her skull. The scar that throbbed in time with each rapid beat of her heart.

Edi was unimpressed. 'I've heard every explanation you can think of, every justification under His smog-choked sky. You know how many rek-heads and blissed-out junkies I've seen scraping through the gutter for slivers, all the while saying that they don't have a problem?'

'I'm not a damned addict, Edi.'

'No?'

A Har Dhrol flunky appeared from the corner ahead of them, and they both fell into angry silence. Melita waited until he passed. 'Let's not do this now,' she hissed.

'No, not now,' Edi agreed. 'But soon.'

Shame and anger competed within her, each impulse desperate for her to have the last word. But nothing would come. 'You had no right,' she finally said.

Edi was evidently far from finished, but he followed Melita in silence along the tall stone corridor.

Like many Imperial churches, St Eurydice's was dominated by its vast, open nave, onto which joined several multilevelled transepts. In the seminary's former life, these had been the haunts of Adeptus Ministorum priests and curates, tending to the training of their acolytes and young charges. To be called, or to be sent, to the Church of His Holy Ecclesiarchy was considered a prestigious honour for those fortunate few who achieved a modicum of education, and a convenient way for the gilded houses to rid themselves of unclaimable bastards and indiscreet siblings. As such, seminary chapels were a common feature in many districts. Missionaries were, Melita had once learned, one of Varangantua's more notable exports. Several prominent subsector deacons and Frateris Militia crusaders had begun their paths to greatness, or infamy, in halls such as these.

The once hallowed passages of St Eurydice's now played host to a different class of criminal, and Melita strode through them with little reverence. Quick familiarity and her biting headache had banished any sense of awe she might first have felt upon entering the God-Emperor's church.

She made her way towards the north-eastern transept, where she had left Bai a few hours earlier. Melita heard the huff and sigh of mechanisms from the far end of the corridor that led to Bai's workshop. Though the dark stone and heavy carpets were no different here than in other parts of the church, the air was warmer, and scented with the tang of machine lubricant and ionised air. Like any adept of the Machine Cult, Bai could not occupy a space for any length of time without imprinting their character upon it.

As Melita raised her hand to the summon-chime, the heavy door swung back, pulled open by a grey-skinned servitor that leered from the doorway.

Pallid flesh clung to its face, emaciated to the point of horror. Limp strands of hair trailed back from its head, mingling with thin cables that ran from connection ports across the lumpy, misshapen skull. The eyes were real, grey and bloodshot orbs in lidless sockets. There were no teeth in a mouth that was fixed in a partially open rictus, as though they had been mid-speech, or mid-scream, at their moment of lobotomy. A grey robe, distressingly similar to those worn by the church's sentient servants, mercifully hid the rest of its body.

'Magos Bai?' Melita called into the workshop. She had managed not to lurch back at the servitor's horrifying appearance, but the fright had set her pulse pounding, and her headache throbbed in time.

'Enter, please.' The servitor spoke for Bai, the grey lips moving despite the words crackling from a vox-emitter embedded in its throat. Melita suppressed a shudder, and entered. Edi followed her inside, also keeping a judicious distance from the mind-wiped servant.

The open mouth worked again. 'Does this unit's appearance disturb you?'

While Melita was perfectly at home around mechanisms, and with the interplay of machine spirits, she had never shaken her dread of servitors. Oriel was different – the servo-skull had been her companion for as much of her life as she could remember – but the vacant eyes of the lobotomised slaves made her skin crawl, particularly when they spoke in a macabre puppetry of human speech.

'Yes,' she admitted.

'A common response,' said Bai, this time from their own lips.

The magos appeared from between two rows of tall shelves lined with components, carrying what looked to Melita to be the partial workings of a metriculating engine. They were cloaked in the familiar crimson of their former order, and seemed to be unaffected by the day's ordeal.

'I must confess, the unit is intended to evoke that particular reaction. As a doorkeeper, it excels at ensuring my time remains uninterrupted. However, as a gesture of gratitude for your aid, I will dismiss it.' The servitor turned from its post at the door, and lumbered off towards the rear of the workshop.

Melita appreciated Bai's attempts to make her feel welcome, and she was happy to see the back of the servitor, but the headache knifing into her brain was cutting through what little patience she usually had.

'The clave-captains are arriving.'

'Indeed.' They waved at a bank of imagifiers as they walked towards a workstation, which flickered into life. The feeds were from picters mounted around the church's grounds, and as Melita watched, a pair of groundcars rumbled beneath the gatehouse entrance. She didn't see Vasimov's aircars on the screens and assumed that he had prudently, if somewhat surprisingly, moved them to a less conspicuous location.

'I need to know who the slate belongs to,' she said. She had left the stack of slate she had retrieved from Horvaç's pay-off in Bai's possession. They had, as she'd expected, not allowed her to access their safeguarded databases herself.

Bai placed the cogitator on a worktop, and dipped a thin-fingered hand into the depths of their robe to withdraw the slate. 'I cannot say.' They held out the jumble of chips, and Melita took them, automatically responding to the gesture. 'The pieces you provided have never circulated through any of the syndicate's stores.'

Melita was bitterly disappointed. She had pinned all her hopes of tracking down the architect of Sorokin's death on this lead.

'However, I consider your line of enquiry valid.'

Melita looked up.

'As such, I have extended the investigation beyond those specific pieces.'

She followed Bai's gesture. A second servitor was working with inexhaustible patience in front of a cogitator. It was passing one chip after another across a palm-sized slate-scanner, and with each slate a new line of alphanumeric runes appeared in warm green tones on the connected imagifier. The rumpled sack that Melita had inspected in the church's dungeons lay on the workbench, and every slate it had contained was set out in neat stacks on either side of the cogitator. The stack to the right of the machine was smaller than the one on the left, but was growing steadily as the servitor carried out its rote task.

Fresh hoped dawned. 'And?'

Bai had begun to assemble, or possibly disassemble, the device in their hands, and did not look up from their work. 'Given the magnitude of the accusation you will level on the strength of this evidence, it would be irresponsible to draw precipitate inferences from an incomplete dataset.'

Melita's grip on her patience slipped. 'Magos, there were hundreds of slates in that bag.'

'Three hundred and eighty-six,' Bai said compulsively. 'With a combined value of forty thousand, six hundred and–'

'We can't wait until you have catalogued every single one,' she interrupted. 'Are any of the chips you've reviewed so far in the system?'

'Eighty-two per cent have been registered with one or more accounts of syndicate members.'

'And?' she said again.

'I do not yet have sufficient data to reach a conclusion that would be mathematically robust.'

Melita's frustration must have been clear, even to a devotee of the Machine Cult who was elbow-deep within the mechanisms of whatever they were working on.

'It is not my intention to obstruct your investigation.'

'I know, but the captains are gathering. And one of them had Sorokin killed.' She had no way to be sure of that, but surprisingly Bai chose not to point that out. Melita thought for a moment. 'Is it possible for you to transfer that data to my iris?'

There was the merest hesitation as Bai computed an answer. 'It is.'

'Please do so.'

They finally looked up from their task, evidently discomfited. She forestalled their next objection.

'I don't need complete access to the banking database. Just which account each slate was last associated with.'

Bai considered this, then bowed their head in consent. 'Very well. I will establish a data-stream via your familiar.'

Finally. 'Thank you, magos.' She turned to leave.

'Mistress Voronova?'

'Yes?'

'I am grateful for your intervention earlier. And for your continued efforts to identify Andreti's killer.'

There was such unusual strength of feeling in the magos' voice that Melita was compelled to turn back. They used no title for Sorokin, no awkward formality, and she said as much.

'That is a symptom of significant familiarity,' they said.

By dint of long experience, Melita could tell when someone had something they needed to say, but would have to be coaxed towards it. Bai, she thought, wanted to talk.

'Why were you exiled from the Machine Cult, magos?'

The ghost of a smile surfaced in the recess of Bai's hood. 'You must resign yourself to some things remaining a mystery, Mistress Voronova.'

That was too tempting, even with her head pounding and the fate of the Spoil about to be set.

'There are many rumours regarding how you came to join the Har Dhrol.'

'Indeed.' They still did not look up from the innards of the metriculating engine.

'When did you first meet Sorokin, Magos Bai?'

That, finally, seemed to be enough to break the reserve that Bai had evidently been desperate to shed.

'Many years ago, Mistress Voronova.'

They withdrew their hands from the machine's workings and turned to face her, though she could see few details of their features within the shadow of their robe.

'My parents were minor warlords within the Redfort. The

Turnward Quarter. I was fortunate, if such things can be measured objectively, in the chance of my birth. Their relative affluence ensured that I lived through infancy, and that I was privileged to receive what approximated an education in the essential competencies.

'They were deposed while I was still a juvenile. They were betrayed, in fact, though ineptly, for they and I were permitted to live. We were driven from the Redfort, and suffered many ordeals before evading our pursuers by crossing the Hanub Waterway.'

Melita realised that they had referred to the Rustwater Canal by its original name, a piece of lore that had always escaped her enquiry.

'My parents did not endure our exile with particular grace. Narcotics abuse claimed them both a year after our escape into Korodilsk.'

Melita felt Edi's stare on the back of her head.

'After my parents expired, I determined that I would not. I possessed a fascination with the machine and the Motive Force even as an infant, and with youth's monomania I resolved that I would survive to wear the crimson, in defiance of my low birth and indigent state.'

Bai noticeably drew themself up as they spoke, their thin form rising to its fullest. Whether this was a conscious act on their part, Melita would never know.

'I journeyed to Nearsteel, as challenging a feat then as it is now, and presented myself for enlightenment at the Naesmeth Enclave.' They smiled, a flash of iron teeth, so wry and warm that Melita found herself smiling in reply. 'I was, as you would expect, immediately turned away.

'I would not be deterred. Employing low cunning and base ingenuity, I brought myself to the attention of a sufficiently senior adept of the enclave. I believe I impressed them with my tenacity, and, with their sponsorship, I was admitted to the lowest mysteries of the order.'

Melita burned to know more. The Adeptus Mechanicus was the most secretive of all the innumerable ordos, departments and sanctioned organisations on the planet, and the most proof against her powers of insight. Bai evidently saw her desire, but was not moved.

'There is much that I cannot and will not speak of. Some oaths remain inviolate, even when one party breaks the faith that binds them. But suffice to say that I embarked on a long, if not storied, existence among and along the manifold paths of the most holy Cult Mechanicus.

'I did not rise to any rank of particular note. Despite my fervour and, dare I say, my ability, I was never wholly accepted into the enclave's social orders. I was resistant to the Cult's dogma and rigid hierarchy. Too frequently did I challenge my peers, my seniors. This was, I think, a consequence of my origins. I think regularly of those times, and wonder what might have unfolded had I excised, or better restrained, my more antagonistic neural patterns.'

Bai stopped, the silence extending for so long that Melita feared they had lost themselves in evidently oft-revisited memories. But then they looked up, resentment or defiance burning in their gaze.

'I was exiled from my order, as is now common lore. I am acquainted with your familial circumstances, Mistress Voronova, and so you may understand a fraction of the distress of that moment. To be severed so completely from all that you had known, from your plans and aspirations for an expected future. Coupled, of course, with the trauma of augmetic confiscation, and the attendant disfunction and dysmorphia that follows. The ceremony is not swift, nor painless. Exemplars... hold great value within the Cult.'

Such potent bitterness could not be concealed by any amount of pretended detachment.

'In my desolation, I clung to those aspects of my identity that had been left to me. I excised emotion from my speech and manner, as far as unfettered organic functions would allow. I walked the streets in a torn bedsheet dyed with my own blood.' They fingered the rich, scarlet fabric that swaddled them, indistinguishable from the few examples of Mechanicus cloth that Melita had seen.

'But, as you might expect, these pale echoes of habit and manner could not sustain me, and swiftly the weakness that plagued my progenitors consumed me as well. Solace in narcotics is a vice that stalks my genomics. Sharpened, if anything, by the lingering traces of my stolen existence, and their vulnerability to such stimulants.'

The surprise must have shown on her face.

'Indeed, Mistress Voronova. The sin of biological degradation and data contamination is not unique to the unenlightened. You would be intrigued and appalled by the depths of degeneracy to which the devotees of the Omnissiah can lower themselves.'

They looked away, wearing an expression that was uncomfortably familiar to Melita.

'I am not wholly aware of how I came to return to the Spoil. But by some strange pedesis – perhaps the will of the Omnissiah, if it is not blasphemy to believe that I still lie within their sight – I returned to the corroded ruins of my past. It was there that I was found by Andreti.

'He was at the beginning of his career, one warlord among many, but with grand ambitions. My utility to him was obvious and immediate. My skills, turned to the arts of factional warfare, proved quite decisive. But as our familiarity grew into trust, and idle chatter became intimate conversation, it became clear that our thoughts, opinions and ideals were aligned to a degree I had never before experienced, even within the depths of the Sacred Commune.'

Bai stared at her, grey eyes sharp amid the depths of their cloak. 'I lost much in my excommunication, Mistress Voronova. You cannot begin to conceive of what was taken from me.' The ferocity of their stare became leavened, slightly, with bitter amusement. 'But knowledge and ambition are more challenging to extract than mere machinery.

'Andreti was always going to take the Spoil for his own. It was in his nature. But I hastened his rise, I think. I was his vindication, as he often said. He seized a crown from a river of blood so that I might build a kingdom. For him, and for those whose lives are unacknowledged by the city at large. We were united by that purpose. By the desire to build, and to make better this forsaken sector.'

Bai took a distinctly human breath, a deep inhale and sharp exhale, to shed themself of memory's grip.

'We were friends,' they said finally. 'Thirty years of companionship is a long time, even for someone whose thoughts were once devoted to the study of planetary motion.'

'It is,' said Melita. She, too, let out a long breath. 'Thank you, magos.'

She spoke sincerely. Melita had not dared interrupt their reminiscence. She doubted there were more than a handful of people in the Spoil, or anywhere, who were privileged to know Russov Bai's story.

'Of course,' they said. They turned back to the metriculating engine, an unspoken signal that Bai had finished their... retelling? Their confession?

She and Edi turned away, but evidently the exiled adept had one final thing to say.

'I have one request to make of you, Mistress Voronova, if I may.'

CHAPTER 18

Liocas Boscan and his friends had been staring at Haska since she had boarded the hauler.

They were sat at the far end of the trailer, their heads together in sly chatter that was inaudible beneath the grumble of the hauler's engines. The crew – five of them, all of them the same age, more or less, as Haska – had been bitter rivals with hers for years. They had fought a dozen times, and traded insults and threats on an almost weekly basis. The scar on Haska's lip had been given to her by Boscan in their first fight, and he had a hand's span of taut, puckered skin on his forearm from when she had pushed him onto a red-hot steam pipe.

Fortunately, they were squeezed in at the back of the Raxis, and everyone was so packed in that there had been no chance of a disagreement breaking out. So far.

They had been driving for over an hour. The three haulers from the junction had been joined by several more, forming a convoy of heavy vehicles that rumbled unchallenged through the last hours of the day. A few enginebikes had sped by at one point, but Haska had no real notion of how many others had volunteered for Saitz's escapade, or where they were heading.

The mood among the forty or so occupants of the hauler's interior had been strangely jubilant as the haulers grumbled into life and set off, but had soured almost immediately into an awkward kind of quiet. The engines were so loud that it was impossible to have a conversation with anyone but their neighbour, and what was there to say?

Haska, for her part, was as close to peace as she could remember. Lira's head was resting on her shoulder, and Katryn's legs and hers were intertwined, the younger girl's boots knocking against the outside of her thigh. Haska had been surprised to find that she was glad Aryat was with them. He and Katryn sat in an easy silence, their hands clasped, as the tenements and workhouses fell away behind them.

The hauler's frame juddered. Lira jerked her head from Haska's shoulder, woken from her state of half-sleep by the change in the engines' droning pitch.

'By the Throne, I need a piss.'

Haska's own bladder was telling her the same thing. 'I expect that's why we're stopping.'

They were, indeed, slowing down. Though it was hard to tell with the next hauler in line so close behind, they had evidently turned off the main arterials and onto some derelict scrubland. Tufts of snake grass broke through cracked asphalt, and low heaps of rockcrete rubble were piled haphazardly. A few buildings, black shapes against the orange-grey of the clouded sky, were a way off, and the Redfort was an imposing silhouette to the south. The hauler behind them began to swing out of line, and she assumed that the whole convoy was pulling to a stop.

Their vehicle finally ground to a halt. The absence of the constant vibration and growling engines made Haska feel strangely alone, until a chorus of complaints from the hauler's occupants filled the silence. After a minute's pause, one of Saitz's men appeared at the Raxis' rear. He pulled the pin holding the loading gate in place, and let it swing open with a squeal and crash of ungreased metal.

'Everybody out.'

Haska was the first to jump down. She staggered immediately, cramp shooting through her ankles. She limped a few yards, cursing each step. She heard similar grunts of pain from Lira and Katryn, and from others to her left and right. A total of six haulers had pulled up in a rough line, and bodies were spilling from their rears with overlapping moans. They were men and women of every age and condition. Haska spotted at least a dozen Pit Snakes that she recognised from tense nights among Lopushani's gang, and several juve crews that had competed for their attention. Rek-heads and sleeper-fiends stumbled along beside elderly couples, all of them believing they had so little to lose that they would see where Saitz led them.

Haska did the sums in her head as the blood started flowing to her complaining limbs. She reckoned around two hundred and fifty Spoilers milled about on the scrubland, none of them with the slightest idea where they were, or why.

'Do what you've got to,' shouted the man who had released their vehicle's rear. 'You won't get another chance.' He strode back towards their hauler's cab.

Her crew gathered to her, gravitating to the familiar in the face of the uncertainty into which they had chosen to plunge. Haska saw Boscan and his fellows climb down, the last ones off.

'Well, I don't know about you, but I'm going to take this

opportunity.' Haska stumbled away into the dark, trailed by the others.

There was a convenient heap of rubble, a grey shape in the night, that provided as much privacy as they were used to. Haska and her crew took turns to relieve themselves, and were rounding the heap to head back towards the line of haulers when they ran into Liocas Boscan and his gang.

'Jovanic.' The juves were evidently waiting for Haska's crew. They had knives in their belts, but their hands were empty.

'Boscan.'

The youth was of a height with Haska, but much heavier, thickly muscled in the neck and chest. Someone, most likely Boscan himself, had spread a rumour that he had acquired a pack of growth stimms, but that was almost certainly dross.

'I think the last time we saw you, you were running away with my property.'

That was true, to a point. Haska and her friends had stripped out several bales of communications-grade cable from the walls of an old commercia unit inside what Boscan and his crew laughably considered their territory. Yurin, the youngest of them, had come across Aryat acting as lookout, and rather than risk their find in a fight they had fled before Boscan could rally his troops.

'And a tidy profit we made on it, too.' Lira set her feet, radiating thuggish energy.

'Then that slate's ours by rights.'

Haska could sense an audience gathering behind them. 'Do you want to do this now?'

One of Boscan's lackeys – she couldn't bring his name to mind – leaned forward, grinning. 'We do.'

Haska sensed her friends reaching slowly for weapons. She felt something like a headache building, as though her whole body were vibrating like a plucking string.

'Don't push me, Boscan. I'm not in the mood.'

He leant forward and shoved his fingers into the meat of her shoulder. 'Or what?'

With a distressingly easy motion, she pulled the gifted pistol from her belt and swung it up into the juve's face.

'I killed someone today, Liocas. I said, don't push me.'

'Put it down!'

The words snapped across the scrubland with such force that Haska froze, rather than letting her arm drop.

'I said, put it down!' A woman, chest and shoulders made blocky by body armour, did not wait for Haska to comply. She barged into the two crews, splitting them apart, and snatched the pistol out of Haska's grip. Both sets of juves immediately backed off, except for Haska, who was pinned to the spot by the woman's angry stare.

'You lot, back to the hauler.'

Boscan's crew fled immediately, but Haska's friends loyally held their ground.

The woman was huge. Even without her armour she would have been imposing. She was much older than Haska, older than her mother, even. The lines and scars on her face told a story of past violence. Her voice was low and powerful, her breath carrying the scent of cheap slatov.

'Am I going to have a problem with you?'

Haska's heart was pounding, her breathing coming in hard, sharp bursts. 'No.'

'Good.'

She held out Haska's pistol. 'Can you be trusted with this?'

Haska felt Lira's hand on her shoulder, and she let out a long, deep breath. 'Yes.'

The woman checked the pistol's safety was on, then passed it over. 'Get back there with the others.' She roughly spun Haska by her shoulder, and shoved her towards the haulers.

The crowd was being divided into groups, and Haska's crew hurried over. The four of them were directed into a clump of twenty or so volunteers. To her dismay, Haska saw that Boscan and his band were on the opposite side of their huddle.

A pair of large metal crates were carried into their midst by two gangers, both kitted out in the same body armour that seemed to mark Saitz's picked crew. The woman who had scolded Haska pushed into the centre of their group, dragging a third crate behind her. Each one was stamped with a broad-winged aquila on its top, and the sigil of a manufactory collective that Haska didn't recognise.

'Sit.'

A few junkies lowered themselves to the ground, but most of the assorted men and women were still disoriented, and were more intent on getting their bearings than following orders.

'I said, sit down.' The sharp bark of command got their attention. 'Get your knees in the dirt.'

They all knelt. This was an unwelcome start, although Haska knew she shouldn't have been surprised. Every gang had a hierarchy, and everyone who had boarded one of the haulers had, whether they knew it or not, signed up with Saitz's band.

'I'm Leonida Andrysi, and you'll do what I say.' That seemed to be all the introduction they were going to get.

She kicked open one of the crates with her heel, and lifted out an autogun. She held it up for them to see, the way the Astra Militarum recruiting placards showed, with one hand on the fore and the other wrapped around the grip with her index finger safe against the trigger guard.

'Who knows how to load one of these?'

No one answered, because their attention was on the weapon.

It was immaculate. All of them were. The crate held a dozen solid-shot rifles on its upper layer, and each one looked freshly stamped, like it had just been picked off the assembly line. Every weapon in the Spoil had passed through countless hands, each one leaving a smear of blood or dirt, a new nick or scar to show its use. This was untouched. Haska would have bet that the last hands to touch that autogun had belonged to the servitor who loaded it into the packing crate. It even had a slight sheen of gun-oil on the barrel.

'Anyone?' she asked again.

Liocas Boscan was the first to shake off the awe, and raised his hand like a child at scholam.

'Come on, then.' She held the autogun out, and plucked a magazine from the third crate, which was full of slab-sided boxes of ammunition.

Boscan climbed to his feet, and tentatively took the rifle from her. Fortunately for him, he managed to get it the right way on the first try, and took only a second to get the magazine to crunch home.

'Good enough, but you need to pull back that lever to chamber the first round.'

She took the rifle from the boy. Then she demonstrated unloading, and how to clear the chambered round and replace it in the magazine.

'Everyone, pick up a gun and two – two! – mags. Practise loading until you know what you're doing. Keep quiet, and for Throne's sake, keep the safety on, or the second shot will be for you.'

They all leapt to their feet, crowding towards the crates. Haska was among them, and managed to come away with both a weapon and a third sleeve of bullets, which she tucked into the inside pocket of her jacket as she emerged from the scrum. Soon the sound of metallic clicks and crunches carried over the scrub, along with a few laughs from the more excitable members of their group.

No one asked where the guns came from. That kind of unguarded curiosity was beaten out of Spoilers at a very young age. But everyone wondered. It was plain on their faces, as Haska was sure it was on hers. These rifles, Andrysi's body armour, it was all far finer than anything anyone on the Spoil should have had, particularly in such quantity.

Of course, there were the exceptions to the rule; the stuff of street rumour on any given day. The discharged Astra Militarum soldiers who left the Imperium's service with more mementos than was strictly allowed. The well-connected hired guns whose patrons provided access to the wealth of arms produced by Varangantua's countless forges. The few truly dangerous individuals whose past had brought them into contact with some of the more exotic means of killing that a hostile galaxy could produce.

But in the main, the firepower that ended up on the streets of the Spoil was second-rate, and second-hand. They tended to be cast-offs from the gangs and cartels in the tri-districts. There was a robust trade in weapons that had been used in places where the enforcers' verispexy would sniff out any forensic clues left by the user. Har Dhrol crews were responsible for their own arms, and any stockpile or deal to import a sizeable quantity of weapons did not remain covert for very long.

Haska ejected one of her magazines for the tenth time, feeling confident that she had the motions down. She pushed her way out of the huddle, and looked around.

There were at least a dozen clusters of Spoilers up and down the low rise of scrubland, each the size of Haska's group. All of them were arming themselves, practising the motions as she was. How had Saitz got hold of enough guns like these to arm not just Andrysi's little mock-platoon, but the hundreds who had followed his rhetoric out into the middle of nowhere?

'Haska.' Lira said her name in a pitched whisper. She realised she had wandered a little way, and was halfway up a low berm. She could see the glare of Setomir to the north, lighting the underside of the smog-bank in dull orange. This close, she could see individual towers and spires, illuminated like earthbound star clusters across the horizon. She knew the district was rich, a centre for commerce and finance, luxury trade and high technomancy. A place where deals were done, and slate changed hands in quantities beyond her imagining. And all of it sheltering behind a squat line of dark shapes and unseen guns.

'Haska,' Lira said again. Andrysi was back in the midst of the tooled-up men and women, and was gesturing for them all to kneel down again. She had acquired a heavy-duty shot-cannon, and had draped a bandolier of shells across her body armour. Haska trotted down the slope and joined the rest of her crew, squatting at the edge of the half-circle of Spoilers.

'I don't know you, and you don't know me.' Andrysi looked around at the assembled Spoilers. Evidently, she would have preferred to keep it that way. 'I don't know why you stepped forward, but you did. You're here now. We're all here now.'

The joking and enthusiasm had died down. Everyone was holding their new weapons with a lot less gusto.

'Some of you will have been in fights before. Remember what it's like, because it'll help. Keep your heads. Look before you shoot. Look before you move. Hells, look before you breathe, because there's going to be a lot of death in the air, and I don't want to catch a piece of it because you don't know which way is forward.'

They had all fallen completely silent. Haska looked at the

faces in the half-circle, hoping that hers didn't show the same mix of fear and confusion that was painted on the others.

'Some of you will be thinking you can't fight. You're look-ing around at the guns, at the scary bastard next to you, and thinking that you've made a terrible mistake.' She paused. 'Maybe you have. But it's too late now. Now it's kill or be killed. Those are your only options. Make your peace with that, or when the time comes I can guarantee you will be on the wrong side of that exchange.'

She let that sink in, then straightened, evidently finished with her attempt to rouse them.

'We're ditching the haulers here. I don't suppose any of you know what light and noise discipline is, but it means that if you light up a lho-stick while we're on the march, be prepared to eat it without making a sound.' There were some chuckles, but Andrysi's expression silenced them swiftly. 'If you get lost, you stay lost. Keep quiet, keep together, and for Throne's sake, don't shoot at anything unless I tell you.'

With that, she slung the shot-cannon over her shoulder, and stomped through the centre of the crowd, which split in two to let her pass. Lacking any other instruction, Haska picked up her own gun, and looked around at her crew.

'Let's go, I guess.'

The platoon, such as it was, fell into a shuffling column in Andrysi's wake. Boscan and his boys quickly ran to the front of the line, so Haska made sure that her crew drifted back until they formed the rear. To their left and right, almost lost in the darkness, the other knots of volunteers were also on the move, trudging north with unordered purpose.

'Last chance to turn back,' said Haska.

'Do you want to?' Lira said. She seemed to be sincerely asking. All of Lira's usual front was gone, stripped away by the reality of what they were embarked upon.

'No.' Unlike her friend, Haska felt certain, for the first time in many years. Stepping out of her hab had felt permanent, decisive, regardless of whatever lay ahead for her. Andrysi's speech had not deterred her from facing whatever came next. 'You?'

'Not a chance,' Lira said, her infectious smile returning as a flash of white in the darkness.

In something approaching silence, Haska marched towards the pillars of light on the horizon.

CHAPTER 19

Vasimov was not far.

The transepts that budded from the church's nave were topped by ornate, tiered galleries, looking out over the pulpit and processional path. When St Eurydice's had been the centre of worship for the nearby habclaves, these balconies had been private boxes, given in gratitude by the church to its wealthiest patrons for their largesse.

The ornamentation and privacy fields had been stripped away along with the proselytising priests and hypocritical sermons. Now, from the stark comfort of one of these balconies, Tomillan Vasimov watched gangsters assemble to decide an empire's future.

Melita approached from the box's rear, after being waved through by a pair of Reisiger mercenaries guarding the entrance. Vasimov stood at the heavy stone balustrade, arms clasped in the small of his back. Nedovic was a few steps to his right, affecting the same manner of stern disdain as his master. The shorter man turned at her approach, and she saw him give a minute nod of acknowledgement to Edi. She could not see Edi, just behind her, but she wondered at the extent to which the mercenary's respect for her bodyguard was reciprocated.

'I trust you are well rested,' Vasimov said, without turning.

Melita stopped. The tall securitor radiated cold, clinical disdain, and she preferred to keep a discreet distance from him at the best of times.

He ignored her silence. 'While you slept, I did this.' He swept an imperious hand out over the church's grandeur. Reluctantly, Melita stepped up to the balustrade.

Dozens of gangers had assembled in the nave, and more entered through the massive doors at the church's far end. Each clave-captain was identifiable by the train of leather-clad soldiers at their back. They moved like the formations of avians Melita had seen in off-world cultural reels. The tight knots of men and women milled about uneasily, though some were clearly taking the opportunity to speak with their peers.

Vasimov smiled, as though inviting a child at scholam to step up and be tested. 'Tell me what you see.'

From the moment she had approached the balustrade, Oriel's ocular sensor had been capturing each ganger's face, and her iris cogitators had been matching features to her patchwork organigram of the Har Dhrol's hierarchy. More than half the known leaders of the Har Dhrol gangs were in attendance. Several more had evidently sent deputies, or else had been deposed in the day's chaos. Those that she recognised were, if Melita's information was correct, among the weakest of the clave-captains, or those considered to be the most loyal to Sorokin. The older captains, those few who had ruled Spoil gangs before the Har Dhrol's rise, were conspicuously absent.

'More came than I would have expected.'

'Yes, quite the coup,' said Vasimov dryly, as though he expended greater effort summoning his morning meal.

'How did you do it?' She didn't want to ask, but the question tumbled out anyway. When she had left the church on her mission to retrieve Bai, the Har Dhrol had seemed on the brink of collapse.

'Slate,' Vasimov sighed. 'A great deal of slate. Too much, perhaps, although it was instructive to see the variance from man to man. A few required more... tangible inducements, but nothing that we were not able to provide.'

He glanced at her.

'You seem surprised. You of all people should know that everyone's pride has its price.' He turned back to the assembling gangers.

Melita could not let that stand. 'I could have helped with this, you know.'

She waved a hand towards a group of gangers huddled beneath the statue of an armoured angel. They eschewed the typical uniform of the Spoil streets, and were instead dressed in black tabards covered with crude attempts at Imperial iconography, a parody of the Ecclesiarchy cassocks and habits that belonged within the seminary's walls.

'Branis Sokol has a daughter addicted to bliss.'

She pointed to another group, whose leathers were covered in plates of metal stitched into long chains.

'Loni Pleško of the Forge Kin owes substantial sums to Korodilsk creditors.'

Another crew, as hulking and gruesome a set of street-blades as Melita had encountered.

'I have it on good authority that Albin Milić's lieutenant is an informant for Bastion-K.' Melita thought briefly of Mattix, but she put him from her mind. 'Manipulating these people was what I did for a living.'

'Yes, before we so generously adopted you into our organisation, and put your meagre talents to better use.'

Vasimov's superior smile provoked a spasm of anger so fierce that it bled into her connection with Oriel, causing a flare in the servo-skull's power systems. The brief whine of overloading suspensors drew the securitor's eye. His lip twitched from its sneer to show a flash of white teeth, bared like a challenged animal. Vasimov's dislike for the servo-skull did not arise from fear. Nor was it distaste for Oriel's macabre nature, although Melita knew that he was an adherent of the Cult of the Immaculate Design, a notorious sect within the Imperial Church that opposed all forms of augmetic modification and deviation from the perfect template laid down for humanity by the God-Emperor.

Rather, it was the more deep-seated loathing of a bully faced with an equal. A predator whose prey had a potent defender.

His smile turned colder. 'As I said, I have read your reports extensively. The back-street gossip you have passed on has been taken into consideration, for all that it is worth.'

They lapsed into silence. The growl of conversation carried up to the balcony, but neither of them made any effort to eavesdrop on a particular discussion.

'What's the purpose of this expensive little gathering?' she asked, doing her best to mimic Vasimov's haughty tone.

'The selection of a replacement for Sorokin. I have a marked distaste for democracy, but the Kadern insisted on it.'

It was the logical course. Though Iliev, Amadan and Toskanov were known and respected by the clave-captains, none of them could fill the void left by Sorokin. A new name had to rise from among their ranks if there was any hope of the alliance of gangs enduring.

'And you've stacked the deck in favour of a candidate who will do the Valtteri's bidding?'

Vasimov saw no need to dissemble. 'One who appreciates the nature and value of our relationship, yes.'

'This will lead to civil war.'

'Internecine conflict is unavoidable,' said Vasimov. 'This way, with our assistance, it will be brief, and serve a greater cause.'

Melita was dismayed to find that she agreed with him. Avoiding a long and protracted war in the Spoil was in the interests of all. For that to happen, one side had to lose, as swiftly as possible.

She was surprised so many of the gang praetors were willing to participate in what was, effectively, a declaration of war against their more belligerent comrades. There were dozens of factions and lines of trust and mistrust within the Har Dhrol, aligned by territorial integrity, shared antagonisms, and what was essentially dynastic interrelation. But even so, the assembled gangers would be sanctioning the destruction of their fellows, with the undisguised support of the Valtteri cartel.

'And they came despite not knowing which of them killed Sorokin...'

'Do you?' asked Vasimov.

'What?' Melita hadn't realised she had spoken aloud.

'Has your investigation yielded anything of consequence?'

Throughout their conversation, Oriel's cogitators had been working through the drip-feed of information from Bai. A growing web of connections drew together the slate, its last owners, and their affiliations with the assembling gangers below her. The query was working, but, as Bai had said and she had feared, it was far from conclusive.

'Not yet.' She said it absently, distracted by the nagging sense that something was wrong.

Vasimov gave a performative sigh. 'I continue to be struck by the magnitude of your failings, Voronova.'

Melita ignored him. She stared down at the assembled

gangers that were shuffling in the direction of the church's apse. Intuition, so hard to quantify yet so often right, was telling her that Vasimov's blithe confidence was far from justified.

CHAPTER 20

The ground under Haska radiated heat, hours after night had fallen. It seemed to smother her, enveloping her like a blanket. She had stripped off her jacket and was using it as a barrier between her stomach and the flinty ground, but the heat was still oppressive.

They had walked for an hour into the night, a task that she and the rest of her group had found more difficult than Haska would have imagined. Though the thick banks of smog above them were lit by the blaze of lights from Seto-mir, they did little to illuminate the ground beneath their feet. More than one person fell during their march, and the entire journey had been accompanied by a chorus of soft complaints and barely suppressed curses. The lumens that studded the mile-high Setomir starscrapers had at least served as an unmistakable landmark, drawing the column north like a cluster of compass needles.

And then, all of a sudden, someone had ordered a halt. Haska's mock-platoon, and the hundreds of Spoilers that were ahead and behind them, were spread out along the stony stretch of ground and ordered to lie down and keep quiet.

That had been an hour ago, by Haska's vague reckoning.

Someone off to her left was snoring. Haska was quietly impressed that anyone was able to sleep on the rocky ground. They had been lying in silence for an age, waiting for... something. Haska had no idea what signal or order they were expecting, or what to do when it came. Andrysi, the ganger in charge of their section of the massed volunteers, had said nothing on their march north beside the occasional pitched demand for quiet, and Haska wasn't going to be the one to break the silence.

'I don't know about you, but I thought a raid would be more exciting. All I've done so far is wear a hole in my boot.'

Lira had shed her jacket as well. She and Haska lay as they had as children, their faces just inches from one another.

'Takes you to interesting places, though,' Haska replied. In the darkness, she could just make out the flash of Lira's smile.

Neither of them could quite believe that they were in sight of the Line. For all of Haska's life, it had been one of the boundaries of her world. Beyond was the city, with its wealth and excess and industry, concealed and kept out of reach by rockcrete barriers and men with guns. The Line was an emphatic statement of Varangantua's contempt for the Spoil, and those the city chose to put beyond its sight.

'Which one is that?' Lira asked.

Haska thought that they had walked almost directly north, and the shadow of the Redfort had been behind them the entire time. 'The Praetorian,' she said.

The Praetorian's Gate, the Angel's Gate and the Regent's Gate. Grandiose names for the three passages through the Setomir Line.

The Line was not a single, continuous wall, but rather a

boundary drawn in the earth with metal and rock. Around the three gates, stone and iron stretched in a las-straight line, rising from the scrubland like the mythical Walls of Terra. The tops of the Praetorian's Gate towers were a hundred and fifty feet above Haska's head. The mass of the Binas-tri Arterial was a dark shape against the smog, flying on its massive stanchions over the Spoil and the scrubland to meet the gun-metal grey face of the gate itself.

The wall's enormity stretched away from her, east and west, but she knew that there were vast tracts between the three gates where the earth itself had been sculpted into a barrier. Sheer-sided hills and valleys had been carved into the flinty soil. Fields of razorbriar and steelthorn and bittergrass covered the slopes, as impenetrable a barrier as the rockcrete walls and iron-faced ramparts of the Praetorian's Gate. The valley depths were lined with countless miles of coiled flaywire, and gun-servitors patrolled the hilltops in packs. Flocks of roaming monitor skulls raced to investigate unexpected movement or body heat, bringing squads of Grenze Guard in their wake.

The scale of what faced them made Haska's skin prickle, as if a cold wind had blown across her body.

They had no chance at all. Saitz's army, if that's what they were, was waiting to throw itself onto the city's guns, a bloody charge of defiance that had a single, obvious end. And yet she was here, shoulder to shoulder with hundreds of other Spoilers, all apparently willing to throw their lives away on the strength of his word that they could win where others had fallen.

Had Saitz created this desire in her, in everyone who lay in wait along the ridge, to stand together and strike back at a city that despised them? Or had the Spoil always been waiting for someone to give voice to the anger that they all pretended was not there?

Haska had heard zealots before, the mad fanatics who stood on street corners and preached anarchy and uprising against Sorokin, against the city. Against the God-Emperor Himself, although even in the Spoil such blasphemy was the route to a short and bloody end at the hands of His faithful. Haska had listened, but until now had done nothing.

It was Sorokin's death that had broken the dam. The order he had imposed upon the Spoil had been stripped away, releasing not just the gangs but everyone to explore their suppressed desires. Saitz had been right, back in the Soldier's Square. The king had fettered the ambitions of the praetors, and tempered the excesses of the street-blades. That had been good, in a way. It had brought slate into the Spoil, even if only the merest trickle reached the hands of those, like Haska's mother, who worked the hardest for it.

Above all else, Haska feared a wasted life and a pointless death. That was all she had been offered by Sorokin's order. By the Har Dhrol and their bloody infighting, by Ludoric Erastin and those like him. Saitz, for all that she mistrusted him, offered Haska something more. If she was going to die, she would do it fighting for a cause, to spit in the eye of those who built walls to keep what was theirs by rights.

Haska heard the crunch of gravel, and she and Lira awkwardly twisted over, their unfamiliar autoguns in their arms. Someone – Andrysi, from her heavy footfall and growled whisper – passed behind them.

'It's time. Be ready. Pass the word along.' She moved on, and Haska just made out her repeating her order. 'It's time. Be ready.'

Lira looked at Haska. 'Be ready for what?'

CHAPTER 21

'My fellow captains, join us.'

The conclave would take place beneath St Eurydice's great dome, watched by the murals, reliefs and statuary of the once sanctified centre of the chapel. Wooden pews, which must have been worth their weight in precious metal, had been hauled from wherever Sorokin had secreted them, and were set out in a large square under the dome's centre. Amadan, Toskanov and Iliev stood at the centre, each wearing outfits that straddled the line between gilded finery and Spoil street practicality. Mercy Iliev looked particularly fierce, a collar of stiffened lace rising from her shoulders like the crest of a predatory avian, and a knife so long and curved that it was practically a sabre hung from her waist.

As the gangers slowly filed beneath the balcony, Melita stepped back from its edge.

'Who decided which captains to invite?' she asked softly.

'What?' Despite his calculated air of derision, Vasimov's attention was wholly on the gathering clusters of gang leaders.

'How was it decided which praetors would be invited to the conclave?'

'Runners were sent to all of them, where they could be reached. Most responded via proxies, but evidently their greed outstripped their fear.'

'And you didn't question why so many came?'

'No.' He looked at Melita, the briefest turn of his head. 'If you are going to persist in this fretting, go elsewhere to do it.'

Harol Toskanov waited until each praetor had taken their place at the pews, their small collection of bodyguards lining up behind them.

'A day has passed since Andreti Sorokin was taken from us. We mourn his loss. Let it be clear, the harshest vengeance is reserved for the coward who took him, and any who abetted her.'

The assembled gangers stomped their boots in approval.

Iliev took over from Toskanov. 'For thirty years, we benefited from Andreti's strength, insight and wisdom. He forged the Har Dhrol out of nothing...'

Melita was familiar with the edited and, no doubt, embellished history Iliev was embarking upon. She retreated further into the box. Edi, his brow knotted in concern, followed her.

She opened her iris interface. > Magos, are you there?

> Indeed, Mistress Voronova.

> I need you to interrogate your records. Have any clave-captains logged unusually large amounts to their accounts in the last month?

Thankfully, they seemed to pick up on the urgency in her words. > That will take some time.

> Just the headlines, anything that stands out.

> Working.

What she had asked for was a poor indicator of the clave-captains' loyalties – anyone with the slightest sense would keep an illicit payment off any records that could be interrogated. What else could she check?

Melita scanned through the list of praetors in attendance again. The cartel kept a tight record of its transactions with the Har Dhrol, but they were all delivered centrally, via Sorokin and his staff so as to preserve the feudal nature of the gang's structure. They would be no help.

Her iris feed flickered into life.

> No significant deviations, although with such loose parameters I cannot say whether I have truly resolved your query.

> I understand, thank you, magos.

'Andreti Sorokin is dead,' Juri Amadan said from the church's floor, concluding for Iliev. 'It was his wish that his successor be chosen from among your ranks. It is for this purpose that you have been summoned.' He looked around the square. 'Which of you is worthy of that honour?'

'I am.'

Parviz Dragović stood immediately, to the stomps of several captains seated closest to him.

Melita wasn't surprised. Dragović was the leader of the Ataren Blades syndicate, whose subsidiary gangs controlled the greater part of the southern reaches of the Spoil. He was the son of Junia Dragović, one of the warlords whom Sorokin had first fought and then brought to his side during his rise to power. He had practically grown up in Sorokin's household, a hostage against his mother's continued loyalty. He was the natural choice, at least from among those who had historically supported Sorokin's leadership.

He, evidently, was the Valtteri's man.

'I knew Sorokin, better than many assembled here. I respected him as an adversary, and as a friend.' Parviz Dragović could have been no more than twelve when his mother handed him over into Sorokin's dubious care, but such rhetoric was expected.

'There is much that we must do if we are to continue his legacy, and become more than we are. His killer must be hunted, no matter how far they run. Those praetors who did not heed the summons must understand the consequences. It is through our collective strength that we hold against our enemies, and ensure fair dealing from our friends.'

He stopped abruptly. A short, sly-faced man wearing a red baldric across one shoulder had climbed to his feet while Dragović was speaking.

'It is interesting that you speak of friends, Parviz. You have always had so many of them.' That raised a chuckle from several clave-captains who regularly crossed blades with Dragović's syndicate.

'Who is that?' asked Nedovic.

Vasimov answered before Melita could speak. 'Damor Saitz. A minor figure from the Deiten claves, with few allies.'

Saitz continued. 'Tell me, will you be receiving an annual stipend from the Valtteri, or equity in one of their combines?'

A few more laughs greeted the jibe, but there were more grim faces than amused ones among the gang leaders. They may have taken the cartel's slate, but they still clung to their traded pride. Dragović's fury was plain to see.

'Sit down, Saitz.' Dragović said tightly.

'I will not. I happily took their bribe to come here, as you all did.' He looked meaningfully at the assembled gangers, then up towards the balcony from which Vasimov watched. 'Stealing from a thief is no crime at all. But I will not let this sham proceed for a second longer than it must.'

'Sham?' Toskanov thundered. 'If you came to this conclave to mock and self-aggrandise, Saitz, you will play no further part in it.'

'I came to spare the Har Dhrol from you!' countered Saitz. He looked round at his fellow captains, who sat in various states of naked anger and impassive curiosity. 'We came because we know what the Har Dhrol is, and what it can be. Sorokin brought the Spoil together in a way no one thought possible, and we–'

'You were barely birthed from your mother's sour womb when Andreti claimed the Spoil!' Iliev spat.

Saitz glared at the old woman, but he would not be deterred. 'There is such strength in us when we have a united purpose. What could we have done had Sorokin not been so willing to accept the Valtteri's leash?'

'Did you kill him?' Mercy Iliev could no longer contain the accusation. 'Did you kill Andreti?'

Saitz's face was a picture of angered innocence. 'No.'

'You lying bastard!' screamed Iliev.

'Let him speak!' shouted more than one voice from the encircling gangers.

'This is getting out of hand,' murmured Nedovic.

Vasimov was still sanguine, though the deepening crease of a scowl marked his brow. 'I expected some resistance, from a minority. It may even be useful, to give the proceedings the appearance of influencing the outcome.'

Melita was not concerned by the vocal minorities who either cheered or jeered Saitz, but rather the silent majority who gave every appearance of listening to what he had to say. She could see that Amadan, Toskanov and Iliev could sense it too. Too few voices were raised in agreement with them, or in denouncing Saitz.

'I did not kill the king, nor did I wish him dead. But he is, and it is for us to decide what comes next.'

'That is why we're all here, Damor,' Amadan said, one hand raised as though calming an agitated animal.

'But how can we do that while shackled to these preening bastards!' Saitz practically shrieked. 'Look at them!' He
pointed up at their box. 'They watch from on high, as if we
were livestock to be bought and sold. And we are! They paid
us all to attend this conclave, as if we needed their bribes to
stay true to the ties that draw us together. How many indignities must they heap upon us before we will throw them from
our backs? Will any of us stand and demand to be treated as
equals? Will any of you?'

His wild gaze swung across the assembled gangers, who
mostly continued to sit in unnervingly receptive silence.

'Can you see beyond the narrow path they set for us?
Will you dare to stray beyond the bounds of what they
will allow?'

'We need the Valtteri,' said Dragović. He looked far from
happy to be forced into defending the Har Dhrol's ties with
the cartel.

'We need them? For what? What do they give us that we
cannot claim for ourselves?'

'Sir...' Melita caught Nedovic's whisper of concern in his
master's ear.

'Alert the men,' said Vasimov. Saitz's rhetoric had gone far
beyond principled objection to the cartel's presence within the
Spoil. Vasimov was gripping the balustrade with both hands.

'You have no vision.' This, even more than his accusations of thraldom, was clearly Saitz's most venomous insult.

As if on cue, one of Saitz's bodyguards pulled a hololithic
plate from beneath his coat and passed it forward. The projector was the size of Saitz's stretched handspan, and heavy
with the arcane mechanics of its workings.

'I have a vision. For us. For the Har Dhrol. For the Spoil.'

Saitz placed it on the table before him, and pressed a thumb
to its controls. A tri-D image, fuzzy with static, filled the air

above the assembly. No sound accompanied the image, but none was necessary. The church was silent, as the image resolved into the distorted outline of an enormous cargo hauler. The hauler shrank within the haze of light. The image was evidently being captured by a servo-skull that was keeping pace with the huge vehicle as it raced along a wide arterial roadway.

'I will show you the world that Dragović says is impossible.'

Mercy Iliev was the first to find her voice. 'Saitz, what have you done?'

The slight, unimposing man who had upended the Har Dhrol conclave tilted his face towards the three regents, lit by the hololith's glare.

'I have done what you would not.'

CHAPTER 22

The crew of the Cratos were exhausted. The two-day passage across the Binastri Wastes was a gruelling, mind-numbing affair, beset by brutal heat and dust devils that could over-turn a groundcar. There was also the distant but ever-present concern that enterprising engine-gangers might defy the Har Dhrol's edict, and strike their convoy while it was mired in the unremitting emptiness between the districts.

And so, as the morning dawned and the arterial finally rose out of the ochre desolation of the Wastes and into the grime-streaked grey of the Spoil, the giga-hauler's crew and their escorts could be forgiven for allowing their attention to wander and their guard to drop. Andreti Sorokin's aegis was a powerful deterrent; no one had been foolish enough to attack a Valtteri caravan within the borders of the Spoil for years.

The engine-gangers took them at the Slahin Junction.

A dozen groundcars and flatbed haulers roared onto the arterial without warning. The caravan's escort vehicles were immediately struck by improvised explosives and strings of tyre shredders, flipping the racing groundcars over in clouds of promethium and metallic scraps. Others were rammed off the road, bursting through rockcrete guard-rails to plummet a hundred feet or more to the ground, or into unlucky hab-blocks below the roadway.

The Cratos, however, was a different proposition. Its armoured prow shattered the paltry resistance offered by a groundcar, and its enormous wheels were proof against the makeshift caltrops that were dropped in its path. Its crew were well trained, if momentarily complacent, and put up a ferocious defence. As they fought, their urgent squawks of alarm into vox-units went unheard, swallowed by an invisible blanket of electronic noise broadcast from one of the pursuing hijackers.

Boarding a Jujen Cratos, a huge, multi-engined giga-hauler towing five enormous cargo units, while the great beast was in motion was no simple task. Nevertheless, a swarm of young and impetuous gangers made the attempt. Most fell beneath the drive-unit's huge wheels and were instantly crushed. Others leapt for the trailing cargo carriages, and were struck by sprays of hard rounds from the sponsons that studded either side of the hauler's flanks, or by small-arms fire from the crew.

But enough made it aboard.

The crew of East Tower, Praetorian Gate Company, Setomir Grenze Corps had been tense all day.

First, the news about Sorokin had reached them. Additional readiness checks had been run in between the gossiping and speculation, and Major Molka, the company commander, had made a number of unscheduled visits to the tower and the nearby wall crews.

Nothing had come through from the Spoil, and that was

the problem. A caravan for Bech-Ulysses Agri-Tech had been scheduled to reach them at midday, but after an hour's wait, Molka had authorised a reconnaissance. A trio of Ramparts, armoured groundcars in the proud gold-and-green of the Grenze Guard, had roared out from the gate, speeding along the length of the arterial. By nightfall they had not returned nor reported in, a clear violation of protocol.

Now, as the tower's upper deck chron ticked over to a new day, men and women stood at the casements, staring urgently but impotently through magnoculars in hope of spotting any sign of the convoy or their missing comrades.

Sergeant Sileny Fiala bent down to tug the cuff of her trousers straight, and in the same motion slipped a dataslug out of her boot and into her palm. It had sat there for twelve hours, since she had begun her shift, tugging at her focus and her conscience.

She knew what would happen. What she was about to do. She had not allowed herself the luxury of pretending that what she had been asked to do was a victimless act. People would be hurt. Some of her fellow guardsmen might even die.

But it was a price she could accept. She had to. The medicaes at St Arlo's who had diagnosed her rare, terminal blood disorder had given her three months to live. But with the slate the anonymous agent had paid her to betray her uniform, her comrades and her duty, her husband could get their daughter, Milani, the genomic grafts she needed to avoid her mother's fate.

Fiala slowly straightened, and placed her hands against the flat of her control console. She sucked in a breath, held it, and pushed the dataslug into the matching socket.

Alarms instantly wailed, as the tower's cogitators detected the hostile code and attempted to shut down. But it was already too late. Even as Fiala was tackled to the deck, the scrapcode tore through the gate's interconnected systems, sowing logic bombs and data-phages in its wake. Lumens flickered and consoles died as the corrosive code did its work, disrupting the carefully tended machine spirits and the vast mechanisms they controlled.

While the tower crew frantically tried to assess the damage to the gate's systems, a bank of flood-lumens appeared on the horizon.

The architects of the Line had predicted the gates' vulnerabilities, and had designed appropriate countermeasures. For the final two hundred yards of the approach to the mighty steel face of the Praetorian's Gate, the surface of the roadway was studded with retractable bollards. Each was a massive column of rockcrete five feet thick, encased within a shell of steel, mounted on vast pistons that would lift the top of each post a full twelve feet clear of the road's surface.

With the gate's cogitators degrading, the defenders were powerless to raise the final line of defence as the Cratos bore down on them.

Tiny figures spilled from the giga-hauler's flanks, landing in open-topped groundcars that screeched to a halt as soon as the last ganger was free. The giga-hauler's enormous flood-lumens lit the face of the Praetorian's Gate and surrounding wall with blinding brilliance. Las-beams spat from the nearest turrets, slashing through the empty pilot's cabin and bursting a tyre with a detonation that was heard a mile away. But each flash of las was a needle set against the face of a descending hammer.

The hauler's drive-unit struck the point where the gate's edge met the eastern tower with the force of a macro-cannon's shell. Layers of armour crumpled like so much vellum, but the massive engine blocks hammered through the reinforced rockcrete stanchions and on into the tower's innards. Metal shards peeled back like leaves from a dying tree. Pulverised rock formed a lethal bow-wave as the hauler ground its way into the building's core. Dozens of Grenze Guard and Administratum officials died without ever knowing what killed them, their bodies crushed by sundered walls and collapsing ceilings and an irresistible tide of shrieking metal.

The dying vehicle came to a slow, grinding halt as the awful inertia of its charge became equal to the weight of hundreds of tons of shattered masonry. Cogitators, furniture and bodies tumbled through fissures that suddenly gaped between the levels. Those fortunate few who had survived the initial impact also fell, as floors dropped into the void that had opened up in the heart of the gate tower.

The titanic squeal of rending metal finally stopped, replaced by the screams of the dying and the rumble of subsiding stone.

There was time enough for the Line's defenders to register the shock of what had happened, and then the giga-hauler's fractured engines exploded.

CHAPTER 23

The explosion lit the darkness, bright enough to paint the smog-bank above Haska in vivid shades of red and orange and illuminate the scrubland for hundreds of yards in every direction. Eyes aching from the sudden flash, she got an impression of a wide-open slope, its barren surface blanketed in coils of wire, leading to the Line that stretched from the arterial's stanchions to far into the west. And then the shockwave hit.

The detonation sundered the world. A roaring, howling blast of dust and air crashed over Haska, pressing her face into the dirt. It was like nothing she had ever seen, nothing she had ever felt. The crash of Aryat's shot-cannon beside her ear was like a whisper next to the cataclysm that erupted barely half a mile from her head. Someone nearby was screaming. She could taste clumps of dirt filling her mouth when she sucked in a breath. Lira's hand clutched hers with desperate strength, as though she were afraid the howling wind would pull her from the ground.

After an hour, or a minute, or a second, the pressure on her back lifted. Haska spat the dirt from her mouth and looked up.

The Praetorian's Gate was a shattered ruin. The tower nearest Haska was devastated, obliterated by the calamity that Saitz had somehow engineered. Each level of the cracked tower was open to the elements, the slumping internal floors lit by flames from the arterial's roadway. It was as though the God-Emperor Himself had taken His sword to the building, cutting it vertically in two.

Through the darkness, Haska could see that the broken half of the tower had collapsed, dropping into a great pile against the structure's foundations. The mass of rubble had slumped into a crude ramp. The rockcrete slope led from the scrubland where hundreds of would-be fighters massed to the level of the roadway and the broken gate beyond.

'Let's go!'

Haska had no idea who gave the order, but she obeyed. Some force, from outside or beyond her, simply lifted Haska from the ground and set her sprinting towards the scree. Elation seized her, wild and terrifying, and she let out a whooping yell as she ran.

Haska was not alone, in her run or in screaming sudden joy into the ruptured sky. Hundreds of cheering Spoilers to her left and right were charging across the rock and dirt, aiming for the heap of rockcrete and stone. Others were heading for the thick legs of the arterial, intending to reach the ladders that led up to the maintenance gantries that ran beneath its immense bulk.

No raid, no stealthy sortie, had ever achieved anything of this scale. Nothing like this had ever happened before, and mad joy coursed through Saitz's army as they surged across the distance.

Another explosion, much smaller, cast a moment's glare

over the scrub, and Haska saw the fields of flaywire in her path. She checked her run, and reached out to grab Lira's arm as she sped past.

But she need not have worried. Figures moved in the half-darkness, dragging long coils of the viciously sharp wire aside to create corridors through the lethal ground. Saitz and his lieutenants had prepared the ground for their headlong charge.

Lira spotted the closest gap, and grinned. 'Come on.' She shouted at Aryat and Katryn, pointing the way, and set off again. Haska and her crew ran side by side, full of breathless exhilaration and sudden conviction towards the rockcrete slope, the broken gate, and the city's riches.

Gunfire stitched the darkness, and the cheers turned to screams.

Thick bursts of tracer rounds and eye-aching beams of las-fire burst out of the darkness, slashing through the charging mob. Men and women fell, some screaming, some already dead.

Haska dropped, skidding and rolling over the hard-packed earth. Another painfully bright burst of las lanced into the flank of the charging masses, and she had the briefest glimpse of limbs tumbling before Katryn's knee struck her head.

Hard rounds chattered from turreted emplacements along the top of the eastern wall, raking over the dead ground and the hundreds of running figures. The attack lost its joyful momentum in an instant, as factorum workers and dock-yard labourers and drug-addled vagrants were struck by the horror of heavy-weapons fire.

A boot thudded into Haska's ribs, and a hand hauled her up by the collar. It was Andrysi, her shot-cannon clutched in one hand. She was standing above Haska's crew, glaring at the gun emplacements.

'Can't stop here.'

They clambered to their knees, staring fearfully up the slope and the stalled attack. Aryat hefted his autogun into a firing position, and Haska remembered her own weapon just as Andrysi barked at him. 'You won't hit anything. Save the rounds for when they matter. Keep moving!' This last was yelled across the scrub, louder than the pops and crackles of the wall-top guns and the sporadic return fire.

'To where?' Haska asked. There was still a quarter-mile of open ground between them and the wall, and yellow lines of tracer fire reached out every few seconds to cut down men and women who had nowhere to hide. Bursts of muzzle flash from the top of the roadway suggested that whatever forces Saitz had sent along the arterial were similarly embattled.

The woman appeared to scan the distance, then pointed. 'You see that big hunk of wall, to the right of the scree? That'll give all the cover we need. Get up and get moving, or stay here and die.' And with that she was off, running towards another knot of Spoilers.

Haska's friends looked at her, their faces barely visible in the darkness. They were afraid. Haska was afraid – she had never felt terror like it. Not in all the back-alley fist-fights, break-ins, and frantic flights had her heart hammered so heavily in her chest. Everything was too loud, too chaotic. Her thoughts were a jumbled mess of sensation and impulse.

A flash of las scarred the air a hundred yards to her right, and a knot of would-be fighters fell, immolated.

The sound of their screams reached Haska, and something changed inside her. The fear boiled away, incinerated by a blaze of anger and hate that welled up in its place. The chattering guns that casually swept the field were aimed by men and women, flesh and blood just like her. It was as Andrysi had said – now, with weapons in their hands, it was either kill or be killed.

Haska gripped her gun, the sudden strength in her fingers enough to make her feel like she would flex the metal. She bared her teeth in a savage, primal snarl that matched the animal anger in her heart.

'Let's kill them. Let's kill them all!'

She saw the same change come over her friends, fear turning to ferocity in the face of so much death. The four of them rose.

'Kill them!'

It was a rallying cry that came easily, the oldest human instinct roared from peeled-back lips and aching lungs. It drove Haska through the darkness, through the gunfire that seemed to be all around her. Every step could have been her last. She would never see the shot that killed her, and so she ran, the resolve she had felt as she left her hab hours before turned to a fatalistic drive to hurt before she was hurt. To kill before she was killed.

'Kill them!'

They passed others who had leapt for cover, but found only the razor-sharp grip of the flaywire. They were trapped, screaming piteously for help, but Haska could do nothing for them. Nothing but silence the guns that had driven them onto the wire, and return their pain to the Line's defenders with interest.

'Kill them!'

Others were renewing the charge, finding their own reserves of courage or else berated into movement by Andrysi and her fellow gangers. To her left, Haska saw Boscan and his crew, heads down as though they were running into a gale. She pushed harder, pumping her legs, suddenly determined to be the first to reach the rubble.

A dark shape loomed over Haska, the shadow of the wall against the grey-orange light of Setomir's sky. They were so close.

The slope was littered with shards of rock and rubble, and Haska slipped on a loose hunk of the tower's outer face. Their charge was no longer a sprint, but an awkward hobbling climb as they negotiated the debris. Soon it was a matter of hands and feet, clawing their way up the loose stone and broken rebar.

Haska finally had to pause to catch her breath, and turned to look for her friends. They were with her, perhaps ten yards back on the mound of rubble. Dozens more Spoilers were behind them, a few still cheering but most grunting wordless defiance, teeth clenched in the grim determination that they would not die in this place.

Leonida Andrysi appeared out of the darkness, chest heaving in and out like a blown equine. She nodded a brief acknowledgement as she came alongside Haska's crew.

The line of the wall was now out of sight. They were in the lee of the hab-sized piece of the fallen gate tower that Andrysi had pointed out from across the scrubland. That colossal chunk of masonry was almost half the height of the arterial that loomed to their left, and it gave them cover from the small-arms fire from the closest embrasures. The heavier guns were firing less frequently now. Evidently, they didn't have the angle to shoot along the face of the wall, and most of the fighters had made it across the killing field and into cover.

Haska sucked in a breath that tasted dry and bitter. A cloud of rockcrete dust hung in the air, thick as wet-season fog. Haska grinned at the sight of Katryn and Lira's olive features coated with a fine layer of white where the powdered stone was sticking to their sweat. She raised her hand to her own face, and her fingers came away covered in the same gritty dust.

Andrysi climbed up a few yards ahead of Haska, and turned

with one hand holding on to what looked like the back of a locker. Equipment and furniture of every description was layered into the rubble, protruding at odd angles where it had come to rest amid the collapsing building.

'All right, up.' She led by example, throwing her shot-cannon over one shoulder.

The sounds of battle slashed and coughed and chattered from the gate above them. The instinct to stop here, to cringe back from the strange and unfamiliar, returned. Haska turned, and saw that she was at the head of the crowd of Spoilers, all waiting for their turn to climb. All seized by the same fear.

Haska shrugged the autogun's sling over her head, and pulled it tight until she felt the weapon press hard against her back. Then she started to climb.

CHAPTER 24

The silence endured for moments, before the church erupted.

'Saitz, what is this?'

'What have you done?'

'You madman!'

Every member of the gangers' conclave was on their feet, shouting accusations and recriminations, but Melita's attention was fixed on the hololith.

She recognised the distinct form of a Cratos giga-hauler, each one of its carriages large enough to hold three ground-cars abreast. The hololith blurred in a way that Melita recognised as the skull panning, turning to focus its sensors on a new and distant target – the colossal shape of the Prae-torian's Gate, the entryway into the heart of Setomir.

Saitz continued, speaking over those who shouted him down. 'As we speak, an army gathers. It is united by pur-pose, not bribery or fear. They see, as I see, that this will be the dawning of a new day for the Spoil. We will take back what is rightfully ours.'

Though the hololith was awash with static, Melita thought she could see figures leaping from the flanks of the Cratos into groundcars keeping pace alongside. The vehicles suddenly braked and fell back out of the recording servo-skull's field of view. The hauler itself started to shrink in the feed, as it outpaced the skull.

'Join me in this great endeavour. Under Sorokin, we were bound together by fear, slaves to the scraps tossed to us by his masters. Now, let us become a brotherhood of the free!'

The giga-hauler thundered into the gate. Saitz's declaration fell into stunned silence, as every person present watched the world change.

Steel and rockcrete shattered beneath the Cratos' titanic bulk. The carriages heaved, bursting into splinters of metal as they tried to force the hauler's drive-unit further into the hollowed-out shell of the eastern tower. Then the projected feed flashed, bathing St Eurydice's statues and frescos with cobalt light. When the image returned, the giga-hauler was wreckage, and the Praetorian's Gate a shattered, broken thing. The first gangers were already visible, clambering over the rubble in a frenzy.

Saitz turned, arms raised, flushed and victorious. There was a wildness to him, his movements jerky. But the shock receded, eclipsed by the triumph that galvanised his wavering voice. His gaze lifted towards the private box, seeming to look Vasimov directly in the eye.

'The people of the Spoil have but one demand. Cede to us what you stole.'

'Shoot him,' said Vasimov.

The cartel's contingent had been just as rapt as the Har Dhrol, but Vasimov's order broke the spell.

The securitor stepped from the balustrade, his clenched fists the only sign of his fury. Nedovic took his place at the balcony, and levelled his lasgun.

A pair of shots, muted by stone walls and heavy ironwood, made Melita turn. Bodies struck the floor outside their box, and something hard rapped against the wooden door.

Edi hit Melita at a run, hurling her to the floor. In the same moment, shot-cannon blasts turned the door to splinters, and gangers burst inside.

CHAPTER 25

Haska was just a few yards from the mound's summit when she met her first enemy.

He was lying upside down, half-buried in the rubble. The back of his head was a black, viscous mess. She froze.

He didn't look so different to the faces she saw on the street each day. A bit better fed, perhaps. His skin was bone-white, but dark underneath the dust. His green Grenze Guard uniform jacket was torn at the neck, revealing a patch of bare chest. The exposed skin seemed strangely intimate, more so than the terrible damage to his head.

Someone below shouted at her to keep moving. She tore her gaze away, and hauled herself up the final feet. The climb had been a nightmare of jagged spurs of metal and rough stone, and her palms were raw and bleeding.

Finally, with her arms trembling, she felt something new, smooth and unyielding. It was the surface of the arterial, still warm with the day's heat. Haska gripped something, stumbled when the loose chuck of rock came free, then reached up again and hauled herself onto the roadway.

She rolled onto her back, and looked up at the open levels of the tower directly above her. Papers, dust, and debris of every kind fluttered from the rooms that were suddenly open to the elements, caught in the weak breeze. Andrysi was ahead of her, kneeling in the lee of an enormous heap of grey-black rockcrete. With undeserved luck, the south-west corner of the tower had crashed down bare yards from the arterial's edge, creating a barrier just taller than Haska that would shield the climbing fighters from the wrath of the gate's defenders. The sound of fighting lapped over the heap of cracked rebar. Up close, the high-pitched squeal of heavy lasweapons made Haska's teeth ache.

Haska climbed to her feet, and took the chance to step onto a hunk of debris and tentatively peer over the top of the cover.

Battle's fury enveloped her, deafening and awful. Rifles chattered, men and women shrieked in pain and anger, and the constant whine-snap of las-fire overlaid everything.

She ducked back, having seen nothing at all. A fire was burning inside the hauler's wreckage, taking up most of the road's width, and her eyes had not seen past the flames. Haska rose, more slowly, and took in the battleground of the Praetorian's Gate.

The gate itself was enormous, a vast slab of iron ten yards tall and thirty across. The colossal metal face loomed above her, the spread wings of the Imperial aquila flickering orange and red in the light of the flames where it wasn't obscured by smoke. It evidently retracted into the road's surface to permit passage, although it would never do so again.

The giga-hauler had struck the Praetorian's Gate at the edge nearest Haska. Either the titanic force of the hauler's impact

or the monumental explosion of its engines had punched a
dent in the thick plates of metal. A space, perhaps two yards
wide, was visible between the gate's edge and the remnants
of the tower's face.

That space was under continuous fire from the intact
western tower. More bodies than Haska could quickly count
lay in a carpet running towards the gap, although bodies
was too generous a description for the broken ruins that
continued to be struck by wild shots whenever any Spoiler
made a run for the opening.

The brave and foolish souls making the attempt were
emerging from the remains of the giga-hauler's cargo units,
which were all that stood between the undamaged tower
and the main bulk of the Spoil's army. There were at least
two hundred people behind the overturned trailers, frightened figures huddling together in the darkness. Half a dozen
black-clad gangers were trying to urge men and women out
into the fight, but it was clear that none were making it
through. The Spoil's attack had relied on surprise and sudden,
overwhelming momentum, but now it had stalled in the face
of the Grenzers' constant, desperate defence.

Something grabbed Haska's belt and hauled her from her
vantage point.

'Get down!' Andrysi released her. 'We're in defilade here.' She
gestured at the dark interior of the shattered tower. 'If there's
a way through to the other side of the gate through the tower,
we can get round them without even having to fight.' The
woman set off, without waiting to see if Haska was following.

Lira, Katryn and Aryat had made the climb, and together
they set off after the ganger. Haska and her friends ran in a
crouch along the narrow stretch of paving between the fallen
rockcrete and the sheer drop that promised a bloody end to
any who missed their footing.

The darkness inside the tower was almost total. As her eyes adjusted, Haska realised they had entered through an ablutorial; broken tiles were scattered underfoot, and there was a reek of cracked plumbing. Aryat led them towards the room's exit, which took them into a narrow corridor. Haska tried not to be distracted by the signs of life and occupation that had survived the giga-hauler's impact. She felt the press of bodies at her back, and not just her crew. More Spoilers were reaching the summit of the artificial slope each moment. Some were winded from the climb, and others were clearly intending to huddle in the ablutorial and wait out the fighting. But more joined the single-file string of fighters that was working its way into the tower, following Haska for no better reason than the age-old human herd instinct.

They caught up with Andrysi at the bottom of a wide stairway. The corridor beyond was blocked, and she knelt at the foot of the staircase with her shot-cannon covering the summit.

She whispered. 'Up, two at a time. Watch the corners.'

The staircase turned back on itself. Haska and Lira let fighters flow past them, then set off to seek any way through to another route back down.

They searched each level, ducking into offices, a refec-hall, and dormitories holding three-high tiered beds. The roof of one such room had collapsed, and Haska felt her stomach churn at the sight of arms and legs protruding from beneath slabs of rebar.

There were other bodies, strewn beside or more often pinned beneath mounds of broken building. If any Grenzer had lived through the giga-hauler's annihilation, they had fled the broken tower before Andrysi's force had made their ascent.

On the fifth level, fluttering shadows on the far wall

crowned the staircase. The steps abruptly ended, and the exterior wall gave way to the madness in front of the Praetorian's Gate. There was no way to climb higher.

Andrysi was at their shoulder. 'Cover the gap.'

Aryat and Katryn ran past her and crouched at the corner, their weapons levelled towards the sounds of battle.

'You, check that way.'

One of Boscan's crew ran in an awkward crouch to the far end of the corridor, evidently hoping to see another route up to the level above. But even from where Haska stood, she could see that the fallen masonry had blocked the hallway's end. The juve looked back, shaking his head.

'Shit.'

'There's a way up,' said Haska. She was staring at the jagged edge of the tower's ruined wall. She could see it, more or less, through the pulsating bursts of light and shadow that rent the darkness. There was a route of hand- and foot-holds up the exposed rebar and onto the level above.

'What?'

'There.'

Andrysi followed Haska's gaze, evidently seeing the same path she did. Then they both ducked as a hail of rounds cut the air above them.

'You wouldn't make it.' It was no more than eight or nine feet, but any climber would be in full view of the defenders in the western tower.

Haska looked around. Dozens of Spoilers had followed them up, and were huddled behind whatever cover they could find, clinging to the dubious solidity of walls and furniture, or just the body of the person beside them.

'I can do it.'

This was what Haska had wanted. Lying in her hab, sitting in a joy house, the countless, interminable hours she had wasted in bitter doubt, had been spent waiting for this moment. For a chance to step forward and be seen.

Andrysi looked at her, seeing her resolve. Someone had to make the attempt. 'Once you're up there, look for a way for us to join you.'

Haska nodded.

'We'll cover you.' The ganger turned, and started pointing at frightened faces. 'You, you, you and you. Get over here.'

Haska rested her autogun against a fallen cabinet, and stripped off her jacket. The heavy novaplas would only slow her down. There was a rustle of material beside her as Lira followed her motions.

'No.'

Lira grabbed her, thin fingers hard around her forearm. 'The hells I'm not.'

'Two people will draw more fire.'

'Then I'll do it.'

'I said no!' Haska shouted. 'I have to do this.'

Lira's eyes were wide, full of unfamiliar fear and desperation. 'And I can't lose you.'

Haska grasped a fistful of Lira's shirt and kissed her. Her lips tasted of dust and sweat. For the heartbeat instant that Lira's body softened into hers, there was nothing else in the world.

She shoved Lira back into Katryn and Aryat's arms. 'Don't let her follow me!' She threw her autogun over her shoulder, spun, and ran for the first step.

From behind her, Andrysi bellowed. 'Covering fire!'

A storm of hard rounds erupted from the broken stairwell, hammering the far tower's embrasure, but Haska was aware of none of it. Her boot ground against the loose grit on the first step, the second, and then she leapt for the rebar. She caught the rusted metal, flakes jagged against her palms. She heaved, feet scrabbling at the wall, and heaved again. She made it to the next pillar of shattered masonry, tottered, and pulled herself towards the next outcrop.

A heavy stubber sprayed rounds towards her, but only blasted chips of rockcrete free above her head. The fragments rained down on Haska, wickedly sharp. She screamed, but kept climbing, hauling herself up with desperate speed.

The wall's surface vanished, and her hand found the flat, carpeted floor of the level above. Arms and legs and chest all screaming with the effort, Haska threw herself up. With the last burst of fading strength, she swung a leg, found a toehold, and pulled herself in through the gap.

She rolled onto her back, agony pulsing from every limb, every nerve in her body. Her hands were bleeding, her fingernails torn away. Something hot and sticky was in her eye, but she didn't have the energy to raise her hand to wipe it clear. Bullets slashed the dust, but they couldn't reach her. Or perhaps they could; she had nothing left in her to move either way. Her breath sawed in and out, acrid with the dust. Stars burst in her eyes, and her head swam.

But she was up.

It took more effort than she'd ever known to lift her shoulder and roll herself further into cover. She forced herself to stand, arms and legs screaming with cramp.

She was in the remains of an overseer's office. She could make out dark green carpet, torn and dust-caked, and the remnants of a desk, cogitator, and whatever else upclave types filled their working spaces with. There was a pillar near each corner of the room, and they were clearly the only things that had stopped the ceiling from collapsing.

The south face of the office had fallen away with the rest of the tower. The view was incredible; Haska could see for miles into the Spoil's interior. Patches of darkness and light marked where the Har Dhrol's influence extended, or else where the claves themselves had set up generatoria as a shield against the many threats that hid in the night. The silhouette of the Redfort rose into the orange-grey smear that was the sky.

Haska carefully stepped towards the void in the wall. With one hand gripping a knurl of rockcrete, she looked out over the edge.

A dizzying drop yawned below. There was nothing between Haska and the bottom of the valley from which the Spoil fighters had climbed. A gust of wind made her fall to her knees, suddenly fearful that she would be sucked out into the empty air, or else that the office would follow the rest of the building and topple down onto the bloodstained scrubland.

From her position near the top of the wrecked tower, she had a better view of the hundreds of men and women sheltering behind the hauler's broken bulk. It was clear that they still had not made any progress; the guns of the western tower dominated the blood-soaked stretch of road before the gate. Below her, there were still Spoilers climbing up the scree, and more were lined up with their backs against the fallen rockcrete.

She needed to let the others know she'd made it.

'Hey! Hey!' She swung her autogun around her body and loosed a burst of shots into the night; the first she had fired since the battle had been joined.

Katryn's head appeared, looking up at her from the floor below, her smile beaming through the grime that coated her face. 'Haska!'

'I know! Tell Andrysi!'

There was a bundle of cables, half as thick as her wrist, curling from a plastek cover that lined the eastern wall of the office. Haska ran over and pulled, and a length came free. She stumbled, and pulled again. More and more cable came free, until finally there was resistance. With a firm yank, she tore the wires from the broken wall.

Haska pulled the snaking bundle of multicoloured cables across the floor. It was at least thirty feet long. She had no idea how best to secure it, so she just wrapped one end around the closest pillar, knotted it inexpertly, and prayed with an intensity she had never felt before that it would hold. She paid out a length and threw it into the void.

The first person up was Lira. Haska took her friend's hand and pulled her the rest of the way. They both stumbled as Lira found her feet, and they fell against one another. Haska pulled away, embarrassed.

'I don't–'

'Later.' Lira smiled, and pushed Haska's autogun into her hands.

Andrysi had been behind Lira, and more Spoil fighters followed, breath rasping from the effort of scaling Haska's make-shift rope. The ganger had to take her own moment of respite, then started pointing fighters to the far side of the room.

'Get over there and get their attention. Short bursts, and keep your heads down.'

The crackle of autoguns started up almost immediately. It sounded like a dust-dry thicket of steelthorn set on fire. Lira and Haska waited until Aryat and Katryn made it up the cable, then the four of them ran to join the fight.

Las and hard rounds chewed the rockcrete, and the air above their heads. They had succeeded in splitting the tower's fire, but the Grenzers had guns enough to fight on two fronts. Haska's crew popped up every few moments to loose bursts of fire across the narrow gap, but with little effect. The gate tower was crowned by a wider top, which was broken by a thin balcony that ran the length of the flank that Haska could see. Heavy weapons had been mounted at intervals inside the embrasure, and were raking the wreckage of the giga-hauler and anywhere else a Spoiler dared to show themselves.

Haska ducked down to reload. Her arm already ached; each shot punched the autogun's butt into the tender meat of her shoulder.

Andrysi thumped into cover beside Haska and Lira, boots crunching on the rubble. Another flak-armoured ganger was with her, carrying a green metal tube the length and thickness of his arm. Andrysi took it from him, and connected a length of wire from a panel on its side to somewhere at its end. Then she passed it back, and took a few steps into the room's interior.

'What can we do?' asked Lira.

Leonida Andrysi grinned, as the ganger lifted the tube to his shoulder. 'Cover your ears.'

The rocket leapt the short distance and was swallowed by the embrasure. There was a loud bang, a puff of smoke, and then a colossal gout of flame burst out of the casement, hot enough to crisp Haska's hair as she ducked down behind the ruined wall. She looked back, autogun scraping on the window's edge.

Black smoke poured from the gate tower's top. Something moved in the roiling cloud, and then a shrieking figure, hair and clothes ablaze, fell from the embrasure. Their scream ended with a grim crunch that Haska should not have been able to hear, but did.

Behind her, Aryat cheered; he hadn't seen the falling Grenzer.

Beneath them, the army that had been held back by the tower's guns surged forward. A few defenders still fired, but with none of the fearsome power or weight of the emplaced guns that had been reduced to twisted ruin.

Haska saw the running crowd, heard the cheers as they reached the far side, and slumped back against the broken wall. She was exhausted. All strength seemed to leave her.

Her stomach roiled, but nothing came up. Even vomiting would be more effort than she could imagine.

'Throwing down that cable was a piece of quick thinking.'

Andrysi stood over her, the empty tube of the rocket leant against her leg.

'You were in the Guard, right?' Haska blurted out. 'You were. You've done this before.'

The smile faded. 'I was, and I did.' Andrysi gave a huge sigh, and looked across at the smoking gate tower. 'Hadn't planned on doing it again.'

'So why did you?'

She gave Haska a hard, appraising stare. 'For the same reason as you.'

She offered her hand to Haska, who took it, and was hauled to her feet without apparent effort.

'Let's keep moving. The fight's just beginning.'

CHAPTER 26

The Kadern of the Har Dhrol were not fools. Each clave-captain had been allowed five lieutenants and bodyguards to accompany them inside the walls of St Eurydice's seminary – sufficient to make them feel moderately safe, but not so many that the regents' own men did not heavily outnumber each praetor that had answered the summons. It was a wise precaution, but predictable.

Damor Saitz had made his plans with care. It only took a few allies, like-minded praetors who saw the truth in the unassuming clave-captain's fervent words, to tip the scales towards his design. As Harol Toskanov began to speak, a dozen gangers, men and women who killed as easily as others breathed, peeled away from their clave-captains and made their way out into the fragile darkness. They crossed the seminary grounds between the church and the encircling boundary wall in a silent sprint, and entered the honeycombed structure through a doorway left unlocked for their purpose.

They slaughtered all they encountered. Kiren Rasyn,

warden of St Eurydice's and loyal to Sorokin even beyond his death, died with a blade across his throat in a grim echo of his king's murder. His crew were similarly butchered, their bodies tossed from the gatehouse windows or else left where they fell. Their deaths were the signal to the scores of Red Knives, Pit Snakes, Breccia's Chosen, and other impatient street-blades lurking on the edges of the Saint's Square to flood inside and complete Saitz's coup.

Saitz had sent the most trusted members of his alliance to secure the gatehouse. The rest had been dispatched to kill the Valtteri interlopers in their midst.

Melita hit her head as Edi tackled her to the floor. Stars burst before her eyes, and one half of her skull blazed with agony along the faultline of her scar. Weapons snapped above her, punctuated by the heavy pounding of Edi's hand-cannon.

She rolled over, gripping her head with both hands. It felt like the bones of her skull were splitting apart. Above her, around her, lasguns snapped and hard rounds cracked, but Melita saw none of it. She felt blood trickle from a cut to her forehead.

As the worst of the pain passed, Melita opened her eyes, blinking through tears. Vasimov had been pushed down onto the far side of the balcony, and one of the mercenaries stood over him in the same way that Edi shielded Melita with his body. Nedovic lay between them, firing from the floor, his back pressed against the square-cut supports of the balustrade. Oriel hovered above her, awaiting her order to engage their attackers.

Through the white wall of pain lancing through her brain, Melita opened her iris. With a sharp wave of her hand, she targeted every human biorhythm beyond the balcony's shattered doorway and ordered Oriel to open fire.

The subtle click of the servo-skull's needler was lost beneath the crash of Edi's hand-cannon. In seconds, he and the Reisiger men ceased fire. Oriel returned to its mute vigilance above Melita.

'Are you hit?' Edi was on his knees beside her. She shook her head, and a wave of nausea joined the spike of pain that drove into her temple.

Edi hauled Melita to her feet, grunting with the effort. She looked around, still dazed. One of the mercenaries was down, a horrendous wound torn from the side of his head. Her senses seemed to snap back into focus, and she noticed her palm was wet where she leant on Edi's chest.

'Holy Throne, you're bleeding!'

His coat was awash with blood, pouring from a narrow hole in his shoulder. 'I'll be all right.' He pushed Melita ahead of him.

'We have to seal it.'

'I'll be fine. What we have to do is get out of here.'

In the brief moment before Edi shoved her up the balcony's steps, Melita glanced over the railing at the chaos below. The apse was a riot of overlapping gunfire. Saitz and his allies, whoever they were – Melita could not believe a minor clave-captain could orchestrate a putsch of this scale alone – had cut down many of the assembled praetors, and more gangers were racing into the church's nave to finish what they had begun. Parviz Dragović was still alive, sheltering behind the heavy bulk of an upturned pew and thumping stub-rounds into anything that moved.

Melita spotted Amadan, Toskanov and Iliev. They had fallen in the centre of the square of benches, no weapons in their hands. Las and hard rounds buzzed through the air above their broken bodies.

One of Nedovic's men was at the private box's door, lasgun

levelled, but it seemed as though Saitz had underestimated the strength of Vasimov's guard. Although not by much – every one of them had taken a wound before the gangers had fallen. Only Vasimov and Melita were unharmed.

Nedovic, who had a hard round lodged in his thigh, set his helmet straight and pressed the vox-emitter to his ear. He listened for a moment, then pulled Vasimov upright.

'Sir, we have to go.'

Vasimov nodded. If he was shaken by the sudden violence, he gave no sign. 'Skala, Černy, take the lead.'

They piled out of the box, and ran at such speed as Nedovic could manage. Melita felt the urge to look everywhere at once, sensing ambush at every alcove and junction, until she registered Oriel's familiar presence at her shoulder. She reopened her iris, and hooked its scanner feed into a corner of her vision.

She still had an open vox-link with Russov Bai. She had no idea how far their quarters in the seminary extended, but she had only seen the one door.

> Magos, if you have not yet fled, you must do so now.

If Bai received her message, they sent no reply.

The fighting in the nave was barely audible, but as they reached the aisle's end a dull crump travelled through the church's stone that made Melita's heart sink. Vasimov put a finger to the micro-bead in his ear as he ran.

'Molchanov, report.'

Melita had no micro-bead, but her iris fed vox signals directly to her cochlea. She opened the standard frequency used by the Reisiger combine.

'–are heavily engaged. Sigil Four *has been destroyed.*'

'What strength?'

There was a delay before the reply came through, overlaid with the snap of las-fire. '*Significant. The compound's gates are open.*'

'The other aircars?'

'Inbound, two minutes.'

The aisle opened onto a wide corridor that Melita thought ran around the southern end of the church. Any gangers, hostile or otherwise, had wisely run at the sound of approaching strangers. Melita called up Oriel's scans of St Eurydice's interior, and pointed towards a stone arch that opened onto one of the many spiral staircases that wound through the church's ribs. The stairs led to the nave, and Vasimov sent two men down ahead of them.

If they had hoped for any kind of stealth, they were betrayed by their laboured breathing and grunts of restrained pain. Nedovic was sweating, and his limp was becoming pronounced. To Melita's complete surprise, Vasimov lifted the man's arm and draped it over his shoulder, and helped him down the narrow stairs.

A wooden door stood opposite the staircase's end, and the two mercenaries stood with their weapons trained on it. Once the last of their party had made their way down, one of them darted across the corridor.

'Wait.' Oriel's auspex had detected the powercell of a lasweapon on the far side, and Melita's iris had thrown up a warning. She mimed levelling a rifle, and pointed at the heavy wooden door.

St Eurydice's seminary had been built at least five hundred years before Andreti Sorokin had claimed it for his own. The wood for its pews, altars and doorways had been hewn from a grove that had been blessed by Arch-Cardinal Láska, on a world that lay far, far from the faded might of Alecto's star. It had crossed the vastness of humanity's empire in the hold of a vessel whose construction exceeded the impossible dreams of the species' ancient forebears, in order that it might honour the holy saint and the generations of faithful scholars who would be trained within her seminary's walls.

Edi's hand-cannon and the combined weight of four lasguns punched through the ancient wood, blasting a hailstorm of priceless splinters into the hapless ganger who lay in ambush.

Hot night air and the Spoil's reek were waiting for them, along with over a hundred men and women locked in a pitched battle. Flames curled from the broken frame of one of the Teridons – *Sigil Four*, Melita assumed – and gangers in colours and uniforms of every description advanced beneath the glare of the aquila that crowned the church's face. Reisiger mercenaries were in cover behind thick stone buttresses and a clutch of outbuildings nestled in the enclave's expansive grounds.

As Melita emerged, another of the Reisiger Teridons swooped overhead. One of Vasimov's men stood at the aircar's open rear door, spitting heavy fire from the interior that shattered the courtyard's paving slabs and hammered ruinous wounds into grey-clad bodies.

'Bring them in!' Vasimov shouted into his micro-bead.

The mercenaries were fighting a holding action, no more. The two sides were evenly matched, but would not be for long. The Reisiger mercenaries were better trained, working in pairs to cut down charging gangers, watching out for one another as they lined up each shot. But the Har Dhrol gangers – Saitz's gangers, now – had superior numbers, and some had comparable equipment. Every other man or woman charging across the seminary's courtyard was not clad in the eclectic styles of the Spoil's various gangs, but instead was bulked out by flak armour and held weapons that looked strangely uniform to Melita's eye.

The scream of overworked turbines announced the Teridons' approach. Two were landing, as close as the pilots dared to the church's black stone walls. The third remained overhead, the punishingly deep crumps of an autocannon marking a grim backbeat to the engines' howl.

Something streaked up from the courtyard's gatehouse, tracing a hazy line of smoke.

The rocket struck the hovering Teridon in the centre of its open ramp. The gunner disappeared in an instant, immolated by the fireball that burst from its interior. The aircar dropped like a stone. The pilot dipped its nose, using the last gasps of thrust to angle the terminal flyer away from the other two Teridons that were touching down.

Melita watched in horror as the aircar fell. The plex-enclosed cockpit crumpled instantly, sparing the pilot from the explosion that followed. The night was banished as the Teridon's fuel ignited. The fire roared like an apex predator as liquid promethium sheeted from the ruptured tank, drawing an impassable inferno across the compound's courtyard.

'Run!'

The dying aircar had given them time, creating a barrier no ganger would be willing to cross. The other Teridons were down, their rear gates juddering open on hissing hydraulics. Vasimov set off, all trace of dignity and reserve abandoned. Melita was on his heels, driven on by Edi's hand in the small of her back.

Vasimov ran for the closest aircar, and Melita followed. A gust of wind lifted the promethium flames, carrying heat that stung her face like a spray of scalding water. Melita threw up an arm to shield herself and she shied away. She found herself heading for the farther Teridon, but ran on regardless.

There was a grunt behind her, and Edi's hand fell away. Melita leapt the final steps, and tumbled into the aircar's interior. She rolled onto her back and looked out at the firelit courtyard.

Edi Kamensk was lying face down on the paving, no more than twenty yards away. He wasn't moving.

'Edi!'

Melita struggled to her feet, but a mercenary's restraining hand closed on her shoulder. She tried to shake him off, but irresistible force pressed her into a seat.

Her hand slapped at a micro-bead that wasn't there, terror stealing all thought of her iris and its array of functions. 'We have to get him!'

Melita saw Nedovic angle his own limping run towards Edi, but his leg finally gave out, and he crumpled to the ground beside him.

Vasimov's flyer was closer to the fallen men. Skala and Černy rushed out of the Teridon, lasguns cracking at the gangers who had advanced as close as they dared to the burning fuel. Melita sent Oriel to join them, suspensors whining as its needler spat a hail of darts at the few gangers who were willing to brave the flames.

The two men reached Edi and Nedovic, and one of them dropped to his knees to continue firing. The mercenary captain let the other help him to his feet but then he hobbled on alone, pointing at Edi's prone form. Skala and Černy slung their guns, and lifted the old sanctioner between them. Oriel followed, covering their retreat with yet more neurotoxic shards.

A shot-cannon punched out a spray of slugs, its report deeper than the dry-twig snap of Reisiger lasguns and the cough of the gangers' autoguns. The cone of shot lashed through the flames and struck Oriel in a shower of sparks and splintered bone. The skull dropped instantly, its silver leer deformed by the impact.

Melita let out a scream of primal anger. She pulled free of the mercenary's grip, lurched out of the aircar's interior with her laspistol in hand, and stabbed death at every ganger she could see. Each shot was matched by a snarl of fury, a keen of pain, a moan of anguish. The pistol's charge pack whined empty, but still Melita tried to fire.

Skala and Černy, Edi's slack form held between them, reached Vasimov's aircar in the same moment that gloved hands hauled Melita back inside her flyer. Melita pressed herself against the tiny viewport in the Teridon's flank. She couldn't lose Edi too.

'Vasimov? Vasimov, is he alive?'

Melita's panicked cries into the vox went unanswered. Her stomach lurched as the flyer leapt into the air.

INTERLUDE

Major Argus Ranić was in the air when Setomir fell into darkness.

He had been staring out of the aircar's passenger viewport ever since the flyer had lurched free of its landing platform. He clutched the sheaf of wafer-thin papers that had been thrust into his hands by a mute, unblinking figure who had disappeared into the promenade's swirling crowd as swiftly as he had appeared. Ranić was about to open the plastek wallet to read them again, to confirm that the time of his testing really had come, when he became aware of the change that had swept across the world.

Below him, where there should have been a kaleido-scopic field of light stretching to the horizon, there was only yawning blackness.

Sudden dread threatened to take hold, born of a primal fear. A change to something known to be unchangeable. The unimagined absence of the familiar.

No, not a complete absence. As Ranić's eyes adjusted to the

sudden gloom, he could make out broken, indistinct lines of light, running like veins through the night. They were arterial roadways and busy streets, sketched against the darkness by groundcar headlamps. Each vehicle was a tiny iridescent insect following the paths of a vast, multilevelled nest. Here and there were tight knots of light, isolated beacons within the black. Ranić was able to identify the imposing form of the enforcers' Bastion to the east, the illuminated spires of the Basilicum Lateransus to the north, and the winking navigation beacons that climbed the flanks of the vast starscrapers at the heart of Setomir's corrupted mass.

This intellectual challenge, locating the few structures that had not succumbed to the cataclysmic power outage that had struck the district, allowed Ranić to regain his self-control.

She had done it.

He had never doubted. Not since he had faced those haunting, void-black eyes, which burned with a fire that went beyond passion, beyond devotion. He was ashamed of his scepticism when he had first been brought before her, mystified as to how his wife had obtained an invitation to such an exclusive gathering. But once he saw her, heard her, he had believed.

The memory unfolded all at once. The dark orbs, unyielding, unwavering. The agony of the brand, sealing his allegiance to this woman who had seen the truth that lay behind the Imperium's lies. Who had revealed to him the hypocrisy of the Ecclesiarchy's unquestionable gospel. Ranić clutched his chest as the mark she had placed within his flesh began to throb in sympathy with the recollected pain. There was no physical blemish or impression – he had torn open his shirt to look for one many times, when the needle stabbed and he felt her touch upon him.

She had taken Ranić into her trust. Shared her vision. He

would not falter now that he was called upon to fulfil his part of her design.

Below, more lumens were reappearing, bursting into strained brilliance as local and emergency generatoria took up the unexpected burden. Ranić stared down through the viewport, ignoring the flicking lights in favour of the emptiness between them. That was where the truth was found, she had told him. Not among the gaudy decadence of the city's decaying edifices and its miserable, suppurating masses, but in the darkness, in the space between the stars, where only the brave dared to tread.

He had shared her vision with his men. First his closest officers, those comrades who had been with him since the first days of cadet training. Then they had worked together, disciples bound by secret faith, sharing the revelations and forbidden words she gave to him alone. After many months of furtive discussion and whispered oaths, every man and woman under Ranić's command was a loyal adherent, trusting Ranić as he trusted her.

More flashes of colour caught his eye. Brief bursts of orange and red boiled into the night, or else settled and began to slowly spread. Flames, Ranić realised, either spontaneous or the work of her agents.

'Sir,' his pilot said shakily, through the aircar's vox-link. 'Setomir.'

Ranić settled himself in his seat, and tried to calm his racing pulse. 'On to the barracks, Cedrich.'

There was much to be done.

PART 4

CHAPTER 27

Whatever discipline Saitz's makeshift army had possessed had been lost the moment the gate was breached. Haska had watched from a shattered window in the eastern gate tower as men and women, flush with unfamiliar victory and the rush of survival, raced away in all directions. The wide, dark expanse of the Binastri Arterial stretched away to the north, and the Spoil's fighters had run to see what they had won.

The Grenze Guard had been utterly routed. Though the night was disturbed by the background snap and clatter of gunfire, as far as Haska could tell they were shots of celebration rather than battle. The defenders of the Praetorian's Gate were dead to a man. Those who had been posted to the wall turrets had either retreated or died, although the few who had stood their ground had taken many Spoilers with them. Haska had seen one group of fighters – street-blades from the Black Canids, going by the stiff tufts of fur pinned to their leathers – gathering ropes and cables to hang some of the bodies from the wall. She had steered her crew well away from them.

While the rest of the Spoil's army rampaged, Haska and her friends walked east between slab-sided storehouses and animal pens, following their curiosity by the glow of stolen stablights.

Boscan's crew fell in with them as they drifted away from the gate's ruin. At first Haska watched them nervously, fearful that they would take the opportunity to finish what they had started so many hours before. But it quickly became clear that the battle had changed Boscan and his juves, just as much as it had Haska's crew. In this alien place which they had won, there was comfort in the familiar, even if both crews were more used to glaring at one another with knives in hand.

Haska's friends certainly felt the elation that had gripped the army. Katryn and Aryat grinned as they walked hand in hand, weapons slung across their thin bodies. They had fought, they had lived, and they walked where no Spoiler had ever been – at least, not without being shot at while doing it.

Haska was more sombre. She replayed every moment of the battle in her head, seeing herself as though from outside her body. The pulse-pounding run across the slope. The fearful climb to the gate itself.

Kissing Lira, before leaping to what she had believed was her death.

She and Lira walked apart from one another, each embarrassed and awkward. Haska caught Lira shooting glances her way, but in the dark it was impossible to tell what she was thinking.

The Line plunged into darkness about an hour after the Praetorian's Gate fell. All at once, the lumen strips and tall sodium lamps that stood at the crossroads between each sheet-metal building failed, and crushing blackness swallowed them. Haska had no idea if it had been accidental or by design, but if anything the whoops and screams of Saitz's volunteer soldiers only rose louder.

They continued to wander, running their hands along corrugated metal cladding and trying to make sense of the signs that marked each doorway and intersection. Almost at random, they stopped in the shadow of an enormous white oblong, easily twice the height of Haska's hab-block. Vast Gothic runes stencilled across one face proclaimed it to be under the ownership of Dalibor Agri-Tech. No crew appeared to have found it yet, and, without any debate, they decided that this building contained their prize, whatever that might be.

The nearest service door was locked, but Aryat had claimed one of the Grenzer lasguns as a trophy during the battle's aftermath. One shot turned the lock and bolt to slag. A second burned right through the thin metal.

The smell, ripe and entirely unfamiliar, struck them as they pushed the door open. It was rich, thick in their nostrils, easily overwhelming the seared ozone waft of the fired lasgun.

It rose from the plants.

The building was hollow, its walls a thin shell to define a cavernous interior that stretched up and away from Haska and her friends, who ventured inside with weapons raised. The darkness was broken by the harsh glare of emergency lumens, which cast their light over hundreds of precise, ordered rows, stacked in tiers that reached from floor to ceiling, from one side of the massive agri-plex to the other.

The juves walked over to the nearest row, almost fearful of their discovery.

'What are they?' asked one of Boscan's friends.

'I have no idea,' Haska replied.

Each plant was a thick green vine, the length of Haska's arm. Strung out along each sinuous coil were fruits; or, at least, Haska guessed that was what they were. Each one was the size of her clenched fist. The taut red skin seemed almost swollen, but there was a glossy sheen to them that suggested health and vitality.

Katryn reached out and plucked one from the vine. She held it in both hands, and with her thumbs pushed until it burst open. Red juice spilled out, covering her hands. The smell reached Haska instantly, and she broke into a smile. She pulled one off the vine for herself, split it in two, and bit into the flesh.

It was... She didn't have the words. Nothing in her life had ever prepared her to describe it. It was sweet, but completely different from the chemical sweetness of a carb-bar. Tart, enough to make the back of her mouth ache. Haska took another bite, savouring the sensation of sticky juice dribbling down her chin.

All of them were smiling, giggling like children. Aryat was pulling the fruits from the vine two at a time and stuffing them into his pockets beside his knife and pistol. Boscan had flicked open his own knife and was cutting whole bunches free from the trunk of the vine.

Haska looked up and around the enormous building. The emergency lumens, stark against the dark ceiling, ran the length of the growing racks and above the metal gantries, where even now servitors rattled from one vine to the next, oblivious to the change in ownership Haska and her fellow Spoilers had won. There must have been ten levels at least, each of them groaning under the weight of green vines, black soil and red fruit. Hundreds of thousands of the sweet fruits, and this was just one building amongst hundreds.

'Hey, don't waste it!' Katryn called. She was joking, but Haska realised she had crushed the last of her fruit in her hand. Sticky juice and pulp oozed between her fingers.

She was trembling with rage. It flared up out of nowhere, sudden and ferocious. It was different from the battle anger that had driven her across the scrub, up the face of the gate tower. That had been desperate, frenzied madness, with no thought behind it at all. This was cold, calculated rage, born of intellect rather than emotion.

They had had to kill just to see this place. To know that it existed. Hundreds of Spoilers had died without even knowing that this was the prize. And there were hundreds more agri-complexes like it. Probably thousands, if they stretched the full length of the Line. Haska had the sudden urge, almost painful to resist, to pull down the vines. To tear them to green shreds, to stamp on the fruit until it ran like blood into the sluices. The unfairness was like a physical weight dropped upon her shoulders. She thrust a hand into the soil, fingers curled like claws, feeling the unfamiliar touch of wet earth and questing tendrils. Haska gripped, arms shaking, ready to rip the vine free.

'Haska!' Her friends immediately stopped laughing. Aryat and Katryn clustered round, confusion clear.

'It's alright.' Aryat and Katryn pulled away, giving Lira space to stand beside Haska. 'It's alright.'

Her fingers encircled Haska's wrist, and gently pulled her hand from the soil. She smiled softly at the dark clumps that clung to Haska's skin.

Haska's heart was pounding, from the rage, from Lira's touch. Neither of them said anything. Tears stung Haska's eyes, and the smell of earth and growth and Lira's sweat were in her nose. Lira's fingers traced a line along Haska's bare arm. Up to her neck. Into the matted mess of her hair.

This time, Haska tasted sweet fruit, and the salt of her tears.

Someone coughed, close by.

Leonida Andrysi stood in the doorway, leaning on the jamb, a broad, unashamed grin on her face.

Haska and Lira broke apart. They had found an overseer's tiny office, and had been lying in shared, wordless joy while the world turned about them.

Andrysi's grin faded, just a little. 'Gather your crew. We need to start preparing for the counter-attack.'

Haska frowned. She had let herself forget about the fighting. The Line. Everything that was not the warmth of Lira's body pressed against hers.

'I'll get them,' Lira said. She squeezed Haska's hand, then climbed to her feet and set off into the building's interior, shouting for Katryn and the others.

Haska stood as well, conscious of Andrysi's stare. 'I–'

'None of my business,' the older woman said, her smile returning.

'That's right,' replied Haska, a little more defensively than she'd intended.

Andrysi waited while Haska shrugged on her jacket, then together they went out onto the agri-plex's wide floor. They walked in silence, Haska awkward and Andrysi amused. Andrysi reached out and plucked one of the fruits that had escaped Haska's crew's pillaging. She tucked it into a pouch on her flak armour beside her spare magazines.

'Did we turn out the lights?' asked Haska.

She nodded. 'Part of the plan. This…' She gestured at the enormous agri-plant. 'This was the reward. But the objective was the geothermal generatoria to the east. Half of Setomir runs on the Line's power.'

'What happens now?'

'Now the city takes it back.'

Haska felt herself tense. 'It doesn't have to be like that.'

'Maybe, but it's how it is. We can steal it…' Andrysi reached out and stroked a finger along one of the vines. 'We could even put the torch to it. But we can't keep it.'

Haska felt the rage return. 'So all of that at the gate. Everyone who died. That was for nothing?'

Andrysi shrugged.

'If it's futile, why fight at all?'

'To be defiant. To stand up and be seen.' Andrysi's eyes burned. 'For twenty years, I carried a lasgun and followed the standard. I've walked on three worlds. I've fought orks.' Something dark passed behind the woman's eyes, but she shook it away. 'When I was discharged, and found myself back here... Fighting's a habit, but if you do it long enough, you learn what's worth fighting for.'

Haska turned to look along the row of vines, to where Lira had caught up with the rest of her friends. Boscan and his crew were running back, lobbing the red fruit at one another like grenades.

'I understand.'

Andrysi's smile was now a sharp, hollow thing. 'Gather your crew.'

CHAPTER 28

The Valtteri cartel did not formally exist. It was a name, adopted by an association of merchant-combines and businesses to validate a hierarchy of power that was not acknowledged on any ledger or roll of incorporation. The Valtteri, as an entity unto itself, possessed no assets, nor claimed any property as its own.

But if it had, the Xeremor would have been its headquarters.

The starscraper was one of the tallest in Setomir, a mighty pillar of steel and plex that lanced almost a mile into Alecto's smog-choked skies. Most of the cartel's directors and executors maintained their primary or secondary residences within its opulent hab-levels. To support their demanded standard of living, the tower boasted fine dining, rejuvenat therapeutics, an exclusive and highly secure brothel, and every other form of comfort that the gilded mind and body could conceivably require. These nestled above, below, and alongside medicae facilities, barracks for the building's standing garrison of Reisiger mercenaries, agriponics, power generatoria to rival a large-scale manufactorum, a sanctified chapel to the Emperor in His aspect as Industry, and hundreds of dormitories for the tens of thousands of indentured servants that kept the entire edifice functioning. The Xeremor could not be called a city in miniature – that right belonged solely to the long-dead hives of Alecto's southern pole – but it was, at least, one of the greatest concentrations of wealth and power in the tri-districts.

It was to the Xeremor that the Teridons flew.

Air rushed around the aircar's hold, filling Melita's world with the howl of the wind and the drone of the engines. The two Reisiger men sharing the hold were silent; or, at least, they had nothing to say to Melita. They had ignored her frantic demands to communicate with the other Teridon since they had escaped the catastrophe at St Eurydice's. Even worse, the pilot had locked her out of the aircar's dataveil relay, presumably on Vasimov's orders. Ordinarily, Melita would have been able to bypass the securitor's pettiness, but the first time she had tried she had automatically reached for Oriel's supplementary computing power, and then her iris interface had fuzzed with tears.

The absence of her guardian servo-skull was a knife through her heart, and Edi's unknown condition worried that pain like a cyber-mastiff hauling down its prey. The two of them lying broken on the pale paving stones was all she could see. Edi's grunt of pain, and the sound of Oriel crashing to the ground, chased one another around her head. All the strength seemed to have fled her body; she sat immobile and unrestrained in the Teridon's rear, head slumped against her chest.

Fortunately, the Reisiger men's disregard was total, and they left Melita to her misery.

The aircar landed in the early hours of the morning – her iris chron would have told her precisely, but Melita was too deep into her sorrow to check. The Teridon's rear hatch hissed open almost immediately, and Melita was stunned from her self-absorption by a gust of frigid wind and the shriek of cycling turbines. One of the mercenaries unceremoniously pulled her to her feet, and she didn't resist.

They stepped out onto a landing platform somewhere in the middle of the tower – both the ground and the building's projecting spire were hidden by darkness and the thick haze of smog that pervaded even amongst Setomir's grandeur. Skirling wind snatched at her as they made the short walk from the Teridon to the open maw of the platform's hangar. For once, Melita was glad to have a restraining hand gripping her arm.

A brace of Reisiger men, all wearing well-cut but functional suits rather than the flak armour of their comrades returning from the Spoil, were waiting for her inside the hangar's door. The man at her arm artlessly deposited Melita in their midst and then turned back to the aircar.

'Your weapon.' The squad's leader held out a hand to accompany his brusque demand.

'What? Where's Vasimov? I need to speak to Edi Kamensk.'

'Your laspistol, now.'

'I want to talk to Edi!'

The man pulled a short-handled shock goad from his belt, his gloved thumb held over the activation stud. 'I'm not going to ask again.'

'Back away, all of you.'

Andela Nedovic limped across the hangar. He had shed his damaged flak jacket, but his greaves and the clothes beneath were caked in sweat, dirt and blood.

He spoke before Melita could repeat her demands. 'Kamensk is alive. He is being taken to the chirurgeons.'

'How bad?'

'I don't know.'

'Nedovic!'

'I don't know. We couldn't stop the bleeding with the Teridon's trauma kit. But he was conscious when they took him.'

'He's alive?'

'Voronova, give him your gun. You need to come with me.'

'Why?'

The man's expression was the twin of Vasimov's familiar sneer. 'You still have a job to do.'

It seemed that Nedovic's superior had lifted his vindictive punishment once they landed; Melita's iris latched on to the Xeremor's dataveil relays the moment she attempted to make the connection. A storm of information flowed in, no less buffeting than the blasts of cold air that had assailed her on the landing platform. The squad leader reached forward and tugged her laspistol from its holster. Even as Nedovic and his men pulled her towards the nearest transit-shaft, Melita was lost in her feeds.

The Xeremor's role as residence for the executors of the Valtteri cartel was only a minor aspect of its function. The majority of its two hundred and forty-seven habitable levels were taken up by the offices of its constituent merchant-combines, and all the attendant spaces they required. None of these were designed to coordinate a response to an unprecedented, district-wide calamity, but, regardless, one had been pressed into use.

The conference chamber was crowded with aides, each of them rushing to and fro in purposeful activity. The chamber was not large, intended to seat perhaps a thousand selected investors and shareholders in its gently tiered levels. The luxurious furnishings had been hastily removed and portable cogitators wheeled in, along with hundreds of operators to manage the flow of information into, and orders out from, the host of cartel officers trying to come to terms with the scale of the challenge they faced.

The room was centred on a wide dais from which speakers could expound, but which was now crowded with gilded notables desperate for answers. Half a dozen directors of the Valtteri's most powerful member organisations were leading proceedings, along with representatives of the enforcers, the Ecclesiarchy, and the other major branches of district government.

It was telling that this room, and not the vladar's palace, was the centre of the district's response. The vladar himself, Vojta Sobol, had arrived shortly after Melita, accompanied by a large and energetic staff who had immediately clashed with that of the Valtteri's directors.

Amid all this, Melita went unregarded. Nedovic's men had marched her into the conference chamber, but Vasimov, who appeared to be coordinating the activity of many of the cartel's functionaries, evidently had no role for her. She had been hustled to one side, with a Reisiger man set to guard her, and then promptly ignored.

The only positive of her captivity that Melita had to hold on to was that Edi was in the tower's medicae levels, which were surely some of the best facilities in the tri-districts. She had bombarded the chirurgeons' aides with requests for information until they had surrendered. Nedovic's trauma aid had evidently been better than he had let on, and it seemed that the medicaes had been successful in stemming the bleeding from the wound in Edi's side. Melita's attention flicked to her iris chron every few minutes, desperate for the news that he had emerged from the chirurgeons' care.

While the Valtteri could disarm and disregard her, they were powerless to stop Melita working. She had hooked into the Xeremor's manifold, and absorbed every scrap of information that came in from streams and feeds across the tri-districts. Her own feeds were fizzing, each hastily written missive from her informants adding to the picture she was building of the utter chaos that had engulfed the tri-districts.

The battle at the Line had only been the start of the night's mayhem. An hour after Dmitriy Zemskov, the Grenze Guard's district commander, had confirmed that the Praetorian's Gate was lost, a message had been delivered via dataveil to the vladar's private node. It had stated, in language that was immediately declared heretical by the district's bishop-praetor, that the Spoil had reclaimed the territory of the Line as its own. It further stated that only when this claim, made in the name of Damor Saitz on behalf of the people of the Spoil, had been ratified by all relevant powers, would negotiations begin regarding access to the resources of their recovered holding.

Moments after the message was delivered, power was severed to half the district of Setomir.

Crisis had become catastrophe. The Xeremor was receiving regular updates from Bastion-S, for all that they were worth, but it was clear that order had been lost across entire sub-districts. Spontaneous riots had erupted across Setomir, just as deployment orders had dispatched every enforcer who could stand and wield a weapon to muster to retake the Line. These orders had been hurriedly reversed, which only added to the anarchy on the streets. Several subdistrict blockhouses were under siege, but in the main the rioting citizenry had shied away from concentrations of the Lex's power in favour of softer targets. Most alarmingly, at least to the thunderous bishop-praetor, half a dozen sites of Imperial worship had been vandalised. The Shrine of St Jocasta had apparently been set ablaze, a fact the bishop had, by Melita's count, mentioned fifteen times in the past hour.

As ever, the troubles of one district spilled over to its neighbours. Korodilsk was too far to share much in the way of civic infrastructure with Setomir, but Dragosyl was certainly embroiled in its own chaos. Melita wondered what role Probator Mattix had in his Bastion's response. Somehow she couldn't believe that he would be pulling on riot armour and heading out onto the streets.

Only one thing appeared certain. The tri-districts were in turmoil, and the fault lay with the Valtteri.

She corrected herself. Wherever the fault truly lay, it would be placed at her door, if Vasimov had any say in the matter.

The securitor was attending his masters on the chamber's central dais. He never strayed far from one man in particular, the slim, austere figure of Kriskoff Tomiç. The two of them might have been father and son, their resemblance was so profound. The two men were silent, stoic figures amid the cluster of shouting, panicked cartel directors and city officials. It was clear from Vasimov's stiff stance that he ached to clear the dais of the whole pack of them, whereas Tomiç had more patience, or, at least, greater command of his temper. While the cartel's leadership squabbled, Tomiç observed dispassionately, and occasionally bent his head towards Vasimov to ensure that an order of actual importance was dispatched from the fray.

Melita stared over the heads of hurrying adjuncts, watching Tomiç and the other executors. How had it come to this? Only a handful of years ago, Melita had imagined herself killing them all. Not these men specifically, perhaps, but the idea of them. Every organisation had its head, and for years the imagined leaders of the Valtteri had been the object of so much hate that Melita had thought she would die from it.

Melita had been born the first child of Eumenides and Arelis Voronova, the masters of Voronova Atmospheric Shipping.

This relatively small trans-orbital haulage combine had been a prominent player within the thriving smuggling networks of the Dragosyl voidports for generations, and under Melita's parents' guidance had risen to even greater prominence. Smuggling was a competitive industry, but everyone who thrived in Varangantua did so because they found a niche and widened it sufficiently until slate poured in. Melita had been raised in relative luxury, with a maid, tutors, and the favour of proud parents who had prepared her to inherit the family business.

The Valtteri had taken all that away from her. Like every industry in the tri-districts, the cartel had their own interests and operators at the voidports. They were willing to tolerate competitors, provided they squabbled amongst themselves for the scraps the Valtteri left them. As VAS shuttles began to carry a greater percentage of contraband to and from Alecto's void-stations, the threats had begun. After the threats had been ignored – Arelis Voronova had been a proud and ferocious woman – the deaths had begun.

The Valtteri had struck with what Melita came to understand as their characteristically overwhelming force. Nothing direct, of course – not that tangible evidence of murderous conspiracy would have mattered a damn in Varangantua's corrupt courts. But the gangs acting as proxies for the cartel's wrath had done their work well. Melita lived only because her parents had smuggled her away before the worst had started to take hold.

For years she had planned her revenge. Elaborate schemes of infiltration, assassination and espionage had blossomed in her mind, fuelled by an implacable hatred for the nigh-omnipotent organisation that had robbed Melita of her family and her future. She had started down the path of an info-broker merely as a means of learning more about

their organisation and how she might best sabotage its workings, until she had learnt of her talent for the work, and the
practical needs of a hungry belly had overtaken plans for
vengeance.

She looked around the conference chamber. How had it
come to this, with Melita Voronova waiting passively for the
Valtteri to pass judgement on her actions?

A report slid into her iris from the chirurgeon who had
been operating on Edi, and she blinked it open with fear's
urgency. Edi was alive, and out of surgery.

That was the impetus she needed. She stood sharply, surprising
her guard, and pushed her way through the milling crowd to the
dais' steps. Vasimov did not deign to acknowledge her.

'I'm going to see Edi.'

Vasimov did not look up, but flicked a hand, as though
shooing an insect. To the Reisiger man at her elbow he said,
'She doesn't leave the tower.'

Melita took that to be all the permission she was going
to get.

She was about to step away when Andela Nedovic, still in
his scorched and battered fatigues, appeared beside her. She
was close enough to overhear his whisper.

'Sir, a Valkyrie-class flyer has landed at platform four. It
bears the insignia of the Adeptus Arbites.'

'What?' His attention divided between three different imagifiers, Vasimov seemed not to register his subordinate's urgency.

'Tomillan,' said Nedovic. 'The Arbites are here.'

Now he turned. Even Vasimov, the austere and redoubt-
able Tomillan Vasimov, paled at the name of the Emperor's
law-bearers. As Melita edged away, she saw the securitor step
forward to request the attention of the assembled civic and
civilian leaders so that he could relay the news.

They had less than a minute to wait.

A figure swept from one of the level's lift-units like an avenging deity. An ink-black cloak flared from his shoulders, draped over immaculate charcoal carapace armour. A silver icon – a clenched fist holding the scales of justice, mounted within the Imperial 'I' – hung on a thin chain from the collar of his armour. He was bare-headed, allowing piercing, slate-grey eyes to take in the room with a single intense glare. His black hair and beard were both clipped short and scattered with grey. The touch of age to his face only heightened the aura of overwhelming authority that seemed to roll ahead of him, like the bow-wave of an ocean-fording liner.

A pair of arbitrators, similarly armoured but with their faces concealed behind imposing helmets, followed a few steps behind. They each held a double-barrelled shot-cannon tight against their chests, with brutally flanged shock mauls hanging from their waists, while their leader carried an eagle-headed baton of office.

No one moved. Every person in the room was stilled instantly by the sudden presence of a man whose word could condemn all of them to immediate execution.

The figure stopped at the chamber's entrance, and raised a gauntleted hand in a gesture of benediction. His voice was a rich baritone, suited to that of an operatic singer or a Defence Corps drill instructor.

'Please. Continue.'

The room's activity immediately returned. Beneath that adamantine gaze, no one wished to be seen to give anything less than their complete effort.

Tomiç and Vasimov recovered themselves first, and both men stepped down from the dais to greet their unexpected visitor. Melita made every effort to inconspicuously retire. Her natural curiosity was silent, curbed by the incarnation of Imperial justice that had stepped into their midst.

Hierarchy suffused everything in the Imperium. Every citizen knew their place, knew whom they could abuse and to whom they must yield. That hierarchy was not limited to the vulgar masses. While the vladars and burgraves administered the collection of the tithe, and the sanctioners and probators of the enforcers applied the Lex Alecto with shock maul and excruciation, the Adeptus Arbites answered to a far greater authority. The men and women despatched from Fort Gunlysk, the great citadel at the heart of Alecto's Praesidium Quarter, were charged to enforce the God-Emperor's own laws.

'I am Arbitrator Hakon Karadiz.' Each syllable fell into place with the weight and irresistible energy of continental motion. 'Who is responsible for this situation?'

'I am.'

Melita's regard for Kriskoff Tomiç increased substantially. His voice had not wavered at all.

Karadiz's stare steadily swept over each of the figures around the hololith, which included a district vladar, three enforcer castellans, the most senior officiant of the Imperial Faith in Setomir, and the directors of four merchant-combines whose contributions to the planetary tithe could be individually discerned. Finally, his gaze settled on Tomiç, who had planted himself in the arbitrator's line of advance, Vasimov loyally at his shoulder. Tomiç was a slender man, resembling nothing so much as a fluted amasec glass. While he might have stood eye to eye with Karadiz, it was impossible to match the man's physical presence.

'You are?'

Watching Tomiç summon his full reserve of dignity was like seeing a thunderstorm gather. 'Kriskoff Tomiç. Director of the Aspiry-Tomiç Trading House.'

'And you speak for the association known as the Valtteri?'

Tomiç paused momentarily before responding, in a way that seemed calculated to tread the line between modesty and authority. 'In this matter, yes.'

'I see.'

The assembled worthies waited in silence. Karadiz's every movement projected absolute, unquestioned supremacy. It wasn't simply the effect of the armour he wore, or the sigil he bore. The man himself exuded an air of unyielding judgement. In the brief moment his stare passed over Melita, she felt a tremor start in her core. Her contrarian nature, which would usually rankle at such assumed dominance, completely failed.

'The Praesidium Council has formally requested that I assess whether this situation can be contained and resolved by local forces.'

In that voice, everything sounded like a threat, but there was no mistaking the danger inherent in his words. The figures gathered together on the dais held almost unquestioned authority within their own spheres, but Karadiz could unmake any of them with a word.

'Does that mean you will be deploying your Arbites to the Line?' squeaked Castellan Hauf, a representative of Bastion-D who was nominally in command of the enforcers seconded to their neighbouring district. The man had been sweating profusely throughout the night, but now he looked as though he might soon expire of heart failure before dehydration did him in.

Karadiz's head turned slowly. 'Do you feel you require our involvement?'

'No,' said Tomiç smoothly, as Hauf wilted beneath the arbitrator's gaze. 'I am grateful for your presence, arbitrator, but we' – he gestured at the assembled power behind him – 'will bring this matter to its assured conclusion.' His gesture turned into a deft inclination of his hand, as though magnanimously giving Karadiz permission to join them. 'We would, of course, welcome any observations you feel might hasten that end.'

Karadiz nodded, and tucked his baton under one arm. 'What is the disposition of the enemy force?'

Vasimov stepped back, inviting him to approach the hololith.

Melita took that as her moment to leave. She headed for the lift-unit that had brought in Karadiz, her escort in tow. She had to step between the two arbitrators, both at least a head taller than her, to access the elevator. The slight creak of a leather gauntlet tightening around a shot-cannon's grip made her almost leap through the open doors.

As the doors closed and the lift-unit rumbled into motion, Melita was certain she heard the Reisiger man exhale in relief.

CHAPTER 29

The Xeremor's medicae facilities were roughly thirty levels below the conference chamber, occupying a significant section of the starscraper's waist. She rode the elevator in silence, trying to ignore the mercenary beside her. Melita tried to see Vasimov's pettiness as a point of pride, rather than the insult he intended. Someone with her skills and nothing to lose could do an inordinate amount of harm if allowed to roam around the cartel's headquarters.

The elevator doors grumbled open onto a corridor that stank of incense and counterseptic fluid. The strange combination of sweet and sharp scents brought back memories of her iris implantation. The disquieting sense of her anticipation twisting into fear as the attendant took his razor to her hair. The feeling of helplessness as she lay on the chirurgeon's table and surrendered to the anaesthesia. The reassuring presence of Edi Kamensk at her side as she lapsed into unconsciousness.

Apart from her recent surgery, Melita had gone out of her

way in life to avoid spending time in such places. Dragosyl's sanatoria ran the gamut from private clinics that provided common treatments for those who could pay their exorbitant fees, to feculent hospices run by well-meaning charitable foundations and missionary orders, where the diseased and the destitute could be left to die by hollow-cheeked family members. They were uniformly bleak, hopeless places, wreathed in stinking smoke to combat the stench of death that stalked their halls.

The Xeremor differed from that template, in some ways. The corridors were brightly lit, in adherence with the common understanding that illness and decay thrived in darkness. But the lumens here cast soft, refined light from artful sconces, unlike the harsh overhead bars so common elsewhere, that stripped all hope of dignity from the dying. The medicaes that haunted the Xeremor's halls were followed by servitors laden with the sterile instruments of their art, and armed with all the assembled knowledge of the city's elite biologis academies. The best a foundry labourer in Dragosyl might expect was a harassed attendant to refill their supply of soporifics, and the benediction of a stern-eyed Ecclesiarchy pastor.

Like everything else controlled by the Valtteri, the medicae facilities were stocked and staffed to a level only available to the gilded. They occupied that world that overlaid but was entirely divorced from the realities of Varangantua.

The level was quiet, at least, which was a relief after the chaos of the conference chamber. A woman in a heavy smock was walking towards the corridor's far end, where a pair of chirurgeons had their heads together in low conversation. Incense burned in a censer at the end of the hall, wafting from the small shrine to the God-Emperor in His aspect as Restoration. Melita headed that way, following the coils of cloying smoke to the end of the corridor.

She passed a sign that directed the way to the level's medicaments vault, and the stencilled runes roused the subtle barbs
of temptation and need. The last of the sleeper's after-effects
had been drowned in the flood of adrenaline and shock that
had carried her out of St Eurydice's. The past few hours had
left her hollowed out, overwhelmed by the scale of what
had overtaken the city and the dawning realisation that
she would be blamed for it. Though she walked in silence,
the cacophony of memory, censure and recrimination rang
around the inside of her head. The need for respite was an
almost physical pain in her core, gnawing at her insides as
a punishment for unwillingly enduring her daemons rather
than fleeing from them. Had Edi not robbed her of the option,
she knew she would have already evaded her captors and
lost herself in the sweet oblivion of topaz, or the numb peace
of sleeper.

The corridor opened into a junction, where a dour-looking
attendant in an unstained smock laboriously entered data
into a brass-bound cogitator. Melita asked him for directions
to Edi's ward, and he wordlessly pointed at the door opposite the station.

She looked through the pane of plex in the door, but
couldn't see Edi. She pushed the door open, but stopped
when her escort started to follow her through.

'Give me a moment, for Throne's sake.'

The guard tapped the attendant on the shoulder. 'Any other
doors into the ward?'

He looked up in irritation, shook his head, and returned
to his work.

'Fine.' The mercenary took up position beside the door,
falling into a stance that was likely as familiar to him as
breathing. Melita pushed the door open softly, hesitant as a
parent entering the room of a sleeping child.

The ward was a narrow, vaulted space. Its stone-flagged floor and the relief icons of Imperial saints on the walls reminded Melita of the side chapel in which she had interrogated Nurem Babić, not twelve hours earlier. Melita wondered what had happened to Babić, and whether he had escaped the catastrophe that had cost her so much else.

Steel gurneys lined the walls, five on each side of the room, with an array of medical cogitators looming like brass headstones above each one. At the far end of the ward, a sculpted grotesque held an autocenser in its cupped hands that steadily puffed counterseptic-infused smoke into the air. Its mouth was shaped into a vox-horn, from which droned a low, monotone recitation of Saint Clara's Homily to the Infirm.

All but one of the bays were empty. Guilt, bright and bitter, flared in the pit of Melita's stomach.

Edi Kamensk lay motionless on the wheeled bed, propped into a mostly upright position. The bullet wound in his shoulder was covered by a bright patch of synthskin, too pink and conspicuously hairless against his pale and wiry torso. Plastek tubes ran from his collarbone and from somewhere in his side, flowing with what she hoped was pain medicaments.

His hands were pale, the skin puckered and hairless up to his wrists. Melita realised that in the six years Edi had worked for her, she had never seen his hands. He habitually wore heavy gauntlets that came up to his elbows, or else thin synthleather gloves when the dry season's heat was at its peak. Nothing in Edi's background had mentioned injuries like this, not in his enforcer service record or the checks she had run when she had first hired him.

Through the fog of pain suppressants, the old sanctioner became aware that he was not alone. Edi's eyes opened slowly, flickered, and then gradually focused on her face.

'Good to see you.' His voice was slow and weak, the same familiar gravel but robbed of its strength.

'And you.'

Edi noticed her curious stare, and twitched the white blanket that covered his chest so that his hands were beneath it. Melita flushed, embarrassed. She stood awkwardly beside the bed, listening to the sound of the vitae-monitors and Edi's rhythmic breathing.

'Sit down, for Throne's sake, before you fall down.'

Melita obeyed, and crumpled into the hard plastek seat beside his bed. For a while, neither of them said anything. The tramp of feet outside the room intruded on the silence that stretched out between them.

'How do you feel?' she asked, aware of how inane her concern must sound. The guilt was a smothering weight, making her hesitant and timid.

'Nothing permanent. They found the slug easily enough.' He glanced towards the table beside his bed, and the small plastek bag with a deformed hunk of metal inside. 'And as for that,' he looked down at his side. 'No lasting harm.'

'That isn't what I asked.'

He sighed. 'It's not the first time I've been shot.'

He was evidently set on playing the stern veteran, so Melita tried to force a bluff cheer to match. 'Well, don't get comfortable. I don't know for how long Vasimov is going to cover the bill.'

His grin seemed less forced than hers. 'Shame. Of all the medicae-wards I've woken up in, this is the cleanest by far.'

Melita smiled weakly, and they lapsed back into awkward silence.

'What's going on out there?' asked Edi.

'Why did you take the topaz?' said Melita, in the same moment. She hadn't meant to speak, but the question had burst from her unbidden. Now it was said, hanging in the air between them.

Edi nodded slowly, his forced smile fading into solemnity. He didn't answer immediately. His gaze roamed the ward as he gathered his thoughts.

'Because I needed you to know I'm serious,' he said finally.

Melita sat back in her chair. 'Serious about what?'

He pushed himself up on his elbows, drawing himself together like a herald about to deliver an edict. 'If you can't get it together, I'm not going to watch you circle the drain.'

'What does that mean?'

'It means the narcs have to stop.'

The hard edge to his voice was a goad, a lash against her fraying self-control.

'I'm fine.' She said it as a reflex, without any thought at all.

'No, you're not. For Terra's sake, yesterday I was holding the bucket that you were puking into.'

'That was because of your damned detox shot!'

'And if I hadn't given it to you, you'd likely still be dead to the world, face down in your cot while the Spoil goes insane.'

'That would–' she started, then stopped herself.

'No, go on.' Edi was merciless, his eyes boring into hers. 'That would be better. It'd be easier? That's what you were going to say? Tell me again, please, about the hard life of Melita Voronova.'

If Edi saw the anger in her eyes, he ignored it. Whatever dam inside him that had kept this tirade pent up had finally broken.

'I turned a blind eye to the cotin. To the occasional blister or vial. Hells, I did that for my entire career.' Bitterness was a new side to Edi. 'When you said you needed something to help soften the aftermath of the cortex and whatever else you pump into yourself to keep working, I understood, even if I didn't like it.

'But these past few years, you've got out of control. I know where you're going. I've seen it before. Hiding in a haze of narcotics is the first step on a path that always has the same end.'

'Are you trying to save me, Edi?' Melita said, pouring venom and spite into each word.

He shook his head. 'No. I can't stop you throwing your life away. But I won't help you do it.'

Melita lurched to her feet. Her heart was hammering, a fresh headache making stars burst behind her eyes. She had not come here for this.

'You picked a bad time to lecture me, Edi. This life that I'm ruining is about to be cut abruptly short. The world has fallen apart, and I'm going to get the blame. Between Vasimov and the Throne-forsaken Arbites, I'll either be found dead in a Setomir alley or shackled into a damned Bulwark before the sun rises. So, yes, right now seems the perfect time to crack open a vial if I had one.'

'The Arbites?' he repeated, the invocation of the Imperium's lawbringers momentarily derailing him.

'Edi, these people are going to *kill me*. I'll be lucky if it's a lasbolt in the back or a wire round my neck.' A stray hand touched her throat as she spoke, her imagination making the blood flow hot over her fingers. 'More likely that they'll turn me over to the vladar. Vasimov might even tie me in with Saitz, make up some kind of conspiracy to save himself from scrutiny.'

As he had so many times before, he let her rant until she finally ran out of breath.

'So what are you going to do?'

'Do? Edi, didn't you hear me? I'm measuring what's left of my life in hours.'

'And what are you going to do with them?' The harsh edge
had receded, leaving his voice an intense whisper. 'In this city,
few people get to control what happens. It's too big. All we
can do is react. Everything is a decision, minute to minute,
day to day. Hiding from it helps no one. Least of all yourself.'

'I can't help anyone, Edi. It's all fallen apart.' She felt the
first threat of tears in her eyes and, as ever, anger at such a
pathetic display of weakness rose with them.

'It has,' Edi said. 'But that was beyond you. Nothing we
could have done since we crossed that stinking canal could
have averted what has happened. As I said, a few people get
to shape events, and the rest of us have to react.' He reached
out with his strangely scarred hands, and took one of hers.
'So find whoever it is that had the control. Find Saitz – that
bastard has a reckoning coming. Find the evidence that makes
all this make sense.'

Melita looked at him through the haze of tears. 'If you
hadn't noticed, we're in the middle of the Valtteri's damned
headquarters.'

'That's hardly going to stop you, is it?'

Edi's forced cheer, the bluff strength that had so often lifted
Melita from her doldrums, could not pierce the depression
that settled on her shoulders.

The door to the ward suddenly rattled and her Reisiger
escort entered. Melita quickly cuffed at her eyes before she
turned.

His hand was at his micro-bead. 'Yes, sir.' He looked down
at Melita. 'You need to go back up to the directors.'

'Okay.' She didn't move.

'Now.'

'Okay.' She stared at him until he backed out of the ward.

Edi looked at her for a moment, then awkwardly pulled
himself straighter on his bed.

'There's an old tradition in the Corps. Or a superstition. Call it what you like.' Edi reached over to the side table and unsteadily picked up the bullet that the chirurgeons had retrieved from his flesh. 'There's a shot out there meant for you, and this is it.' He spoke as though reading from a script, or from an old, precious memory. He placed the plastek bag in her hand.

'And this is going to keep me safe from Vasimov's wrath?' Melita said bitterly.

Edi tucked his scarred hands back under the sheet, fighting to keep the hurt from his face. The old sanctioner seemed to sag back into the medicae bed, the last of his strength – or patience – worn through. 'It might.'

Melita gave a half-hearted smile, and folded her fingers over the bullet.

Edi didn't offer any platitudes, no injunction to be careful or to look after herself. He simply watched her slowly stand and leave the room.

The door to Edi's ward clicked shut.

Melita wanted – needed – some time to stop, to rest, to think. But the mercenary was impatient to obey his order.

'Come on.'

She put a hand in her pocket, feeling the bullet Edi had given her. It was deformed into bluntness by its impact with his body. She regretted her reaction to his apparently sincere gesture. It was hard, at times, for Melita to remember that for all of his decades of experience enforcing the Lex upon a resistant populace, Edi Kamensk was a deeply, perhaps even charmingly, naive man.

The guard gave her a firm push in the shoulder, his hand sitting meaningfully on the shock goad holstered at his belt. 'I said, move.'

Melita looked up at him, but said nothing.

He marched her down the corridor, back through the coils of incense. They passed the sign to the narcotics vault, and Melita burned anew with the shame and anger she had felt throughout Edi's lecture. All she wanted was to escape. She had nothing left to give; not to Edi, not to the Valtteri. Not to the imagined hordes in the Spoil, facing another new day with even less certainty than the one before.

Her fingers tensed around the hunk of metal in her pocket. It was well for Edi to tell her to keep going, to rage against the trap that had closed about her. His... talisman was meant to be a reminder of that, of her assumed obligation to keep fighting, even without him. Without Oriel.

She resented that. Wasn't she entitled to feel hopeless? To give in to the despair that lingered on the edge of her thoughts. What right did Edi have to demand that she carry on in the face of Vasimov's implacable hatred? It was humiliating to take the slate of the people that killed her parents, that robbed her of her promised future. Why shouldn't she welcome the end of that, and accept the death the Valtteri had intended for her?

Melita slapped the lift-unit's call button, and waited for the elevator to arrive. She stepped in first, and slumped against the rear of the unit. Her escort followed, taking up position just in front of her. There was room for about ten people, but fortunately no one else attempted to join them. The elevator doors closed, and Melita's stomach fell as it began to climb.

She had thirty seconds, maybe less, before they returned to the conference chamber.

Melita took a deep breath, tensed, and grabbed the handle of the guard's shock goad. It half-caught on its loop of synth-leather, and then it was free and Melita thrust its end into the mercenary's armpit. A loud snap of electricity turned his shouted objection into a yelp of pain.

He staggered back, one arm cradled against his chest. He groped with his other hand for Melita's wrist, but his grip closed on the shock goad's end instead. She reflexively thumbed the stud, but the power pack was still whining. It released a half-charge into his clenched fist. He howled, arm numbed up to the shoulder.

In the moment's distraction, Melita had enough presence of mind to reach up and slap the micro-bead out of his ear. Then he was on her.

He lunged for her neck, and Melita stumbled away. She tried to punch the way Edi had shown her, fingers clasped tight, but he took the blow on his jaw and kept coming. His numb fingers caught her by the throat, and bore her back into the wall. Melita kicked, struck him with the charging goad, clawed at the thumb that was digging into her windpipe. Her world started to go black at the edges.

Somehow she worked her foot up between them, and kicked out. Her boot in his solar plexus was enough to throw him off, and he crashed into the far side of the lift-unit. Melita fell to her knees, sucking in an aching breath.

He rebounded and leapt for her, just as the shock goad's whine reached its apex. Melita stood, the goad thrust up and out before her. The baton's end struck his forehead, and another crack erupted. The mercenary dropped like a stone.

She released the shock goad, which pinged back on its power cable to his belt. Melita rubbed her throat with one hand, and reached out to cancel the level request to the lift-unit with the other. She swallowed painfully, and sent the unit racing back down the tower.

Melita rode the lift-unit in panicked silence. Her knuckles throbbed, and every breath through her bruised throat was agony. Through the pain and panic, Melita held on to her anger. She had forgotten it, or buried it beneath a narcotic haze and the day-by-day trivialities of survival in a hostile world. But now it was rekindled, ignited by the pitiful thoughts to which she had been so willing to submit.

She would take Vasimov's contempt and throw it in his face. She would show the Valtteri how foolish they were not to trust her counsel. She would find Saitz, and Sorokin's killer, and the gilded swine who had wanted to start a war with the Spoil.

But to do that, she first had to get away from the tower. That was up to chance now. She knew the security picter in the corner of the elevator had seen everything, and there was no way she could conceal the unconscious body at her feet. The Xeremor's internal security systems were densely layered, enough that any on-the-fly attempt to subvert the picter through her iris would likely draw more attention to herself. Melita simply had to hope that whoever was monitoring the elevator's feed was not paying particularly close attention.

The levels flicked by, as Melita willed the elevator to drop faster. Her stomach lurched as the unit started to brake. She thought about trying to push the mercenary's body into the corner of the lift-unit, but then the carriage hissed to a halt and the doors opened.

The Valtteri, naturally, had their own mag-train terminal. The Xeremor served as the arrival and departure point for tens of thousands of merchant-combine functionaries, further enhancing the cartel's headquarters as a locus of power within the district. Several lines met inside a huge chamber that occupied the lowest levels of the tower. The east and west faces of the building were massive plex-and-stone facades, which kept the noxious city air at bay while admitting maglev lines through artfully crafted portals. Dozens of enormous pillars, each at least twenty yards in diameter, held the colossal weight of the Xeremor above the terminal.

Fortunately, the city authorities had restored power to the maglev lines as a matter of priority, and even in the small hours of the morning there were several trains entering or making ready to depart.

Melita entered the terminal at a fast walk, resisting the urge to bolt. Setomir's Officio Travectura had its own security services, and their dun uniforms patrolled the vast chamber in abundance, but they were the least of her concerns. Her gaze was on the recessed alcoves that lined the walls, from which would pour Reisiger mercenaries and weaponised servitors at the first sign of a disturbance.

She scurried down a staircase, then doubled back beneath the overpass she had just crossed. She took turns at random, hunting for any unobserved route through to a departing maglev. The early hour was both a boon and a hindrance; at busier times, there likely would be more transport authority figures on duty, but Melita would have given a lot for a crowd in which she could shelter for a moment.

Melita climbed back up another set of steps, which took her within just a few yards of a crowd-control barrier and a maglev platform. The train waiting there was evidently preparing to leave; the hum of its suspensor plates changed tone as the pattern of magnetism shifted to begin propelling hundreds of tons of metal and passengers forward.

She looked around, waiting until the last possible moment, then awkwardly scrambled over the barricade. She crossed the platform at as close to a run as she dared, and boarded the train without a backwards glance. The doors closed behind her a second later.

CHAPTER 30

The maglev wended its way between several minor towers, a hundred feet or more above the district's streets. Melita did not sit, but stood at the door, watching through the carriage's window as the Xeremor's outline shrunk from dominating the skyline to merely being one vast edifice among many. In a few scant minutes, the train had carried her several miles from the Valtteri starscraper and the wrath of its senior securitor.

The mag-train was barely up to speed before it began to slow for the next station. She was moving the moment the carriage doors rattled open. She did not run, but only because there was nowhere for her to run to.

The wan glow of morning could just be seen, adding a touch of colour to the glassaic in the lancet arches high upon the station's walls, and the platform was thickly crowded with finance clerks, auditors, and the thousands of others that poured in from Setomir's residential claves to the centre of commerce for the tri-districts. Even in the midst of riot

and catastrophe, the business of commerce and trade did
not cease.

There was a heavy sanctioner presence to ensure that the
anarchy that gripped so much of the district did not take
hold here. Pairs of enforcers roamed the platforms, stocky
impediments that drew curses that became quickly muted as
the mass of bodies flowed around them. Melita was acutely
aware of the monitor skulls that patrolled with the sanctioners. If Vasimov and his underlings had moved quickly, her
biometrics could already be with them, and there was no
way to obscure her features from the skull's facial recognition
systems without drawing even more attention to herself.

A pair of sanctioners was coming straight towards her,
moving purposefully. Panicking, Melita ducked out of the
crowd and beneath a tall stone archway.

The cloying funk of Imperial worship greeted her. Melita
realised she had entered one of the station's altar houses. They
could be found in public spaces throughout the tri-districts,
typically in recessed spaces near thoroughfares where busy
commuters could receive their daily benediction without
interrupting the more vital work of commerce and industry
that occupied their days. Without thinking, Melita joined
the line of queuing administrators and merchant-combine
retainers, her heart still racing. She sagged with relief when
someone else stepped into line behind her, shielding her from
any searching stares from the platform.

There were several people ahead of her, and Melita used
the time to calm herself. So far, she had acted solely on
impulse, but now she needed to slow down, to think and
plan. She tried to put Vasimov and his vendetta from her
mind; with luck, his pursuit would be slowed by the need
to focus on the disaster that had descended on the Valtteri.

Melita had no faith that the chaos that had engulfed the

Spoil and the Line would die quickly. Nothing about Saitz's attack was rational. Yes, it had made him a rallying point for the clave-captains, and legitimised his coup. But there was no chance that he could hold the Line, or even a fraction of it. Varangantua would not, could not, permit it. To allow such a revolt to succeed would be to invite anarchy to engulf the entire city.

There was something else behind everything Saitz had done, an angle she couldn't see. It was clear now that the gang captain was behind Sorokin's death, his necessary first step to gaining control of the Har Dhrol. Melita thought again of Sorokin's guard, struck dead by a digital laser. Who was backing Saitz? Perhaps it was a play by one of the Valtteri's rival conglomerates, to destabilise the cartel and win control of the Line's factories and power plants for themselves. If so, it was a remarkably high-risk strategy, not to mention bloody.

She needed more information, and there was only one place she could go to get it. It was not without risk, but there were no other options she could see.

The first obstacle, if not the one weighing heaviest on her mind, was how to get there. Passage between the districts of Varangantua was heavily policed at the best of times. In practice, of course, the physical delineations were far from strict, particularly in the tri-districts. Dragosyl, Setomir and Korodilsk were really one greater part of the city's unfathomably vast body. The borders between them were the scars that marked past disputes of jurisdiction, rather than the sharply demarked perimeters found in other parts of Varangantua. The Regio Custos units that monitored travel between the tri-districts occupied checkpoints, not fortifications, but were no less rigorous or remorseless in the discharge of their duties. Boundary transgression, to use the term favoured by the Lex, was subject to harsh and often immediate sanction.

Fortunately, this was one challenge for which Melita was prepared. The Spoil had, until recently, been the easiest way to avoid the Custos' scrutiny, but there were plenty of smugglers who took a more direct route, and Melita was owed favours by many of them.

The man ahead of Melita, a secretarius tattooed with the baroque sigil of the Brumail Mercantile Association, received his blessing, and she found herself at the head of the queue.

She shuffled forward and knelt on a scarlet cushion, its fabric worn thin by the weight of countless petitioners. A plastek screen was between her and the altar, a thin stone plinth inside an ornate wooden box that was intricately carved with votive scenes of devotion. A printed prayer book, its fragile pages contained within a cover of green real-leather, was given pride of place at the altar's centre.

The pastor working the altar's diurnus-shift was a young man, a pair of green eye-lenses perched at the end of a long, thin nose. He gave her ragged, sweat-stained clothes a curious glance; his petitioners were more typically attired in clerical robes and dynastic livery. He made the sign of the aquila, and spoke in a tone that was more bored than reverent.

'The Emperor grant you wisdom and fortune, child. Use these gifts in furtherance of His design.'

Melita swallowed, unexpectedly feeling the weight of the pastor's words. 'I'll do my best.'

She guessed that the sanctioners would have moved on. As she climbed to her feet, the pastor's eyes narrowed behind his smoky lenses. 'Ahem.' He tapped the slate-scanner beside the altar, and the conical receptacle for physical donations.

Melita froze. Her slate-stick was tied to one of her accounts. By now Vasimov had to know that she had escaped; any transaction in her name would draw Reisiger men to her as fast as an aircar could fly.

She panicked, patted her pockets, and felt the unexpected clink of hard plastek. She still had the stack of high-value slates from Troian Horvaç that Bai had returned to her. That was something. It was more than something – the handful of slate probably equalled the donations received by the clave's diocese in a month.

She chose one of the lower denomination chips and dropped it into the receptacle. 'My thanks, frater.'

Melita cautiously edged her way out of the chapel, then dove into a cluster of commuters. She let them carry her towards the far side of the platform and onto another waiting maglev. She didn't look at its destination, but once it was moving she found that it was a slower service, acting as a shuttle between the smaller clave-stations and the transit hubs like the one she had just left. After three stops, Melita was hemmed in on all sides by clerks and workers of every description.

At the fourth, Melita alighted, darting quickly between bodies as the crowd shifted to admit more people. This time, she had to wait a few minutes for a train to pull in, its drive-unit hissing and repulsor plates groaning as it struggled to bring its great mass to a halt.

She did this twice more, fighting the bustling crowds to cross from train to train as inconspicuously as possible. By accident as much as design, the maglev system took Melita on an oblique path away from the Xeremor and the other monuments to Varangantua's industry, and deeper into the urban wilderness of Setomir.

Finally, she alighted at a small regional station in a clave she had never heard of. From the elevated platform, she could see the dark tops of row-houses stretching away beneath her. The congregated starscrapers at Setomir's centre were massive pillars of iron and stone and blazing light, still enormous but less imposing, their threat dulled by distance. No sanctioners or monitor skulls patrolled here, and the local security was minimal.

Melita stood for a moment, leaning against the metal railing that was just starting to warm in the morning's heat. Sweat caked the inside of her jacket. Her chest ached from the many elbows that had collided with her.

She had escaped. Now, she had to make use of her hard-won freedom.

CHAPTER 31

'Don't bother printing the orders, Anto, for Terra's sake. Just get them into the field. We'll get Hauf to authorise everything later.'

The probator-novus took back the thin sheaf of data-wafers that he had placed on Mattix's desk, and retreated out into the bullpen. The babble of voices raised in anger and alarm briefly intruded as Mattix's junior opened and closed the door.

Mattix had been at his hab when the crisis broke, nursing his wounds and his slightly bruised ego. He had not expected the Valtteri's agent to have tracked down his safehouse in the Slahin clave-hub. He was fairly sure that Babić was to blame for that. He should not have been overly surprised – the man was far from reliable – but retribution would have to wait.

In a single night, the tri-districts had been swallowed by chaos. Even Mattix had been shocked by the size and scale of the calamity that had engulfed the Setomir Chimneys.

He, like so many others, had taken Sorokin's control of the Spoil for granted.

Dragosyl had, fortunately, been spared the worst. A few sub-districts on the Setomir border had briefly lost power, but nothing like the anarchy that had taken hold in their neighbouring district. Requests for support had roared across the dataveil, and every sanctioner not already on duty had been summoned across the border to help contain the spreading riots.

Mattix, being Mattix, had managed to avoid being deployed to the street. The first hours had been intense, imposing order on the chaos, the first duty of all enforcers. Now, with the curfew in Setomir in effect and the riots more or less contained to their original claves, there was still plenty to occupy him within the Bastion's walls. Reports were coming in from blockhouses across the district, and from the few roaming sanctioners who had not been sent north. Mattix and his junior were hurriedly collating this information to identify where the next disturbances might erupt.

He poked his head out of his office, holding a sheet of vellum that summarised a number of active investigations into subversive worker collectivisation.

'Anto, I need you to get hold of Captain Kudrnova over at the Aravas blockhouse. I'm sending him a list of names for pre-emptive arrests, and he needs to make them right now.'

The young man took the pages without question, and made his way back to his desk. Anto was well on his way to earning his elevation to full probator, another graduate of Mattix's little apprenticeship for scholam cadets who showed the kind of attributes he valued in a junior. There were quite a few now, quietly serving the Lex in the blockhouses and bastions of the tri-districts. They were an investment, as Mattix saw it, in the future.

He shut his office door, and took a moment to breathe.

The wound in his side was still raw beneath a hastily applied layer of synthskin, a reminder of his lucky escape just a few hours before. Mattix counted it as a poor day whenever he had a pistol pointed at his head, and even more so when it had been his own damn gun.

His iris pulsed a notification into his eyeline, the little icon surrounding by a high-priority corona that caught his attention. He flicked open his feed, and found that a terse message from an unlisted ident had made it past the firebreaks into his personal dataveil node. Mattix's instinct tickled, and he blinked it open.

> We need to talk.

Melita stood in the public entrance of Bastion-D, a cavernous chamber that smelt of hot, stale air and desperate, sweating bodies. Despite the early hour, dozens of citizens were inside, most in slow-moving queues that wound their way between thick metal barriers. Above them, dominating the chamber, was a pair of vast obsidian plates, each at least fifty feet tall. Carved upon the face of one were the nine central tenets of the Lex Alecto, the first words each child in Varangantua was taught upon entering their scholam. Inscribed upon the other, in far smaller runes, was a list of names: the name of every enforcer assigned to Bastion-D who had fallen in service to the God-Emperor and His laws.

A few sanctioners in the heavy armour used for riot suppression were on guard duty at the long rail to which the public presented themselves, and others watched from the balconies that overlooked the hall on three sides. A few luckless citizens in manacles were being escorted with due hostility across the polished granite floor towards a set of caged iron doors, to disappear into the labyrinthine interior of a Bastion of the Lex Alecto.

'Unauthorised weapon detected.'

Melita jumped at the artificial growl. A monitor skull was descending rapidly, vox-emitter blurting its three words of alarm even as the light of its ocular sensor half-blinded her. Through the red haze, she could see the articulated length of spinal column that draped down from the skull's underside, which ended in a viciously curved barb that curled up towards her chest.

'Unauthorised weapon detected.'

Melita heard boots on stone as sanctioners rushed to the skull's summons, but could see nothing through the ocular's stab of light.

'On your knees!'

'I–'

'Lace your hands behind your head and drop to your knees!' The sanctioner's shot-cannon appeared through the red glare, no less threatening than the servo-skull.

Despite the shouted order, Melita backed away, hands raised. She wondered briefly if this was finally the mistake that would get her killed.

'This is your final warning!'

'Stop!'

A young man in civilian clothes appeared beside her, disrupting the servo-skull's position. He carefully interposed himself between Melita and the sanctioner, who grudgingly lowered his weapon.

'Mistress Voronova. My name is Burian Anto. The probator asked me to escort you to his office.'

The sanctioner cleared his throat. 'This woman has a weapon. Sir.'

Anto gave her a questioning look. Melita nodded.

'You'll need to give that to me.'

* * *

Melita's business, both for the Valtteri and in her yearned-for past as a free agent, had rarely taken her inside the Bastions of the Lex Alecto. Her interactions with probators and sanctioners typically took place on the street, or, better yet, without any direct contact at all.

The face the Bastion presented to the city was one of black stone, sheer iron, and the brooding symbols of Imperial aquilae and the skull-and-coronet icon of the enforcers. The public hall proclaimed the authority of the Lex, overawing those who entered through grand scale, forbidding design and stern presence. All this was as she expected; the first duty of all limbs of the city's government was to make manifest the Imperium's overwhelming authority over the lives who served it.

Stepping behind the facade revealed a strangely – almost disappointingly – mundane reality. The corridors through which Anto led her were functional, depressing, and desperately in need of a coat of paint. Bulletin boards with notices about refectory rotas and shift patterns hung between familiar devotional placards. Melita passed offices that were as ascetic and functional as any she would expect to find in a merchant-combine spire. More so, in fact. Within the Xeremor there was a distinct aura of slate that permeated the building to its bones. Bastion-D's character was one of almost deliberate neglect.

They climbed several flights of stone stairs – Anto explained that the lift-unit for the section was broken – then along a beige corridor that Melita suspected housed some of the Bastion's secretariat staff, and finally into a working elevator.

'I assume it's not always this empty,' she said as the lift-unit juddered into motion. The hallways had been remarkably quiet. The Bastion was the centre of Lex enforcement for the entire district, the place of work for tens of thousands. Aside from the white-coated figures of verispex and their orderlies, and the occasional clerk, the route Anto had led her through was almost entirely depopulated.

'Not usually,' he replied.

'Everyone's deployed to Setomir?'

'Some.'

Anto was more or less Melita's age, and had wide, innocent eyes and an easy smile. He was also evidently smart enough to be tight-lipped around new faces. They rode in silence, except for the occasional alarming grind of metal as the elevator climbed through the levels.

'Anything I should know about your boss?' she asked as the lift-unit juddered to a halt. She had little to lose from such blunt questioning.

Anto's polite smile broadened into a roguish grin, but he said nothing.

She followed the junior probator out of the elevator and across a stone atrium, its surface scuffed smooth by decades of footsteps. They passed beneath a sandstone arch inscribed with a faded High Gothic epigraph, and into Mattix's domain.

The heat struck her first, followed immediately by the smell. It was an almost physical fugue of recaff and lho-sticks, made worse by the foetid warmth of too many bodies and too little ventilation. This chamber, at least, was busy. Enforcers of every rank and age were seated at stamped-metal desks, and each of them was either shouting into a vox-horn or striking brass-bound runeboards with too much force.

Anto gave her a moment to adjust to the sensory assault of the probator's chamber in action, then took her elbow and guided her around its edge towards the row of offices that formed the far wall.

Mattix was waiting outside his cubicle, a lit lho-stick burnt almost to the filter in one hand and a wad of papers in the other.

'Mistress Voronova. I had not expected to renew our acquaintance so soon.'

Without a muzzle-bound stablight in his eyes, Mattix was a good deal more handsome than she remembered. A growth of silver stubble marking his jaw and the rearmost portion of his scalp were evidence that he, like Melita, had had a long night since last they spoke.

'Nothing is going as expected right now.'

'Very true. Come in. Get these to the blockhouse captains.' This last was to Anto, who took the stack of vellum and retreated to his desk.

She stepped inside and Mattix shut the door behind her, muting the worst of the racket. He gestured towards a pair of hard plastek chairs, then rounded his desk but did not sit down.

They stared at one another in silence. Melita broke first. 'You're not out on the street, keeping the riots in check?'

Mattix lifted his left arm, bound tightly against his chest. The cuff of his civilian-cut jacket hung limply at his side. 'I was sadly injured in the line of duty a few hours ago.'

'In the line of duty? Really?'

'Quite so.' He did not attempt to expand on that. 'You know that a writ of seizure in your name has been sent to every blockhouse in the tri-districts.'

She had assumed as much, but the confirmation was still chilling.

'Have you come to turn yourself in?'

She forced a smile, although she felt icy pricks of fear climb her spine. Melita had no reason at all to trust the probator, but she had stepped willingly into his control. 'No.'

Mattix slid into his chair, and made an expansive gesture with his free hand. 'Then, with the greatest of respect, why are you here?'

She took a breath. 'I think there is a larger conspiracy behind Saitz. Behind Sorokin's death and the destabilisation of the Spoil.'

Mattix raised an eyebrow. 'Larger, you mean, than orchestrating the biggest citizen uprising the tri-districts has seen for a century?'

Melita returned his stare. 'Yes.'

'Do you have any evidence of such a conspiracy?'

She didn't answer him immediately. 'What do you think Saitz hopes to gain from this? What's his endgame?' She leant forward, ticking off her thoughts on her fingers as she addressed them. 'If it was to control the Har Dhrol, he's thrown that away. I don't think there will *be* a Har Dhrol after this.' Melita paused for a moment, thinking of the scale of what had been lost in the past few hours. She shook the thought off, and continued. 'If his intention is to somehow hold the Line for good, he's a fool. The Grenze Guard may have run, but the Valtteri are unchaining every weapon the city has. No Spoil mob, however flush with victory, is going to be able to hold out once the vladar calls in the Defence Corps. To say nothing of the fact that the Arbites are overseeing the situation.'

Mattix was not quite good enough to keep the surprise from his face. 'Who?' he asked after a moment.

'Karadiz. Hakon Karadiz.'

Melita saw the probator's gaze unfocus as he fed the name into his iris. They both understood what Karadiz's arrival meant for the conflict, as, Melita was sure, did Vasimov and the cartel's executors. The Adeptus Arbites were empowered beyond the tenets of the Lex to enforce its greater meaning – order, at any cost. If he considered it necessary, Karadiz could rend the Valtteri cartel to its foundations, or have the entirety of the Spoil razed to the ground.

'It is, of course, right that the honoured Adeptus Arbites should oversee the response to a crisis with such far-reaching consequences.'

She wondered whether Mattix was paranoid enough to believe his office was wired for vox-theft, or just wanted her to think he was.

'As you say,' she agreed, just in case. 'But it adds to my point. There is no possible way that an improvised, untrained force could hold even a section of the Line for more than a few days. If the Arbites get involved, call it a matter of minutes.'

Mattix nodded as he plucked a lho-stick from a case on his desk. He noticed the hungry look in her eyes, and lit a second stick and passed it across his desk.

'Did you voice these thoughts with your superiors at the Xeremor? That is, before you fled their custody.'

Melita ignored his jibe as she took a long drag on the stick. It wasn't topaz – it wasn't even the soothing balm of cotin – but it was something.

'After the past few days, my opinion carries very little weight up there. If it ever did.' She drew in another lungful of hot, bitter smoke.

'So, I think we return to my first question. Why are you here? If you're looking for protection, I'm afraid you've come to the wrong place. The cartel's reach undoubtedly extends inside our walls.'

Melita played her high card. 'I'm certain of it. Your commanding castellan receives an annual payment equal to half his stipend directly from the Valtteri's coffers.'

Mattix blinked, and Melita suppressed a small, victorious smile. Finding that fact had not been easy, as the smuggler's rickshaw had rattled its way through the Dragosyl streets and Melita's probes raced across the dataveil. She had only found the connection thanks to two years of subtle, halting infiltration of the Valtteri's sprawling affairs, and because Hauf had done a rather poor job in setting up the anonymous account into which his bribe was paid.

Mattix rallied quickly. 'Only half? I'm surprised.'

'I don't think they value his contributions all that highly.'

Mattix snorted, but a degree of wariness entered his eyes. 'If you know my castellan is in their pocket, why do you assume I'm not?'

She took her time before answering. 'Three reasons. First, the Valtteri have a tendency to confuse hierarchy with power. They assume that by buying the person at the top, they buy the whole structure.' She was staring hard at Mattix, and he back at her. 'Oftentimes, they're right. But they make no account of the individual. They forget that everyone gets to make their own choices.'

'That's rather naive, wouldn't you say?'

Despite his reflexive cynicism, Melita sensed she had struck a chord. 'Second, if you are on their payroll, you're better at concealing it than your castellan.'

'You've done your digging?'

'I have.' Mattix had received no direct payments from the Valtteri, at least that she had been able to find.

'And the third reason?'

Melita felt like she was stepping out on a narrow ledge over a high drop. 'You wouldn't have been out at the Slahin Junction if you were taking their orders. You were out there to investigate for yourself. You needed to know what was happening. And so do I.'

Mattix took his time in nodding, but there was a sincerity to the gesture. 'So you trust me?'

'I didn't say that.' Now she stepped off the ledge. 'Why did you pick up Magos Bai?'

'What?' Mattix appeared to be genuinely surprised by the question.

'You snatched Russov Bai from their domicile, and took them out to Slahin. Why?'

Mattix shifted in his seat. For the first time since Melita had entered his office, he looked uneasy. 'For the same reason that you came and so effectively retrieved them.'

She shook her head. 'No. Vasimov tried to grab Bai to use as a bargaining chip to secure his preferred candidate to succeed Sorokin. I came because I needed their help to trace a lead in Sorokin's murder. You didn't have a stake in either of those.'

'I'm a probator. Solving murders is what I do.'

'And that's why you were interrogating Bai, out on the very edge of the Spoil? When you could have run them back across the Rustwater and into one of your extremely secure blockhouses?'

Mattix didn't reply to her sarcasm. Whatever his motive, he would hold on to it.

'You took their robe,' Melita said instead.

Again, he seemed confused. This was the root of her concern about the probator. There were many stripes of enforcer, and Melita wanted to know what kind he was.

'You took Bai's robe, because you knew it would make them uncomfortable. Put them on the back foot. Make them yield to your questions that bit easier.'

Melita left the accusation hanging. Mattix stared at her for several seconds, then scoffed.

'If that's your idea of intensive interrogation, I should show you the chastener levels.'

She almost walked out. Melita felt the urge to stand and abandon this last, desperate attempt to redeem herself and undo the damage she had watched unfurl. Bai may not have been harmless, armed as they were with the forbidden lore of the Adeptus Mechanicus. But they had aided Melita when she had least expected it, and were not deserving of casually inflicted torment.

Melita almost walked out. But she didn't.

'I see.'

Mattix saw the judgement in her eyes, but if it wounded him he gave no sign. 'So, we've established why you won't trust me. Why should I trust you, Melita Voronova?'

She had been braced for it, but the emphasis he put on her family name made Melita freeze.

Mattix continued, watching her carefully. 'I've done a little digging myself. I thought it was rather unusual that a scion of Voronova Atmospheric Shipping would be happy working with the Valtteri, of all people.'

She knew this was a test, but she couldn't help gritting her teeth as she replied. 'I wouldn't say happy.'

'What would you say?'

'Coerced,' she said eventually.

'Interminor?' He used the High Gothic term for blackmail.

Melita said nothing. She had given him all that he would get, and after a moment the probator leaned back, satisfied that he had her measure.

'Very well, Mistress Voronova. Let us, for the moment, assume there is a wider conspiracy behind Damor Saitz's rebellion.' He stubbed out his lho-stick. 'What evidence is there to prove it?'

Melita reached into her pocket, and pulled out the plastek bag containing the bullet that Edi had given her.

'What's that?'

'A bullet from an autogun used by one of Saitz's men. They are far better armed than any Spoil gang has the right to be.'

'A single bullet?' He reached for another lho-stick. 'I'd like to say that I've broken cases with less, but the truth is, I haven't.'

It was not much – in truth, it was an appallingly slender thread – but it was all Melita had. 'We have to start somewhere.'

He shrugged, and picked up his vox-horn.

'Probator-Senioris Mattix for Verispex Razinn.'

CHAPTER 32

'Shoot them! Just fucking shoot them!' Haska screamed. Thunderous blasts of shot and las answered from the barricade. But it was all too late.

Haska and Liocas Boscan grabbed Andrysi's arms and heaved her back from the barricade. Haska stumbled. The woman was heavier than the two juves combined, and the ground was slick with dust and gravel.

Leonida – Haska couldn't say at what point the older woman had become Leonida to her – gave a weak moan, as their jerking efforts tugged at the wounds in her side. She had been caught by the full weight of an enforcer's shot-cannon. Haska had seen it all, like a vid stuck on stuttering slow motion. The sound of the blast, the punch to her midsection that bent her in half like a prize-fighter's body blow. The dark blood that welled from the cluster of holes that perforated the lames of her flak armour.

They pulled her inside the door of the pens. As the morning had dragged on, their small company had been pushed back,

from one barricade to the next, as the city's forces pressed
on. They were now fighting over a wide junction between a
set of holding pens and the neighbouring abattoir.

The smell of Leonida's blood set the grox snarling and
crashing against their restraints. Haska clawed at the broken
shards of armour, coating her hands in horribly warm gore.
Leonida tried to speak, but all that emerged was a wheeze.
Haska scrabbled at the wounds, pressing her hands hard
against the shredded muscle.

She wanted to cry for help, but there was none. No medicae
or chirurgeons were among the Spoil's ranks, and even if
they had been, they had nowhere to take the wounded, and
nothing besides street narcotics to treat them with. Anyone
hit either died, or stayed on the barricades and fought on,
possibly with the aid of a blister of topaz or a shot of bliss.

Haska felt Liocas' hand on her shoulder. She looked up at
him, then back at Leonida. She was gone.

Hot tears cut runnels through the dirt and dust on Haska's
face. Liocas had no tears, but that was because he had already
shed them. Two of his friends had been killed in the first
counter-attack by the city's forces, cut down by long-distance
las-shots that had burst their skulls in a horror of gore and
bone. Liocas had been standing right beside them, too focused
on the fight to even register that they had fallen until Aryat
had tackled him to the ground and out of the line of fire.

After the bloody havoc of that first attack, Haska had found
him behind a tool shed. Despite the threats they had made
to one another not half a day before, she had wrapped her
arms around his broad chest and held him until his sobs had
finally run out.

Outside, the crackle of gunfire from the barricade was
dying down. There were no cheers this time, nor had there
been since the breach of the Praetorian's Gate and the wild,

whooping race through the alleys. The morning's battle had made veterans of them all, grim and stubborn in defence of their conquered ground.

The first counter-attack had come as day broke, and now the dry, diffuse heat hammered at them from the gravel paths, from the sheer metal sides of warehouses, from the air itself. Splashes of dried blood and viscera marked the places where the waves of enforcers and mercenaries had broken, and where the Spoil's fighters had fallen in the effort. The city's forces had advanced behind enormous armoured groundcars, under the cover of snipers, and even accompanied by deafening wails that screamed from vox-emitters.

Each time, the mob of Spoil gangers, factorum workers, and drug addicts had pushed them back, and ransacked their bodies for weapons, ammunition and armour. Haska was wearing the cuirass of a particularly short sanctioner, and had been firing the woman's shot-cannon for the past two hours after her autogun had run dry. The barricade that blocked their stretch of alley was formed predominantly by the burnt-out husk of a Bulwark riot-wagon, and extended by enforcer riot shields and whatever furniture and sheet metal could be stolen from the agri-plants.

The pent-up grox lowed, mournful hoots of frustration and pain. With the power shut down, the air filters that kept them cool were silent, and the beasts were suffering in the heat just as much as those fighting outside.

'It'd be a mercy to just shoot them.' Lira appeared from around the corner, her autogun gripped by its middle and a plastek water bottle in her hand. They had been drinking from the pipe that filled the grox's troughs. It was almost certainly laden with growth hormones and chems to keep disease in check, but it was the closest source to hand and was surely no worse than what they had been drinking all their lives from the corroded pipes of the Spoil.

'It'd be a waste,' said Liocas, taking the bottle.

'I meant a mercy for me. I don't want to listen to them any more.' She said it with a grim smile, but it died when Lira saw Haska's face, and the body at her feet.

They stood in silence. That was all the ritual they could give the fallen. A few seconds of stillness, the time a sacrifice to their memory.

The moment was ruined when a cart pulled up with a heavy crunch of gravel. The flimsy machines had evidently been used by the Line workers to move from building to building, and the Spoil army had quickly adopted them to speed messages back and forth to the disparate sections of their line.

'Where's Andrysi?' asked the runner behind the control column.

Haska wiped the last tears from her eyes, and gestured at the ground.

The runner glanced down, then nodded tersely. 'You'll do.'

'For what?' asked Lira, instantly suspicious. She stepped up beside Haska, switching her grip on her gun. Haska put a hand on her arm.

The runner didn't react. 'Saitz wants someone from each section for a meeting back at the gate.'

Haska sniffed, and nodded again. She had, in effect, been Leonida's second since the first counter-attack. It was right that she go back, and see what Saitz had to say for himself.

Lira gripped her hand. They had not been apart since Lira had pulled Haska out of her hab.

'I'll be back,' Haska said.

She nodded. 'You'd better be.'

Haska handed over her shot-cannon to Liocas – none of the

Spoilers were precious about their scavenged weaponry, and her section would have more need of it while she was gone than she did – and climbed into the cart's passenger seat. She looked at Lira and Liocas as the cart's motor coughed into life.

'Look after them.'

The Praetorian's Gate was a ruin.

In the stark light of day, the gate and its broken towers seemed less imposing. It was not just because the western tower's summit was still wreathed by black smoke that billowed from its cracked embrasures, and the eastern tower was a broken husk. Seen from behind, the gate seemed smaller, less daunting.

The bodies of slain Grenze Guards and fallen gangers had been cleared away, but blood stained the rockcrete dust that coated the ground in a layer thick enough for bootprints to mark its surface. Haska's driver took them across the wide space behind the fractured gate, the start of the huge highway that ran north towards the district's heartland. Haska couldn't see the barricades that must have been erected somewhere on its stretch, which she took to be a good sign. This was the greatest point of vulnerability in the Spoil's line, and if they hadn't yet been pushed back here, then perhaps they were holding out better than Haska had imagined.

There were two dozen new volunteers huddled together behind the western tower, evidently waiting for someone to organise them. None carried any weapons that she could see, although that wasn't a surprise. The last batch of volunteers that had appeared at her company's crossroads had been similarly unarmed, and had had to pick up the guns and ammunition discarded by the dead of both sides.

They drove on, the Line's great bulk oppressive above them. Haska said nothing, letting the messenger steer the cart. Cuts and bruises she hadn't realised she'd taken had all begun to throb as they'd driven away from her crossroads, presumably having waited for their moment to ambush her. Although she had not been fighting continuously – the city's forces seemed to come in waves, probing each barricade in turn for any weakness – this was the first time in hours that she had allowed herself to unclench, to let her eyes close in rest. It was not the relief she had hoped for.

Saitz had set up his headquarters, such as it was, near the Praetorian's Gate. The messenger swung their cart around the corner of a squat stack of offices topped by a protruding landing pad for aircars, and slewed to a stop. More of the two-person carts and a pair of dusty groundcars were drawn up in the lee of the stack, and fifty or so gangers were spread out across the building's parking depot. Spoilers were awkward in a crowd at the best of times, and everyone present had learned that to stand too close to their fellows was to invite a grenade into their midst.

'Who are you?' One of the gangers nearby turned as Haska joined the back of the crowd. Most of the gathered section leaders were the veteran gangers that presumably came from Saitz's own crews, distinct in the black flak armour that Leonida had worn. Haska was a new face, and Spoil-bred instincts had only been heightened by a day and night of close-quarters combat.

'Andrysi's dead,' she said. It was all the reply she could muster, and all that was needed. The ganger nodded, and turned away.

Saitz appeared from the office stack's door, wearing a black flak jacket and a wearied expression. Haska was oddly pleased to see that he looked as tired as the rest of the Spoilers. Had he appeared fresh and untouched by the battle's trials that she and the rest of the Spoil's army were enduring, she might have shot him then and there.

He seemed to like having a stage from which to speak. In the Redfort he had stood on the body of a groundcar, and here someone had found a collection of crates and had piled them so that he could stand above the shoulders of his bodyguards and look down at the assembled fighters. A few of them, volunteers like Haska rather than the veteran gangers who led most of the army's sections, cheered as he appeared from the office block's door. Haska didn't join them.

He acknowledged the scattered applause with a wave of his hand. 'Thank you, my friends, but I do not deserve your praise. It is you who have won so much. You have done everything that I could ask, and more. You've shown courage beyond anything this city could have expected. Your ingenuity has stymied their vengeance at every turn.

'But courage alone will not be enough to carry the day. Ingenuity will only get us so far. Now,' he said. 'Now is the time for guile.'

He smiled, as though he had admitted Haska and those around her into a secret.

'We will be receiving reinforcements. Not more volunteers, although the God-Emperor knows that every fighter is welcome and valued.'

Saitz paused, inviting his audience to think of the comrades they had left back on the barricades.

'Breaching the Line was not just the first necessary step on our path to victory. It was a symbol, a statement to the city that their walls will hold us back no longer. Now we need another statement, to show that where we now stand is ours, and will remain ours. We will match fire with fire until the city relents, or all about us burns.'

Saitz's zealous smile faded, replaced by grim and sombre determination. 'I need you to go back to your crews and your sections, and ask them to hold. Hold on, just a little bit longer. They must find their last vestiges of strength, and continue to defy this city that would erase everything they have achieved.

'Because before the sun sets, we will take what the city would not share. By the end of this day, we will show Varangantua something that it has never seen before.'

This time, the cheers were unforced, and Haska joined them.

She felt renewed. Of course they would win. Her aches and pains were still there, but they were ignorable, less sharp and all-consuming. The empty void left by Leonida, the memory of Liocas' tears for his friends, seemed that bit more bearable, because their sacrifice had not been in vain. The treasures of the Line – free power, untainted water, the chance to dictate terms to a city that had spat on the Spoil – they were worth the pain. Haska wondered what her mother would make of the red fruit she and her friends had found. Of course they would win.

Saitz raised a hand in silent thanks, and stepped down from his makeshift podium. Gangers nodded to their fellows, or embraced arm to arm, before starting back to the carts that had carried them from their positions. Haska didn't know any of the other fighters, and so simply stood for a moment, revelling in the restored sense of purpose Saitz had given her. It was a strange and alien thing for Haska to admire someone. Besides Lira and Katryn, she had never known what it was to draw strength from seeing someone, from hearing them speak. Perhaps her mother, when she was younger, although that was the shadow of a memory if it had ever been the case at all.

Haska shook herself, and turned to look for the driver that had brought her to the brief meeting. As she turned, her gaze caught on someone among the small huddle of gangers surrounding Saitz.

He was standing beside Karlo Karamenko, arms folded impassively. She couldn't say why he stood out, but he did. His ochre skin was dusted with the same off-white powder that coated Haska and the gangers around her. His black hair was clipped down to a fine stubble in the manner of so many Spoil street-soldiers. But there was something about his manner, the way he stood. He wore the same body armour as the rest of Saitz's closest fighters, but he seemed detached from them. They stood slightly apart, their stares wary rather than welcoming. He was a stranger in their midst.

He and Saitz were speaking; or, more accurately, Saitz was speaking, gesturing with forceful motions of his hands, and the stranger was listening in silence. She watched Saitz offer the man his hand, and the moment of hesitance was unmistakable. Despite his costume, the man was no ganger.

Now she understood. Whoever this interloper was, he was not of the Har Dhrol, which meant he was upclave. He was the link with the reinforcements Saitz had promised, which would also be upclave – maybe gangs from outside the Spoil, although Haska didn't think that this man was born to the streets. He was likely responsible for the crates of autoguns and ammunition Haska and the other volunteers in the first wave had received.

For all his talk of independence and pride, Saitz had a sponsor. Disappointment crashed down on Haska, all the worse because it swept away the admiration she had allowed herself to enjoy just moments before. That feeling offered up excuses: Saitz was merely using the outsiders for their resources; it was naive to think that something so enormous could be done alone. Nevertheless, she couldn't shake her dismay in the hypocrisy of preaching defiance and autonomy while taking aid from outside the Spoil.

She kept watching until the two men broke apart. Either by

CHAPTER 33

She hated to admit it, but watching Mattix work was an education. For all his cheap smiles and half-truths, the man knew how to work an investigation.

Within minutes of a verispex orderly arriving to collect the bullet that had struck Edi, Mattix had sent out demands for reports from a dozen enforcer units. His junior, Anto, had been pulled from whatever duty he had been absorbed in, and set to work collating active investigations into gunrunners, arms dealers, and the nest of smugglers that was the Dragosyl voidports. Mattix had dispatched subtle but urgent messages to informants in the most organised of the district's gangs with requests for all news of caches opened or deals made.

Melita worked alongside him. The probator had begrudgingly granted her limited access to the Bastion's noospheric network, and she had spent the past two hours scouring the dataveil for any plausible sources of high-grade weapons, armour and supplies. She had cracked the production records of the six largest manufactoria licensed to produce arms, and traced the delivery of every shipment within the last month to their intended destinations. Her own network of sources had been roused, although she doubted whether any of them would provide her with anything useful at such short notice.

She was pushing the micro-cogitators and logic engines of her iris to their limit. Melita knew it was just her imagination, but she could almost feel the heat building in the tiny machines embedded in her skull, such was the frantic pace of her work.

Reports from sanctioners deployed to the Line came in piecemeal, and they made for grim and shocking reading. Close to eight thousand Spoilers were estimated to be inside Setomir's border, dug-in – Astra Militarum parlance was the only vocabulary that seemed to fit the circumstances – across a four-mile front of fortified warehouses, agri-complexes, and especially the vital Setomir geothermal power plants. More were arriving all the time, ferried north from the Redfort and all across the Spoil.

The effect on Setomir was unprecedented. The official feeds from across the district told a tale of mass chaos, as the enforcers were pulled back and citizens took their chance to run amok. There were reports of blockhouse captains who were triaging sub-claves, letting the riots in some run unchecked while they massed to stamp out those that threatened any sensitive precincts.

The city was gaining ground in the Line, albeit agonisingly slowly. The Valtteri had unleashed the strength of their Reisiger mercenaries, the tri-districts' Bastions had been all but emptied of their sanctioners, and the shamed Grenze Guard units were fighting to restore their lost honour. But for all their gathered might, they were frustrated by the close-quarters nature of the fighting, and the creative tactics of the Spoil's fanatic army. Mattix had shared with her the helmet-picter footage of a charge led by a Bulwark riot-wagon which was countered by a stampede of grox released from their holding pens. A dozen men had died, and the Bulwark was a battered wreck that formed the centrepiece of a new barricade for the cheering Spoilers. The city could not even deploy Zurov gunships or Reisiger Teridons to circumvent the line of battle, due to the volume and ferocity of fire that greeted any such attempt. Somehow the battle had degraded into block-by-block, alley-by-alley fighting, and while the city had the edge in equipment and discipline, the Spoil's ranks were swollen with zealots who refused to back down until they were put down.

Melita blinked her iris away, fighting a fearsome head-ache. She had co-opted a folding table and chair and had occupied a corner of Mattix's office. In short order, the table had become a graveyard of lho-stick butts and recaff mugs to equal the probator's own desk.

She suddenly thought of Edi, lying in the Xeremor's medicae facility. A hostage, now, in all likelihood. She hoped that the connection he and Nedovic had formed would shield him from Vasimov's anger towards her.

'Who were the Pasc Scorpina?' Melita asked, into the silence.

Mattix looked up from his cogitator's runeboard. 'One of my first cases.' He rubbed his face, then pushed himself away from his desk, stretching to relieve the cramp that had set in. 'I had just made full seal. I was looking into unlicensed flesh-dens. More than usual were popping up across a few of the eastern claves, near the voidports. I drew the case.'

'And?'

'And, we sent thirty-two people to the mortuarium, and

another twenty to the justicius. The Pasc Scorpina never recovered.'

'Why did Edi know the case?'

'This may shock you, Mistress Voronova, but enforcers gossip. Particularly about one another.'

She smiled, as he expected her to.

Mattix stood up, fighting the aches that came along with hours spent bent-backed at a cogitator, then slumped back into his chair.

'If we're asking questions, let me put one to you. Who killed Sorokin?'

Melita mirrored Mattix's slouch. In the midst of all the destruction and devastation that had followed the conclave, she had almost forgotten the death that had set it in motion.

'It had to be Saitz.' She had tried to push her anger at Vasimov aside while she worked, but it was still there, simmering. Thanks to him, Melita had spent a day and a night chasing shadows and vague hopes of bank records, and all the while Saitz had been preparing to unleash chaos.

'No, I mean, who specifically? How close were you to identifying the actual killer before everything exploded?'

'I wasn't.' She relayed her conversations with the two men locked up in St Eurydice's dungeons, and her hunt to trace the source of the pay-off that Troian Horvaç had received.

'And that was a dead end?' Mattix asked.

Melita shrugged.

'So, what do we actually know?'

'We have a description, from Babić.' Melita couldn't help but give Mattix a hard glare as she named their mutual informant. 'We know a digital laser killed one of Sorokin's guards.'

'There can't be that many people in the city who would have access to a weapon like that.'

Melita leant forward, picking up Mattix's train of thought. 'The Mechanicus, obviously.'

'I've heard of half a dozen gilded families that have one in their vaults.'

'Arch-Deacon Sakić has a ring on every finger during his Sanguinala address each year. I'd put hard slate on one of those being a weapon.'

'General Kurtsyn, probably,' said Mattix.

Melita gave a sudden start. 'General Kurtsyn.'

Mattix frowned. 'What about him?' General Vadim Kurtsyn was the overall commander of the Alectian Planetary Defence Corps, and one of the more powerful members of the governing Praesidium.

'No, not him specifically. But what did I say earlier? That there's no chance the Spoil mob will be able to stand up to Defence Corp troops.'

The two of them sat in silence, considering the implications of Melita's thought.

'We've run down every other lead,' she said. 'Where else would you get Guard-grade material in the quantities Saitz has?'

Mattix's eyes unfocused for a moment, and he grunted.

Melita looked up. 'What?'

'With an uncanny sense of timing, Razinn has finished the report on your bullet.'

'And?'

Instead of replying, he pushed the report from his cogitator into the noospheric node she had set up to aid their collaboration. The report blossomed into her vision, a wash of green runes, diagrams and complex chemical strings. It took the verispex until the fourth page to finally provide a conclusive statement.

Summary analysis

Based on the specific alchemical combination
of lead, stannum, and stibium present in
the projectile, and analysis of trace res-
idue of fyceline primer, the sample's origin
can be estimated with a 97.6% probability
of accuracy.

This projectile originated at the Saladie-XV
Manufactorum (see appendix for loc-ref).
Registered ownership: Trismodine Consortium.

This projectile was registered as delivered to Tertiary Magazine, Sixth Armoured
Company, Second Defence Corp Regiment (see
appendix for loc-ref). A summary of the shipment contents is appended to this report.

Thought for the Day: The Emperor's light
leaves no shadow in which the wicked and the
heretic may hide.

She blinked the report away and looked up at Mattix. 'How
would you contact an arbitrator of the Adeptus Arbites?'

He took a gulp of recaff before replying. 'I wouldn't.'

'I'm serious.'

'So am I. This is not conclusive. It's a sad fact that there
are any number of ways for equipment like this to reach
undesirable hands.' He gestured at the sheets of vellum and
data-wafers littering his desk. 'As we've seen.'

'But this fits. We've eliminated every other possibility. The
verispexy report–'

'Defence Corps regulars are always trading their gear for a
sheet of black ice or rekanine. A single bullet traced to this
armoury proves nothing.'

'Are you being deliberately obtuse?'

He grinned. 'It's a requirement of the service. They run special training courses at the academy.' He saw that Melita was not in a mood for jokes. 'You and I can see where this points, but this is not grounds to mobilise a detachment of the God-Emperor's Arbites. And even if there is a rogue quartermaster arming Saitz's mob, that doesn't lead us any closer to a wider conspiracy.'

'Doesn't it?'

Mattix looked away for several seconds. As the day had worn on, Melita had noticed that he had the habit of rubbing his hands together while he was thinking.

'Shit.' His callused hands continued to work back and forth. 'You said Karadiz was at the cartel's starscraper?'

'Yes.'

Mattix stood, and poked his head around the office door. 'Anto, I need to get a message through to Hauf.'

Castellan Alber Hauf wiped an already saturated kerchief across his face. The Xeremor's conference chamber was an oven, its ventilation systems outmatched by the volume of bodies running back and forth, and the number of cogitators that occupied almost every tier of the room.

So far, Hauf's role in the city's response to the chaos had been limited. He was representing the Bastion-D enforcers seconded to riot suppression and to the fighting with the Spoil's revolting mob, but besides agreeing to whatever requests that the Bastion-S commanders made, he had not been asked to make any contributions to the overall strategy. The castellan was, in equal measure, offended and quietly grateful for this lack of regard.

As a matter of course, he had been monitoring the feeds from his units in the field, and the discussion among the assembled civic leaders to which he was privy. And so, when his iris winked with the arrival of a priority message from Kerimov, his secretarius, he did not immediately blink it open. Only after he had duly considered – and approved – the latest set of deployment orders for his men did he turn his attention to the waiting bulletin.

Hauf read the missive, then read it again. Then he opened the appended report, and carefully read each word and examined each chart, despite lacking an understanding of the arcane mysteries verispexy involved.

He returned to Mattix's request. It was plainly written, but asked much of his superior.

Hauf was not ignorant of how closely Mattix had tied himself to his castellan's rank and standing within the Bastion. Hauf was forever covering for the man's insubordination; he had been required to retroactively sanction many of Mattix's investigations when it became clear that their consequences would fall well beyond what would ordinarily be expected of a single probator, even one of senioris rating.

What cost might there be to Hauf in supporting Mattix's theory? That was always the question, when Mattix brought one of his overreaching activities to him. But then, what might be the benefit, if the probator proved to be correct? Mattix was a renegade, but he had a sense for these things. And in such unprecedented times, surely one could be forgiven for advancing an outlandish notion that, upon examination, proved untrue?

Castellan Alber Hauf mopped his brow, and stood on unsteady legs.

The chamber's dais was crowded with functionaries and the forbidding figures of Valtteri executors. Hauf was all too aware of the proprietorial, almost disdainful stares several of them gave him as he awkwardly made his way to the stage's far side.

Karadiz and Tomiç had been in near-constant discussion since the arbitrator's arrival, with the director's forbidding advisor hovering close at hand. Although, as far as Hauf had observed, Tomiç had done most of the talking, while Karadiz stood in silent judgement of all that the Valtteri did to rectify the disaster that had been unleashed upon their holdings.

Hauf stood to one side of the line of cogitators and hololiths at which they worked, a child at scholam awaiting their tutor's attention. Finally, the grey eyes flicked up from a data-slate gripped in one gauntleted hand.

'Yes, castellan?'

'M-my lord arbitrator, I must beg a moment of your time.'

Karadiz waited. 'Yes?'

Hauf cleared his throat. 'I believe one of my probators has uncovered something that bears your consideration.'

CHAPTER 34

Melita's stomach lurched as the Zurov gunship tipped violently. A rush of rockcrete raced past the passenger hold's open hatch as the pilot banked around a tall hab-block, replaced swiftly by wan sunlight diffused by the city's polluted air.

Before the pilot levelled out, Melita caught sight of the hunched, ominous shape of the Adeptus Arbites Valkyrie that led their formation. She had been slightly surprised by how swiftly Arbitrator Karadiz had accepted the argument advanced by Mattix. Melita's presence within Bastion-D had gone unmentioned, but, listening in, she was sure that the Arbites had made the connection between her flight from the Xeremor and Mattix's sudden revelation. In any case, it had been all of an hour between Mattix sending his message to Castellan Hauf's aide and their growling exit from the Bastion in one of the few enforcer gunships left in its primary hangar.

The memories of taking off from St Eurydice's courtyard came unbidden, making her hands twitch in and out of painfully tight fists. The crash of gunfire, and Edi's grunt of pain. The sight of Oriel falling broken from the air.

She missed them both. Edi was the solid, reassuring presence she always needed in times of difficulty, even if she would never admit it to him. But she felt the servo-skull's absence the way she would a missing limb. Melita kept reaching out to it with her iris, and each time, an error code flashed in her sight, and a spike of loss stabbed her heart. Oriel had been the only constant in all the mad years of her life, and she had left it cracked and broken in St Eurydice's courtyard.

It was with these maudlin thoughts for company that Melita soared over the city. Although she was far from alone. A squad of sanctioners, enormous in their riot plate, filled the gunship's interior, while Mattix stood at the Zurov's door, tightly gripping a handhold to brace against the worst of the gunship's motion. Melita shifted in her borrowed armour. Mattix had ordered his junior to turn over his flak jacket to her, and fortunately Burian Anto was a slim man. Even so, the straps were at their tightest extension, and her jacket fitted poorly over the top.

The howl of the gunship's turbines made conversation impossible. Melita had a helmet on, mainly for the padded ear defenders to protect her hearing from the deafening drone of the engines, but it was not connected to the gunship's vox-network. Mattix wore a headset, and occasionally spoke with the Zurov's pilot and Sergeant Kalishk, the sanctioner squad's sergeant, but Melita was left to face her growing, restless anxiety alone.

She had pinned all of her hopes for redemption, for a reprieve from the death sentence that Vasimov had undoubtedly arranged for her, on uncovering a grand conspiracy. Something that justified her failure to foresee the chain of calamities that had struck the cartel. But if that was what the traced autogun round pointed towards – every bit the tenuous data-point that Mattix said it was – Melita feared that they would be too late to undo whatever plot was at work. Or, worse, she was wrong, and she had convinced Mattix to mobilise a squad of the Emperor's Arbites with an accusation of treason against loyal Varangantuan soldiers.

Either outcome was unlikely to buy her the goodwill she needed to escape Vasimov's petty vengeance.

At some point in the flight, a combination of the hull's vibration and flat-out exhaustion combined to let her sleep. She awoke when Mattix tapped her boot with his, and she saw that the Zurov was descending between a cluster of grey tenement towers.

It had surprised Melita to learn that the Defence Corps magazine was located in an urbanised clave. Before departing Bastion-D, she and Mattix had retrieved the building's schematics from the Setomir Administratum's archives, and had discovered that the magazine and its storerooms were all underground. Only a squat rockcrete bunker, with several large gates and loading depots to accommodate flyers and haulers, gave any indication of the wealth of munitions that were stored below.

Melita shook the cramp from her legs, and craned to see out of the passenger hold's narrow viewport. The two flyers had pulled into a hover, and Kalishk's sanctioners were checking and rechecking their riot plate and armaments.

'What's going on?' Melita shouted. There was no way Mattix could have heard her, but he gestured at a panel behind Melita. She plugged the trailing end of a cable into the port that Mattix indicated, then waited for Kalishk, at the probator's insistence, to flick a switch on the Zurov's communications array.

'–tiary Magazine, Sixth Armoured Company, you are commanded

to stand down by order of the Adeptus Arbites. All personnel must surrender themselves for interview, and all materiel on site be relinquished for inspection.'

The voice over the vox could have been the twin of Karadiz's, except broken by tinny distortion; the same unhurried, unchallengeable tone of authority.

Long seconds dragged by, with no response from the armoury.

'Tertiary Magazine Control, acknowledge.'

Still no answer. Melita caught Mattix's eye, and for once his cocksure amusement was absent.

'Soldiers of the Alectian Planetary Defence Corps, this is your final warning. Power down all defensive systems, unlock the primary loading bay for ingress, and surrender yourself to our judgement. Failure to comply will be taken as admission of complicity in crimes against the Lex Imperialis, and punished in accordance with His Will.'

Whoever was in command in the Valkyrie waited ten more seconds, and then clearly exhausted their supply of patience.

'Take us down. Zurov-D-Sixty-Two, hold in position.'

'Acknowledged.'

The enforcer pilot kept them in a hover, a hundred yards distant from the descending Valkyrie. From the passenger hold's viewport she watched armoured figures appear at the gunship's sides, shot-cannons cradled in their arms.

The Arbites evidently had some means of remotely overriding the magazine's controls, as the hangar doors that took up the bulk of the armoury's roof began to slowly grind open as their flyer carefully descended. The arbitrators at the doors leaned far out from the hull, held in place by anchored rappelling lines, to peer into the armoury's unlit interior.

The Valkyrie was ten yards from the opening doors when the hangar exploded.

A pillar of fire erupted from the rockcrete Bastion. It seemed to swallow the Valkyrie, swirling about the gunship with raging jaws. Secondary explosions coughed from within the inferno. Melita saw the briefest impression of flickering shapes leaving the flames, and then the Zurov's hull sang with the impact of hull fragments.

'Gah!' Mattix cried as he fell back into the passenger hold, both hands gripping his knee.

'Holy Throne!'

The probator's thigh was laid open, and blood poured in sheets onto the decking. A pair of sanctioners gripped him around each arm, keeping Mattix inside the Zurov as its pilot threw the gunship into a tight roll away from the detonation.

Mattix reached around the restraining arms to shout into his helmet's vox. 'Take us up! Up!'

The pilot fought to obey. The turbines howled as the Zurov struggled to lift itself away from the sudden destruction. Alarms wailed and lumens flashed. Melita had no idea what any of them meant. The gunship rocked, levelled out, and rocked again, caught in the tormented updraught of the blaze that raged below. Melita crashed against the plex of the hold's viewport, and looked down at the stricken Arbites flyer.

The burning husk of the Valkyrie seemed to fall slowly, as though the flames of the burning hangar were fighting to hold it aloft. But, inexorably, the armoured frame dropped from the sky, trailing a column of smoke, into the heat-hazed maw below. Another gust of flame belched from the magazine's mouth as the Valkyrie disappeared inside. And then Melita could see no more, as the Zurov hurled itself up into the chem-rich air.

She slumped back, heart racing. There was no chance any of the Arbites on board could have survived the initial blast, let alone the horrific destruction of their flyer. Of all the ways Melita had hoped to be proven right – an empty munitions crate, an inconsistent storage manifest – this had not been among them. Never had she imagined treachery on such a scale.

The sanctioners heaved Mattix into the Zurov's rear. Kalishk shoved Melita aside to give herself space, and slid a thick plastek band up the probator's leg. She manoeuvred it into place around the torn meat of his thigh, then hauled on the band's end to pull the ragged lips of the wound closed.

Mattix was shaking and ashen-skinned, too far into shock to even register her treatment.

'Sir? Mattix? Thaddeus?' Kalishk finally tried his given name, and slapped him across the face. His eyes swam into focus. He nodded thanks, and with a hand coated in his own blood reached for his helmet's vox-bead.

'Pilot, put me through to Bastion command.' He waited for three of Melita's thumping heartbeats. 'This is Probator-Senioris Thaddeus Mattix, authentication K-46-32-Invictor. I need you to connect me to Arbitrator Hakon Karadiz, right now.'

CHAPTER 35

The Bastion-S primary medicae ward was close to being overwhelmed.

At least fifty sanctioners were strapped to gurneys, or sat in rigid plastek seats if their injuries permitted it. The level's ventilation system was unequal to its task, and so the air was streaked with the coppery stink of blood, the vicious tang of counterseptic, and the nauseating reek of ruptured guts. Melita had seen half a dozen enforcer gunships approaching or leaving the Bastion as their flyer had arrived, acting as evacuation craft from the ongoing battle on the Line. Evidently more were coming in as the day wore on, as every few minutes more wounded walked or were wheeled in to wait for exhausted medicaes to assess the extent of their injuries.

The dead, presumably, were taken elsewhere.

Mattix had been given one of the tiny individual rooms at the far end of the ward. They had been met on the Bastion's main hangar deck by a pair of weary orderlies, and whisked along busy corridors and past sanctioners whose injuries seemed, to Melita, to be far more severe. This, she supposed, was a privilege of his rank.

Sergeant Kalishk had been dismissed shortly after they reached the ward. She had administered morpholox during the flight, which had kept the probator on the edge of consciousness but brought the pain down to something close to bearable. The sanctioner sergeant had not wanted to go, but a harried senior chirurgeon had ordered her away while inspecting the tourniquet she had applied. Melita had been permitted to remain, but made herself as unobtrusive as possible as the medicaes set to work, pinching the lacerated flesh of his leg closed with enormous metal staples. Mattix had been fortunate, they said, that the shard of Valkyrie hull plating had avoided all the major arteries. He was cleaved to the bone from kneecap to hip joint, but it seemed that the God-Emperor smiled on the probator.

With their crude work complete and a bolus of blood hooked up to Mattix's veins, along with another of obscurine to take over from the morpholox, the chirurgeon had pronounced him stable. He would undergo proper surgery later, but it appeared that he had received all the special treatment due to a probator-senioris while others waited and bled.

He and Melita had been left alone, with only the irregular clunks and whines of the vitae-monitors beside his bed to fill the silence. For a while Mattix appeared to sleep, but then the probator's eyes fluttered open.

'You look worse than I do,' he rasped.

Melita gestured at the alarmingly large bag of blood that was steadily bringing the colour back to his face. 'You know that stuff is harvested from executed prisoners?' It was a common bit of street rumour. 'I hear there are whole levels in each Bastion given over to reclaiming the organs of anyone the sanctioners take a disliking to.'

Mattix gave the shadow of a smile. 'They're not using them any more.'

Melita snorted, although it wasn't the least bit funny.

He licked parched lips. 'I could use a drink.'

She stood, cramped limbs complaining. 'I'll see what I can find.'

She pushed open the door to the main ward in the same moment as Karadiz arrived.

The arbitrator swept into the medicae level with the force of an advancing thunderstorm. Chirurgeons and their attendants attempted to scatter from his path, but they were hampered by the gurneys loaded with wounded sanctioners. The pair of arbitrators who followed in his wake, the peals of thunder to Karadiz's lightning bolt, did not help matters.

The arbitrator ignored the cries and the blood, and the few timorous voices raised in protest at his disruptive arrival. He evidently knew where Mattix had been billeted, as he marched with purpose towards his private room.

Melita ducked back inside. 'Karadiz is here.'

Through the fog of pain suppressants, Mattix nodded understanding. He tried to sit straighter in his bed, but with little success. Melita backed away, half expecting the door to disintegrate into a hail of splinters beneath the weight of shot-cannon fire and the wrath of a vengeful arbitrator. Instead, the door swung open, admitting moans of pain and the frantic demands of orderlies. The arbitrator's armoured frame almost filled the narrow doorway.

'I am Hakon Karadiz.'

'Thaddeus Mattix, sir. Probator-senioris, Bastion-D.' Mattix made his best attempt at a salute. Karadiz gave the briefest nod of acknowledgement.

'This is–'

'Melita Voronova,' said Karadiz, in a tone that made Melita

take a few involuntary steps back, to put Mattix's gurney between her and the arbitrator. 'Your departure from the Xeremor starscraper was much remarked upon.'

Melita stammered, entirely lost for words.

Karadiz continued, ignoring her inarticulate fear. 'For the moment, I could not care less about the circumstances of your flight, or your relationship with the Valtteri.' He stepped into the room, leaving his two arbitrators outside to deter any duty-bound medicae from intervening.

'Tell me what happened to my men.'

Karadiz, for all his haste, had arrived too late for Mattix to be of any use to him. The drip-feed of obscurine that numbed the agony also fogged his mind. He swam in and out of lucidity, although never falling into complete unconsciousness.

As a result, the full force of the arbitrator's interrogation had fallen on Melita.

Karadiz listened with more patience than she would have expected as Melita laid out the chain of logic and evidence that had led them to suspect the Setomir garrison of the Defence Corps. He had already heard some of this from Mattix, via Hauf, but he had her go over everything. Occasionally he would ask a question, or demand further clarity when she faltered in her retelling.

'Describe the wound caused by this digital laser.'

'Have you retained the data provided to you by the Har Dhrol's rogue Mechanicus adept?'

'What did you expect to find at the magazine?'

Melita thought about that for a moment. 'A rogue quartermaster. Perhaps a corrupt unit, given the scale of the materiel Saitz has in his possession. Evidence of misappropriated weaponry and ammunition, enough to tie them to Saitz and whoever is backing him from outside the Spoil.'

'You believe there is a conspiracy acting against the cartel?'

Melita had considered this as the Zurov tore through the smog-choked sky. 'I didn't, until the armoury exploded.'

The arbitrator's scowl deepened. 'And now?'

'We believe it to be a cult cell, sir.'

'We?' Karadiz glanced towards the groggy Mattix, who appeared to be slowly surfacing from his dazed state.

Melita conceded that point. 'I believe.'

The violence the corrupt soldiers had unleashed at their discovery. The planning and precision that underpinned Saitz's coup. The fanatical zeal with which the Spoil army fought. A cult was the only logical answer.

Karadiz nodded again, saying nothing. That a violent sect could have grown under the noses of the tri-district authorities was a damning indictment of their vigilance.

'The armoury corpsmen will not have acted alone,' Karadiz said finally.

'No,' Melita agreed. While possible, it was highly unlikely that the rot stopped with the armoured company's munitions depot.

'My Bastion can handle this,' said Mattix, defending the pride of fellow enforcers despite his stupor. 'It will take hours for more of you blackcloaks to get here.' Fort Gunlysk, the much-feared fortress of the Adeptus Arbites on Alecto, was several hundred miles to the north of Setomir, reassuringly close to the high Praesidium spires in the planetary capital.

'My troops will be here in eighty-seven minutes,' said Karadiz, ignoring Mattix and his use of the slang term for the Arbites order. 'I summoned them from Fort Gunlysk the moment your first message reached me.' Karadiz lifted a gauntlet to his armoured chest, and briefly held the icon of the Arbites order that hung above his sternum. 'A cancer has been allowed to grow and fester in the Spoil, and now

ten of the God-Emperor's arbitrators have been killed. I will
see their murderers brought to justice.'

'What about her?' asked Mattix, his voice starting to slur
again as another measure of obscurine flowed into his system.

'I would prefer to remain here in the Bastion,' said Melita
quickly.

Karadiz's stare made clear the extent to which he valued
her preferences. 'You will be accompanying me.'

CHAPTER 36

The waning orb of Alecto's sun was sinking in the sky, throwing the narrow silhouettes of the racing aircraft ahead of them as harbingers of their wrath.

Melita clutched the metal struts of her seat as the flyer rocked in a gust of turbulence, and tried to appear calm. Beside her, Arbitrator Hakon Karadiz sat in silence, sable cloak across his knees and eagle-topped baton of office held tightly in his lap. His attention was on a data-slate mounted on the arm of his seat. Occasionally he glanced up, and Melita was subjected to the full force of his grey, piercing stare.

Their flyer led the point of a V-shaped flight of ten Valkyrie transports, with a pair of aquiline gunships that Karadiz had named as Vultures above and ahead of the formation. Below them, a column of squat, coal-black armoured personnel carriers, bullish Bulwark wagons, and sheer-sided haulers used for the transportation of prisoners surged along emptying streets, their clarions warbling a dire warning to any who did not heed the approaching might of the Lex Imperium.

Melita doubted that the traitors had imagined they would rouse the ire of the Emperor's Holy Arbites. But rouse it they had.

The now annihilated Tertiary Magazine had served the Sixth Armoured Company of one of the two Defence Corps regiments on Alecto, and it was to the company's barracks that Karadiz's vengeance flew. Unlike the armoury, the garrison occupied a wide, purposefully barren expanse of land near the Dragosyl border. Its boundaries were tall, double-layered earthworks, its entry points guarded by servitor-controlled weapons turrets and a company of Defence Corps auxilia.

Melita had no idea what to expect. The traitorous soldiers that had shipped munitions from the magazine to Saitz could have been working alone; as she and Mattix had reflected only a few hours before, the corruption endemic to Varangantua did not confine itself to civilian agencies. But it seemed unlikely that the Sixth Company's command structure would have been ignorant of such betrayal. And the spectacular act of sabotage that claimed the lives of Karadiz's arbitrators had not been arranged merely to erase the evidence of their thievery, although it would be days before anybody would be able to enter the armoury and confirm the absence of materiel. The explosives had been set to make a statement. Of intent, perhaps. Of defiance, clearly.

Of hubris, certainly.

Why? The question was lodged in Melita's mind. Corruption was one thing, but the ringleaders of whatever conspiracy was unfolding could not be so foolish as to believe there would be no consequences. What could compel Defence Corps soldiers, men and women who had sworn loyalty to the city and to the Imperium, to abandon their duties – and their lives – and throw in with a Spoiler rebellion?

'What, precisely, is the nature of your involvement with

the Valtteri organisation?' Karadiz asked suddenly over the Valkyrie's vox. His voice was distressingly powerful, like the breaking of a thunderhead, even beneath the crackle of vox distortion.

Melita's attention shifted with fear's rapidity to her own, more immediate concerns. 'At this point, sir, I really don't know.'

'Indeed.'

He might have intended to continue, but Melita was given a reprieve by the gunship's co-pilot.

'Sir, we are approaching the target.'

Melita watched him lean forward and flick on a grainy imagifier. She guessed that it showed the view from a picter mounted in the Valkyrie's nose.

'Our quarry is on the move.'

The armoured company was, indeed, moving out from their barracks.

The first of the tanks had already cleared the series of gates through the fortress' fortifications. Melita counted sixteen Leman Russ-class battle tanks, enormous slab-sided machines all painted in the blue-and-grey of the Alectian Defence Corps. They were drawn up in a single column, while behind them a caravan of armoured personnel carriers, haulers and other vehicles queued. The entire company, down to the spouses and children of the turncoat soldiers, was abandoning their barracks.

Karadiz's command was simple. 'All squads, engage and detain. Assume hostile intent from all targets.'

The Arbites flyers fell upon them like the airborne predators they were. Bunched up at the barracks' entrance, the armoured company was ripe for slaughter; it was well for the traitors that Karadiz had restrained the ire of his men. Melita's Valkyrie shook as a Vulture gunship, rocket pods affixed to its stubby wings, roared past. It whipped over the clustered armoured vehicles, low enough to rock them with the force of its downdraught. Vox-horns blared from the hulls of every Arbites vehicle, hammering the turncoat soldiers with overlapping demands for immediate, unconditional surrender.

Chaos raced through the column in the Vulture's wake. Most of the armoured vehicles were hemmed in by the narrowness of the fortress gates, and those at the rear could not reverse without flattening the waiting haulers and groundcars.

The first Arbites leapt into their midst, rappelling from their gunships directly onto the hulls of the tanks at the front and rear of the column. Every motion of an Imperial officer of the Lex was covered by the guns of the hovering Valkyries and Vultures, traversing to track their nose-mounted rotary cannons left and right as the arbitrators hauled unresisting soldiers from their hatches. The howl of engines holding the flyers at a hover was deafening, even through Melita's muffling headset.

The civilians were running. Some, most, leapt from their haulers and transports and fled for the assumed safety of their squat hab-block homes, while those that could gunned their vehicles' engines, turned out of the line, and raced away towards the base's interior.

They did not get far.

A pair of cruciform shadows overtook the fleeing vehicles almost immediately, and that brought many to a stop. Melita started at the ripcord buzz of one of the Valkyries' wing-mounted weapons pods unloading, even at a mile's distance and over the din of her own flyer's engines. It was like the gunner had unchained a vast swarm of enraged insects. The cannon stitched a line of craters in the asphalt across the path of the fleeing vehicles. Without exception, they slewed to a stop.

As though the hammering gunfire had been a cue, the Defence Corps tank crews that had not yet surrendered slammed hatches shut, and gun turrets projecting from the Leman Russ tanks' hulls started to traverse. Arbitrators leapt from their fields of fire, dragging their prisoners with them as human shields.

Melita grabbed a handhold above her as the gunship slewed suddenly. As it turned, Melita saw the turrets of the tanks that had already cleared the barracks' gates turning to point along the wide arterial road, up which the combined Arbites and enforcer column raced.

Karadiz plucked a vox-emitter from a cradle on the equipment in front of him.

'Open fire, and you condemn your souls to the Emperor's fury.' The words bellowed from a vox-horn mounted somewhere on the gunship.

There was a second's hesitation, then smoke and flame punched from the lead tank's barrel. In the distance, a black armoured vehicle erupted into flames, and somewhere beneath and below Melita, heavy weapons started to chatter.

Karadiz switched back to his command vox. 'I want prisoners.'

'Sir, this is the company commander. Major Argus Ranić.'

Ranić would have been tall, had he been able to stand up straight. One eyebrow was crusted with blood, and he hunched forward around a pain in his chest, though his hands were bound behind his back.

'He has no rank now.'

Hakon Karadiz stalked closer, the hem of his cloak catching on slivers of broken glass and shattered armour.

'He abandoned the honour of his rank the moment he turned his back on his city.' He lifted the man's chin with the end of his baton, until Ranić's one good eye met the arbitrator's. 'You killed my men.'

Melita expected fury, rancour, possibly even raving from one so mad as to lead treason against the city. But he met Karadiz's glare steadily, and said nothing.

'Where were you going?' the arbitrator asked.

Ranić jerked his head away from Karadiz's stick, and spat on the ground. He smiled around bloody teeth. 'I am prepared for what you will do.'

The arbitrator's shot-cannon thundered into his cracked ribs, and Ranić dropped to his knees. Melita turned away, but over the crackle of flames and the wet sound of body blows, she heard Karadiz speak.

'No, you are not.'

The massacre had taken moments. Most of it was a blur of sound and movement smeared across Melita's memory. The scream and hiss of the Valkyrie's weapons. The horrific crumps of detonating tanks. The violent lurches as the gunship evaded what little return fire had been thrown up by the traitors.

Melita had wanted to remain in the Valkyrie after they had landed. She had no wish to see the devastation in greater detail, but Karadiz insisted that she follow him. Several of the huge Arbites personnel carriers, of a size with an intact Leman Russ, had managed to force a path through the wreckage that choked the gates, and more black-clad arbitrators were marching from ramps at their rear to assist in taking charge of the Defence Corps barracks. Isolated gunshots echoed every few moments, as the remaining resistance was pacified. Melita could see lines of civilians, the families of the soldiers who had betrayed their uniforms, being marched across the enormous open space towards waiting transports.

Having finally been allowed to return to the Valkyrie after

her reluctant tour, Melita reclaimed her seat. The hold rocked slightly as Karadiz climbed back into the gunship's interior.

'Pilot, take us back to the Valtteri.'

The engines' whine grew almost immediately.

'I am grateful to you, Mistress Voronova,' said Karadiz as he settled back in his seat. 'Had this corruption been allowed to play out, the outcome of the conflict across the Setomir Line might have been entirely different.'

Melita looked out of the gunship's hatch at what remained of the Sixth Armoured Company. She swallowed. 'I am the city's servant, arbitrator.'

'However, I believe that this treachery presents an opportunity to bring that situation to its resolution.' Karadiz reached forward and began keying his vox-unit to a different frequency.

An icy premonition fell through Melita's centre. 'What do you mean?'

For the first time since she had encountered the forbidding arbitrator, Karadiz smiled.

'The insurrectionists are expecting tanks. We will provide them.'

CHAPTER 37

'Haska.'

She woke with a start, despite the gentleness with which Lira shook her awake. Haska clutched the shot-cannon cradled across her body, the butt between her knees. She had been asleep beside the grox pens, the first time she had closed her eyes in almost two days of murder, fear and confusion.

She looked up at her friend with bleary eyes. 'What?' Then she heard the crash of distant thunder, and staggered to her feet.

'It started a minute ago.'

The explosion shivered the air, carried by the hot wind from the west. Then another, quieter, and then a rapid tattoo of several rolling detonations.

Haska coughed, ignoring her body's many complaints. 'Send someone across to Jolana, see if they know what's happening.' Jolana Kalui was the fighter commanding the section holding the neighbouring junction, another volunteer who had somehow become the person others looked to as the fighting dragged on.

'Liocas is over there now.'

Lira's face was grey with fatigue, streaked with dust and dirt, and riddled with tiny cuts from the vicious sting of gravel shards thrown up by stray bullets. Despite all that, and the grim expression with which she had woken Haska, she was still the most beautiful person Haska had ever seen.

On an impulse, she reached out and took Lira's hand, who squeezed it back, and held up Haska's jacket. Haska pulled it on and staggered on cramped legs out of the warehouse.

Her fighters were all sheltered behind their barricade, listening to each detonation. Darkness had fallen in the hours since Lira had ordered Haska inside to rest, to take advantage of the tense peace that had descended on the Line.

The fighting had intensified as the day reached its peak, and the wicked, sapping heat had risen to its apex. Haska's section had fallen, one person at a time, until there were barely two dozen of them left, firing back with whatever ammunition the attacking enforcers and mercenaries dropped when they died. Then, all of a sudden, the city's forces had withdrawn, retiring to their own junctions and barricades. Some had even been seen pulling back entirely, presumably to be redeployed elsewhere along the Line.

That had been almost four hours ago. Haska had been sceptical of their reprieve, which had not been helped by a messenger from Saitz who had made it clear that this was not the end. She supposed that she should have tried to push forward, advance the Spoil's territory, but she knew her fighters were spent. Either the city would give in to Saitz's demands or they would come again. There was no point forcing more fighting where none was needed.

Liocas appeared beside her, keeping low for fear of snipers. Katryn and Aryat, who had been slumped together with their backs against a piece of sheet metal, looked up as he and Haska knelt.

'Kalui doesn't know anything. They've sent two people back to the gate in a cart for answers.'

They sat in silence, Haska, Lira and her friends, listening to the dull crumps that echoed along the alleys between the workshops and agri-mills. Each explosion was a shocking and concussive blast, a brutal punch followed by an eruption of something out of sight.

'I can hear something,' said Katryn suddenly.

'What?'

'I said, I can hear something.'

Haska heard it too, now she tried. It was constant, low, but growing in strength beneath the punctuation of detonations in the west.

One of Liocas' friends was a few paces down the barricade, keeping a lookout across the dead land between the lines. 'What the hells is that?'

Haska forced herself to move. She looked over the lip of the piled metal and wreckage, and stared in stunned silence at the thing that was steadily, implacably coming towards her.

She recognised it from the propaganda reels and vid-projections broadcast in joy houses. Haska had seen dozens of images of stalwart Imperial soldiers, standing atop or beside slab-sided war machines, their swords raised and rifles levelled towards humanity's many enemies. To see a Leman Russ battle tank advance towards her, metal treads pulverising the gravel beneath their bulk, was far less stirring.

Haska drew breath to order a retreat in the face of this new, impossible threat, when Liocas shouted, 'They're pulling back!'

It was true; the combined force of Grenzers, sanctioners and cartel mercenaries was hurriedly running out of the path of the approaching tank. The Bulwark that was parked in the centre of the alley, no more than two hundred yards down at the next junction, rumbled into life, and started to retract its extended armour plates that had given such effective cover to Haska's gunfire.

Cheers erupted from every Spoiler throat. This was the reinforcement Saitz had promised, the unlooked-for support that he had somehow engineered from outside the Spoil. How had he done it? The hostile eyes of the stranger shaking Saitz's hand came back to Haska. Was the man a renegade Defence Corps officer? Some district leader turning traitor on the city? How had Saitz done this?

Even as Lira and her friends cheered, Haska's suspicions grew. Someone had managed to scavenge a long-las on one of their brief forays forward into the city's lines, a horribly lethal weapon that had reaped a fearsome tally until its bearer had been struck by a counter-sniper. Haska had unceremoniously plucked the scope from the precious weapon, and pulled it now from a pocket on her scavenged flak armour to stare down the roadway at the approaching tank.

It was huge. The path between the two rows of warehouses was barely wide enough to accommodate its bulk. Through the scope she could see two columns of men and women advancing ahead of it, their grey-and-blue flak armour matching the colours daubed across its plating. Its main hull was at least twice the height of the tallest soldier who led the way. A fearsome gun projected from its sloped front, although Haska's eye was drawn to the enormous cannon and turret on top. Her arm would have fitted down the cannon's mouth without touching the sides.

The Spoilers around her continued to celebrate. The enemy were beaten, pulling back, but Haska continued to stare. The Grenzers had split apart and the Bulwark was grumbling out of sight, but they were not running, not firing at the newcomers. Through the scope she could see the city's soldiers cheering, a match for the jubilant whoops and shouts that echoed around her.

Dread slid its knife into Haska's core.

The turret disappeared behind a sudden burst of white smoke, and an instant later the wreck of an agri-hauler at the centre of their barricade exploded. Shards of metal plate burst from its flank, scything down the Spoilers nearest the blast, tearing through the flimsy protection of their barricade. Haska felt hot wind and a spray of splinters strike her face, and her scream joined others.

The force of the explosion, even from twenty yards away, was enough to knock her back. Haska clambered to her feet, scrabbling for her shot-cannon. Others were firing, each round rendered insubstantial and meaningless after the world-breaking thunder the tank had unleashed. Haska joined them, firing at far too great a distance to be effective.

'What do we do?' Someone – Aryat, she thought – shouted. 'What do we do?'

'We can hold!' Liocas roared. Something vital had broken behind his eyes; he looked like a canid straining at its leash.

'Are you mad?' Katryn shouted back. 'We have to fall back!'

Haska's fighters were already running. Most were throwing down their weapons to free their arms so they could flee faster. There would be no rallying them, no ordered retreat. This was the breaking of their fight.

'Haska!' Lira had run to the far side of the barricade, grabbing at the collars of the Spoilers who were wavering. She turned, her face a mirror of Haska's own horror.

The tank fired again.

'Haska, what do you want to do?'

The shell landed.

Something sharp dragged its edge across Haska's head, and the world vanished. An immense weight punched her to the ground, and drove the air from her lungs. She was helpless, blind. Blood dripped into her eyes, warm and wet. Her head hurt.

With limbs that felt like they belonged to someone else, Haska pushed herself upright. A violent wave of nausea shuddered through her, and she fell back. There was nothing but pain. A hot bar of raw agony pressed its way into her forehead. She gaped, lacking the breath to move and the strength to scream. Hands were at her back, heaving Haska to her feet. She raised a hand to her face, wiped away a streak of red from her eyes, and looked along the line of the barricade.

Lira was gone. A dust cloud drifted slowly aside, revealing the spot where she had stood. There was nothing there. A void had been punched through the piled sheet metal and agri-equipment, leaving a shallow crater in the ground and a blackened fan of gravel strewn back towards the Line. It was as though the hand of the God-Emperor had reached down and snatched Lira out of her world.

'Haska, we have to go. We have to go.' Katryn was by her side.

Haska felt her lips move, but she made no sound. Lira was gone.

She started towards the gap in the wall, but hands grasped her, pulling her back. She fought them, nails and teeth becoming claws and fangs, but the hands were stronger. Someone was screaming, loud in the empty cavern that had swallowed her thoughts. Her boots were scraping on the ground, leaving trails in the gravel. Lira was gone.

Something snatched at Haska's side, tearing open her jacket. She felt the pain as a knife across her ribs, but it was far away, irrelevant. Blood dripped into her eyes, steadily hiding the barricade, the bodies of her fighters, the last spot where Lira had stood.

Step by step, yard by yard, Haska was dragged away from the death that advanced between the warehouses, rumbling towards the shattered remnants of Saitz's uprising.

CHAPTER 38

Haska would carry the scar to her dying day.

She sat in silence, staring at her reflection in a small hand-mirror. Her mother was standing over her, watching with open concern. A few days earlier Haska had been offered some stamp broth, and she had broken the ceramic bowl and tried to turn the jagged edge on herself. Haska recalled none of this, beyond a vague memory of shouts of alarm, and unyielding hands bearing her down into the mattress' foam.

She ungently probed the raw, red line that creased her forehead, deep enough to etch a wrinkle into the bone of her skull, running from her hairline across to the tip of her eyebrow. She was lucky, she had heard several voices say, not to have lost her eye. The skin on either side of the line was puckered and inflamed where it had been pinched together to seal the wound. Her mother had been warning her, repeatedly, to keep her face immobile – every twitch and frown tugged at the medicae-grade glue that kept the cut closed.

Haska had no memory of how it had happened. Katryn

and Aryat had visited the day before, and told her that something – a chip of stone, a shard of metal, a brittle fleck of broken bone – had slashed the furrow across her forehead, in the same moment as... In the moment the shell had landed. The pain in her forehead was all-consuming, dull and deep and nauseating all at once. But worse, somehow, were her eyes. They were red-raw, and seemed to rasp against the inside of her head when she looked from one place to another. Verka said that she had sobbed for two days, not pausing to sleep, to eat, to clean herself of the salt and snot drying on her face, or wipe away the gore that was already there.

Haska dimly recalled that on the third day, when her body had finally given in to exhaustion, her mother had pressed a wet cloth to her face, moistening the crust of tears and blood and dust so that she could wipe it away. She had deftly sutured her head, and tied a bandage made from a folded strip of realweave fabric she had stolen from Ludoric Erastin's garment manufactory. The expensive cloth lay beside the bed, soaked through with blood and pus.

'It's getting better,' Verka said, full of forced optimism. Haska became aware of her mother's hand in her periphery, reaching for the mirror. She mutely passed it over.

'I have to go,' Verka continued. 'Mhari on the level below has a line on a cache of medicaments and water purifiers, and I need to be with them if we're to get our share.'

Haska said nothing. She longed to say something, to make it clear that she saw what Verka was doing for her, for them both, but the words wouldn't come. Verka had done all that a mother could and more to keep her daughter alive. Haska could not imagine what the past few days had cost her.

She had heard the guns, even through her sobs and screams. The ceaseless pounding had rumbled through the hab, day and night. Each detonation took her back to the shell's explosion, forcing her to relive the fountain of dust and dirt, the slash of pain, and the second's blindness that had erased Lira from her world. When she had finally risen from her mother's bed, forehead wrapped in priceless realweave, Haska had known what she would see from the window.

The Redfort was a cracked ruin, bleeding smoke from dozens of rents in its fractured walls. The city's retribution had not ended with retaking the Line. The Defence Corps' tanks had rolled on, shrugging aside the few acts of resistance the brave remnants of Saitz's army had tried to offer. They had paused at the Redfort, and let their guns speak the message of Varangantua's overlords: challenge us, and die.

Though insignificant beside the city's wrath, the Spoil's own guns had not been silent. But they had, as ever, been turned against their own. All semblance of order had collapsed. Verka had told Haska pieces of the truth, and she had overheard the rest in conversations between her mother and their neighbours.

The Har Dhrol was nothing but a fresh memory, its gangs dissolved into the petty factions they had always been. Some hab-blocks and clave communities had formed their own gangs in response. A few, Haska had overheard Verka say, were still managing to assert their independence, but the gangs had the stores of food and weapons and narcotics, and little reason to hold back from gunning down anyone who tried to take them.

'I'll be back tonight,' said Verka, doing her best to stifle the beginnings of one of her wet, rattling coughs. Haska heard her back out of the room, then the clatter of the hab door and the sound of the worthless lock clicking shut.

Sometime after, Haska rose on unsteady legs. The dry season's heat had not abated, and both the dorm-chamber and the hab's communal space were like the inside of an oven.

The hab was as she had always known it, albeit untidier. A folded pile of cloth on the narrow bench that ran beneath the window showed where Verka had been sleeping while Haska had monopolised the hab's only dorm.

Haska found her jacket across the back of a chair and shrugged it on, slowly and carefully, feeling warmth spread across her back and arms from where the novaplas had lain in the sun. The sensation felt alien, as though her mind were detached from her body. She fingered the repaired rent in its side, where another whickering shard of shrapnel had caught her.

She walked to the hab's door, remembering all the times she had opened it to find Lira's mischievous smile waiting for her. A hand reaching to pull her out into whatever violent and heart-pounding misadventure lay ahead.

That would never happen again. Haska felt the rage awaken, the same agonising fire that had sustained her through the hours since she had returned to her mother's hab. Not just rage. Hatred. Hatred for everything and everyone. For Katryn and Aryat, for living. For dragging her away from the Line, and the death she would have welcomed. For her mother, for her patience and love of which Haska was so undeserving. For Lira, for the crime of dying. For leaving her to face the cruelty of the world alone.

No, that was wrong. Lira had not left. She had been taken.

The nihilism she had felt just days ago, standing on the same spot, seemed so petty and small when compared with the raging inferno that now blazed in her heart. The memories of rich, black soil in her hand, of liquid-sweet softness on her lips, were needles in her head, poisonous and vicious. The hab was a collection of grey shapes, without joy or meaning. Everything had fallen away, consumed by a roiling, burning fury.

All her resentment, undirected for the long years of her short life, now had a target. When she had finally emerged from the void into which she had plummeted after Lira's loss, one thought, one need, had been waiting for her.

Vengeance.

It was all that was left to her. The Haska of a few days before would have called that small-minded, selfish. An excuse to fight, when fighting was what she wanted. But what else was there? What use was hope when she had seen everything she cared for, everything she had fought for, erased in a single moment of overwhelming violence?

She remembered the ganger who had not belonged, who had stood at Saitz's side and pretended to be one of them. He stood out in her memories of the uprising, as he had amongst the gangers whose appearance he had tried to imitate. Whoever he was, he had been an emissary of the clave-captain's sponsor. Whoever they were had been behind the upclave weapons that Leonida Andrysi had pressed into Haska's hands, and no doubt had been moving behind the scenes even as the blood of the Spoil ran red across the Line.

Haska would find the person whose goals were aligned with her own. If they had helped Saitz, she would make them help her as well.

She didn't try to look for her pistol. The pistol that Saitz had pressed into her hand, for which she had been so pathetically grateful. It wasn't with her jacket, so she assumed that Verka had taken it, either out of fear of what her daughter would do with it, or to win her place in the hab-block's emerging crew.

Somewhere at the back of her mind, guilt surfaced from beneath the roiling waves of bitterness. Verka had kept her alive, was out on the street at that moment fighting in a way that she never had to, to claw the necessities of life from hoarding hands. Haska owed her something more than to return home to an empty hab.

But this time, she could not summon the energy to leave a note, to sketch out words of hope for her mother to believe in. Better that Verka think that Haska was ungrateful, or wandered. Better that she harden her heart to the idea of her daughter, than to live with the fool's hope that she would one day return.

What Haska was setting out to do would kill her. She had seen what the city did to those who tried to take a piece of it for themselves. It would defend itself even more viciously against anyone who sought to tear the entire edifice to splinters.

Haska opened the hab's door, stepped through, and pulled it closed behind her.

Mattix stepped out of the lift-unit, his limp too real for his liking. It would keep him consigned to his desk for several more weeks, and for the first time in a long time, Mattix resented the excuse that would keep him off the street. Not, he thought as he made his way along the corridor with his cane thumping on the worn carpet, that he had been inactive over the past few days.

He stepped up to Kerimov's desk, too slow with his limp to simply breeze past as was his habit. The secretarius regarded him over the top of his bank of imagifiers. It might have been Mattix's imagination, but was that grudging respect he saw in the man's eyes?

'You can go straight in, probator-senioris.' The clerk pressed a button on his desk to alert Castellan Hauf to Mattix's presence.

'His Hand,' said Mattix, his face a studied picture in collegial courtesy. He would have to save the city more often, if it would coax a display of deference out of Markus Kerimov.

He stomped through into Hauf's office, leaning just a bit

more heavily on his ironwood cane than was strictly necessary. Hauf, though, was not in a sympathetic mood.

'What the hells is happening, Thaddeus?'

Mattix had expected this. 'The city does as it wills, sir,' he said as he lowered himself into a chair.

Hauf shook a sheaf of data-wafers at him, then cast them onto his desk in disgust. 'It's all gone to the hells! I have reports from the Grenzers that five thousand people a day are crossing the Rustwater. And those are just the ones they're catching! The God-Emperor alone knows how many are actually sneaking into the district.'

'They are fleeing rather significant instability, Alber,' said Mattix gently. The Spoil had degenerated into a bloody and multisided war in a distressingly short space of time, and everyone, both inside and out, was struggling to catch up.

The Har Dhrol was no more, that much was clear. What was left of its factions seemed to ally, break apart, re-form, and betray one another on an almost hourly basis, as the clave-captains traded territories and scrambled to claim control of the principal infrastructure sites that Sorokin had built. Running battles and sudden, brutal ambushes were the norm, trading lives over so small a thing as a box of carb-bars, or as grand as a promethium generator.

Worse than the violence was the privation. With the sudden closure of the Spoil's borders, the flow of goods in and out had dried up. That meant little to the tri-districts, but represented an existential threat to the hundreds of thousands who subsisted on imported starch and stamp. There was a catastrophe happening on the far side of the Rustwater, and it was clear to Mattix that the city was going to do nothing about it.

'I don't give a shit about instability!' Hauf bellowed. 'When's it going to end? The vladar is demanding I stem the tide. As if that were my responsibility!'

Not for the first time, Mattix wondered just how powerful and intemperate Hauf's familial connections were, to justify their need to promote such an inadequate creature to a position of high office.

'I am sure a new equilibrium will assert itself in the next few days.'

'What the hells does that mean?'

'The Spoil will adjust, sir. The Grenze Guard will remember how to do their jobs. And I understand the merchant-combines with interests in the Spoil are working to stabilise the situation.'

Mattix understood far more than that, but he would not tip his hand now.

'We have to take proactive measures, Thaddeus,' said Hauf in a manner that suggested he was echoing a command he had recently received himself.

'And indeed we are, sir. The Bastion's sanctioners are working with the Grenzers to control the bridges and the east bank of the canal. Monitor skulls have been redeployed, and I am making progress in identifying the new Spoil gang bosses.'

'Just get it under control, Mattix.' Hauf gave no sign of having listened to Mattix's report. 'What about the ringleader of this fiasco? This...' Hauf trailed off, and started picking through the data-wafers spread out before him.

'Damor Saitz, sir. Confirmed under excruciation by multiple captives. We don't have him yet, but there are many bodies still to be identified.' Just as likely that Saitz had scurried back into the Spoil's warren, but Mattix saw no need to point that out.

Determining the ganger's whereabouts was the foremost of his concerns, in no way due to Hauf's demands. Arbitrator Karadiz had contacted Mattix three times since the Redfort's destruction to make clear his expectation that the probator would secure Saitz for interrogation by the Arbites' own questioners. The evidence of a cult within the tri-districts would keep Mattix under the arbitrator's unwelcome scrutiny for the foreseeable future.

'Well, find him quickly, Thaddeus! The vladar demands results.' Hauf shuffled the data-wafers back together as a cover for his nervous energy, and made a show of consulting his desktop cogitator.

'Through His strength and grace, sir, all things are possible.' Mattix touched one hand against his chest as a limited form of salute, and rose to begin his slow journey back to his office.

Mattix had, of course, kept the full extent of his knowledge from Hauf. The Valtteri were hard at work on every front, trying to salvage their reputation and stabilise their damaged claims to hegemony within the tri-districts. But they had not yet risked sending another convoy across the Wastes, and his new source informed him that the lack of imported material was causing severe tensions within the cartel's senior ranks, to say nothing of the economic costs.

Mattix smiled to himself. He was not indifferent to the suffering of the Spoil's denizens, but from his perspective, it was very useful.

For years, he had looked at the map of the tri-districts and seen the tragedy that lay at its heart. The catastrophic waste of potential. Sorokin had seen it, and for three decades had made the most of what he had conquered. But the gang lord had been working with a fraction of the resources the city could bring to bear, if properly motivated. The Har Dhrol's success had, ironically, been to the Spoil's long-term detriment. With the border region stable, or at least under sufficient control to keep its troubles from spilling out into Dragosyl and its neighbours, the city authorities could ignore the Spoil. They could even factor its permeable borders into their activities; it was not just criminals who had made regular use of the Spoil as a means of circumventing difficult questions at the district boundaries.

Mattix stomped back into the lift-unit, and prodded the level selector with his cane. The next few days would be a delicate time. He had cultivated careful relationships with select figures within Dragosyl's Administratum, positioning himself as an authority on the Spoil and its troubles. He had to be seen to work tirelessly, and successfully, to quell the chaos that boiled at its edges, lest that cultivated reputation become tarnished.

But he could not be so successful that the disorder died down completely. Mattix had great plans for the Spoil. He only waited for those with the power to bring them into being to see their need.

'We are at twenty-eight per cent effective strength, but that should rise to forty within the week as men are discharged and cleared for duty. It's all detailed in my report.'

Tomillan Vasimov took the data-wafer from Nedovic's outstretched hand. 'Thank you, Andela. You are recovering quickly, I trust?'

'Yes, sir,' said Nedovic, around the bandage tightly wound about his face.

At its height, the situation on the Line had become so severe that Vasimov had been forced to dispatch his own second-in-command to oversee the Reisiger units that spearheaded the fighting. In the course of prosecuting the battle, Nedovic had been struck by a hard round that had come within a hair's breadth of shattering his jaw. The left side of Nedovic's face was still swaddled in a thick layer of gauze. The man had refused treatment with synthskin in order to retain the scar. Vasimov firmly approved of his decision; it was good for a man to wear his wounds, to show others what he had endured.

'And how are you faring, sir?'

The pitying tone in the man's voice was enough to make Vasimov look up sharply. 'That will be all, Andela.'

'Sir.' Nedovic clicked his heels in lieu of a more formal recognition of deference, then marched out with admirable precision.

Vasimov stood, his hands falling into their customary clasp in the small of his back. He turned, regarding the smog-shrouded expanse of the city from his suite's window on the hundred and thirty-third level of the Xeremor.

At length, he let out a long, slow breath.

Voronova had earned herself a reprieve through her actions with the damned arbitrator. It had been necessary for the cartel to retroactively sanction her activities, though it was plain to anyone who looked into the arrest orders that had flowed from the Xeremor that she had been acting outside her role as an agent of the Valtteri. That was a source of profound embarrassment for the executors, who moved in circles for whom such information was entirely within their grasp.

The scapegoat for the cartel's humiliation was Vasimov himself, and he burned with the injustice of it. He had done all he could to avert the catastrophe that had erupted from the cesspit of the Spoil. He had rightly used all means to return Voronova to the Valtteri's confinement; the men responsible for allowing the woman to abscond from their custody had already been dealt with, regardless of the shortage of manpower on the Reisiger's books.

However, Vasimov's punishment was also held in abeyance. The executors needed him and his Reisiger men, even at their diminished strength. The cartel was besieged on all sides, fighting with every tool in its arsenal to retain its prestige and position as its rivals circled. Competitor banking houses had begun to buy up assets the Valtteri would rely on to shore up their recovery. Cipher-knives – Voronova's cursed ilk – had been detected probing the cartel's data-bunkers. Individual merchant-combines and heavyweight conglomerates alike were wooing Setomir's fickle vladar, intent on breaking the Valtteri's monopolies while the manufactories and agri-plants along the Line were rebuilt. Worst of all, the cartel's privileged berths on Alecto's tropospheric void-stations had been revoked. At any other time, that alone would have been crisis enough to drive the executors to desperation.

But the cartel, like Vasimov himself, was a wounded beast, and they were the most dangerous. Voronova, he promised himself, would learn that before too much time passed.

CHAPTER 39

The sea-green steel of Melita's office door swung open, and she reached out and flicked on the lumens.

A tremor passed through Melita, so strong that she had to reach out and grasp the door's handle for support. Her desk. Her cogitators. The child-sized set of Voronova Atmospheric Shipping coveralls – Melita had worn little else until her twelfth natal day – mounted with care beside her cot. They were all as she had left them.

Oriel's alcove was silent and empty. Almost everything was as it should be.

She had spent a day and a night in the Xeremor waiting for Vasimov to bow to the inevitable. Karadiz's influence had saved her from whatever retribution he had planned. The arbitrator had thrown his cloak over everything Melita had done after her escape from the Xeremor, directly linking her – as well he should – to uncovering the Defence Corp company's betrayal and preventing a potential disaster. As such, the cartel had taken no action against her, although that did not mean that she was safe. Not at all.

Edi stomped in behind her. He was still hurting, but he had tired of feeling like a hostage, and so had discharged himself from the starscraper's medicae facilities when Melita had visited him on the second day. They had been given use of a Terilli flyer to avoid the chaos that seethed at the district borders, and to speed them away from the Xeremor and Vasimov's sight.

He made his way over to the culina counter, opened the fridgerator, and withdrew two bottles of jeneza. He passed one to Melita, then sat down heavily on her cot. She folded into her chair, its cold synthleather as welcoming as the embrace of an old lover. They sat in silence for some time. Exhaustion settled on Melita like leaden weights, pressing her into her chair. But she dared not close her eyes.

When she looked up, Edi was watching her carefully.

'What?' she asked.

'You feel guilty.'

After a few seconds, Melita nodded.

'About me?'

She smiled, slightly. 'Hardly. You should have run faster.'

Edi scoffed, but seemed pleased that she had made the attempt at humour. 'About what happened with the Arbites?'

The memories had faded, but not disappeared, try though she might to push them away. They had dissolved into still images, picts in her mind that cascaded one after the other. Bleeding bodies, lying beneath the cannons of black-clad figures. Children walking in manacles because of the sins of their fathers and mothers. Black smoke boiling out of broken armour.

'I do.'

'You shouldn't.' He turned stern. 'They were rebels and

traitors. There was only one fate for them when they took up arms against the city.'

'What about being humanitarians?'

Edi's expression did not change. 'Sympathy only stretches so far.'

'I suppose.' She took a long pull on her jeneza. 'They're dying over there.'

Most of Melita's contacts in the Spoil had gone quiet, she assumed due to the violence knocking out vox-masts and noospheric relays. The few that had been able to get messages through had all begged for her help, to get them out of the Spoil.

She hadn't responded to any of them. What could she do?

Edi nodded solemnly. 'It's going to be bad for a while.'

Melita felt the beginning of a scream, somewhere deep in her core. Such a mild way to put the disaster that was unfolding on the far side of the Rustwater.

'Do you think Saitz is dead?' she asked.

'If there's any justice.'

There wasn't, Melita knew. In Varangantua, there was vengeance, not justice.

There was no justice for Sorokin. His killer was still at large, an anonymous assassin with ties to a cult that had moved men to betray their most steadfast oaths. There would be no justice for the Grenzers who died at the Praetorian's Gate, true to their duty to defend their district, though their fellow border guards had fought tooth and nail to exact their revenge. None for the Spoilers who died within sight of what should have been theirs by rights; only the city's retribution against their kin for their temerity.

As guilt-ridden and jaded as all that made her, it was Edi's ultimatum that rang the loudest in her mind. She knew he'd meant what he said from the Xeremor's medicae-ward; if she continued on her path of self-destruction, he would not remain beside her to watch her fall. It was too much to ask, even if he had been willing to give it.

'I think you ought to have this,' she said suddenly. Melita held out the bullet Edi had given her, which Mattix had managed to smuggle out of the hands of Bastion-D's verispex archive and couriered to her. It had been a dead weight in her pocket ever since it had been handed to her.

'You need it more than me,' he said.

'I don't want it.'

Edi frowned, and looked at her thoughtfully. 'You have a role in what comes next. It'll be hard. These things always are. But if you care about those poor devils, you'll dig in.'

'Even so.'

He nodded. She placed the deformed hunk of metal on the cot beside him, and he slipped it into a pocket. The back of Melita's palm itched. She tried to scratch it with the cuff of her jacket, but that didn't get it.

'It's getting late,' she said. It was; the dry season's furnace had not yet abated, but darkness had at least descended.

Edi took the hint, and pulled himself to his feet with the aid of Melita's arm. 'You'll sleep here?'

'I don't trust their place.' The Valtteri had given her a hab in one of their buildings in Dragosyl when she was first taken into their fold. She hadn't liked it before everything that had happened, and she certainly didn't trust it now.

'I'll see you tomorrow.'

Melita smiled, because that was what he wanted to see. The old sanctioner stumped out of her office, the heavy thump of his cane marking his progress down the steps.

She checked that the door was locked, then, on trembling legs, staggered back to her desk. She fell to her knees and wrenched open one of its many lockers. She tossed aside a stack of folded vellum pages, groping for what she knew was there. Her fingers touched a chrome cylinder and a glass vial. She lurched upright, then collapsed onto her cot.

She had returned Edi's talisman to him because she had her own. Melita loaded the sleeper into the injector and pressed it to her arm.

EPILOGUE

The Bastion-S primary hangar deck was a punishing assault on the senses. Arc welders cast their glare, metal grinders shrieked, pneumatics strained beneath the weight of fractured engines and crumpled bodywork, and everywhere men and women worked at a pace that was well beyond frenetic.

The Setomir Enforcers' fleet of vehicles had suffered immensely during the chaos at the Line. The vast majority of their Zurov gunships were out of action, to the extent that the commanding castellan had ordered round-the-chron shifts by the Bastion's technical department to restore his enforcers' mobility. To meet that demand, the hangar chief had been authorised to admit civilian contractors to augment his own crews.

This would prove to be a serious lapse in judgement.

Halfway through the morning shift, a matt-black Valkyrie emblazoned with the fist-and-scales of the Adeptus Arbites burst into the hangar on roaring turbines, causing uproar among the labouring engineers. A squad of armoured figures emerged, led by an imposing arbitrator in a swirling black cloak. Their appearance provoked a brief lull in the hangar's work rate, as every head turned towards the avatar of the Emperor's judgement.

The rumour mill had anticipated the Arbites arrival. It was known to every clerk and menial in the Bastion that the ringleaders of the traitorous Defence Corps company were being held in the deepest gaol levels. While the precise time of their extraction to Fort Gunlysk was a closely held secret, the fact that they would be transferred into the Arbites own custody was obvious.

Soon after the Valkyrie's arrival, a crew of technicians drove a refuelling wagon across the crowded hangar towards the grimly avian gunship. The two arbitrators guarding the flyer allowed them to approach with a wave of gauntleted hands, and the crew set to work. A pair of servitors had the unenviable task of hauling a heavy polymer hose from the wagon over to the gunship's thirsting fuel tank. The hiss and gurgle of flowing promethium joined the overlapping sounds of mechanical activity as supervisors set their crews back to work.

Unknown to any of the crew overseeing the refuelling procedure, the fluid sloshing into the flyer's tank had been contaminated with a highly volatile chemical, which would go on to cause spectacular damage to nineteen enforcer vehicles before the taint was discovered. Once the Valkyrie's primary lift engines were ignited, the fluid would begin to react to the rise in fuel temperature. Approximately two minutes after that, the flyer's fuel tank would convert itself into a high-explosive bomb.

The technicians retired, and the servitors hefted their burden back onto shoulders rubbed raw and bloody by the chafing polymer and caustic promethium vapour.

On the far side of the hangar, a mechanic set down her

tools, and stepped away from the engine block at which she had been working. Later – much too late – her crew foreman would be subjected to the harshest examination by the Bastion's chasteners for his failure to observe that one of his technicians had absconded from her duties.

Marzanna Veles had been forced to expend a great many resources to reach this place in such a short space of time, to say nothing of the considerable time and energy invested in Major Ranić's recruitment to her cause. She smiled at the memory. It had, in fact, been Ranić's spouse whom she had first turned, and then allowed marital strife to do much of the rest. Kuranov was dealing with those details, eliminating by root and branch anyone who might have knowledge of Ranić's unseen benefactor. But she could give the challenge of infiltrating an enforcer Bastion to no one but herself. Ranić had no documentation, no evidence of Veles' instructions. Only his testimony, and she would silence that.

It was an unsubtle act, liable to attract the scrutiny of those in Varangantua's various orders who watched for such things, but that was unavoidable. She could endure a period of forced inactivity, if she must. The past week's strife had sown the seeds of much with which she could work. She had found that an untended garden yielded, on occasion, greater results than one trimmed and coaxed towards a particular path.

The smile behind her welding mask became a good deal colder. Events had not run as she had intended. But this, she reminded herself, was the nature of her calling. Saitz's insurrection may have failed, but her part in it would – must – remain unseen. Her cause had been furthered nonetheless. That was the gift, the extraordinary power of that which she served. Every plan was mutable. Change was the only constant. Every apparent setback or purported failure was merely a new twist in the design.

GLOSSARY

BASTION	Enforcer stronghold and base of operations, usually one per district
BLACKCLOAKS	Slang term for the Arbites of Fort Gunlysk
BULWARK	Enforcer armoured wagon
BURGRAVE	A relatively high-level official (beneath a vladar)
CARB-BAR	General source of cheap sustenance, can be eaten hot or cold. Bland but filling
CASTELLAN	Bastion commander
CLAVE-CAPTAIN	Low-level gang leader
CLAVE-HUB	Sprawling complex of interconnecting hab buildings, with a comparable population to a clave but more compact
CULINA	Kitchen (domestic, also referred to as 'refec')
DATAVEIL	System of city-wide comms/archive files, accessible to anyone with an iris augmetic
DORM, DORM-CHAMBER	Bedroom
GRENZE GUARD CORPS	Regiment of watchmen who protect the border between the tri-districts and the Spoil
HABCLAVE	Urban district
HAB-UNIT	Apartment, in a hab-tower/spire
HAR DHROL	The alliance of the Spoil gangs (prev. under Andreti Sorokin's leadership)

'HIS HAND'	Common greeting between enforcers, referring to the Emperor's holy will and judgement
JAEGER	Freelancer, private detective
JENEZA	Heavy, dark malt beer
JOY HOUSE	Den of iniquity where patrons partake of the pleasures of the flesh
KADERN, THE	Andreti Sorokin's criminal inner circle
PROBATOR	Detective rank
PROBATOR-NOVUS	Low-ranking detective, usually probationary (note: pre-dataveil)
PROBATOR-SENIORIS	Experienced detective of high rank
RAMPART	Sanctioner up-armoured patrol groundcar (not to be confused with the anti-riot tank, the Bulwark)
REFEC-HOUSE	Common eatery
REFEC, REFEC-CHAMBER	Kitchen/kitchen-diner
REISIGER	Hirelings/mercenary unit
REGIO CUSTOS	The border 'police'/customs in Varangantua
SECURITORS	Private security guards
SPOIL, THE	No-man's-land in the centre of the tri-districts
TZARINA	Service autopistol, used by probators
UP-CITY, UPCLAVE	Referring to better quality habitation and overall standard of living in the city
VERISPEX	Part of enforcer ancillary staff, a forensics expert
VLADAR	A local district commander responsible for the safety and prosperity of the district

ACKNOWLEDGEMENTS

First and foremost, I am forever grateful to Nick Kyme, Kate Hamer, Richard Garton-Wills, Will Moss, and everyone in the Black Library editorial team. Their support and patience have been unfailing, their advice and guidance invaluable.

I am indebted to Chris Wraight, Guy Haley, Alec Worley, Marc Collins, and every author who has had a hand in sculpting Varangantua into the bleak, oppressive, fascinating setting in which I have been permitted to roam.

Particular thanks are owed to Marc Collins, who forged the path that I now follow.

My thanks to Victoria Hayward and the members of the Scriptorum Recaf Station, for solidarity and support when I needed it most, and to Sarah Cawkwell and the members of the Black Library Bolthole, for creating the best community a burgeoning Black Library fan could have asked for.

My deepest thanks to my family and friends, for everything.

Finally, and most importantly, my unending thanks to Alice. You are the light of my life, and I couldn't have done this without you.

YOUR
NEXT READ

Bloodlines
by Chris Wraight

An investigation into a missing member of a wealthy family leads Probator Agusto Zidarov into a web of lies and danger amidst the criminal cartels of Varangantua. As the net closes in, Zidarov falls further into darkness from which he may never return…

An extract from
Bloodlines
by Chris Wraight

Down, down below, down under the flyovers and the transit arches, down to where the lumens floated on wheezing suspensors and the windows were steamed with condensation. People packed in on all sides, some high on topaz, some exhausted, all smelling of euphoria.

She breathed it in. She let her fingers graze along the rockcrete of the close wall, feeling its coldness against the wet heat of the night. She looked up, and saw the smear-glow of private club entrances, vivid in neon. She heard the rumble of turbine traffic overhead, and the hiss of groundcars on damp asphalt.

She'd taken it. Topaz. It was as good as she'd hoped – she was giddy, enjoying the freedom. Every face she looked at was one of a friend, smiling back at her, rouged, whitened, darkened, flared with photoreactive pigments, glittering with augmetic baubles. Music thumped away, spilling from the open doorways of the sanctioned haze dens, threatening to drag her in, smother her in the heat and the noise.

She could have walked along that street forever, just drinking it in. She liked the smells, overlapping one another, competing like jostling suitors for her attention. She stuck her hands in the pockets of her overcoat, pushed her shoulders back, slipped through the crowds.

She didn't know what time it was. The deep of the night, for sure, a few hours before dawn. It didn't matter. Not any more. That was the point of freedom – make your decisions, stupid ones, good ones, get out, do your own thing.

A man lurched into her way, grinning and drunk. He shoved up against her, and she smelled his breath.

'Hello, young fish,' he slurred at her, swaying. 'Come to swim with me?'

He had plastek-looking hair, too clean, too sculpted. She kept on going, sliding past him, out into the middle of the street. The press of people swept him away, giving her more faces to gawp at. Fireworks went off in the sky, dazzling, smelling of chems, picking out high arches overhead engraved with skull-clusters and fleur-de-lys finials. Commercia chameleon-screens flashed and whirled, spinning pixelated images one after the other – a woman smiling, a man gazing at an altar, a Navy drop-ship wheeling across a starfield, troops in uniform marching under a crimson sky on another world.

For the first time, she felt a spike of danger. She had walked a long way, away from the friends she had come with. She had almost forgotten about them entirely, and had very little idea where she was.

She looked back and saw the plastek-hair man following her. He was with others, and they had latched on to her.

Damn.

She picked up the pace, skipping on her heels, darting to the street's edge, to where the grand avenue, scarred with twin steel ground-tracks, met another one, cobbled and glinting, that ran steeply downwards.

If she hadn't taken topaz, she'd have stayed, by instinct,

with the crowds, where the press of bodies provided its mute kind of safety. But it got darker quickly, and the lumens faded to red, and the old cobblestones underfoot got slippery. The beat of the music felt harder – dull, like the military dirges they transmitted every evening over the communal prop-sets.

Down, down, down.

She felt a bit sick. She shot a glance back and saw that they were still coming, only jogging now, four of them, all drunk on jeneza or rezi or slatov. They all had those sharp, fake haircuts, smart dress, clean boots. Defence-corps trainees, maybe – officer-class, full of entitlement, untouchable. She'd come across the type so many times before. Hadn't expected to find them down here – perhaps they liked to slum it from time to time as well, to skirt against the grime for fun, see whether it stuck to their uniforms.

Just as she began to worry, someone grabbed her by the arm. She pulled back, only to see a girl smiling at her, a girl her age, pale emerald skin, orange hair, a metal serpent-head stud in her cheek.

'Come on,' the girl said, her irises glittering. 'I saw them too.'

She followed her. She went down a narrow passageway between two big hab-blocks built of dark, crumbling prefab slabs. It soon smelled of urine and old sweat, of drains and discarded carb-bars. As she wound further down the alley, the noise of the men's footfalls, their laughter, faded. Perhaps they'd gone straight on past. Perhaps they'd never really been that close.

It got hotter. She felt the boom of the music well up from under her, around her, as if the walls themselves were vox-emitters. She needed a drink. For some reason she was very thirsty.

The girl brought her to a door – a heavyset door in a

blockwork wall, one with a slide panel in the centre. She activated a summon-chime, and the slide opened, throwing out greenish light from within.

'Elev in?' the girl asked.

'He is,' came a man's voice.

The door clunked open. Warm air billowed out, and music came after it, heavy, thumping music. She felt it move through her body, make her want to get going, to get back to that place she'd managed to reach a while back, where everything was forgotten save for the movement, the heat, the heartbeat of escape.

The girl pushed her inside. They were at the head of a long flight of plastek-topped stairs. The walls were bare cinder blocks, the floor sticky with spilled drinks. It was hard to hear anything at all over the music, which seemed to be coming from everywhere at once.

'Down,' said the girl, smiling at her again, encouragingly.

They went together. Soon they were in a bigger chamber, one full of bodies moving, throwing shadows against lumen-scatter walls. What had this place once been? An assembly chamber? A chapel, even? Not now. The light was lurid, vivid, pulsing in time to the heavy smack of the music. She smelled sweat fighting with commercial fragrances. She smelled the acrid tang of rezi. There was a high stage with murals half-hidden in a haze of coloured smoke, men and women dancing on platforms surrounded by kaleidoscopic lumen flares. The floor was jammed, crushed with damp bodies in motion. It was hard to breathe.

'Just keep moving,' said the girl, taking her by the hand.

They somehow threaded through the crowds. A drink was passed to her and she took it. That made her feel better. She started to look for the source of the music. Faces swelled up out of the dark, flustered and glowing, all grinning at her. They were nice, those faces, and interesting, with their slim metal exo-frames and their holo-halos that waved and flashed like prisms. Where had they all come from? Did they work in the manufactories she had heard about, during the drab day? Or were they all the sons and daughters of the gilded, writhing down here until they collapsed into narc-induced sleep? They were like exotic beasts, feathered, horned, wrapped in silks and sequins, coming in and out of the flickering shadows, fragments of strange bedtime stories, moving in unison under old gothic arches.

She danced for a while. The girl seemed to have gone, but that was fine. She thought back to the past, to the rules that had kept her in her chamber every hour, all the hours, at her studies, learning the catechisms and the rotes, and wanted to scream out loud for the joy of being free of it. Her limbs moved, clumsily, because she had never been able to do this before, but she learned fast, and the topaz made it easier.

They pressed around her, the others – reaching out for her hair, her arms. She lost track of time. More drinks appeared, and she took them again.

And then, much later, the girl came back. She led her from the chamber of lights and heat, and down some more narrow, slippery stairs. That was a relief, for she was getting tired. It would be good to rest, just for a moment. Away from the music, it was cooler, and she felt the sweat patches on her shirt stick to her skin.

'Where are we going?' she asked, and was surprised to hear how the words slurred.

'Time out,' said the girl. 'I think you need it.'

It was hard to follow where they went. Some stairs went down, some went up. At one point she thought they'd gone outside, and then in again, but she was getting very tired and her head had started to hurt.

'Do you have any water?' she asked.

'That's where we're going,' came the reply. 'To get some.'

And then they were through another heavy door. She had the impression of more people around her, though it was very dark, and increasingly cold. They went down yet more stairs, a well so tight that it scraped against her bare arms, even though she wanted to stop now, just sit on the floor, clear her head.

Eventually they ended up in a narrow, empty room with bright overhead lumens that hurt her eyes. She really wanted a drink.

A man was there, one with sallow skin, a tight black body-suit and collarless shirt, a knotwork tattoo just visible at the base of his neck.

'What's your name?' he asked, pleasantly enough.

'Ianne,' she replied.

'Ianne. That's unusual. I like it. Are you having a good time?'

'I could use a drink.'

'Fine. Come with me, then. We'll get you something.'

By then, the girl seemed to have gone. She felt hands on her arms, and she was heading down again. The lumens were turned down low, and she struggled to make anything out.

She had the vague sense of being surrounded by people again. She heard a noise like breathing, in and out. She shook her head to clear it, and saw metal shelves, many of them, all with glass canisters on them. She saw tubes, and she saw machines that had bellows and ampoules and loops of cabling. She saw the padded couches, in rows, running back into the dark, and it looked like people were sitting on them.

She felt a lurch of worry. There was no music. It was quiet, and cold, and she didn't know the way back out.

'Where am I?' she asked.